THE
WITCH
OF TIN
MOUNTAIN

ALSO BY PAULETTE KENNEDY

Parting the Veil

THE
WITCH
OF TIN
MOUNTAIN

PAULETTE
KENNEDY

LAKE UNION
PUBLISHING

Published by Lake Union Publishing, Seattle

www.apub.com

Amazon, the Amazon logo, and Lake Union Publishing are trademarks of Amazon.com, Inc., or its affiliates.

ISBN-13: 9781662507625 (paperback)
ISBN-13: 9781662507632 (digital)

Cover design by Faceout Studio, Amanda Hudson
Cover image: ©Des Panteva / ArcAngel; ©Nikola Pavkovic / 500px / Getty; ©Thitisak Mongkonnipat / Getty; ©LUMIKK555 / Shutterstock; ©sema srinouljan / Shutterstock; ©getgg / Shutterstock; ©BGSmith / Shutterstock; ©Niccolo Bertoldi / Shutterstock

Printed in the United States of America

CONTENT WARNING

While potentially triggering content is mostly referenced and not depicted explicitly, this novel contains references to child abuse and neglect, including sexual and physical abuse. Sexual assault, dubious sexual consent, self-harm/suicide, addiction, alcoholism, death and dying, racism, homophobia, murder, attempted murder, fire/arson, and abortion, adoption, and childbirth are also mentioned within this novel.

For Paul . . . who knew how to tell one hell of a story.

Wherever a witch's blood is spilled, a curse remains on the land . . .

PROLOGUE

ANNELIESE

1831

It is too late for her. She knows this, and so she finishes her writing, scrawling the last few lines of hurried script across the parchment. A shout comes from outside, followed by the steady rumble of male voices. Her son ceases spinning his top across the floor and looks up at her, his brown eyes wide with fear.

The woman closes the book and takes the little boy by the hand. "Come, Liebling."

She leads him to the trunk at the foot of her bed—hewn of strong cedar carved by her father's hands and protected by her wards for such a time as this. She lifts the boy into it, then gives him the book. He hugs it to his chest. "You must keep this and go on, Jakob. For her sake."

A rock sails through the cabin window, smashing the warped glass to shards. The wind filters through the ragged opening, bringing the sweet fragrance of rose verbena and the fiercer scent of burning tallow. Flickering light glances off the cabin walls. The little boy whimpers and reaches for his mother. She smiles at him, presses her lips to his forehead, and buries her face in the soft darkness of his hair one last time.

She closes the lid and stands, then walks to the door and opens it, a defiant smile on her face. The man in black does not smile in return. He grasps her by the wrist and hauls her out into the night, where her death awaits.

Hidden inside his grandfather's trunk, the boy remains. And the book remembers.

ONE

GRACELYNN

1931

Thursdays are town days, and it's town days I dread most. People's eyes
swarm all over me like flies on a wet dog, their mean words humming
like hornets around my head. They hardly wait until I've passed by before
they spit in my path. Granny tells me to ignore it—that folks here have
their superstitions and it's nothing for me to worry over. But I've learned
enough to know you can't put much trust in people who want what you
have on Thursdays but won't talk to you come Sunday morning.

If it weren't for Granny, I'd be long gone from Tin Mountain and
the people here who'd break me if they ever got the chance.

I pick my way down the slump-drunk shoulder of the hillside, mud
seeping through the holes in my Salvation Army boots. My yarb bag
swings low and heavy at my hip. Inside, there's a whole pound of fresh-
picked morels and a screw-top jar full of green sludge that'll get old Bill

Bledsoe's bowels to moving and buy us enough food for a week—if he's feeling generous, that is. We never charge for our cures. We take whatever sort of payment folks can give. Sometimes that's money. Sometimes it's no more than a can of beans or evaporated milk.

At the edge of town, the sweet, half-burnt smell of sawdust curls up my nose. Northrup's Mill sits at the end of Main Street, as it has for the last fifty years. Timber and sharecropping are about the only work folks can find in these parts. And if you don't do one of them things? I reckon you ain't worth too much around here.

"Well, lookie here. If it ain't the high and mighty Miss Doherty." The low drawl is followed by a puff of blue tobacco smoke, and a lanky form unfolds from the shadows next to the sawmill. A slow smile spreads across a pockmarked, narrow face that wears its twenty years hard. Harlan Northrup. All sorts of trouble, and none of it the good kind.

I ignore him and keep on walking. He follows me, his big feet punishing the dirt. "Where you goin', Gracie? Too full of yourself to stop and talk to me?"

I spin to face him. "Get on your way, Harlan. I got deliveries to make."

"Is that right?"

"I mean it. I'm in no mood for triflin' with you." I draw myself up tall and cross my arms, glaring over the edge of my scarf.

"Easy now. I don't mean no wrong." He tosses his cigarette butt into the gutter and widens his stance, trying to block me. The old men jawing on the mercantile porch fall silent. Their eyes skim past us like dragonflies skating across a pond. "I jus' want to bend your ear for a spell. Maybe see that pretty hair of yours." He edges closer and reaches for the scarf tied over my braids. I jerk away and he grins, showing his yellow, crooked teeth.

A raw, fierce burning starts low in my spine. The same burning that haunts my dreams. I don't quite know where it comes from, but every time it happens, I feel like a baby copperhead, newly hatched and lethal. The air shimmers in front of me and my eyes start stinging. I clench my fists. "Get out of my *way*."

Harlan's squinty eyes go big, and he takes a step back. I step forward. That's when he laughs. But it ain't like he's laughing at a joke. He's nervous. I can almost taste his fear, sour as gooseberries on my tongue.

"All right, Gracie," he says, putting his hands up. "Another day."

I shake my head and stand firm in my spot. "No, Harlan. Not another day. Not ever."

"Witch." He hacks and spits at the dust, then turns on his heel to go back inside the mill. When he's gone, I let my breath out in a shaky rush. I've won. For now. But Harlan Northrup ain't the only person in Tin Mountain I need to watch my back around. Ever since I came here, as a girl of fourteen, folks have treated me different. It started the first day I showed up at the schoolhouse, freshly scrubbed with lye soap, pale braids pulled tight by Granny's fingers, my eyes watering from the cold. I'd climbed down from Tom Kellogg's school wagon, slipped on a glaze of ice, and fell flat on my back with my skirt up around my bloomers. Only one girl came to help me up, while the others laughed. Abigail Cash. No matter how hard I tried to make friends, to fit in, Abby was the only one who ever treated me like I belonged. But it was the day Clyde Millsap said I'd killed my own mama that hurt the most . . . because he wasn't half-wrong, his words sharp as rocks in a shoe. I hauled off and hit him so hard his nose is still crooked to this day. After that, there was no more school for me.

The kind of learnin' I got from Granny was a far sight better, anyways.

I keep my head down and hurry up the road, not stopping again until I come to the big house on the corner. It's three stories of painted timber decked out with peeling gingerbread and stained glass—proof that old Bill Bledsoe was once the richest man in town until the Northrups stripped him of that honor. I hoist my bag with its sloshing liquid and climb the steps trimmed with splintered millwork.

Calvina, Bledsoe's maid, flings open the door before I have a chance to knock. "Come on in, Miss Gracelynn. Mr. Bledsoe's been 'specting you."

I step over the threshold, blinking from the sudden change in light. Calvina's dark eyes flit nervously from mine to the stairs. "He's in mighty bad pain. Been tryin' the castor oil like you said. Ain't nothing moved."

"Locked up tight again, ain't he?"

A loud groan filters from the floor above. "Goddammit, Calvina! Bring that girl up here!"

Lands. Old Bledsoe is in *mighty* rare form.

I follow Calvina up the stairs to a room draped in scarlet silk. Faded pink wallpaper curls at the corners. Mr. Bledsoe's propped up in a bed as wide as a railway car, sweat sliding down his wrinkled face in rivulets. He squeezes his eyes shut and rolls onto his side as another cramp seizes him. "I'm dyin', Lord Jesus," he groans.

I cross the room and kneel next to the bed, unwinding the scarf from my hair and locking eyes with Mr. Bledsoe. "Now listen here, sir. You ain't dyin'. You just need a good shit."

"It hurts! Bloody Judas, it hurts!"

He rolls again, clutching at his pajamas. Ah, hell. Granny once told me Mr. Bledsoe had a tragic past, and that's what's made him the way he is, but all I see is a bitter old man with too much money and time on his hands. I rummage through my bag and pull out the jar with its fern frond tisane. "Drink as much of this as you can muster. It won't taste good. But it'll get things to moving."

Calvina holds out a teacup, and I fill it with the thick green liquid. She offers it to him. He takes the smallest of sips, then pulls a face like a gargoyle. Another cramp rolls through him, and he flails around, cursing a stream of filthy words. The flimsy teacup nearly flies from Calvina's hand. She purses her lips and shakes her head.

If there's one thing I've learned over the years I been helping Granny deliver babies and work her cures, it's that ladies are miles tougher than menfolk, and much nicer patients, too.

"Now, Mr. Bledsoe," I say, "if you don't drink that, you'll have to go see Doc Gallagher. He'll give you something called an enema. That means up the rear with a rubber hose." His eyes get real wide. "I don't reckon you want that, or the bill that'll come with it, so if I were you, I'd drink up."

He pushes out his lower lip like a pouting baby, but this time, when Calvina offers the cup, he chugs it down. A few minutes later, a rumbling sound comes from under the covers. A stench stronger than a day-old bloated deer wafts through the room.

Old Bledsoe *really* starts howling then.

"Them cramps just mean it's working! I'll help you get him to the privy, Calvina. Otherwise, you'll be washin' his sheets for a week."

༺৪⊹৪༻

After we've gotten Mr. Bledsoe settled back in bed, Calvina presses a silver dollar in my palm and walks me out to the street. "You heard anything about that evangelist comin' to town tomorrow night?"

"I sure haven't."

Calvina reaches into her apron pocket and pulls out a folded sheet of paper, smoothing it with long brown fingers. I take it, scanning the boldface headline:

Reverend Josiah Bellflower

Miracles and Wonders

Are you sick? Crippled in body or touched with infirmities of the mind?

Reverend Bellflower has a message of healing and prosperity from The Lord.

Below the circus-like script is a date, May 1, and a photo of a tall man with longish hair and sharp features, one hand pressed to the forehead of the woman kneeling before him, the other up to God. I sniff and hand it back to Calvina. "Looks like a bunch of Holy Roller hogwash to me."

"All the same, I'm thinking about bringing Mama. Her hip won't stop gripin' her."

Something prideful in me rears up. "She been doing the Epsom soaks and taking the willow bark Granny prescribed?"

Calvina looks off somewhere above my shoulder and nods. "Been following your granny's advice to the letter, but there ain't no change. And we can't afford no doctor."

I gesture up to the bedroom window, where Mr. Bledsoe's lying in a bed bigger than our kitchen, on down pillows and satin sheets. "You can't, but *he* can. Pardon me, Calvina, but you sure do put up with a lot from that old man."

She shakes her head. "He lost most of his money in the crash, just like them city folk did. I'm thankful to have the work. Mr. Bledsoe is cranky, sure enough, but at least he keeps me fed—keeps Mama fed, too."

She ain't wrong. *Any* work is better than no work in these times.

By now, the sun is sliding under the broad-hipped roof of Mr. Bledsoe's big, soulless house. I've got about an hour to do our trading at the mercantile before it closes. If I hurry, there'll be just enough time to see Abby before Aunt Val and the cousins get home from the fields, their bellies aching for dinner. I reach for Calvina's hand. "Don't you worry about your mama. Granny'll figure something out. She always does."

ᴄᴏ⋆ꙮ

I hear Abby before I see her.

"Dang it, Hortense! Come *on!*"

An angry mooing echoes over the hillside. Hortense is a cow. A temperamental, milk-poor Guernsey that Abby raised from a calf. If she were mine, she'd have been stew meat a long time ago.

I undo my braids as I walk, letting my hair spill down in waves over my back. I'm wearing my best dress—the one I made two years ago with daisy-print fabric from the Woolworth's down in Fayetteville. I try to look as pretty as I can when I go to see Abby.

Up the hill, I spy her tugging on Hortense's lead. She has on her work bibs, the patched denim straining over her curves.

"If you wait a minute, I'll fetch Morris's shotgun," I holler. "We'll have steak for dinner."

Abby turns. The setting sun catches on her dark curls. Her lips widen into a grin. Ah, hell. *That smile.* "Gracelynn Doherty, quit your damn gawkin' and come help me."

I shrug off my bag and hang it on the fence post, relieved to be free of its weight. The mercantile was stocked full today. With what I earned from the morels, I got salt pork and three whole pounds of navy beans. There was even half a loaf of rye bread left from the weekly breadline.

I join Abby in the corral and take hold of Hortense's leather bridle. The cow blows a huff of steamy air into my face and rolls her eyes. "Now you listen here, you bitchy old heifer, you're gonna get in that barn and bed down for the night. Hear me?" I give the bridle a shake, and Hortense takes one measly step forward, her tail swishing like a mad cat, but she starts moving steadily, bony hips swaying from side to side. We tether her inside the barn, where she promptly lowers her head to chomp on the hay.

"She's been more cross than usual. Ain't givin' any milk at all now," Abby says.

"Animals act up when there's something brewing."

"Weather?"

I nod. "Maybe."

Abby gives me a long, sweeping look. "You sure look nice. Go to town today?"

"Yep. Bledsoe's bowels."

"Again?"

"He won't eat his damned prunes. Locked up tighter than the county jail."

"At least his money's good, ain't it?" Abby shakes her head. "Come up the tower with me. I got some cigarettes. Pall Malls. Chocolate, too." There's a naughty quirk to her grin that makes me go all warm inside.

"Lands, Abby. That's rich. You rob a bank?"

"No, but I can save a dime for somethin' special now and then, just like you can."

We pass through the back pasture, nodding with cow parsley, and top the hill, the shadow of the lighthouse long and narrow on the grass. It's at least a hundred feet high and made of whitewashed field rock Abby's great-great-granddaddy Hiram Cash quarried from the hillside, its peaked top crowned with copper shingles. High windows blink in the setting sun, reflecting the clouds and purple-tinged sky. It's like something from a fairy tale—out of place compared to the dusty shantytown feel the rest of Tin Mountain has.

When I first came here five years ago, I thought it strange for a lighthouse to stand in the middle of a forest, hundreds of miles from any ocean. But compasses don't work at all in these hills. They just spin and spin. Every now and again, teams of engineering students from the School of Mines come down to *investigate* and go back to Rolla scratching their heads and muttering about ley lines and magnetic fields, but no one really knows why Tin Mountain is the way it is.

If it weren't for the lighthouse, people would get lost all the time. And when people get lost here, they don't come back the same. If they come back at all.

We pass by the stone cottage that sits at the lighthouse's base, and a wet, ragged cough comes through an open window.

"How's your pa?" I ask.

"He's been in bed for a week. Ain't eatin' much."

"Any blood with his cough?"

"Nah. None I've seen. Yet."

10

"I'll tell Granny. Maybe she can get her hands on something more potent than elderberry syrup."

A shadow slides across Abby's round cheeks. "Ain't nothin' for it, Gracelynn."

"Now, don't say that."

"I took him to a doctor up in Springfield. It's tuberculosis."

The taste of sour metal skates over my tongue. Me and Granny might have lots of cures, but there ain't no cure for tuberculosis. Abby sniffs and turns away, but not before I see the hurt pooling in her eyes. She undoes the latch on the lighthouse door and bumps her hip against it. The door judders open, sweeping an arc of dirt in its path. Inside, spiraling steps twist upward into the darkness.

"I'll get the lamp," she says, her voice husky. "There's matches in my back pocket if you'll fetch 'em."

My fingers dart into Abby's pocket. I fish around for the box of matches and pull them free, my face heating at having touched her in such a close way. She holds the paraffin lantern steady while I light it, the sharp scent of sulfur sparking between us.

I follow her up the winding rockwork staircase, the cool walls growing close as we near the top. On the last step, she passes the lantern to me so she can push the hatch open with both hands. The hinges creak as the trapdoor falls back against the floor. Light floods into the tower, washing the steps gray. We emerge into an octagonal room, with glinting windows on all sides. Ever since her pa first took sick, the job of lighting and tending Old Liberty fell to Abby. She's proud of the lighthouse and it shows. She spends every morning carefully polishing the windows and brass lantern fittings so Liberty will shine bright and true.

She climbs the ladder leaning up against the lantern housing. Watching her gets my head all woozy, even though I've seen her climb that rickety ladder dozens of times. "There you go, starin' again," she teases, throwing a smile over her shoulder. Her fingers dip into the slippery tallow, then stroke at the cotton, prepping the wick. "Bring me that jug of kerosene over by the catwalk. Reservoir's dry."

I walk carefully over the planks, trying not to look out the windows. I ain't never told Abby I'm scared of heights. If I did, she might never invite me up here again. I'm pretty good at faking brave. When something or someone is important enough to me.

I heft the metal jug of kerosene, leaning back slightly to hug it to my belly as I waddle back to Abby. She leans down from her ladder and takes it. As she fills the reservoir, the sharp smell of kerosene stings my nose and sets my eyes a-watering.

A few seconds later, there's the sharp pop and the wick ignites. Flames shoot high within the lantern and heat fills the glass-walled room. Abby sets the Fresnel lens and mirrors to turning, then climbs down from her perch. I shield my eyes from the brilliance of the reflected beam. It's like being too close to the sun.

"Go on out, Gracie. I'll be there in a minute."

I open the glass door that leads to the lighthouse's gallery and step out. The wind blows a gust up my dress. I hug the curved side of the tower, my heart beating fast as a bumblebee's wing. Together, we move to the railing and look out over the landscape. It's quiet up here. Pretty, too. The mountains ramble off in the distance like slow purple soldiers, the setting sun tinging their peaks with gold. But as much as this land is a part of me, I crave the sounds of an ocean I've never seen. A place where there's work and plenty of rich people's money to keep a hungry belly fed.

"Your top button's come undone," Abby says. I glance down, where the barest hint of my lace slip shows. My flesh pimples. To button it up, I'll have to let go of the railing. Below me, the trees start spinning at the thought.

Abby gives me her crooked grin. "Here. I'll get it." She reaches over and slides the thin mother-of-pearl button back through its hole. Her fingers linger on the skin above my collar. A rush of blood heats my face. Our eyes meet for just a second, and I think about taking her hand and kissing the callouses on her palm. Then the moment's gone and she's digging in her pocket for a cigarette.

She lights one and sits, feet dangling off the edge of the balcony. I lower myself slowly and curl next to her, knees hugged to my chest. She passes the cigarette to me. I take a short drag and wince as the smoke burns through me. I pass the cigarette back to Abby. "I'd rather have the chocolate."

Abby pulls a square of foil-wrapped chocolate from her bibs and hands it over. The sweetness explodes on my tongue, taking away the bitter taste of nicotine. I close my eyes and sigh with pleasure. This is the berries, being here with Abby, enjoying such luxuries. I could almost forget about all the thankless work waiting for me at home. Braver now, I unfold my legs and let my holey boots drape over the edge of the platform.

"You look like you're far away from here, Gracie. Whatcha thinkin' about?"

"Ah, nothing much." I've never told Abby my dreams of leaving Tin Mountain. I'm too afraid she wouldn't want to come with me, and I'm not ready to think of that. "There's a preacher man comin' to town. Some revivalist who claims he can put a healing on folks."

"I saw that." Abby purses her lips and blows a stream of blue-gray smoke away from me. "You gonna go see what it's all about?"

"I reckon I better. Yarb doctors and hucksters are trouble. Me and Granny can't afford to lose no business."

Abby clucks her tongue. "Them healin' men come and go, Gracie. They blow through with the summer. Your granny *stays*. Folks trust her. Just like they'll trust you someday."

Someday. Someday, like becoming the granny woman of Tin Mountain is some sort of prize. I imagine myself through the long, gray years, handing out cures and delivering babies. An ache of dread claws through me.

Abby stubs out the spent cigarette and leans forward, squinting. "There was a feller got lost the other night. Some banker from Rogers. He was out in the woods when his dog got spooked and run off. He got turned around in the holler and couldn't find his way back to the trail. He finally saw the beacon and made it to the top of the hill. Claims he saw something in the woods. Tried to get him to talk about it, but he just sat at the table, drinking cup after cup of water and shaking. He was so worked up, the sheriff had to come get him."

The unsteady quaver in Abby's voice gets the hair to standing on my arms. The lighthouse beam whooshes overhead, sending a shaft of light dancing over the treetops. My eyes follow it, looking for any sign of movement. Everything is still in Sutter's holler. Too still, as if something's out there, crouched in the shadows.

"You put any stock in them old stories? About the Sutter haint and the witch curse?"

Abby lights another cigarette, and the sudden spark of flame makes me jump. "Maybe. Folks see things all the time in that holler. Pa says it's been haunted from the way-back-when—the Indians even talk about it. They won't go there to hunt or forage."

I ain't never paid much attention to the old folks and their claims that the land is marked by something foul that happened in Sutter's holler long ago. But lately, I've been having strange dreams—visions. A *burning* comes with them. The same burning I felt just this afternoon, squaring off with Harlan—a pain like fire trapped under my skin, as real as a memory, but it doesn't feel like mine.

A memory of fear, anger, and pain . . . so much pain.

It ain't my pain. But I feel it, just the same.

TWO

DEIRDRE

1881

Deirdre loosened her corset laces, then pulled them tight again, clenching the ribbon between her teeth. The corset was nearly worn out—sweat-stained and threadbare between its boning. Money enough for proper-fitting stays might come home with Pa when he returned from Colorado, or it might not. When the roof needed a fresh layer of shingles to keep the rain out, and their mule needed shoes, new corsets mattered very little in the lay of things.

Deirdre buttoned her best muslin over the corset, tucked the small flask of rye whiskey she'd found in Pa's bureau into the top of her stocking, and cast a final appraising glance at the mirror above her washstand. She went down the loft's ladder and through to the kitchen. At the sound of her step on the wide-planked floor, Mama glanced up from her ironing. "You'll be home by eleven, then?"

"Can't I stay later? If I come home afore midnight, I'll miss the bonfire."

Mama grunted. "Fair enough. But I won't take to you coming home with drink on your breath, hear?"

"I don't drink at the music parties, Mama," Deirdre lied. "I done told you that."

"All the same, have care with that Cash boy. He's trouble, that one. People talk."

"I'm only going to listen to the music."

Mama arched a dark brow. "You're of age, Deirdre. Girls younger than you court and marry. Only be mindful of taking your vows before letting any—"

"Yes'm." Deirdre ducked her head and made for the door before Mama could get all het up. At nearly nineteen, she tired of being talked at like a child.

Outside the cabin, the air was lilac sweet and thick with springtime. The moon hung high overhead, whisper thin and curved like a ladle. Deirdre picked up her skirts and nearly ran down the garden path, her heart growing lighter with every step.

Down the mountain, tucked in a bend of Ballard Creek where the water ran deep, old Bartholomew Ray had long ago laid claim to the flattest stretch of land in Boone County—land that had made him and his kin rich with its fertile soil. Everything grew on Ray's two hundred fifty acres—from alfalfa, fescue, and sweet summer corn to peaches and pecans. Deirdre passed through the newly tilled fields, inhaling the loamy scent of black dirt ready for seeding. At the end of the lane, the round barn beckoned, its open doors flooding the ground with yellow light. A strand of wayward music floated out. Someone picked up the beat with a goatskin drum. By the time Deirdre shouldered past the field hands smoking their pipes by the door, the barn was jumping. Folks swung arm and arm in a country reel, their steps cutting paths across the hay-strewn floor. Old Josh's fiddle bow was sawing so fast over the strings Deirdre was sure they'd either snap or catch fire.

Across the barn, she caught sight of Ingrid with two of the Rays' cattle hands, her full cheeks round with laughter. Jolly Ing never lacked for male attention, even though her face was plainer than a gray November day. Deirdre was far prettier, but hers was the kind of pretty that made men nervous and craven at the same time.

A pair of sun-browned arms encircled her waist from behind, startling her. "I been waitin' for you, Deirdre Jane. What took you so long?"

Deirdre leaned back, resting her head against Robbie's shoulder. He smelled of warm hay and sunshine, a scent at war with his looks—all wild dark curls and stormy gray eyes. She turned in his arms. "Mama had to give me a lecture afore I left. Warned me to stay away from you, mostly, lest people *talk*."

Robbie laughed. "It's a little late for that. Besides, my pa is up at your place enough to make tongues wag about your mama. And we both know he ain't just mendin' fence."

Deirdre had done her best to ignore the gossip about Mama and Arthur Cash. When Pa was gone out west, Mr. Cash helped tend their acreage and see to their cattle. He had a way with the land—a kinship with the natural world that Mama lacked. It eased Mama's burden considerably to have him about when Pa was absent. He was a strapping, fine-looking man, like his son. She could see where Mama might be tempted, and the thought rankled her.

Robbie nuzzled Deirdre's neck, the stubble on his chin sending a thrill of desire through her belly. "You sure do look pretty tonight."

"You do, too." And he did, with his cupid's bow mouth tipping upward at the corners and his black curls shining with pomade. He guided her onto the dance floor. The music slowed to a waltz, Josh's fiddle high and keening sweet.

"How much longer, Deirdre?" Robbie's breath flared hot against her cheek. "I been wantin' you so bad I can't stand to wait much longer."

Deirdre sighed. "I . . . I don't want to wait no more, neither."

"We'll sneak away, then. Go off in the woods. Tonight."

A shudder of nervous anticipation wound through her at the thought of what they might do. She'd imagined plenty, at night, alone in her bed. Robbie's hands traced circles on the back of her dress and roamed lower. He was clasping her far too close for it to be proper. They were only pretending at dancing now. "Robbie," she murmured, pushing against his chest, "maybe we'd better—"

"Land sakes. Y'all better be *betrothed*."

At the sound of Reverend Stack's gruff voice, Deirdre sprang away from Robbie, her cheeks heating with embarrassment. The old minister stood in front of them, his arms crossed over his suspenders. "Idn't proper to be comporting yourself this way outside of marriage."

"We weren't doing nothin' but dancing, sir," Deirdre managed, her breath shallow.

He ignored her. Leaned closer to Robbie. "Have you declared your intentions to Deirdre's pa, young Robert?"

"Not yet, sir," Robbie slurred. He looked down at the floor and pushed at the hay with the toe of his boot.

Old Stack raised an eyebrow. "Have you been partaking of the devil's mash, son?"

"I've had a swig or two tonight, yessir." Robbie glanced over at Deirdre, suddenly bashful. So *that's* why he'd tasted so sweet and been so forward in front of everyone.

"That drinking won't lead to anything godly, boy. Best to give it up afore it gets a hold on you."

"Yessir. I won't drink no more, and I'll go to Deirdre's pa soon as he gets home. Ask permission to court her."

"Good. Good." Reverend Stack rounded on Deirdre, eyeing her bosom with a self-satisfied grin, his fat cheeks purple with gin blossoms. "As for you, *Miss* Werner, a young woman is to remain pure and unsullied until her weddin' night."

The music faded until the barn went snowdrift silent. Deirdre dipped her head and longed to crawl inside herself.

Reverend Stack paced in a fitful circle around her, his upper lip glistening with sweat. "A woman of God must hide her charms from all but her husband," he boomed. "To do otherwise is to invite menfolk into temptation. For in this very same way, Bathsheba tempted David and brought him near to ruin. Ain't that right, flock?"

A chorus of *amens* echoed against the gambrel roof. The townsfolk gawped at her, their eyes full of unkind amusement. Deirdre reached for Robbie's hand. He squeezed her fingers, then nudged away.

"Purity is at odds with a woman's true nature," Old Stack railed on, running a hand through his oily copper curls. "Woman's inclination is toward sin and fornication. For when the serpent tempted Eve, he cursed her with a spirit of seduction." His bleary eyes roved over Deirdre. "Such a spirit must be driven out by prayer and devotion to God."

Reverend Stack ceased his pacing and loomed over her, the sour garlic smell of unwashed flesh rolling off him. "I've yet to see you in my church, Miss Werner."

Deirdre lifted her chin. "My pa don't have much use for churches, Reverend. And my mama prays for my soul aplenty."

"Well. I won't be sanctifyin' *no* vows of marriage unless you come to the fold. To be wed under a yoke of sin and fornication is an affront to God."

A wave of defiance swept through her. "Is that so, sir?" She lowered her voice to a whisper. "Nobody but me and Mama know about them babies. I'd suppose you'd like to keep it that way. You *so* sure you want me in your church?"

Reverend Stack took a step backward, his mouth knotting in an angry scowl. For a moment, Deirdre feared he might hit her. She clenched her eyes shut. When the stinging strike didn't come, she opened them. Stack turned from her, angrily stalking to the other side of the barn. Josh picked up his fiddle once more and the townsfolk went back to their dancing.

Deirdre let out a shaky breath. It'd been dangerous to say what she'd said. Foolhardy. Even if it had been the truth.

Two babies had been born this past winter—both with copper hair. She and Mama had delivered them to frightened young girls from Reverend Stack's congregation. They both refused to name the father. No one knew what happened to the babies afterward, though Deirdre had her ideas. She'd learned to hold such secrets close in Tin Mountain. Folks acted their best on Sunday morning—all smiles and hands clasped in prayer. But the same hands hurt and killed, then buried their sins in shallow graves so they might dig them up late at night, after they'd put God to sleep.

There was darkness everywhere in Tin Mountain.

You just had to know where to look.

⁂

The fire clawed and climbed the night sky, sparks cracking as the menfolk fed it with bundles of straw. Deirdre sank down on a hay bale, next to Ingrid. Robbie cast furtive glances her way from the other side of the bonfire.

"Mind you're not mooning at Robbie," Ing hissed. "Old Haystack'll go right to your mama. What were you thinking, käraste? You're taking care, I hope?"

"Yes, Ing. We ain't done nothin' but kiss." But they'd gotten close to doing more, Robbie's hands working her drawers over her hips in the tall grass behind the lighthouse before she pleaded "no" and bucked him off.

"You could tell me if you had. Me and Edgar do it all the time," Ing said matter-of-factly. "Sometimes I even fool around with Albert, but only if Edgar's gone. He's much better at it. Uses his tongue on me."

"What's it like?"

Ing shifted the wad of tobacco bulging under her lip from one side of her mouth to the other. "You know when you've got an itch, in a place high up on your back where you can't scratch, and you lean against the corner of the barn and rub? It's a lot like that."

"Does it hurt? When they put their thing inside you the first time?"

Ingrid gave a quick nod. "*Ja.* Just for a minute."

"Robbie means to sneak me off tonight. To do it, I think."

"In the woods?" Ingrid's brow creased. "I wouldn't."

"Why not?"

"The witch. It's her time. Walpurgis."

"Mama says not to listen to superstition."

Ingrid spat a line of brown tobacco juice between her feet and scraped dirt over it. "Her kin weren't here when the curse first came over Tin Mountain fifty years ago, like my *morfar* was. She remembered that witch. What she did. How the settlers tore her limb from limb, then burned her."

A log cracked on the fire, sending a cyclone of sparks heavenward. Deirdre flinched at the sound and drew her cloak tight around her shoulders. "Who was she? No one ever says her name."

Ingrid shrugged. "I reckon no one will speak her name aloud, for fear they might call her spirit up, though Morfar always said she was Owen Sutter's youngest daughter. People only sought her out for blood magic. Wicked things. The sacrifice of innocents. It all came back on her, I'd imagine."

Innocents. Babies, likely. A sudden disturbing vision of a mewling, red-faced infant held down on a stone altar intruded upon Deirdre's thoughts, unbidden. Her secret visions had become more frequent of late. More troubling and filled with ominous portents. She discreetly pulled out the flask beneath her skirts and took a swig of whiskey to chase the chill from her bones. *Witch* was a troublesome word. People sometimes cast their aspersions about Deirdre's mama, and the word

21

had been whispered more than once in her presence, even though no one feared God as much as Finola Werner. Mama was a midwife, who brought life into the world with her hands, not death and curses.

"Do you really believe in witches, Ing? Pacts with the devil and such?"

Ingrid nodded slowly. "There are those who turn down a dark path. For their own gain."

"But if folks were asking her to work those sorts of spells, don't that mean they were just as bad as she was?"

A pair of hands clapped onto Deirdre's shoulders, sending her heart thudding into her throat. "Would you stop sneaking up on me, Robbie Cash?" she said, turning. "You make me jump clean out of my skin every time."

Robbie smoothed her hair away from her ear, his breath hot and heady with liquor. "Preacher man's gone. I reckon your mama wants you home soon." There was a wolfish gleam in Robbie's eyes as he pulled her to her feet. "I'll walk you up the mountain."

"*Walk*, he says." Ing sniffed contemptuously, her mouth pulled tight. "Stay close to the road. No wandering deep into the woods, Robbie, lest the witch take your pretty virgin for her midnight feast."

"Ain't no such thing as witches, Ing." Robbie's voice hardened. His grasp tightened around Deirdre's waist. "Those old stories change all the time, depending on who's telling them. Come on, Deirdre. Let's go."

As Robbie led her from the warmth of the bonfire and into the inky-blue night, Deirdre sent a knowing smile over her shoulder. Ing lifted her chin, her eyes haughty, and spat an arc of tobacco at the ground.

THREE

GRACELYNN

1931

I lift my hem above the brambles and follow Granny through the pines, my head on a swivel. Even though it ain't rained for three days, with any luck, more mushrooms will have sprouted. Every pound of spongy, dead-ugly morels I gather fetches as much money at market as a slab of red meat. Money that'll get me that much closer to San Francisco and a better life.

Granny suddenly stops, her hair a silver torch in the early-morning murk. "Gracie, come here, child. I want to show you something."

I amble over. "What is it?"

"Just look." She points at the ground and shakes her finger. A wide slab of slate, broad as a tabletop stretches over the forest floor. Moss crawls over the smooth surface in the shape of a man's hand, green fingers gripping the edges. The woods seem to go still around us; even the bright chirruping of the robins falls to a whisper.

I fight the chill crawling over my shoulders, and edge closer, squinting my eyes. "What's it mean?"

"It's a weather sign." Granny clucks her tongue. "Summer's likely to be hard this year and yield poorly at the harvest."

"But it's just now May."

"Sure it is. Walpurgis. Witch's night." A faraway look flits over her face. "We'll need to prepare. Build up the root cellar. Ration our wares. I ain't seen this kind of portent for many a year."

I shift my satchel onto my skinny shoulder. "Didn't hard times and a string of bad weather come through this time of year when you were a girl? I remember you sayin' something about that once. A flood?"

Granny presses her lips together. "That was different. We're just in for a lean spell, honey, that's all. Don't you worry." She plants her gnarled walking stick in the ground and turns toward home. "We've gathered enough greens for the week. Let's head on back and see to our work."

The sun crests the hill, lifting the dew from the grass and turning it into patchy fog draped like a threadbare quilt over the ground. Out over the tops of the trees, the lighthouse beam sweeps in an arc, burning a path through the morning dim. Our cabin emerges from the humid mist, squatted low on the hillside, its porch bedecked with bundles of herbs and wildflowers hung out to dry. A thin spiral of smoke curls from the stone chimney. Morris is up, then.

"Start the coffee, Gracelynn!" Granny calls from behind me. "I got another one of my goddamn headaches comin' on."

"Yes'm!" I go through the side garden, sending chickens scattering, and push through the door into the gray darkness of our lean-to kitchen.

Morris, my oldest cousin, is kneeling on the floor in front of the stove, feeding wood into its pot belly. "Any luck?" He wipes his hands on his trousers and stands. He's so tall his head nearly touches the smoke-stained ceiling.

"Nope. Not a single mushroom this morning. Got plenty of young poke and nettles, though." I hang my yarb bag on the peg by the door and sit to take off my muddy boots, stacking them next to the other three pairs on the rag rug by the door. "Start the coffee. Granny's got a headache, and you know how that is."

He laughs, running a hand through his lop of wavy hair. "Yep. I sure do." He fills the tin kettle with water and sets it on the stove with a wet sizzle, while I measure the meager grounds into our coffee jug.

We're the same age, but not for long, because I'll be twenty soon. We favor each other, but my hair's white as goose feathers and fine as corn silk. Morris's is a warm, burnished gold. Still, our sameness shows in the high tilt of our cheekbones, our blue eyes and long legs, and the deep dimples in our chins. Hallmarks of the Doherty side. The drunken, good-for-nothing side, according to Aunt Val, who once thought well enough of a Doherty to marry one and have two young 'uns by him. My mama must have once thought the same, though my daddy was a far sight meaner than his little brother and worthless as tits on a boar hog.

Granny comes in, wiping her feet on the stoop. She squints in the gloom. "Morris Clyde, you sure are up early this morning. Hosea won't be expecting you at the farm until seven."

A furtive, shamefaced look passes over Morris's face. "Figured I'd go up and check on the still first."

Granny sighs and shakes her head. "I sure wish you'd close up that still and leave that hooch alone."

He scoffs. "It makes the ends meet, don't it?"

"It's your drinking of it that worries me more, Morris Clyde, and don't you dare take a tone with me," Granny scolds, wagging a finger. "Remember who you're talking to."

"The best damn granny woman in Arkansas," I say with a smirk.

"And the fiercest. Don't you forget it. I need to go lay back down for a minute to try an' get ahead of this megrim. Bring my cup, would you, Gracelynn?"

"Yes'm."

Morris pulls on his boots and snugs his hat over his curls. "I'm headed out."

"Don't you want some breakfast before you go? I just need to fetch more water to make grits. Won't take two shakes of a lamb's tail."

"Nah, I ain't hungry. I'll walk you to the spring, though."

I grab the water bucket and go out barefoot, not bothering with my boots. We make our way down to the springhouse, my calloused feet sure on the rocky ground. Morris has gone all quiet, like he's chewing on a thought. I know the real reason he's heading out early, and it don't have a thing to do with checking on his still. "Y'all need to be careful."

He gives a sharp laugh. "I know, Gracie. Believe me, I do. Seth knows it, too."

"If Harlan and his gang . . ."

"Don't start in preaching. You let me worry about Harlan. Long as he gets his cut, he stays off my back. Seth's, too."

"Y'all need to mind yourselves. That's all. Nobody's ever found your daddy's bones for a reason."

Morris frowns. "I know, Gracie. I know." Through the honeysuckle bushes on the other side of the spring, a flicker of white flashes against the green. "I'll see you tonight, kid." Morris lopes away and I watch him until he disappears into the undergrowth. I can't help it that I worry. Harlan and his daddy are in thick with the Klan. They been trying to run Seth's family out of Tin Mountain since before Seth was born and have made it their life's work to cause trouble for anybody who don't kowtow to them. And seeing as Al Northrup runs timber in Tin Mountain and keeps most of the families here fed, it don't take no genius to figure out how he rose to the top like a turd in a privy.

But since Morris is my cousin—my best friend—I'll keep his secrets, even though he's cost me more than one sleepless night.

I prop open the door to the springhouse, the loamy scent of moist earth greeting me. A water moccasin slides out, slow and sinuous, and I step aside to let her pass, then kneel on the ground to put the bucket under the tap. Air gurgles through the line as I pump the handle, then a rush of ice-cold water sputters into my bucket. I fill it near to the top and grab the last log of butter from the shelves.

When I get back, Aunt Val is sitting at the kitchen table, her hair frazzled and her face set in the sour scowl she always wears of a morning. Caro's there, too, impatient for breakfast.

"Mornin'," I mutter under my breath.

"Yup. It sure is." Val lights a cigarette, huffing smoke into the stolid air of the tiny kitchen. Doc Gallagher says smoke's bad for Caro's lungs, but Val don't listen. Some women ain't fit to be mothers, and she's sure enough one of them.

I do my best to fill in the gaps for Caro, but it's hard to know if I'm doin' things right, since I never knew my own mama apart from a name stretched across a gravestone.

"I'm hungry." Caro makes a pouty face, her plump lower lip dipping toward her chin.

"Ain't you always, child? You'll eat soon enough." I slide a pan onto the burner next to the kettle. "Granny says we're in for lean times. You need to learn to do with the feel of an emptier belly."

Lord knows I had to at her age. When your mama dies bringing you into this world and your daddy's so mean you can only find peace once he's gotten to the bottom of his moonshine jar, you'll do whatever it takes to survive. The only thing that'd kept me from starving back then was the Friday train from Springfield to St. Louis and the fine people who rode it. They didn't notice me brushing past them, my hand dipping into their coat pockets and handbags as I went by. I was good at what I did. I had to be.

"Mama got one of her headaches again?" Val asks, pulling me out of my thoughts. Smoke slides out the corner of her mouth, and hovers in a blue-gray cloud over the table.

"Yep. She saw something in the woods. Said it was a portent. A sign of hard times. Came on after that."

"Mama and her *signs*." Val barks a laugh. "We're already in hard times as it is. I ain't worried too much."

"I figure not, with the way you're always smoking them cigarettes and going to sideshows."

Val stubs out her cigarette and lights another. "I reckon people who *work* can do whatever they please with their money, Gracelynn."

I clench my jaw and turn back to the stove to keep my words locked tight within my mouth. According to Aunt Val, the cooking and cleaning I do ain't real work. She's always hated me. I can't reason why she agreed to take me in when my daddy died, other than to have a live-in maid and cook. Lord knows there's never been a shred of fondness between us.

Just as I've finished making coffee, the pan of grits boils over. I curse under my breath, pull the pan off the range, and set it down hard on the table. Caro fills her bowl, then adds three whole spoonfuls of butter, one after the other. I smack her hand. "What did I just say? You need to stop eatin' so much. Once that butter's gone, we may not be able to get more."

"You're meaner than a snake this morning, Gracelynn."

Aunt Val snickers, like we're putting on a vaudeville for her benefit. She blows a slow stream of smoke straight into Caro's face, sending her into a coughing spell. Caro's face goes red as summer poppies.

"Can't you put that ciggie out until after breakfast? Or go smoke outside?" I glare at Aunt Val over my shoulder and open the window over the kitchen sink. A rush of fresh air sweeps into the room. "You're throwing Caro into fits."

"She's fine."

"You all right, Caro?"

Caro nods, still wheezing, but with the fresh air, her face soon returns to its normal pink. I pat her on the back and start smoothing her hair with my fingers. Caro's only ten. It ain't her fault her mama never taught her to be respectful to me or anyone else. "I'll get you some horehound next time I go to the mercantile. It helps your cough." I braid her hair, finish the plaits off with kitchen twine, and kiss the top of her head. "Now, after you're finished with breakfast, wash your face to get the sleep out of your eyes before you go. And don't forget to wash behind your ears."

"Yes'm," Caro says.

I ignore the poisoned look Val shoots my way and pour two cups of coffee—one bitter and black and the other sweetened with sugar—and go out to the screened-in porch where Granny always sleeps, even in the dead of winter, with nothing more than a pile of quilts and a bed pig for warmth. She claims the cold makes her tough.

"You get 'em all fed, Gracelynn?" Granny takes the tin cup I offer her, her hand sun-spotted and wrinkled like the pleats in a fancy lady's dress.

"Yes'm. Caro has the patience of a hungry cat." I sit across from Granny and blow on my coffee to cool it. "There's a new revivalist in town. First service is tonight."

"Revivalist, you say?" Granny lifts a brow. "Another one of them hucksters, I reckon."

"Yep. Josiah Bellflower, he's called. Calvina says she's bringing her mama to his service. I figure I better go—see what he can do."

"Them yarb doctors are full-up with parlor tricks. I ain't worried about losing business. You remember that one that came through two summers ago? He had pig innards in the bucket behind his altar. Claimed he was drawing the sickness out of people, but he'd just put them innards in his hand before he prayed over people. Why—" She pinches her nose, a sharp grimace of pain shooting across her face. "Oh, Lord . . ."

I scoot forward and take the cup out of her trembling hand before it spills. "What is it?"

"No . . ." Granny whimpers. She starts shaking all over. Her blue eyes go wide and fix on something I can't see.

A shiver of panic slices through me. I've been with Granny when she's had visions before, but this one seems worse than the others. A look of sheer terror is stitched across her face as she speaks strange words I can't understand. A slow trickle of blood runs from her nostril.

"Granny!" I squeeze her shoulder. "Come on, now. That's enough."

After a breathless moment, she shakes her head as if to clear it, her eyes suddenly locking on mine. She wipes the blood trailing from her nose with the back of her hand. "You're not to set one blessed foot in that revival tent tonight, Gracelynn. You hear me?"

"Why? What's wrong? What did you see?"

Granny grasps my wrist, viselike. "Listen to me, girl. There's a certain kind of evil in this world that seeks our kind. And I don't mean to lose you to it."

⚜

The revival tent sits in Hosea Ray's alfalfa pasture, lit up yellow against the night. It floats in the darkness like something in a fever dream—out of place and unnatural. A crowd of folks huddle around the entrance, jawin' and smoking. A cow lifts her head from her slumber beneath a sweetgum tree and moos at the intrusion.

She ain't the only one who's less than pleased by Bellflower's arrival.

I'm defying Granny by being here. It don't feel right, but my curiosity's too strong to deny. I snuck out while she was napping, a sprig of rosemary tucked behind my ear and a handful of dried sage in my pocket. Simple wards, just in case she was right and there's more to Bellflower's tent revival than a few hymns and an altar call.

I push through the crowd and duck beneath the open oilcloth flap. The tent is packed with people. Their excited talk hums fierce as a nest of mad wasps. The heat from outdoors is only made worse by the kerosene lanterns set along the walls. Sweat rolls down my temple and drips onto my dress.

May came in hot as August this year, and she ain't showing no signs of letting up.

Aunt Val's in the front row, batting the sultry air with a paper fan, all eager to get her first glimpse of the famed Josiah Bellflower.

What the hell kind of name is Bellflower, anyway?

I slump next to Val, arrange my dress over my knobby knees, and pray she won't rat me out to Granny.

Somehow, Val's gotten herself all dolled up between leaving Hosea's fields and now. Folks talk. They say Val don't work at sharecropping as much as she works in his bed. I wouldn't be surprised, knowing Val. She scowls at me, her lips rouged up like a floozy. "What are *you* doin' here?"

I shrug. "I'm just as curious as you. Figured I'd come see the signs and wonders."

"You know this is a religious service, Gracelynn."

"Yes'm." I smirk. "Maybe there's hope for me yet."

Just then, Calvina and her mama step into the tent. Ma Watterson is looking poorly. Her legs shake with every step, ankles swollen below her rolled stockings. She's leaning heavy on Calvina's arm. Her arthritis is the worst I've ever seen it.

I gesture for them to come sit by us, and Calvina waves me off. Ain't nobody wants to sit in the front row of a camp meeting unless they're crazy or stupid, what with folks flopping around like they do and getting slain in the Spirit. Good way to get a broken toe. Yet, here I am.

A swell of music comes from the back of the tent. It's an accordion, grinding out a tune that sounds more sideshow rag than hymn. A man swaggers up the aisle, his collar-length hair a dark sandy blond, his nose as sharp as the blade on a combine. He's tall and wiry, arms knotted with lean muscle beneath his rolled-up shirtsleeves. He's dressed in fine town clothes that flatter his broad shoulders and narrow hips. Some of the women go all moony as he passes by.

Naturally, Aunt Val is one of them.

I cross my arms over my chest and lean back in the wooden chair. The chair squeaks in protest. He turns at the sound. Our eyes lock, and I swear his widen, just the slightest bit. He smiles, and the jagged scar beside his mouth raises one side of his lips higher than the other. Something akin to indigestion flutters in my belly.

People start to clap along as Bellflower works his squeeze-box with long fingers, expertly coaxing music from its bellows. I finally recognize the tune—"Trust and Obey"—only it's sped way up. He comes to the end of the song and shrugs off the accordion. It wheezes out a long, sorrowful note as he places it on the straw-covered ground.

He makes a circle around the front of the tent, his dark, long-lashed eyes flirting with the crowd. Looking for the greenest rube for his tricks, no doubt. "Good people of Tin Mountain," he begins, his drawl as deep and honey-rich as bourbon. He's a Kaintuck, then, like my worthless daddy. "I have lately been to western Oklahoma, where the fields were withered to dust and the unfortunate folks there labored long in the day, to no avail. To those people, I brought a message of hope and prosperity. A message of redemption. Within weeks of my arrival, children with hollow bellies grew fat with plenty. Folks who had not walked a step for years ran. Barren fields grew fecund and thick with green corn."

What the hell does *fecund* mean?

"I can promise the same to you, brothers and sisters." The tent goes so quiet I can hear the rustle of hot wind blowing through the alfalfa outside. A smug smile plays over Bellflower's lips. He's got these people where he wants them. Already. His eyes fall on Aunt Val and narrow. He ceases his pacing and stops in front of her.

Val pokes at her hair, which she's brushed into rippling waves, the ends touched with gold from the sun. The color is coming up high under her freckled tan. She looks as pretty as she can for a woman near fifty who's had it hard in life.

"Sister," he coaxes, "what is your name?"

"Val . . . Valerie Doherty," she stammers like a schoolgirl. "I sure am pleased to make your acquaintance, Reverend." It takes everything in me not to roll my eyes.

"Valerie." His voice slithers over every syllable. I can see the goosepimples come up on Aunt Val's skin. He takes hold of her hand, his fingers splaying over her skinny wrist. "I have a message for you, sister. The Lord sees fit to bless you. An unexpected calling will fall upon you soon. A calling that will bring prosperity, and much abundance."

Aunt Val gasps. Her arm starts quivering. "Praise Jesus! I can feel the power!"

I just *bet* she can. Hogwash. Every bit of it.

The tent echoes with a chorus of *hallelujah*s. Aunt Val lets loose of the preacher's hand. Tears spring to her eyes. She's still shaking as Bellflower goes back to the front of the tent, opening his arms wide. "Come forward, brothers and sisters. Pray with me and receive your own blessing from the Lord."

The townsfolk start rising from their chairs, drawn forward by Josiah Bellflower's velvet promises. An excited murmuring flows through the tent like a wave. One by one, Bellflower places his hand on their foreheads as he speaks in tongues over them. There ain't a single message or Bible verse being preached—just a never-ending carnival line of needy, desperate people, dropping coins into the offering bucket so Josiah Bellflower might touch them. People I've helped *Granny* cure. With every plunk of a quarter or a silver dollar into Bellflower's tin pail, I think of how lean our own pockets are gonna be if he stays the whole summer revival season. When you can pay ten cents for a healing miracle, who needs our kind of mountain medicine?

33

Still, I can't fault people for wanting to believe in something bigger than poverty and sickness, even though I suspect Bellflower's promises are just as empty as our cupboards.

Calvina and her mama are last in line. Bellflower reaches out and covers the neat coil of gray braids atop Ma Watterson's head with his hand. At his touch, her legs start trembling. I spring to my feet. This damned fool ain't gonna push an old lady to the ground and claim it's God. I rush to her side, ready to help Calvina catch her if her knees buckle.

As he closes his eyes to pray over her, his thin lips muttering low, I take a step closer. There's something funny about him—unnatural. Up this close, there's a brutality to his rangy good looks. My skin crawls. As if he can feel my eyes on him, Bellflower turns to me, his pupils widening until they swallow up the inky brown around them.

A low hum starts in my ears and reverberates all through me. My head pings with sudden pain and the light in the tent flickers like a candle. The congregants' voices fade to silence. Where Josiah Bellflower should be, I can see only spinning shadows—a writhing blackness with nothing human at its heart. I ain't never had a real vision, only dreams, but I think I'm having one right now. Granny was right. There's more to Josiah Bellflower than a Holy Roller preacher who likes big words. Fear crawls over me like a scorpion. I panic, clawing my way back to the real world and away from this darkness.

My head pounds in time with my heartbeat, sickening my stomach. Lands. Is this how Granny feels when she has her spells?

"Praised be the Lord!"

Calvina's shout nearly deafens me. I blink, once, twice. Shake my head. My mouth drops open. Ma Watterson is dancing. She's kicking so hard the hem of her dress flies up over her knees.

Josiah Bellflower is staring at me, an amused expression on his face, his eyes glimmering. He smiles wickedly, and in that smile is a thousand promises. None of them the good kind.

FOUR

DEIRDRE

1881

Deirdre trudged through the underbrush, the moon lighting her path with silver. She was sore between her legs, the wet, warm trickle of Robbie's seed running down her thigh. Their joining had been exciting, but hasty and not at all the romantic tryst she had imagined. Just when things started feeling good, he'd finished with three sharp thrusts, then left her with a kiss and a promise in Charlie Ray's peach orchard, throbbing with the want of something she didn't have a name for.

Ingrid had lied. It hadn't been as good as scratching an itch. Not at all.

Mama's words haunted her. She *should* have waited—made him take vows before giving herself to him, like Mama had admonished. But what good would it do to nurse regret now?

Things would get better once they married. They'd have to.

It was fixing to cut loose a storm. Thunder crackled in the distance, and the first few drops of rain splashed across Deirdre's cheeks. She hurried through the orchard and into Sutter's holler. The old homestead was down here, somewhere. The place where Pa grew up. Deirdre had seen it only once, when she was very little, and even by then the shake roof was throwing its shingles and the porch boards had buckled from years of neglect.

Don't ever go down the holler alone, Deirdre, Pa had warned. *There's a reason we don't live there no more. It's a haunted place.*

Deirdre shoved aside the memory of Pa's warning.

The holler was a shortcut—the fastest way home.

It was rough going down the edges of the gully, with the rain beating hard. Her boots slipped against wet pine needles, and she fell on her rump once, then again. When she finally reached the bottom, she stopped to catch her breath, the bluff curving above her like the edges of a bowl. A locust tree stood in the middle of the clearing, its gnarled, thorny branches purple black against the evergreens. A sharp wind rustled its leaves. Just beyond the tree, she could make out the shadowed roofline of Pa's old homestead. She stopped, still as a stone. A wan light flickered through the doorway of the ruined cabin. Was somebody squatting in the old homeplace?

"Hello?" she called, and moved closer, as if pulled by an invisible thread.

The woods went quiet for a full breath. She listened for a return greeting, but none came.

She crossed the clearing, her curiosity quelling any fear. She gingerly stepped onto the sagging porch to peek through the door. A fire burned in the stone hearth, a pot hooked over the grate. In the corner, a low table was laden with tallow candles. An arbor of dried and braided grapevine arched over it, decorated with animal skulls, chicken bones, and feathers. A knife lay at the center of the table, its slender blade wickedly curved. Was a hunter living there? Fur trappers sometimes camped out in these parts.

"Hello?" When an answer still didn't come, Deirdre lifted her skirts and crossed the threshold. Her pulse thrummed in her throat. She went to the table and picked up the knife, studying it. Such a finely made tool would be just the thing for skinning rabbits or dressing deer. She gently ran her fingers over the blade, testing its sharpness.

Footsteps sounded overhead, coming from the loft. Deirdre dropped the knife. It skittered across the dirt floor. She turned tail and ran, her heart pummeling. In her haste to get away, her skirts tangled around her ankles, sending her to the floor of the holler in a graceless tumble. She scrambled to her feet, sparing a glance over her shoulder. The silhouette of a man stood in the doorway, hands braced against the door frame, his countenance hidden in shadow, but for the glimmer of shine where his eyes might be. A crack of thunder rattled the air. Panic drove Deirdre's feet. She ran the length of the holler and up the hillside as if the devil himself were after her, not stopping until she saw the yellow lights of home.

༼༅༈༽

"Cream'll curdle if you don't keep churning," Ingrid said, scowling at Deirdre. "What's the matter with you today? You're all quiet."

Deirdre rubbed the cramp from her arm and lifted the dasher and brought it down again, trying to match Ingrid's steady rhythm. "I ain't feeling too good. Didn't get much sleep last night." She usually loved sitting on the Nilssons' low-slung porch and gossiping with Ing while they churned butter, but today, her head ached with the worst headache she'd ever had, and Ing's constant chatter vexed her.

"So, what was it like?" Ingrid asked stiffly. "With Robbie?"

Deirdre stilled her dasher once more to swipe the sweat from her brow with a rolled-up sleeve. "Fast."

37

"The first time always is." Ingrid chuckled. "They're too excited to be good for much."

"I reckon it'll get better." Deirdre blushed and ducked her head. "Say, did you know there's somebody squattin' in Pa's old homeplace? I passed through Sutter's holler last night, on the way home."

"You went there *alone?*" Ingrid's eyes grew big as wagon wheels. "Did you see the witch? They say she's all wild-haired with eyes as black as pits and claws for fingernails."

"I didn't see anything like that. There was a man. He saw me, I think. I—"

Deirdre startled. She heard a sudden rustling from the mulberry bush near the porch, as if an animal were trapped in the underbrush. Two small white hands emerged through the leaves, a tracery of fine scratches across their backs. A strange child crawled out from the bush, her long white-blonde hair matted and littered with leaves. Her birdlike mouth was purple with berry juice. Placid green-blue eyes met Deirdre's with curiosity.

"Ebba!" Ingrid shouted. *"Rackarunge!"*

"Who's this one, Ing?"

Ingrid looked heavenward. "My little cousin. She's an animal. A beast." She tapped her temple with a thick finger. "Touched."

The child growled and showed her teeth.

"My, you're fearsome!" Deirdre said, laughing. "Come, Ebba. I have a sweet in my pocket."

"She only understands *svenska.*"

"Tell her, then."

Ingrid muttered a terse line of Swedish and the little girl came forward, wiping her berry-stained hands on her dress. Deirdre withdrew a disk of butterscotch from her pocket and held it out. Ebba snatched the candy and scurried around the side of the house, fast as a jackrabbit.

"She's a bit wild, isn't she?"

"She's ever hiding and sneaking off. And she won't talk. Her *mor* and *far* died of the bloody flux during their passage. Her brothers, too. All three."

"Poor thing."

Ingrid shrugged. "It's the way of it, yes?"

A low rumble of thunder came in the distance. Dark-bellied clouds gathered on the horizon, their undersides laden with rain. A sharp, cold wind blew across the rows of freshly sprouted green corn. "There's fixin' to be another storm."

"A bad one by the looks of it. You'd better get on home. My butter's set. I'll finish yours and bring it to you tomorrow." Ingrid scooted Deirdre's butter crock between her knees and frowned at her. "Remember to rinse with cider vinegar after you and Robbie do it. Won't be no babies that way. He's the sort who won't marry you just because you have his child in your belly."

"I remembered, Ing." She'd gone out to the privy and done what needed to be done as soon as she'd got home. It had burned and stung like hellfire but had purged a small measure of her regret.

Deirdre took her leave from Ing and trundled up the hill, her head pounding with each footfall. Just as she crested the rise, she saw Ebba by the fence row, sitting on the ground. She was drawing in the dirt with a stick, her scabbed knees akimbo. As Deirdre approached, she raised her turquoise eyes and made a small grunt at the back of her throat.

"Hello, Ebba," Deirdre said, stopping to catch her breath. "What are you drawing?"

Ebba pointed her finger at one of her drawings—a bird sitting on a fence post. *"Kråka."*

"Ah. So you *do* talk. But I don't speak your language, remember?" Every now and again, Deirdre could parse a Swedish word or phrase that sounded like Pa's broken German, but this wasn't a word she was familiar with.

Ebba smiled knowingly. With a rush of wings, a crow lit on the fence post behind Ebba as if it had been summoned. It tilted its black head, beady eyes glinting. Ebba pointed from the crow to her drawing. "Kråka."

"Crow!" Deirdre exclaimed.

Ebba nodded. "Cr . . . ow," she said slowly, trying out the sounds of the word. She began scribbling again, her movements frantic. A face emerged from the mud, hair frizzing out from its head in an erratic halo. Ebba jabbed with the stick, once, then twice. Two black eyes peered up at Deirdre from the ground. Ebba pointed at a spot over Deirdre's shoulder. *"Trollkona."*

A chill walked over Deirdre's skin. "What does that mean, Ebba?"

Ebba shook her head, irritated. She pointed at the drawing again. *"Häxa."*

Suddenly, a commotion of hoofbeats came from down the road. Somebody was in a god-awful hurry. She turned from Ebba to look. It was Mama, driving Rosy hard. She brought the wagon up short in the middle of the road. "Come quick," she panted. "Mrs. Bledsoe's in a bad way with the baby. I need your help."

"Lands." Deirdre picked up her skirts and climbed in the back of the wagon as Mama lashed the traces, sending the little mule wheeling into a turn. Deirdre gripped the sideboard to keep from spilling out as they lurched back down the mountain at a breakneck pace.

Mama was scared. Deirdre could see it in her ashen face and in the tense way she held the reins. She had never lost a birthing mother, not in all her years of midwifery. She'd lost babies, sure enough—but that was just nature. Some weren't ready to be born, and some were born too late. But if she lost a mother, especially Mrs. Bledsoe, it would be a black mark on her name, one from which she might not recover. It was one thing for a hill woman to die in labor, but another thing entirely if it was a rich man's wife.

When they got to the Bledsoe mansion, it was nearly dark. Golden light radiated from the window with the fancy balcony, its sash thrown wide. A gut-wrenching cry came from within, then a plea for mercy. Deirdre vaulted herself over the side of the wagon. Mama grasped her wrist like a steel trap, her eyes glinting in the dusk. "That baby ain't turned, Deirdre. I tried to turn it last week, to no help. It's comin' feet-first." Mama's voice fell into a hoarse whisper. "We may have to cut it out. Mrs. Bledsoe will likely pass if that happens. Mr. Bledsoe wants me to send for a doctor, but it's too late. That doctor down in Fayetteville ain't worth his salt, anyhow. We'll do our best, hear?"

"Yes, Mama."

At the sound of their step on the porch, Mr. Bledsoe flung open the door, his eyes red and swollen, his dark hair fanning out in all directions. "Oh, thank God you've returned. Mary is with her, but she's in a terrible way. She says she's dying." He turned his head, but not before Deirdre heard the tears in his voice.

William Bledsoe wasn't the type to cry. He was the type of man who turned every girl's head when he strode down the street, his silver-topped walking cane swinging. Those eager girls had grown sullen when he brought home a young Charleston bride late last summer. Hateful as some of them were to his pretty Hannah, they'd likely welcome the news if he became a widower tonight.

Deirdre shook her head to push aside her grim thoughts. "It'll be all right, Mr. Bledsoe. We'll take every care with your wife. She'll pull through just fine."

He sank onto the fancy velvet sofa by the door. "If the worst happens, will you come for me?"

"We will," Mama soothed. "But I've not lost a mother yet, sir, and I don't plan on your Hannah being the first."

Deirdre followed Mama up the stairs, her heart beating a shivering cadence. She'd helped Mama at many a birth—seen the joy when a squalling, red-faced baby was laid on its mother's breast and felt the weight of sadness when one was born blue and still. But she'd never seen a woman die. And a part of her feared death would visit Hannah Bledsoe like a bird flying through an open window, no matter how hard they tried to stop its wings from beating.

When they entered the bedroom, Hannah's panicked green eyes met Deirdre's. She drew her knees up and howled. One tiny purple foot emerged from her sex. Deirdre's gorge rose. She put her hand to her mouth and turned her head for a moment to quell her biliousness. Mary, the Bledsoes' maid, leaned over Hannah, murmuring placating words. Her pinafore was streaked with blood.

Mama rushed to the bedside, her face like thunder. "Fool girl! I told you she needed to labor flat on her back! We need to slow things down, not hurry them along."

Mary covered her round face with her hands and backed away from the massive bed. "I'm sorry, ma'am. It's only . . . well, she couldn't find no comfort like that."

Mama shook her head. "Go make yourself useful and bring fresh linens."

"Yes'm." Mary rushed from the room.

"These city maids ain't worth a damn when it comes to birthing babies." Mama ran a shaky hand over her hair.

"What do you want me to do?" Deirdre asked.

"Keep her calm so her womb might open. A babe can come this way just fine, if she'll stop fightin' things, but I'll need to turn it as it comes, lessen the cord wrap its neck."

"God help me! Make it stop!" Hannah arched her back, her mouth pulled into a rictus of pain. Deirdre put aside her nausea, made worse by her relentless, pounding headache, and sat on the edge of the bed. She pulled Hannah's hand into her own. The girl's skin was cool and ashy, but her pulse raced faster than a derby stallion. Deirdre raked back Hannah's hair—wavy, thick hair the color of the deepest red maple leaves in autumn—and pressed a wet cloth to her forehead.

"Can I have water? Please."

"A little." Deirdre reached for the cup at Hannah's bedside and offered it to her. "Drink it slow or you might be sick."

Hannah drank too greedily and sputtered, the water dripping onto her sweat-soaked shift. "Am I going to die tonight?"

A sudden vision of Hannah, wasted, still, and pale, intruded upon Deirdre's mind. She shook it off and pulled in a steadying breath. "You won't die, ma'am. Not tonight. Just you lay back now and breathe." She put one hand on Hannah's forehead, and laid the other on the swollen, blue-veined rise of her belly, ignoring the niggle of fear in her own. Deirdre closed her eyes and focused her thoughts until they were sharp as an arrow: *Rest, Hannah. All is well. Let your body do the work and the baby will come.*

Within a few moments, Hannah's breathing settled into a steady whisper and her belly softened. She rocked her head toward Deirdre and blinked drowsily. "You sure do have the prettiest eyes, Miss Deirdre. Blue as a jay's wing. And your hair, so fine and dark. Surely you've a beau?"

Deirdre glanced down at Mama, where she knelt at the foot of the bed. Mama gave an encouraging nod. Right. Keep her talking.

"I . . . I have a beau, though he's yet to talk to my pa," she whispered, low enough that Mama wouldn't hear. "I reckon we'll be betrothed soon." If Pa ever returned from laying track out west. Indian raids on rail crews and accidents were a constant worry that kept her and Mama pacing the floors when too much time passed between his telegrams. Anything could happen out in the western territories. "How did you and Mr. Bledsoe meet? I've never heard your courtin' story."

"How funny, I was most certain we'd spoken of it. At my tea social, after we returned from our nuptials. Remember?"

The Bledsoes had never socialized with Deirdre or her family. Deirdre counted it as labor delirium that Hannah thought they'd shared such an intimate conversation. Hill women and city women didn't mix, as a rule. But for all their differences, Deirdre was certain they were the same age. There was a kind of kinship in that. "I'm sure we did speak of it, but I've forgot. Tell me again, Mrs. Bledsoe?"

"Please call me Hannah. Oh—" Hannah's words were stolen by another contraction. She knotted her hands in the coverlet and howled. The panic flared in her eyes, and she thrashed her legs, nearly kicking Mama in the head. "Holy Jesus! It's like I'm being torn in two!"

"Just breathe," Deirdre soothed, calling forth her healing touch once more as she placed a hand on Hannah's pain-knotted brow. "Don't fight it."

"Don't fight it," Hannah echoed. After a few moments, the contraction eased. Outside, the rain started up, bringing a welcomed coolness to the humid room.

Mama was busy between Hannah's legs, whispering prayers. "Baby's comin' fast now, Deirdre. Get her on her feet."

"All right now, Hannah, it's time." Deirdre scrambled across the bed and grasped both Hannah's legs behind the knee and swung them over the side of the bed. She gathered all her strength and lifted Hannah beneath the arms in a tight embrace.

"I can't stand!" Hannah's knees crumpled and threatened to pull Deirdre down to the floor. She was shaking harder than a spring sapling in a hard wind.

"Then stay right here in a squat and lean against me. We're goin' to have this baby now, hear?" Between Hannah's thighs, Deirdre could see the baby dangling half-born, slicked with birth fluids and blood. It was a boy.

Mama cupped its tiny buttocks in her hands, and gently rocked back and forth, trying to help the shoulders slip free. The baby began to turn, guided by Mama's motions. "Now, when I say so, push hard as you can, Mrs. Bledsoe."

"I can't!" Hannah howled.

"You can and you will!" Mama worked fast, her fingers disappearing inside Mrs. Bledsoe. Suddenly, the pulsing, tangled length of cord unfurled from Hannah's womb. Relief flooded through Deirdre. They were almost there.

"Push!" Mama ordered.

"Push now, Hannah!" Deirdre hollered. "Hard as you can!"

Hannah gripped Deirdre's shoulders and bore down with all she had. She took two panting breaths, gave a hearty cry, then pushed again.

Mama shouted in victory. The baby's head popped free, covered in masses of dark hair. A moment went by. Thunder shook the walls of the Bledsoe mansion. As if startled to life by the sound, the baby gave a lusty cry. His face filled with blazing color. "You've a perfect baby boy, Mrs. Bledsoe," Mama said, laughing. "He's even got your husband's hair."

"Oh, praise be to God!" Hannah sobbed, reaching for her hard-won infant.

Deirdre laid the babe across Hannah's chest while Mama worked at massaging Hannah's belly as deeply as if she were making Sunday bread. The afterbirth slipped free with a wet slop into the basin between Hannah's feet. They'd fry it up with beaten eggs and serve it to Mrs. Bledsoe to renew her strength and help her milk come in fat and rich.

Mr. Bledsoe burst into the room, his eyes wild. He caught sight of Hannah, then the baby nuzzling at her breast. He rushed to his wife's side and bent to kiss her cheek.

"You've a healthy baby boy, sir." Deirdre said, smiling wide.

"Praise Jesus. What shall we call him, Hannah?" Mr. Bledsoe asked, his voice quavering.

"Collin Peter, after your father and mine."

"Yes, my own love. Collin Peter Bledsoe. It's a strong name, for a strong boy." Mr. Bledsoe kissed Hannah full on the lips then, so deeply that Deirdre blushed and had to turn away. With kisses like that, she and Mama would be sure to deliver a whole passel of Bledsoe babies in the years to come. She couldn't help but want the same thing for herself, someday. She imagined the babies she and Robbie might have. The thought cheered her, even through the fog of her aching head.

Mama stood, swaying slightly. A rattling cough tore through her. She turned away, but not before Deirdre saw the fresh spatter of scarlet on her sleeve. "Come along, Deirdre. Let's finish our work and head on home. It's fixin' to come a flood."

FIVE

GRACELYNN

1931

I wake from the dream, sweat slicking my neck and my heart skittering so fast it might burst. It's the same dream I've had for weeks. Two women in a clearing, before a burning tree. They turn to me as one, their eyes lit with fire, beckoning me. Then the flames burn me up from the inside, blazing with an unearthly heat that lingers even after I wake.

I wipe my brow with the corner of the quilt, careful not to disturb Caro, sleeping next to me in the brass bed. A stir of sound comes from across the room. It's Morris, rocking back and forth on the floor, trying to pull his britches on without standing up.

"I can hear you," I rasp. I prop myself up on one elbow. "Better hope your ma's sleeping deeper than me. She'll skin you dead."

Morris smirks in the narrow blade of moonlight coming through the only window. "She ain't here, so I reckon it's all right if I sneak out for a spell."

"What? She ain't never come home from that revival?"

"Nope."

Sure enough, there's no snoring from the loft. The cabin's silent as a grave. Moonlight shines across the floor in a scatter of pale silver. It must be well past midnight by now. Val had shooed me on home after Bellflower was all finished up with his healing train. It didn't take a wise man to figure out what was going on. "She's smitten with that new preacher man. I'd bet she's already laid up with him."

"Good. Maybe she wouldn't be so mean, iffin' she had somebody."

"Yeah, but he ain't just *somebody*. There's dark all around him. I had a vision tonight. One like Granny gets."

"Now don't you start in with all that horseshit, too." Morris stands up and stretches. "Them visions ain't nothin' to worry over. Half of Granny's never come to pass."

"Yeah, but that means half of them *do*."

Morris sighs. "You need to stop worryin' so much and have some fun. Why don't you come out with me and Seth?"

"What if Caro wakes up and finds me gone? She gets scared if she's alone."

"We'll be back before she gets up. Come on. We'll go out through the kitchen, so we don't wake Granny."

Granny was still sleeping when I got back from Bellflower's revival. She sometimes slept for a whole day with one of her headaches. She'd likely never know we were gone. "All right." I swing my legs over the edge of the bed. The springs squeak, and Caro rolls over, smacks her lips, then resettles. I lift myself real slow off the mattress, then pad across the floor on bare feet, following Morris.

We go out into the night, the fog wrapping around our ankles. Morris whistles like a robin. "Y'all need to pick a different bird call,"

I rasp. "Somethin' that actually flies at night. Like a hoot owl or a whip-poor-will."

Morris chuckles. "You're probably right, Gracelynn."

"You know I always am."

The branches part and Seth comes striding out, all skinny legs and arms. "Brought that lil' woman, I see." He runs a hand over his close-cropped fuzz of hair. I look away as Morris leans in to kiss him, fast on the lips. My cheeks flame hot, and I focus on the way the moon slides down low, waxing full as a town whore's purse. I ain't used to seeing two men kiss, but I reckon I'd like to do the same with Abby. The thought of her lips on mine warms my blood. Makes my pulse drum in my ears.

Seth whispers something to Morris, then laughs in a quiet rumble. "You want some of our moonshine, Gracie? It's blackberry. Real good."

"No thank you," I say. I got no use for drink and what it does to a person. "Y'all go ahead, though."

"Let's walk down to the tracks," Morris says. His voice is all nervous and trembly. "Ain't nobody down there this time of night."

Seth pulls a silver flask out of his britches pocket and hands it to Morris. They pass it back and forth as we head toward the one-lane road that winds down the low-slung northern face of the mountain. By the time we pass Hosea Ray's farm, with Bellflower's dark tent looming over the alfalfa, they're jostlin' and jawing, loud as a pair of crows. I try shushing them, but they just laugh at me. Ain't nobody gonna be laughing if the Klan's out tonight.

We make our way past the timber camp's deserted saloon, windows broken by bored hill kids. Granny says it used to be a whorehouse for the loggers, till the county sheriff got wise. The scent of pine and cedar sap hangs sharp in the air. Below, the railroad tracks stretch out in a long curve, next to stacks of freshly mown trees. Some will only go a few miles around the bend to Northrup's sawmill. Some north to my hometown—Springfield, then on east to the Mississippi or out west. Maybe even all the way to California.

We settle at the edge of the tracks, where the clover-strewn grass grows thick like a carpet. Seth folds his pelican-like legs and sits next to me. Morris takes another swig of moonshine and passes the flask back to Seth before settling at his side.

I worry. I worry about Morris's drinking. I worry about him running illegal hooch up and down the creek and sharing kisses with a colored boy—something that could get them both killed. But Morris is grown, and grown folks are gonna do what they do.

"It sure is pretty out here tonight, ain't it?" Seth says, his words thick and slow. "Look at them stars."

I lay back on the ground. Out here, where there's no other light but the moon, the sky is clear as spring water, all indigo blue and draped with ribbons of silver.

"That's Arcturus, there," Seth says, pointing a thin finger at the brightest star in the sky, just beyond the handle of the Big Dipper. "It's in the constellation Boötes, which means herdsman. Like my pa." I hear a sad note in his voice, and I know it's because he ain't seen his daddy in years. John Cornelison left Tin Mountain long ago to work in the wilds of Montana, where he earns a healthy wage as a cowboy—money enough so's his wife and kids won't never have to worry about going hungry. There's love in that kind of sacrifice.

"What's that one next to it? The one that looks like a crown?" I ask.

Seth lights up at my interest, his eyes gleaming. "Oh, that's the Corona Borealis. And you're right—it's a crown. Ariadne's crown. If you like looking at stars, Gracie, I can draw you a constellation map sometime."

Morris belches, loud. I roll my eyes. "Say 'Excuse me,' Morris Clyde."

"Excuse me," he slurs, then flops onto the ground next to Seth. They lace their fingers together and whisper to one another. I feel uncomfortable—like I'm intruding where I shouldn't.

A low whistle sounds from around the bend, and the ground shakes beneath us. We all sit up at once to watch the westbound Frisco rush past. Some of its cars are lit up bright yellow. A few people inside turn their heads to look out at us, and I wave. A pretty woman in a red dress leans out her window and hollers something, her words stripped away by the rush of air. I wonder where she's from. I wonder where she's going.

There's a part of me that misses being on the Frisco, brushing up against those finely dressed ladies in their perfumed furs, my pickpocket hands sly and quick. But that was a different time, when I was just doing what I needed to do to survive. My daddy weren't a good man like Seth's pa. I had to hide everything I made, else he'd blow it on liquor and loudmouthed women.

"Y'all ever wonder what it's like out there, beyond Tin Mountain?" Seth asks, all wistful.

"All the time," I say softly. "All the damn time."

⚜

After a while, I leave Seth and Morris and pick my way back up the hill. Even though they're too bashful to admit when they want to be alone, I know when to take my leave. I just hope they'll be careful.

I thread through the woods, breath straining against the muggy air. Everything's still and silent apart from the whir of cicadas. It's a little early for cicadas, and that don't bode well for summer. If it's already this hot in May, what will July and August be like?

Whitacre Point is just ahead, through a break in the trees shaped like a keyhole. A person can stand out on the point in the clear light of morning and see all the way past Sutter's holler, to where the big Buffalo River winds like a ribbon of gold in the distance. When I first came to Tin Mountain, I used to get up in the early hours and hike to the point to watch the sun come up. Then Aunt Val figured out that all those years of taking care of myself had made me a decent cook and housekeeper. There wasn't much time for leisurely morning strolls after that.

I push through the pine boughs. The outcrop juts from the bluff like the head of a hawk, shining white under the moon. I step out onto the crag, where it's flat and solid. Folks braver than me walk to the edge, but a lot of them folks have slipped and ended up dead at the bottom of the holler. Sometimes they don't find their bodies for months. If they find them at all.

Behind me, Old Liberty's beam sweeps overhead. A stray breeze kicks up, pushing my hair from my neck and raising goosepimples on my arm.

Gracelynn . . .

My ears prick. Somebody just whispered my name, from down in the holler. I could almost swear it.

Gracelynn . . .

There it is again. It ain't my imagination. Or the wind. My belly tumbles over with sick fear. I think of them old stories about the Sutter haint and hightail it out of there, tripping and falling over the knobs of shale sticking out from the ground. Whether I'm imagining things or not, I ain't eager to find out who, or *what*, might own that voice.

Once I've made it back up the ridge, I slow down and catch my breath. As I round the corner on our dirt road, I can see the cabin's lit up bright as Christmas. Granny is up and Aunt Val is home, I'd bet. I'm fixing to catch ten kinds of hell.

But as I get nearer, a heavy, electric feeling of dread thickens the sweltering air—like the eerie calm before a tornado. It's the same dark feeling I had when that preacher man laid hands on Ma Watterson and threw me into that vision.

And then I see him. Bellflower. He's standing in front of the cabin, with his hands held out in front of him in surrender. Granny's on the front steps, Morris's shotgun propped against her shoulder and pointed right at him. The stench of asafetida wafts toward me. A shaky line of yellow powder stretches across the path between the preacher and Granny. It's a ward. A hastily made one, but a ward just the same.

"Hey, now! What's goin' on here?" I holler.

They both turn at the sound of my voice. Bellflower grins at me like he's just beat the house in a hand of blackjack.

Granny's eyes go all wide. She shouts a curse, racks the slide, and shoots.

SIX

DEIRDRE

1881

Deirdre woke to the rattle of thunder, and sat up, wincing as a surge of pain and dizziness swept through her head. Rain pecked at the roof and sluiced hard against the windowpanes, graying the thin light that managed to leak through. Two days since little Collin Bledsoe was born and the rains had yet to cease.

From the kitchen, Mama's hoarse, wet cough rang out. It'd grown worse with the damp weather. If Mama sickened more, Deirdre would have to tend to the townsfolk and deliver babies by herself, and the winter before had nearly worn her plumb through. She'd brought four babies on her own, scared the whole time something might go wrong.

A knock came, breaking through the storm's steady thrum. Mama's chair scraped against the floor, then the front door creaked open to the deep rumble of a male voice. Arthur Cash. Robbie's pa.

"It's gettin' mighty treacherous out there, Nola. The crick's already swole over its banks. Took out the footbridge at Abbott's Crossing. I found a young man clingin' to a downed tree down around the holler. He got caught out in the flood. I wondered if he might come in, sit a spell. Maybe get changed into some clean clothes and have a sip of broth."

"Certainly. I'll gather some of Jakob's things. Bring him in, get him warmed up."

Could it be the same man she'd seen in the holler? Deirdre eased her nightgown up over her knees and sank down onto the floor, crawling to the edge of the loft and parting the curtains to have a better listen. Another set of footprints echoed across the floorboards.

"Mornin', ma'am. I'm much obliged for your hospitality."

Now that was a *voice*—low and sweetly thick like molasses. Deirdre leaned forward, craning her neck to see down the hall. The stranger was tall and lean, his head coming near to the top of the doorframe. She could only see his profile from her perch, but he had handsome features, with high cheekbones and a fine nose under his rain-slicked hair. He certainly might be the same man she'd seen down in the holler, judging by his height alone.

"Heavens, you must be chilled to the bone," Mama said, her skirts rustling as she moved about the kitchen. "I've some of my husband's things here, freshly washed. You can go through the hall and into the room beyond to change. There's a screen and a washstand there, if you'd like to wash up. I'll warm some beef broth for you."

"You're too kind, ma'am. Surely you'll be blessed for your charity."

Deirdre let the curtain fall back into place as the stranger's footsteps neared. The wet slop of drenched clothing hitting the floor filtered up to her. The man hummed softly to himself as he wrung out a cloth and began washing. Deirdre's curiosity got the better of her, and she parted the curtain ever so slightly and peered out again. Her breath hitched. The stranger hadn't gone behind the screen to wash. She'd never seen a naked man before, but she'd imagine this one was as well formed as any, with a muscled back and a rear end to match. He turned, as if sensing she were there, and smiled. She pressed her back against the wall, her heart beating so loudly she was sure he might hear it.

After a few more moments of leisurely washing, he dressed in Pa's clothes, leaving Deirdre's face afire with shameful thoughts. After he'd gone, she dressed, then slowly eased down the ladder and took careful, sliding steps past the hutch filled with Mama's paper-thin Belleek china. She craned her neck to peer around the corner. Mama sat at the kitchen table, her face in her hands, Arthur Cash behind her.

The stranger sat himself across from Mama, folding his tall frame into a hoop-backed chair. "I'm sorry I didn't formally introduce myself upon arrival, ma'am. Ambrose Gentry."

"Finola Werner," Mama replied, offering her hand. Gentry took it, and for a moment, Deirdre thought he might bring her hand to his lips. A faint blush pinked Mama's skin. She pulled away, then offered a bowl of steaming broth to him, which he drank heartily.

"Mr. Gentry here is a pastor, Nola. A healin' man," Arthur said. "He came all the way from Tennessee. Means to start a church in Tin Mountain."

"Is that so?" Mama asked wistfully. "Well, that's fine news."

"Yes, ma'am," Gentry said. "I mean to stay on as long as you good folks'll have me."

A new preacher? In Tin Mountain? Deirdre would be surprised if Old Stack would let that come to pass. He was mighty territorial.

"He'd sure like to pray over you, Nola. I told him of your ailment. I know he ain't one of your Catholics, but a healin' man is a healin' man."

"I have a different sort of ministry than most preachers—a calling," the stranger said. "Mr. Cash says you have a pernicious cough that might be helped by my gift?"

"It's the galloping consumption, sir," Mama answered softly. "There ain't no cure for it."

"It might seem so, but with faith, I've healed such ailments before. May I pray for you?"

"Please. Let him try, Nola," Arthur coaxed, squeezing Mama's shoulders.

As she watched, the stranger cupped his hand gently over Mama's forehead, and closed his eyes. He began praying, his alluring, melodious voice sinking deep into Deirdre's ears. She closed her eyes and listened, hoping that there was some truth to the man's promises.

After a time, the preacher's hypnotic words ceased, and Mama raised her head, tears shining in her eyes. Color flooded her cheeks, driving away her bluish pallor. "I could feel your prayers, sir. I ain't never felt *anything* like that afore." Mama pulled in a deep breath, and Deirdre watched her shoulders rise and fall, expecting the raw cough that nearly always came after. Instead, Mama laughed, hearty and loud. "I can breathe! Truly breathe!"

Arthur Cash laughed with her. "Praise Jesus for that."

"Yes, ma'am." The stranger rose from the table. "I received my gift as a boy, after a vision I had. I healed my own mother from her fits. I've been helping good folks like you ever since."

Mama stood, taking his hands. "I ain't sure how to repay you, sir. We haven't much to give in way of an offering for your ministry. But I made molasses bread last night. There's fresh churned butter, too. Would you care to take some with you for later? You, too, Arthur."

"I'm honored by your hospitality, I'll surely appreciate your broth and your bread, but no other payment will be required, ma'am. I do what I do in service of the Lord. Still, as I mean to stay on in Tin Mountain, I'd be much obliged if you might spread word of my ministry."

"Of course! This town has long needed a *true* man of God."

Arthur Cash ducked his head and whispered something in Mama's ear, bringing a smile. Deirdre bristled. He was far too familiar for her liking.

"Perhaps you might call on us for dinner some other night? It's just myself and my daughter, but I've gathered you're a gentleman not yet married?"

The minister ran a hand through his damp wavy hair. "Why, ma'am, I'd be delighted. It's been far too long since I enjoyed fair company and a square meal."

At this, Deirdre flew around the corner. She would not be offered up like chattel to a stranger, no matter how pleasing his voice or looks. "Mama, what's this all about?"

"Deirdre!" Mama startled. "Mr. Cash has come to call. He brought this young man to pray for me. He has a gift of healing. He means to settle here, in Tin Mountain. Start a ministry. I thought we might have him come for dinner this Sunday."

The stranger turned. His green eyes crawled from the hem of her dress up to her face. A tremor of nervousness went through her at the intensity of his gaze. "Pleased to make your acquaintance, Miss Deirdre. I'm Ambrose Gentry."

Deirdre ignored his outstretched hand, which looked nearly as soft as her own. A learned man instead of a laborer. Something in his manner reminded her of Robbie, though there was a smoothness that Robbie lacked. She had the sense Ambrose Gentry was well honed and clever and knew his own charm, and that made Deirdre wary. Plenty of girls had fallen to the seductions of wandering pastors over the years—promises made in the heat of summer and then forgotten as soon as the harvest fell. "Mama, you know I already have a beau, though I'm pleased to meet you all the same, Mr. Gentry."

"Deirdre!" Mama laughed nervously. "Goodness gracious. No one said a word about courting, although . . ." She cast a furtive look at Mr. Cash. "Arthur?"

Arthur cleared his throat and picked his hat up from the table. "Now, my Robbie does regard you fondly, Miss Deirdre, but he'd need to ask for your pa's permission before courting you formally."

"Pa might be reached by telegram," Deirdre said flatly. "Can't we get his permission that way, Mama? I don't reckon I see a difference whether he gives his blessing from here or from there."

"You and the girl should have a talk, Nola." Mr. Cash cleared his throat again and scratched at his head. "We'll see ourselves out. I'll be back to patch the weak spot on your roof after this rain lets up."

Ambrose Gentry slung his hat down low over his eyes and touched a finger to its brim. He took the packet of bread Mama offered and smiled at Deirdre, sending a tickle of nervousness through her belly. "I'll come another day, Miss Deirdre. Not to call on you as a suitor. Only to read Scripture and pray with you. I'll comport *myself* with the utmost propriety and respect, I assure you."

Deirdre's cheeks warmed. He'd seen her watching while he washed up, and he was goading her. "If it's all the same to you, sir, I'd rather you . . . I'd rather you," Deirdre stumbled over her words, suddenly shy. "I can read the Bible on my own just fine, sir."

Gentry tilted his head back and laughed. "Charming, isn't she?"

"Deirdre is a bit bashful, Mr. Gentry. That's all. You're welcome in our home anytime."

After the men had gone, Deirdre turned to Mama. "How is it you think you can offer me up to any man passin' through?"

Mama fixed Deirdre with a steady look. "I hadn't a mind to do so, but it wouldn't be such a bad thing to keep company with a minister, would it? Mr. Gentry certainly seemed to take a shine to you, and he's very kind. You should choose the most suitable man, not the first one who bends your ear with pretty words. Once vows are taken, a lifetime with the wrong man can lead to heartache. A minister's wife is a fine station in life, Deirdre. Honorable. I worry that Robbie is fickle. Arthur is concerned you may be misreading Robbie's affections."

"Robbie's true, Mama, I swear it. My mind's made up for him." Deirdre closed her eyes briefly, remembering the simple ring Robbie had woven for her out of a daisy stem when they were twelve. He pressed a gentle kiss to her lips—her first—then promised to make her his wife. Deirdre had clung to the memory and set about filling her hope chest with trinkets and treasures for the day she'd become his bride, though the years had stretched on much longer than she liked between his boyish promise and now.

"All the same, once Pa is home, we'll set your courtin' candle in the window, and Robbie can come to speak with your father, just like Jakob did with mine. We'll do things properly . . . so long as it's not too late." Mama's lips pursed. "Arthur's told me about your trips up to the lighthouse, daughter. If you've already given Robbie your virtue, he'll not be inclined to marry you."

So, Mama knew. Deirdre faltered, her face going pale. Then she remembered the way Arthur Cash's hands had rested so easily on Mama's shoulders and a righteous ire boiled up in place of her shame. "And what of *your* virtue, Mama? Since when are you so congenial with Mr. Cash? I reckon he gets lonely, being a widower and all. Is that why he's around so much?"

"Arthur is kind," Mama said. "A friend. Without his help, we'd be in a bad way."

"I've seen the soft looks passin' between you—the way he touches you. What might happen if I told Pa about all that?" Deirdre tossed the words carelessly, not stopping to weigh the harm in them.

Mama's eyes flickered with something akin to fear. She drew back her hand and struck, her wedding band cutting across Deirdre's cheek, sharp as a blade. Deirdre put a hand to her face. When she pulled it away, her fingers were wet with blood.

Mama had been plenty mad in the past, but she'd never struck her before. The room spun. Deirdre's hurt and anger surged hot, leapt like fresh tongues of flame. Away. She had to get away. She flew through the door, ignoring Mama's tearful call.

Outside, the rain lashed her smarting cheek and soaked through the thin fabric of her homespun dress. It was cold. So cold. But anywhere was better than home.

She rushed toward the shelter of the woods, with no mind to where she was going. When the land finally flattened out, heaving water stood where freshly sown fields should have been. Deirdre stopped to catch her breath. She covered her head as best she could with her shawl and went on. To her left, Ballard Creek was a roaring torrent. Uprooted trees flowed through its muddy current, borne away by the angry, frothy water. The bloated corpse of a deer bobbed around the bend where the bridge used to be, stiff, spindly legs catching on the limbs of an ash tree. Its dead eyes stared at her, dim and baleful.

It wasn't safe out here. But she couldn't stand to be in the same house with Mama. Her gut twisted, thinking of the things Mama and Arthur Cash might have done, for months, if not years, right under Deirdre's nose. She thought of poor unwitting Pa, laboring hard to make a living on the Colorado frontier. Pa, old and plain and spare of word, who looked at Mama like she was drink in the desert. It wasn't right. None of it.

Suddenly, the bluff she stood on started to crumble and slide, the dirt and rock at her feet winnowing off into the hungry floodwaters. Deirdre grasped the branch of a nearby sapling and used it to claw herself back onto solid ground, just as the sapling and everything next to it slid into the mire. Her heart hammered, loud in her ears. If she'd fallen into the river, she'd have been pulled downstream, at the mercy of nature.

Deirdre shivered. Her clothes were soaked through, and her fingertips numb. The sky had turned a dark and grayish purple. She needed to find shelter before nightfall. She could always go to Ingrid's. She thought of the Nilssons' cozy log house with its rock hearth, the long table laden with too much food, and the spiced tea Ma Nilsson always offered up.

But nosy Ing, being Ing, would ask too many questions. Questions Deirdre didn't want to answer. In the distance, a twig snapped. And then another. Deirdre scanned the dark row of cedars edging Sutter's holler. A flash of pale corn-silk hair moved through the trees. Only one person she'd ever met had hair like that—Ebba, Ingrid's little cousin.

What in heaven's name was the child doing out in this storm? Was she lost? Ebba didn't know these woods. If she wandered too far, she might end up falling off a bluff. Children didn't fare well alone in the forests around Tin Mountain.

A few summers ago, little Tessa Ray, who had been born and raised right here, on her daddy's land, had wandered off after a Sunday school picnic into Sutter's holler. They'd found her days later, babbling about strange voices and a lady perched in a tree like a bird. Tessa's mind went soft as grits after that. Eventually her babbling turned into endless screaming. The Rays had done their best by the girl, but as far as Deirdre knew, she still lived in a home for the feebleminded.

She doubted the Nilssons would have half the patience with Ebba.

Deirdre lifted her skirts and ran into the woods, calling Ebba's name. Within moments, she spotted a flicker of movement to the side of the logging path. She followed, wet branches smacking against her face. The way grew steep and perilous, rocks slipping under her feet as she edged down the lip of the holler. She leaned against a tree to catch her breath. Her shins were lashed to ribbons by the underbrush, blood trickling from the welted cuts.

From the direction of Pa's old homestead, she heard a shimmer of childlike laughter. "Ebba?"

No one answered her call. Something wasn't right. Her heart juddered as she scanned the blackened cedars. Fear prickled along her arms and gathered low in her belly. She felt watched. Hunted.

In the middle of the clearing, the lone, gnarled locust rustled its leaves. A shape drifted out from behind the tree, unfurling like white smoke. Deirdre squinted through the driving rain. It wasn't Ebba, or smoke. It was a woman, tall and slender and dressed only in a billow-ing white shift, its hem singed black. Her long auburn hair stood out from her head in a wild, messy halo. She lifted her hand and pointed at Deirdre, eyes as blue as the depths of the ocean.

Deirdre . . .

The woman's voice, though soft and beseeching, reverberated through Deirdre. She fell to her knees and howled as a searing pain lanced her temple and thrummed behind her eyes. A horrific vision rushed into her head, unbidden. In it, the woman was being dragged from Pa's old homestead by a man in black whose face was hidden in shadow. Outside the cabin, a jeering crowd stood, wielding torches and shouting. Though the woman had a proud expression, Deirdre felt her pain, her worry for her child, and the sting of her lover's betrayal.

The man forced the woman to the locust tree and lashed her to its thorny trunk as the mob looked on. He took the same wickedly curved knife Deirdre had seen in the cabin from the folds of his cassock. With it, he carved a cross onto the woman's forehead, and it was wrong. It was wrong because the knife was the woman's—and it was never meant to do harm. Her blood trickled down her face and neck, painting her bosom red. The man grasped a hank of the woman's hair and lifted her head.

Promise the child to me. Promise her to me and I will let you live.

The woman had made peace with her death, had known for some time that she must die, yet she gathered enough strength to speak:

Never, Nathaniel Walker. You will never claim what is mine. The land and my blood will remember what you've done. One day, there will come a reckoning and you will reap your own folly.

The man laughed. He took up a torch and held it to the woman's hem. Fire licked at her feet, making her dance. A cry of pain broke free from her throat. Deirdre cried out with her—felt the biting tongues of flame as if she were being burned, too. But along with the burning pain, something else rushed through her, borne on a fast-moving current that lit up her bones with light. Her flesh *sang* with knowing. With power.

The vision faded along with the woman's cries, leaving Deirdre spent and shaking. She lifted her pounding head from the ground. The woman was gone. Rain pelted Deirdre's back, chilling her skin where moments before it had blazed with an unearthly fire. She crawled beneath the locust tree, taking what little shelter she could beneath its branches, and touched her hand to the rough bark. A voice flowed through her mind, like a soft whisper of shadow.

Remember, Deirdre. For her sake and your own, you must remember. Guard your heart from treachery, and beware the one who burns.

❦

Deirdre woke to the muted sound of dripping water. Gray light spilled into the cave from the jagged entrance, where rocks hung like the crooked teeth of some fearsome creature. Her thoughts were muddied. She had slept fitfully, plagued with strange dreams and whispers. Garnet Cave was said to be occupied by restless spirits, though it seemed one couldn't walk ten paces in these hills without setting foot on haunted land. But last night . . . last night had been a thing altogether strange and new. She'd run as far as she could from Sutter's holler after her vision, not caring where she ended up, until her legs trembled and threatened to buckle beneath her. At least the cave had protected her from the storm, even though dark, wet places reminded Deirdre of graves and soft, wriggling things hidden beneath rotten logs.

She hoped that Ebba had made it home. She'd stop by the Nilssons' for breakfast to make sure the girl was safe.

She sat up and washed her face in the trickle of spring water flowing through the limestone walls, then braided her damp hair in two plaits, like Mama had done when she was little. Mama was no doubt frantic with worry by now. Deirdre spared a glance at her clothes, piled in a wet heap on the cave floor, and decided to leave them. She'd borrow a dress from Ingrid. Her stomach rumbled, a reminder she hadn't eaten since yesterday morning. She tied on her boots, donned her half-dry cotton shift, and wrapped her shawl over her shoulders. The thought of Maja Nilsson's pancakes with mulberry butter was enough to get her tired legs moving up the hillside.

It was a soft day, as Mama liked to say. The endless downpour had finally ceased, and a misty fog replaced it, drawn up from the warming ground. She'd nearly gotten to the covered bridge that spanned Ballard Creek when she heard a rustling from behind.

"There you are, you pretty little thing."

She turned, her breath catching.

It was Ambrose Gentry. The preacher strode toward her, an eager grin on his face. Conscious of her immodest state, she pulled her shawl close over her bosom, her fingers trembling.

"Your mama's real worried about you, Miss Deirdre. Sent some of the menfolk out to find you. You been out in this storm all night?"

"I took shelter in yonder cave," Deirdre said, pointing to the bluff, where Garnet Cave yawned like a half-opened mouth.

"Well. You're as clever as you are lovely." He took his coat off as he came near and placed it over her shoulders. It smelled of woodsmoke and something else she couldn't place, though it was pleasant. "Let's see you on home."

Deirdre dug her fingers into her arms beneath the warm wool coat, every muscle in her body tensing. She regarded him shyly from beneath her lashes. Lands, he was handsome, his shoulders flexing beneath his linsey-woolsey shirt as he led the way to the covered horse bridge. She remembered her shameful spying from the day before, and blushed. She would let Mr. Gentry see her home, as it was polite to do so, and then bid him goodbye. She had already given herself to Robbie. It would do no good to entertain the interest of another man.

As if reading her mind, Gentry said, "I met your beau. Spent the night up at the lighthouse with Mr. Cash. Your Robert was a bit surly in my presence, and when your mother came up the hill to ask for our help, he didn't volunteer to come with us."

Deirdre's stomach lurched uncomfortably. "Someone has to stay at the lighthouse. Mind the lantern, especially during a storm. Otherwise, he'd have come, I'm sure of it."

Gentry hummed, his lips tilting into a smile. "I suppose you're right."

They walked on for a bit in silence. Gentry gestured at the canopy of trees. "It's pretty country here. That place, down in the hollow, it could be put right again. The land shored up against flooding and that cabin rebuilt. I've a mind to do so."

"My pa says that land is fallow. Haunted. Are you so sure you want to live there?"

"I'm not the superstitious kind. Land is land. I find that country folk make up all sorts of stories to explain the unnatural when they don't have proper learning."

Deirdre bristled. "If you think your city learnin' puts you a cut above us, sir, you're not likely to build a congregation. Folks are wary of strangers around here as it is. We don't take to those who cast aspersions our way."

"You misread me, Miss Werner. I do not consider myself better than any other man, although the world of faith is filled with such ministers, who exalt themselves over others—those who prance and preen and act as if *they* are the God they purport to serve."

Deirdre's thoughts went to Reverend Stack. Full-up with sin, drink, and himself.

"No." Gentry shook his head vehemently. "I have been disavowed of any such arrogance. When I first left the seminary, I had a pretty young wife, a congregation, and a small farm on the outskirts of town. I was a prosperous and happy man until my wife took ill. I attempted to use my gifts of healing to save her." His shoulders rose and fell, his face shadowed beneath his hat. "It was no use. Each time I heal another soul, I think of how I was unable to heal her. Losing her tested my faith mightily at the same time it humbled me."

Deirdre's sympathy stirred. To be so young and already widowed! "I'm sorry, sir. I'd no idea."

He stopped and turned to her, a silvery sheen to his eyes, which might have been tears. "You remind me of her, a bit. The same blue eyes. Her spirit. I've a feeling you might have even more charming things in common with my Betsy. I've heard talk of your gifts. Your visions. Your healing touch with women in labor. It's a rare thing, to be so blessed."

While the words seemed sincerely spoken, they sent an uncomfortable chill through Deirdre. How did he know of her gifts? She'd never told another soul of them. "I . . . thank you, sir. We should move on along, I reckon."

As they walked, the wary feeling nagged at Deirdre, and her hand trembled when Gentry took it to guide her over the downed branches along their path. They'd reached the bridge. Below, the still-angry creek sucked and pulled at the pilings, the sound deafening as they passed beneath the cover of the bridge.

Deirdre startled. In the sudden fall of darkness, Gentry's eyes shone like a cat's. She stopped in the middle of the bridge, her heart hammering.

"Is something the matter?" he asked over the roar of the water. He faced her fully. The eerie shine faded from his eyes. A slight smile played on his lips.

"I . . . I thought I saw something."

He raised a brow. "A trick of the light?"

"Yes," Deirdre answered, nodding, "that's all it was."

She hurried the length of the bridge, eager to escape the shadows and Gentry's presence. The longer she lingered near him, the more unsettled she became. As they rounded the curving slope, Deirdre caught sight of the cabin, a slender column of smoke threading from the chimney. An even more pleasing sight greeted her as they drew nearer—Pa's worn leather boots outside the door.

He'd returned, weeks before he was due! They could speak of Robbie and make plans for a summer wedding. The sooner the better. Deirdre had her suspicions that Ingrid's methods of preventing a pregnancy might prove untrustworthy, and she could no more deny Robbie's attentions than she could her next breath.

"My pa is home!" Deirdre said over her shoulder to Gentry. "You can meet him. He'll want to thank you for seeing me safely home."

Gentry frowned, his eyes narrowing. "If it's all the same to you, Miss Werner, I'd rather be on my way. I'll call on you some other day."

"Oh, we won't keep you long at all." Deirdre bounced up the porch steps. She flung open the door and burst inside. She blinked, her eyes adjusting to the light. The kitchen was empty.

"Mama! Pa! I'm home. I'm sorry I worried you."

From the back room, where her parents slept, came a soft whimpering. She heard the bed creak, then a hushed tangle of voices. Her folks were likely renewing their affections, and she was thankful she hadn't walked in on them, as she had once when she was a girl. The memory was still too keen for her liking.

A few moments later, Mama came rushing down the hall, her hair loose around her shoulders. Her eyes were rimmed red, cheeks puffed and swollen. Pa followed, a tall gaunt shadow in her wake. Deirdre endured Mama's patting and scolding, then ran to Pa, resting her head against his chest. "I'm so glad you're home."

"Deirdre Jane, you had your mother in fits. I raised you to have more sense than to run out in a storm."

"I know, Pa, I know. I got turned around in the holler, and it was raining so hard I spent the night up in Garnet Cave. That pastor—Mr. Gentry—saw me home, Mama. He said you sent him and a few of the menfolk out to find me."

Mama's brow wrinkled. "I thought of such, but in this storm . . . well, I couldn't have walked up to that lighthouse to ask for help all on my own, or down to town, neither. I spent the night praying and pacing the floor, until your pa come through at dawn. Perhaps the angels sent Mr. Gentry to find you, Deirdre," Mama said. "Let's see him in, husband, so we might thank him."

"Did you say this man is a preacher?" Pa swore under his breath.

"Yes, a travelin' healer," Mama said, grasping his arm. "He laid hands on me and prayed. I haven't coughed since, Jakob, even with this damp!"

"You might as well have let the devil himself through the door, Nola. I'd a feeling I'd tarried too long away." Pa pulled away from Mama, strode to the hearth, and took down his long gun.

"Jakob!" Mama rushed toward Pa. Her expression shifted from confusion to fear. "Surely there's no cause for your gun."

A wash of panic flooded Deirdre. "Pa! What are you doing?"

"Deirdre, you stay in this house with your mother."

"Jakob!" Mama screeched. "This is foolishness!"

Deirdre had never seen Pa so het up. He slapped his hat on his head and stormed out the door, his rifle cocked and ready. Deirdre rushed to the window and parted the lace curtains. As far as she could tell, Gentry had already rushed off on his long legs and was likely halfway to Sutter's holler by now. Pa paced the garden, scanning the tree line, then disappeared around the side of the house, cursing the whole way.

"Lands, Mama, what's got into him?"

"I'm not rightly sure." Mama came to her side, twisting her garnet rosary. "All that man did was pray over me and see you home. I hope Jakob won't do anything foolish. He has a reckless streak when it comes to you, daughter."

A rifle shot cracked and echoed across the hillside. Deirdre flinched. A moment passed by, then another. Pa burst in the door, out of breath.

"I saw him. Shot at him and missed. He ran, like a coward. He won't be gone for long, though. That coat you're wearing—is it his, poppet?"

Deirdre looked down at the wool greatcoat that had kept her modest and warm. "Yes, I reckon so."

"Take it off and I'll burn it. Anything else he gave to you, likewise."

Though she was confused, Deirdre hurriedly shrugged the coat to the floor. Pa gathered it up and tossed it into the hearth. The heavy wool caught and flamed hot, sending a shower of sparks onto the floor.

"Jakob! What's gotten into you?" Mama said, stomping them out. "You're half-mad!"

"There are things you don't understand, Nola. Things I've seen that you can't know the half of." Pa poured a mug of cider and topped it off with his flask before passing it to Deirdre with shaking hands. "Drink, poppet." She took a warm swallow, tasting the bite of whiskey on its tail. "Did he touch you? Did he hurt you, in any way?"

Deirdre shook her head. "No, not at all, though I can't reckon why he lied about Mama going to the lighthouse for help."

"His sort is full-up with lies." Pa grimaced, the wrinkles on his face deeper than she'd ever seen them.

"None of this would have happened if you hadn't run off, daughter." Mama's fitful eyes rested on the wall above Deirdre's head, where the morning sun made a hot white circle on the wall. "She's been rebellious while you've been away, Jakob. Disobedient."

"Maybe that's so, but you invited that man into our house, Finola." Pa's square jaw worked beneath the scruff of his ruddy beard. "I've told you about lettin' men on the place when I'm gone."

"He was polite. Kind. I only thought to be welcoming to a stranger, as the Bible bids us be. The only other man who's been on the place is Mr. Cash, to help with the things I couldn't manage on my own." Mama turned away. A stab of guilt ran through Deirdre, knowing what she'd seen between Mama and Arthur Cash. But she'd keep that to herself, at least for now. There was no use in complicating things.

Pa had always been overprotective, but this seemed rash. Dangerous. Deirdre half rose from her chair. "Fa, what's got you so riled? I didn't care much for the man, but that can't be reason enough to shoot him."

"Like I said, you ain't seen what I've seen." Pa raised his head, rubbed the deep furrow between his brows. "Go on up to the loft and get yourself decent, Deirdre. It's time we talked about the past—about what happened to your Oma."

SEVEN

GRACELYNN

1931

Granny's first shot glances off the sugar maple out by the fence, sending a spray of splinters through the air. The second lands at Bellflower's feet, making him dance. He just laughs. She lowers the gun and racks the slide again. This time when she shoots, it knocks the hat clean off his head. A stray bit of bird shot nicks his neck, drawing a skinny line of blood.

Bellflower's lucky Granny can't shoot fish in a barrel, but she might aim true, yet.

Aunt Val screams. I hadn't noticed her before, lurking in the shadows under the porch. "Mama, stop! You'll kill him!"

"You don't know who this sonofabitch is. I'm tryin' to protect you." I ain't never heard Granny cuss like that. Not ever. "Gracelynn Anne, you get up on this porch. Now."

"Yes'm."

Bellflower watches me cross the yard, his eyes burning into my back.

"Ma'am," he drawls, all slow and syrupy sweet. "I believe we've gotten off on the wrong foot. I mean no harm to you or your girls."

"That's what one of your *kind* told me fifty years ago. I've been on the wrong side of lyin' preachers like you for a long time, Gentry."

"I told you my name's Josiah Bellflower."

Granny harrumphs. "You've always favored a mouthful of name."

He shrugs. "Can't help what my folks chose to call me."

"Is that so?" Granny jabs at him with the shotgun. "You're just a simple country preacher with the word of God on his tongue and healing in his touch. Well. I know better. I've seen what you are. *Who* you are."

"Mama, *please*," Aunt Val wails. She's crying, the kohl she uses to blacken her eyes dripping down her cheeks. I'm wondering *how* in the hell Carolyn June can sleep through all this racket.

Dawn blooms pink on the horizon. Out back, Granny's little bantam rooster starts his crowing. Bellflower picks up his hat, shakes the bird shot out, and puts it back on. The air stinks of gunpowder. "Ma'am, I figure we can talk about all this some other time. So long as you promise to be civil when I come to call." Bellflower tips his hat and turns on his heel. "It's been a real pleasure."

"Go on now," Granny says. "Slither away on your belly. You come 'round here again, I won't miss the next time, I can promise you that. You'll never claim what's mine, devil. Not while I'm alive."

Bellflower stops and turns. His eyes have gone dark and glinting, just like they did at his healing service. A hot, dry wind blows across the yard and hits me full in the face.

"We'll see about that, won't we, Deirdre?"

Something smells awful.

I wipe the sleep from my eyes and head into the kitchen. Green grapevine and holly branches tangle across the table, and Granny stands in front of the stove. Ebba, Granny's oldest friend and Abby's great-aunt, breaks stalks of asafetida in two and throws them into the stockpot while Granny stirs.

"What're y'all doing?"

Ebba turns to smile at me, her long gray braid swaying at her skinny hips. "Come see, Gracie."

She makes room for me at the stove, and I peer into the murky water, wrinkling my nose at the strong, garlicky scent. There's more than asafetida in there. I can see a silver cross, a pair of tin spoons, and a shed ram's horn from one of Ebba's goats at the bottom of the pot.

"Please tell me this ain't soup."

"No. Not soup. We're making *förtrollningar*. Charms," Ebba says, giggling like a little girl.

Granny frowns. She tosses a handful of dried cumin and cloves into the water. The spicy smell don't help matters much. "We're not making charms. We're making wards, Gracie. Strong ones. Against *him*."

"Bellflower? Care to tell me what this morning was all about? Seems like there's some history between you and that preacher."

Ebba glares at Granny. "You have not told her about your preacher, Deirdre?"

"I didn't see no reason to. That was all supposed to stay in the past." Granny angrily chops a bundle of mint leaves and adds them to the pot. "Besides, we fixed things."

"Y'all ain't makin' one lick of sense." I shake my head, fill the kettle, and put it on to boil. We're down to our last few grounds of coffee, and I've already used them twice, so I cut them with crushed acorns and chicory. All of a sudden, my back starts itching something fierce between my shoulder blades. I reach around to claw at it. Chiggers, likely. That's what I get for laying down on the ground next to the tracks. "I think I got ate up with chiggers last night."

Ebba taps her ladle on the edge of the pot and shares a look with Granny. "Let me see. Turn around." She swats my hair over my shoulder and fiddles with the zipper on the back of my dress. As it slides open, a rush of breath hits my skin. Ebba runs a finger down my spine. It might as well be a lit match for how it burns. I flinch away. "She's marked, Deirdre. Just like you. Marked for a *häxa*. Marked for a witch."

⟊⟊⟊

I twist in front of the mirror over the chest of drawers, dressed only in my necessaries. To me, the rash just looks like a bad case of poison ivy. It's all welted up in the middle, with fingers of red trailing out like the branches of a tree. Sometimes it itches, and sometimes it burns. The compress of mud, honey, and cow piss Ebba smacked on it earlier hadn't helped matters. It'd just drawn flies and stung like nettles, so I'd washed it off.

Marked for a witch. I ain't got no idea what that might mean, but after the way Granny acted after she saw the rash—all solemn and serious, I figure there's something I don't know.

I pull on my dress and go back to the kitchen. Every muscle in my body aches, and sweat rolls down my temples from the godforsaken heat. I should sleep, but it's too damned hot and I ain't seen Morris all day. He might have slept over at Seth's place as he does sometimes, then gone on to Hosea's to work, but there's a raw worry around his absence I can't shake.

I strain the coffee into a cup and add two spoonfuls of sugar, then go out to the front porch. Granny's on the steps, looking out at her prizewinning peonies. A cigarette dangles between her fingers. I ain't never seen her smoke before. The wards we made earlier sway back and forth in the trees. Some of them are shaped like men. Some are shaped like crosses or wreaths. I'd painted all of them with the rank tincture Granny and Ebba had brewed up earlier. A protective circle of asafetida still surrounds the house, but this time it's mixed with brick dust, cemetery dirt, and salt blessed with prayer. If Bellflower shows up tonight, he'll have to cross one hell of a spiritual barrier to get to us.

I shudder at the memory of his deep-set eyes and the way he'd watched me cross the yard like I was catnip on two legs. Why is he here? What does he *want*?

I hand the coffee to Granny and sit next to her with a tired groan.

"Thanks for the coffee, child. You always seem to know what I need before I ask for it, just like Ebba. I'm plumb tuckered out."

"It's been a mighty long day." I lean my head against Granny's shoulder. "You mind telling me what Ebba was talking about? *Your* preacher? What did she mean by that?"

She pulls in a deep breath, then takes a sip of her coffee. "I reckon it's time. There's things I never told you about Tin Mountain and what happened to me when I was a girl. My pa never told me about what happened to his own mama and why until it was almost too late."

"His mother?"

She nods. "Anneliese Werner—my grandmother. My Opa Friedrich found her in the woods when she was little more than a babe. Rumor had it she was Owen Sutter's youngest daughter. The only one that survived. You heard what happened to the Sutters?"

I nod. There's a graveyard on the hill on the other side of the holler, its flank dotted with crumbling headstones. Story is Owen Sutter had gone mad in the winter of 1818. Heard voices that told him to kill his wife and two of his three daughters. They're all buried there. All but one. Suddenly, I've got the all-overs. Even though the day's as hot as a cast iron skillet on a stove, I'm chilled to the bone.

"Nobody'd set foot on that piece of land until Friedrich came down with a bunch of fur trappers from around Ste. Genevieve. He was out tracking one day and claimed he heard somebody singing.

Found Anneliese down there in the holler. When he couldn't find her family, he reckoned he'd raise her himself. He fixed up the old Sutter place, and him and Anneliese lived there till he got the sepsis and died twenty-odd years later.

"Anneliese had a queer way about her. A cunning way. Folks were unsettled by her looks and manner, even though she never harmed a soul. She had her son when she was little more than a girl herself—my pa—and after she died, folks claimed he was the devil's boy." Granny chuckles. "If you'd known my pa, you'd laugh yourself to death at the thought. No. His daddy was an Osage scout who Anneliese healed after a skirmish with some settlers. She had a lifelong kinship with the Indians because of that. They trusted her. Traded with her. You can imagine how well that went over with the settlers. That's when the rumors first started to gain their steam."

"Folks always got something wicked to say about people who are different, don't they?"

"They sure do, Gracie. But my Oma never harmed a soul. She helped people. Nurtured the sick *and* the land. She blessed Bartholomew Ray's fields and orchard with her charms, because he was kind to her pa and kept him in work. She'd speak her words over the Rays' cattle and their cows'd give milk so rich you could churn butter with a few turns of a spoon. Even if she was a bit strange, folks cast their aspersions, but they let her be. Until *he* came along."

"Who?"

"Nathaniel Walker. The preacher who drove them to burn her."

"She's the witch from them old stories, then. The reason for the curse."

Granny frowns. "Wherever a witch's blood is spilled, a curse remains on the land. That's the saying, all right. Nobody ever blames the men that do the killing and the burning, do they? Instead, they blame the witch."

Granny's right.

The witch poisoned my well.
The witch cursed my crops.
The witch stole my husband.

And on and on it goes, from the first witch, down to the last.

Granny rises, her knees creaking. "If you really want to know who Anneliese was, there's somethin' I need to show you, Gracelynn. Something my pa gave to me a long time ago."

EIGHT

DEIRDRE

1881

Deirdre pulled her cotton wrapper over her shift and sat on the hope chest at the foot of her bed, carved of cedar and decorated with circular, multicolored hexes. Her mind spun with everything that had happened since yesterday. Gentry and his healing. The sudden flood. Her strange vision in Sutter's holler. None of it seemed to fit together.

Downstairs, her parents were arguing, Mama's voice rising and falling in waves. "You're blind to her ways, Jakob. She's been willful while you've been away." Mama knocked a spoon handle against a pot for emphasis. "She's help to me when her mind's not addled with that Cash boy, but you've spoilt her."

"She's not a little girl anymore, Nola. You were younger than she when we married. It's fitting for her to want her own life. Suitors.

Robbie Cash may not be to your liking, but if he comes to me and asks for her hand, I'll give my blessing."

Deirdre smiled. Pa approved of Robbie! It was all she needed to hear.

"The women talk about what he gets up to." Mama hissed the words low, but Deirdre still heard them. "Don't you want better for her?"

"Mountain biddies talk when they've nothing better to do. My concern is with that preacher you let on the place. A man like that would bring Deirdre worse than heartache, just like he brought my mother. His kind don't fit well with our own."

"A minister? Surely a man of God . . ."

"He's no man of God," Pa said with a finality clean as a postal stamp. "We need to hide Deirdre away. Protect her."

"To soothe your mind, we could send her to the Bledsoes' for a spell, to help Mrs. Bledsoe and the new baby," Mama said softly. "Hannah likes Deirdre and would be glad for the help." Mama sighed. "You and I need time to ourselves, besides. I've missed you, husband."

Pa whispered something too low for Deirdre to hear, and a girlish giggle bubbled from Mama's throat. Deirdre's face blazed with indignance. Mama had used her wiles to sway Pa into doing her bidding once more. But going to Hannah's would give Deirdre the chance to be out from under Mama's watch, and she could earn money of her own to put toward her wedding. She'd seen a fine bolt of ivory satin at the mercantile she could fashion into a gown.

Deirdre would finally have everything she wanted now that Pa was home.

A few moments passed, then Pa's footsteps echoed down the hall. He climbed up the ladder with a book clasped against his chest and sat beside her on the trunk, his eyes weary.

"I heard you and Mama," Deirdre said quietly. "Heard you say you'd give your blessing if Robbie asked for it." She clasped Pa's calloused hand. "Oh, Pa . . . being Robbie's wife is what I want more than any-thing. We could have the wedding this summer—by June, even, if we make things official now."

"There'll be time for wedding talk later, Deirdre Jane. There are more important things we need to talk about first." Pa opened the strange book carefully and placed it on Deirdre's lap. It was old, worn around the edges, with fragile pages made of pressed wood pulp and leather parchment. It smelled of musty leaves. She had no idea Pa even owned such a thing.

"What is it?"

"Your Oma's grimoire. Her *Zauberbuch*. It's a book of knowledge. Recipes and secret charms. My Opa Friedrich brought it over from the old country. His mother wrote all her wisdom on its pages and sent it with him. She knew he would have a daughter someday who might learn from it. My mama studied it and carried on the tradition herself, so that you might have *her* knowledge when the time came. If I'm not mistaken, it's time." He studied her, narrowing his eyes. "You must learn as much as you can from this book, Deirdre, so that you might guard yourself from those who would seek to beguile or harm you. You must always come to the book with clear intentions. As *you* will, the book provides, for good or for ill. Seek always to do no harm."

Deirdre carefully turned the pages of the grimoire, her fingers trem-bling. Some of the writing was in German, some in English. There were recipes for herbal cures and poultices, as well as illustrations of animals and the human form. Deirdre's breath caught in her throat when she turned to a page with a drawing of a locust tree, its branches in flame. She traced it with her fingertip. A strange warmth seemed to radiate from the paper. "It's that tree by your old home place. The one they burned her on."

Pa's jaw clenched. "You saw something down in the holler, didn't you, Deirdre?"

Deirdre nodded. "Yes. I've been having visions for a long time, Pa. But this one was different. There was a woman. They burned her, just like the stories people talk about. Did that really happen? Back then?"

"It did. That woman you saw—Anneliese—she was my mother. Your Oma."

Deirdre shuddered. Pa had never told her how his mother had died. He'd barely even spoken of her. Deirdre had only ever known Oma Elizabeth, who had raised Pa.

"Why did they kill her?"

Pa scrubbed his hand over his face. "I was only five years old. I remember only a little. The nightmares, mostly. Oma Elizabeth told me more, over the years, once I got to an age where I could understand it. A preacher came to town from out east. He took a shine to Mama and started calling on her. She was taken with his ways. At first. And then he changed. Grew mean."

He rose and went to stand in front of the open window. The breeze flicked at the curtains and brought the murky scent of wet earth. "That preacher—Nathaniel Walker—saw the way Mama charmed people and wanted what she had. He wanted her land, wanted her healing gifts for his ministry. Wanted her for his wife. When she spurned him, he grew angry. Turned the townsfolk against her. Claimed she was a witch—the devil's own mistress. He came up the mountain that spring with his mob. She hid me away, in that trunk you're sittin' on, and made me promise to give you her book, when the time came, because she knew he would come back for you, too. The spirit that's inside him . . . has long stalked our kin."

"You're saying Gentry's the same man? How can that be, Pa?" With Gentry's youthful looks, he couldn't be older than Pa. It was impossible.

"Maybe he is, and maybe he's not. There are strange things in this world. I can't seek to explain them all. All I know is, I've been dreaming of Mama lately. Felt a strong pull home. I've always had a knowing—the smallest measure of her gifts, but you have the wealth of them, Deirdre.

The gifts in our family are passed from grandmother to granddaughter. With those gifts comes danger. I've known you've had the healing touch since you were a girl. Do you remember Millie?"

Deirdre nodded. Millie had been their redtick coonhound, her constant companion when she was a girl. "Yes, I remember her."

"She was in labor with her first litter of pups and having a hard time of it. Nearly died. You laid down next to her, put your little hands on her belly, whispered in her ear, and eased her way. She brought four puppies, all of them hale and hearty."

"I don't remember that at all, Pa."

"All the same, it happened. Surely, you've noticed the way people look at you, poppet? It's more than your beauty. It's what you are. *Who* you are. Your gifts make folks covetous—some will pay you for what they want, and pay you well, but there are some who would seek to steal from you instead."

Mama's step sounded from below. Pa took the book from Deirdre and hid it beneath the quilt. Deirdre crawled to the edge of the loft. "What is it, Mama?"

"I've a bath ready for you, child. Come clean up and get into some proper clothes before supper."

After Mama swept back down the hall and into the kitchen, Pa unlatched the trunk at the foot of Deirdre's bed, placing the book inside. "You can look at that Zauberbuch anytime you want, daughter. It's yours now. But I don't want your mama or anyone else reading a word of it. What's written here is only for your eyes."

"I understand, Pa. I do." Mama didn't have much use for magic and superstitions. Deirdre had learned to hide her gifts well—her seeing, her healing whispers—though they aided Mama in her work more than she knew.

She swallowed the lump in her throat and went down. Mama had the copper tub filled with steaming water in front of the hearth. Deirdre shrugged off her wrapper and her dirty, stained shift.

"What's that, on your back? Turn around." Mama reached out to trace a fingertip over Deirdre's spine. She flinched. It burned hot and fierce as a wasp sting where Mama touched her. "You've got a mark. A rash."

Deirdre craned her neck and tried to look. Red welts fanned up her shoulder, like the branches of a tree. "I can't reckon where it came from. It stings somethin' fierce."

"I'll put some lanolin ointment on it after your bath," Mama said.

Deirdre climbed into the tub, the warm water unknotting her sore muscles and soothing her rash as she sank down to her chin. Mama filled the porcelain ewer with water and tilted Deirdre's head back to wet her hair. "You didn't say a word to Pa about Mr. Cash, I hope."

Deirdre sighed. "I ain't said a thing, Mama. And I won't."

Mama took up a cake of lye soap and began scrubbing Deirdre's scalp with her fingernails. She was always too rough. "What did the two of you talk about?"

"He just told me a little bit about my Oma. Anneliese."

"Oh? He's never told me much about her. The old folks who knew her say she was a witch."

"They say that about you sometimes, too, Mama. Ain't true. She was just a midwife like you are." Pa hadn't forbidden her to talk to Mama about Oma Anneliese, only the grimoire. Still, if he'd meant for Mama to know more about his family, she would already know after twenty years of marriage. If she could keep Mama's secrets, she could keep Pa's, too.

"And what did he say about that preacher?"

Deirdre bit the inside of her cheek. "Pa remembered his kin from the war. They were horse thieves and such." The lie came easy enough, almost as if someone had whispered it in her ear.

"Well, when you go to Mrs. Bledsoe's, don't think because you're out of my sight that you can go running off with Robbie. I aim to see change in your manner, daughter. Though your pa turns his head to your ways, I won't soon forget your disrespect."

Deirdre choked back the bitter laugh in her throat. "And I ain't forgot about you and Mr. Cash, Mama. Now that Pa's home, you'll likely fawn all over him until he leaves again. Pa's gettin' up in years. I reckon as soon as he passes, you'll take your widow's pension and marry Mr. Cash, and that's the real reason why you don't want me hitched with Robbie. Just think of the talk."

"Don't you dare test me, girl," Mama hissed. "If you want to marry Robbie, you'll bite your tongue and hold it."

So that's how it was going to be. Tit for tat. Something dark and full of teeth clawed at Deirdre from the inside. Her whole body thrummed with it. She stared Mama down, unflinching.

Mama gasped and backed away from the tub. "Your eyes, Deirdre . . ."

"Leave me be, Mama. Pa's already given his blessing with Robbie. You don't get to tell me what to do no more."

NINE

GRACELYNN

1931

Granny kneels on the floor in the alcove under the loft, one hand to her lower back where her arthritis gripes her the worst. She pulls a folded quilt aside, revealing a cedar chest covered with faded hexes painted in red, green, and yellow. She unhooks the latch and opens it, the hinges squeaking in protest. Inside, atop a layer of musty blankets, sits a tapestry satchel overlaid with a bouquet of dried lavender. She turns to me. "Go on. Take it out. See what's inside."

I kneel next to Granny and draw the satchel out. It's heavier than I expect. Inside, I find a book—its leather cover wrinkled like a corpse's skin. Runes—sigils like the markings over the doorways in Ebba's house, are burned into the spine. Symbols of protection. A faint buzzing plays beneath my fingers as I open the book. The writing scrawls across the pages, faded and nearly illegible. "What is it?"

"It's a grimoire. A book of shadows."

"Lands." A witch's book. I'd heard of such things. Sacred, personal journals full of charms and spells. I turn the pages slowly. They feel fragile and thinner than a Bible's pages, like they might flake into nothing if I'm not careful. Drawings illuminate the text, worked in between the words and symbols. The image of a flaming tree stretches across two pages, its branches licked with red and orange. "It's sure pretty." The drawing seems to come alive under my touch, the fire flickering and moving. Heat blossoms beneath my fingertips, travels up my arm, and sets the rash between my shoulder blades to tingling. I gasp and pull back.

"You felt it? Just like I did." Granny nods. "She's chosen you, all right. That burning you felt, that mark on your back, it's just the beginning." Granny takes the book from me and closes it. "This is a powerful book, Gracelynn. The answers to *anything* you'd ever need to know are found in its pages. Women have had these sorts of books for centuries—it's how they brought their old ways to the new country, so their daughters and granddaughters might learn the kind of work we do and more, besides. This grimoire is a living thing. It's been in our family from the beginning, and in our family it will always remain." The crease between her brows deepens. "It can be used for many, many things, but you must come to the book with clear intentions and a mind not to harm. Otherwise, the work might go wrong."

"But why are you giving it to me? Shouldn't you give it to Val, or even Caro, seein' as they're your blood?"

"Anneliese has chosen *you*. That's why you're marked."

The rash between my shoulder blades tingles again.

"You've had dreams lately, haven't you? Strange ones? Maybe even visions like I have."

I nod.

"It's Anneliese. She's calling you. Just like she called me." Granny runs a gnarled hand over the leather cover of the book.

"Blood ain't got much at all to do with family—family is about love. Anneliese wasn't Opa Friedrich's blood, neither, but he raised her no different. Oma Elizabeth took in my Pa after Anneliese died and loved him like her own son, just like I love you." Granny weaves her fingers through mine and gently squeezes my hand. "Anneliese can sense you're special. *I've* always known you were special, Gracie. Knew it from the first time I laid eyes on you, with your tangled hair, them gangly, long legs, and a spirit made older by its troubles. You looked up at me with your big blue eyes and I felt a tug in my heart that knew no measure. It was me that convinced Val to take you in, because you belonged with us. With me." Tears pool in Granny's eyes and spill over. "The power in our family . . . it's real enough, but the love is even more real, Gracelynn. Power don't always look the way you think it should. I had a lot of learnin' to do, just like you."

I close my eyes for a minute, remembering the relief I'd felt that cold day in January when the Greene County sheriff came to our door with his hat in his hands to tell me what I already knew. I didn't cry one single tear for my daddy. Some things just need to run their course. The only good thing Shep Doherty ever did for me was to lay himself down in that ditch with a belly full of rotgut moonshine and die. I thank all my angels every day for that.

I don't want to think about life before Granny, so I clear my head of the past and drink in everything she just told me instead. Real magic exists? And I might be a witch? It's all so confusing. I glance toward the grimoire, freckled with sunlight streaming through the lace curtains. My fingers ache to turn its pages and read what's inside, but I'm also afraid that it might be too much for me to comprehend. I don't know that I'm ready.

"And what about that preacher?"

"Yes. Him." Granny unfolds from the floor, her joints creaking and popping. "There's something familiar about the darkness behind those eyes. I saw some things when I had my last vision. You were all alone, in an open field, and a black wolf came running at you, with bared teeth. A wolf is a symbol. A symbol for the de—" She braces herself against the doorway and puts a hand to her head. "Lands. Got mighty dizzy all of a sudden. Probably just need a bite to eat."

I grasp onto her elbow to help steady her. Her skin is like ice. My heart starts racing. Granny never gets sick. "You all right? You don't look so good."

"Gracie, I can't feel my . . . I . . . ," she slurs. "Get the . . . grim . . ."

Suddenly, Granny's knees fold and she falls to the floor before I can catch her, her back arching as a froth of drool boils from her slackened mouth.

"Granny!" I drop to my knees next to her, panic twisting sharp as a knife blade between my ribs. For a moment, her eyes widen and meet mine, and I see my fear mirrored there. The fit overtakes her, lifting her hips from the plank floor and wrenching her limbs into unnatural angles as she seizes.

It's like a scene from a play or a picture show, almost as if I'm watching from afar as I crouch over her, wailing and shaking her shoulders. I know I need to do something—that I should run for help. But it's like I'm rooted to the floor—weak, worthless, and scared to death to leave her.

Her eyes roll back, and she shudders one last time as I call out her name.

Outside, a dog begins to howl. It sounds just like a wolf.

TEN

DEIRDRE

1881

Deirdre shrugged out of Robbie's embrace, ears abuzz with the whir of crickets. The cloud-veiled sun was already hugging the ridge. She needed to get back to town, and fast. It had been nearly three weeks since she'd left home and gone to help the Bledsoes. Hannah was an easy mistress. Being in her employ had been the respite from Mama she hoped it would be. Best of all, her outings to gather herbs gave her an excuse to steal more time with Robbie.

She picked up her petticoats from where they lay on the wide slab of shale next to her, uncovering the swath of dark green moss stretched across its surface like a clawed hand. She hurriedly stepped into her skirts, then buttoned her shirtwaist over her chemise. Robbie woke and rolled onto his side, shielding his eyes from the light. "You leavin' already?"

"Already? I've lingered too long as it is." Deirdre wound up her hair and raked her combs through it, piling its frazzled thickness atop her head.

"Mrs. Bledsoe can manage without you." Robbie stood and stretched, then circled her hips with his arms, pinioning her tightly to him. He pulled the unbuttoned collar of her blouse over the curve of her shoulder and kissed her there. Deirdre sighed. "Don't you want to stay here, just a little while longer?" he asked.

Heat flared under her skin, though their couplings still left Deirdre hollow with wanting. She'd learned Robbie was much too eager to catch his own pleasure than coax her body into something she'd only ever caught the achingly sweet edge of.

"I have to go, Robbie. And so do you. You'll need to light the beacon."

"Pa can manage all that without me. Just let me have you one more time."

"All right. But be quick about it." Deirdre sank back down into the grass and gathered her skirts in an uncomfortable wad beneath her. By the time Robbie was finished, her bottom was rubbed raw by the rough ground and the rest of her was well past the point of frustration.

When she left Robbie at the foot of the hillside, it was near dark, and thunder rolled in the distance. More rain. Deirdre hastened toward town. When she got to the covered bridge, she paused before crossing, remembering the strange glint in Ambrose Gentry's eyes. What if he was hiding beneath the bridge, waiting for her in the shadows?

Deirdre shuddered. She'd been dreaming of him every night—rank, lustful dreams shot through with the kind of fear that left her soaked with sweat and trembling as he whispered in the darkness.

Only I can give you what you want.

The skin prickled on Deirdre's arms, but she drew up her courage and rushed across the bridge, the echo of her footsteps thudding in time with her heart.

As she neared the Bledsoe place, she caught sight of Rosy, hitched to the wagon, eagerly munching on Hannah's irises. What was Pa doing here? Deirdre patted her mussed hair and shook the brambles from her skirts. Mary met her at the door, her pale-lashed eyes furtive beneath her ruffled cap. "Your pa's in the parlor. I'm sorry, Miss Deirdre. I made to lie, but . . ."

Panic twisted in Deirdre's belly. "You didn't tell him where I went, did you?"

"No, miss. But he's fit to be tied, all the same."

Deirdre followed the little maid into the half-round room with its yellow wallpaper, her heart thumping. Pa paced in front of the fireplace. When he looked up, relief instead of anger shot across his face. "Where have you been, poppet?"

"I . . . I was out gathering herbs for Mrs. Bledsoe's tea." It wasn't a complete lie. Not really, though the tea was for herself. She'd learned more than a thing or two from the grimoire by lamplight, after she'd put Collin to bed. The book had shown her ways to prevent a child that were more reliable than the stinging vinegar Ingrid used.

Pa's frown deepened. Dark circles smudged beneath his eyes. He hadn't been sleeping. "That preacher came here while you were gone. Mrs. Bledsoe let him in."

Deirdre felt the blood drain from her face. "Oh, Pa. I . . ."

"I've seen him on our place, watching and waiting for you in the woods. Chased him off twice. But now that he knows you're here—well."

"What if Robbie and me got married right away? If I had a husband, he'd leave me be, wouldn't he?" The thought of Robbie's strong arms around her in the darkness, driving away her dreams of Gentry, was a comfort.

"Robbie hasn't come to me yet, poppet, and I can't take the chance that Gentry will leave of his own accord, just because you've married. It's not your heart he's after. He'll turn the townsfolk against you, and there'll be no stopping him once that's happened. I can't take that chance." He squeezed his eyes shut. "I have to protect you. If I send you away—far from Tin Mountain—he'll likely move on at the end of summer, and you and your Robbie can have your wedding at the harvest. All will be well by then."

Deirdre sank down in the nearest chair. "You want to send me away? Where?"

Mary bustled back through the parlor door, a silver-laden tea tray in hand. "Mistress will be down shortly."

"Oh. I wouldn't trouble her more than she's already been troubled," Pa said, scratching his head.

"She'd like a word with you, and with Deirdre, sir. About that man." Mary set the tea service on the console next to Deirdre and bobbed an unsure curtsy.

Deirdre poured tea, her hands shaking, then added two cubes of sugar. She'd been fierce hungry after her hurried flight down the hill, but now her stomach turned at the thought of food.

As the clock chimed eight, Hannah Bledsoe swept into the room, dressed for dinner in a gaudy purple frock trimmed with lace, little Collin tucked beneath her chin. "Evenin' Mr. Werner. Deirdre."

Pa rose, dipping his chin. "Sorry to trouble you, ma'am."

"Oh, it's no trouble at all. I hardly have visitors when Billy's away." Hannah sank drunkenly into the chair opposite Deirdre. Her eyes were feverish, her pupils a mere pinprick. She'd been dosing with the laudanum again. "That gentleman, the one who came to call this afternoon, was surely well spoken and polite, but he was insistent upon seeing Deirdre. I could hardly convince him to leave. It was unsettling."

"He's . . . a suitor," Deirdre murmured. "One I've spurned. He's taking it none too well."

Baby Collin woke and stirred at Hannah's bosom, his mewling cry sharp as a fox kit. She jostled him, too frantic. His crying intensified, carrying up the walls. Hannah had no natural inclination with soothing a baby, at all.

"May I?" Deirdre asked. Hannah eagerly offered the baby to her, and Deirdre perched Collin against her shoulder, shushing him as she walked to the front hall and stood in front of the window to stare out at the gloom. He nuzzled against her neck, falling back to his slumber as gently as a feather on a pond. Rain streaked the leaded windowpanes and pinged hard against the glass. The near-constant storms already had the crops stinking with rot.

"Your daughter certainly has a way with my Collin," Hannah said from the other room. "Having her with me has been such a help, Mr. Werner. I've a mind to keep her on as Collin's nanny. That's what I wished to speak with you about."

"That's mighty kind of you, ma'am. And my Deirdre is good help, for certain." Pa cleared his throat. "It's just that her suitor—the man who came here—he's right dangerous. I thought by letting her come here we might discourage his advances, and he'd move on. But seeing as he knows she's here, he won't leave her, or you, alone. He'll keep coming around."

"I see."

"I mean to send her away for the summer."

The other room went silent, the pitter-patter of rain the only sound. "Do you have somewhere in mind?"

"That's the trouble. We haven't any family outside Tin Mountain. My wife wants to send her to a convent. It may be the most practical thing."

Deirdre rankled. A convent! The last thing she wanted was to be hidden away in a convent filled with somber nuns and silence.

"Perhaps, if the convent is a temporary arrangement. I can't see Deirdre taking the veil. She's not even a baptized Catholic, is she?" The opium had made Hannah's silken voice as high and shrill as a tin whistle. "Surely Deirdre should get a say in where she goes, Mr. Werner. Don't you think?"

Deirdre turned and went back to the parlor, no longer content to eavesdrop while her future was decided for her. She sank back into her chair, rocking Collin gently, and fixed Pa with a frown.

"Just look at that." Hannah smiled. "She's a natural mother. You want a family of your own someday, isn't that right, Deirdre?"

"Yes'm, I sure do," she said steadily. "And Hannah's right, Pa. I should get a say in where I go."

"Oh! I've an idea." Hannah leaned forward in her chair, her green eyes sparkling. "I've a maiden aunt in Charleston. She runs a finishing school for respectable young women. She'd take Deirdre in on my recommendation."

Deirdre's heart jumped. The room seemed to shrink, the walls drawing in around her. Charleston was so much farther than she ever thought she'd go—too far away from Robbie. She'd never even been fifty miles outside of Tin Mountain.

Pa scratched his head again. "I'm much obliged, but we couldn't afford to pay much in the way of schooling, ma'am."

"Nonsense!" Hannah said, leaping to her feet. "Deirdre might repay me later, with her service. She's already helped me so much. Why, you can't say no." Hannah rubbed her frantic hands together. "I'll send Mary to the post straightaway. She can telegram Aunt Beryl to tell her you're coming. It's a marvelous school, Deirdre. You'll learn manners and etiquette—and even dancing! She gives the finest debutante balls. You'll be a proper lady by the time you return."

"I ain't got much interest in all that, ma'am. I—"

"And you're certain your aunt will take her?"

"Of course she will! Beryl owes me a favor. She wouldn't think of turning Deirdre away."

"Pa, I really think we should—"

"Deirdre's much obliged, Mrs. Bledsoe, and so am I," Pa said, cutting Deirdre's words short yet again. He stood and clapped his hat over his hair. "Go pack up your things, poppet. I'll see you to the station.

They've just finished a new depot, closer than the one in Fayetteville. The last train leaves in an hour."

The floor seemed to drop out from under Deirdre's feet. "You can't mean now? I haven't gotten to say goodbye to everyone. I'd like to see Robbie, and Ing."

"It's best if you leave tonight. The fewer people who know where you're headed, the better. Now, go gather your things. I'll wait in the wagon." Pa stalked out of the room in that resolute way he had when he'd made up his mind. Hannah followed him, chattering on about Charleston and all the fine things it had on offer.

Deirdre buried her nose in little Collin's hair and drew in his milk-sweet baby smell. She squeezed her eyes shut against her sudden tears, then handed the slumbering babe off to Mary. She flew up the back stairs to her tiny attic room, locking the door behind her. She'd never once defied her father, but the temptation was fierce. All she'd ever wanted was a simple life—to marry Robbie and have a family of her own. And now, it seemed even her simplest of wishes had flown far out of reach. Pa was overreacting over Gentry. He had to be. And what if Robbie tired of waiting for her, and married someone else?

She'd run away. Go to Robbie, and they'd elope. Pa would understand and forgive her, eventually.

Deirdre lit a lamp with shaking fingers, turning the wick low. Greasy light stretched across the ceiling. She thought of Pa, sitting out in the cold, water drenching his shirtsleeves and running off the brim of his hat as he waited for her. She pushed back her guilt, went to the wardrobe, and began to pack, shoving her dresses and shifts into her carpetbag, then placing the grimoire atop the rest.

She tucked her hair as well as she could into her oilcloth bonnet, and pinched her cheeks for color, wanting to look as fetching as she could before she went to Robbie. As she was finishing her ablutions, a low creaking came from behind her. Deirdre turned from the washstand and faced the corner, where a hoop-backed rocking chair sat beneath the eaves. Though the only window was closed, and no draft came from beneath the door, it rocked as steadily as if someone were sitting in it.

It was merely a silly fancy. Her imagination gone wild.

She turned back to the mirror. The carpetbag dropped to the floor.

There, reflected in the mirror's scratched surface, sat Ambrose Gentry, rocking back and forth, although the chair itself remained empty. His cunning green eyes sparked with mischief at her gape-mouthed expression. Inside her head, his deep voice wound silkily between her ears:

Run little rabbit, run. Wherever you go, I'll find you.

Deirdre tried to scream, but only a feeble whine issued forth. She hurriedly snatched up her satchel and ran from the room, barreling down the stairs and out the servants' entrance, into the frigid rain. She was halfway to the road when someone caught her from behind, grasping her with strong arms. Deirdre thrashed and screamed, kicking out at the air.

It was too late. He'd gotten her. He'd do whatever he wanted with her now.

"Deirdre! It's only me. It's your pa." Pa turned her, steadying her in his arms, his warm brown eyes tender and crinkled with concern.

Deirdre collapsed into Pa's embrace, weeping into his coat. "I saw him, Pa. I'm afraid."

"I know you are. And with good reason. Let's get you on that train, poppet."

ELEVEN

GRACELYNN

1931

Granny ain't dead. But she ain't alive, neither. She's somewhere in between. A place beyond sleep and dreaming, where her pulse beats soft as a butterfly's wings.

So soft even the doctor couldn't find it.

A coma. That's what Doc Gallagher'd said, after he tired of my objections to calling the funeral home and placed a mirror before her face. A cloud of frail breath slowly took away its shine—the only thing that kept Granny from a slow ride down the mountain in Floyd Harris's hearse.

"There's no guarantee she'll live or even come back to consciousness. She won't be able to eat or drink in this state." Doc Gallagher washed his hands and shook the water from them as Ebba and I fretted. "I'll come back to check on her tomorrow and give her another injection of fluids, but we should take her to the hospital. She needs intravenous therapy at the very least. Her vital signs monitored, day and night." He fixed me with a hawkish look. "Deirdre and I have always worked *with* one another, not against. I trust you to do the same, Gracelynn."

But I knew Granny wouldn't want to go to a hospital. She had no trust of city doctors. *Hospital's a good place to go if you're aimin' for the grave,* she'd cluck to her patients. So even as Ebba fussed at me and pleaded, I still refused.

No. I'd take care of her, here at home. It's what she would want.

With Ebba's help, I undress Granny, wring out a cloth and bathe her with warm herbal waters—chamomile and lavender. We dress her in her softest cotton nightdress and prop her head up with pillows on her daybed. The sky through the screens is the purple, orange, and yellow of a half-healed bruise. I need to start dinner before Caro and Val get home. I still ain't seen no sign of Morris. It's mighty strange for him not to be home by suppertime. I rise from the floor, my knees sore from kneeling. Ebba stops stroking Granny's hair and stands with me. She's mad at me. I can see it in the set of her square jaw.

"I need to make us something to eat," I say softly. "You'll stay for supper, won't you, Ebba?"

"Ja. And I will stay until she wakes." There's a challenge in her blue-green eyes as she jabs a finger at my chest. "You don't know enough to help her."

I cross my arms. I feel my anger well up, but I ain't mad at Ebba. She loves Granny as much as I do. I'm angry at myself—for not calling for help faster and for not knowing what to do when Granny fell into her seizure. Despite my pride, I could use Ebba's help, because Lord knows Aunt Val is too busy becoming Josiah Bellflower's hussy to be of any use. "You can stay as long as you want, Ebba. I'll fix up a pallet by her bed."

Ebba waves me off, grumbling to herself.

I go to the kitchen, take down the stockpot, and soak the poke greens Granny and I gathered yesterday in a pan of salty water. They'll be good with the ham hock I was lucky enough to get at the mercantile. Once the water is boiling, and I sit down to peel potatoes, the tears come. I sob into my apron, remembering the first day I came to Tin Mountain, when Granny took me by the hand, sat me down at this very table, and pushed a steaming mug of weak coffee cut with milk toward me. *You're home now, Gracelynn. This is your home. It always will be.* And for the first time in my life, I didn't have to be afraid of Daddy's drunken, wandering hands or worry where my next meal would come from.

I've always sworn I'd never let anyone get too close, lest they hurt me more than I've already been hurt, but I don't know what I'm gonna do if I lose Granny. She's the solid ground beneath my feet. I put the potatoes on to boil, and just as the sky turns dark, I hear Caro's step on the porch. I dread telling her what's happened. The poor kid already has enough on her shoulders.

She pushes through the door and slumps into a chair to unlace her boots. Her hair is dark around the edges with sweat. She should still be in school, not working the fields, but Val put an end to that the day Caro turned eight, though I do my best to teach her what I know.

"Dinner'll be done soon. Have as much food as you want tonight, Carolyn June."

"I'm starved. Morris and Mama didn't come out to the fields today, so I had to work all by myself. Things are real dry. Our parcel's cracked so bad only weeds can push through. Hosea has us bringing water up from the crick. I carried twenty buckets today. My arms are like to fall right off."

"Lands. This heat is somethin' else. Morris never showed up to work, neither?"

"Nope, just me."

If I was worried before, a whole new avalanche of fears falls over me.

I drain the potatoes and mash them, then pile some on a plate for Caro. She digs in, slathering a healthy knob of butter over the top of the taters, until it runs over the edges like a river. She squints at me, her jaw working as she chews. "Where's Granny? And why're your eyes all puffy? You been crying?"

"Don't talk with your mouth full. She's sleeping. Real, real deep."

"One of her headaches?"

I swallow, hard. "No, not a headache. She'll be okay, though. Ebba'll stay with us for a while to help take care of her."

Ebba pushes through the curtained partition like a gray whirlwind and goes to the stove, angrily scooping out potatoes. "She's not sick like a flu, Caro." She sits across from me, her eyes narrowing. "It's worse. Tell her the truth, Gracie. She should know."

Caro looks at Ebba sideways. "What's she talkin' about?"

I take Caro's little hand. "Granny's in something called a coma, and she can't talk or move, or anything else. At least right now."

"Why?" Caro's eyes well up. "What happened?"

"I don't rightly know why she's sick, Caro."

"Is she gonna die?"

"Not if we can help it."

We finish up with dinner and then take Caro to see Granny. Her breath rises and falls in a threadbare whisper. Beneath her crepe-paper eyelids, her eyes roll and flutter like she's seeing something in her heavy veil of sleep. The oil lamp's wan light deepens the creases in her forehead and carves darkness into the hollows of her cheeks.

"Talk to her, Carolyn June." Ebba's voice is thick with emotion. "Her body is here, but her spirit is somewhere else. Dreaming. Seeing." Ebba flitters her hands over Granny's head.

Caro sits on the edge of the bed and takes Granny's wrinkled hand. A tear trickles down her face, but she starts rattling on about her day just like she would if Granny was sitting with her out on the porch swing.

Ebba nudges me with her elbow and motions me back into the house. "Let her alone with Deirdre so she can say what she wants to say."

We go back to the kitchen, and I pour myself a cup of black coffee. My hands are shaking. I could really use one of Val's cigarettes right now. "Tell me what you know, Ebba. About this curse, what happened to Granny in the past, everything. I need to know the truth. Granny only gave me half answers before she got sick." Everyone thinks Ebba's off her rocker. But she's got a feral kind of wisdom I've come to appreciate. She makes her living as a water witcher and knows her way around our conjure garden as well as I do. There's some sort of wild magic running through her veins, too, and she knows Granny in a way few people do.

"Most of the story is in that *häxboken*," Ebba says. "Deirdre finally showed it to you, yes?"

"Anneliese's grimoire?"

Ebba nods, her head haloed with silver in the candlelight. "The past will help you understand what is happening now, better than I can tell you. The women in your family have powers. Sometimes the powers help and heal. Sometimes they hurt."

"And that preacher?"

Ebba turns away, worrying at her sleeve. "A preacher came through Tin Mountain fifty years ago. Ambrose Gentry. Got things all stirred up. There was a flood. Many people died. She has it in her head that it's him, returned to do the same again."

"He couldn't be the same man. He's too young."

"Some men have the devil in them. A darker kind of magic that fools the eye."

I remember what Granny told me about Anneliese and Nathaniel Walker and the origin of the curse that plagues Tin Mountain: Anneliese's murder. Maybe Ebba's right. "When did the trouble start, and when did it end?"

"I was just a girl, but as I remember, it started near Walpurgis Night—witch's night—and ended with the harvest—*freyrfaxi*. Young folks think Walpurgis is just about bonfires and playing pranks. But we old ones, we remember. Walpurgis is a powerful holiday for our kind. It's a woman's time—Frigga's time—a period of fertility and increase. At least, it should be." Ebba sighs. "Fifty years ago, when Gentry came through, there was no fertility. No harvest."

"There was a flood, wasn't there?"

"Yes, what folks call a hundred-year flood. The rain never seemed to stop."

"But it passed?"

"Yes. After a time. But crops failed. Animals and people died, and things took a good long while to settle. I lost my aunt Maja that winter, and two of my cousins died, too." Ebba gazes out the open window, where the cicadas are starting their nightly cacophony. "So much lost that year." Ebba rubs her arms, as if fighting off a chill. "Deirdre tried to set things right back then. She . . . gave up much. But still, it wasn't enough." Ebba's eyes glint, her thin lips curl down at the corners. "Some say it's Anneliese who brought the curse, but it was *him* who brought it. He angered the land with her murder, and now it reacts as if poison's been spilled on it when it senses his return. The curse will only end for good once he's driven out and Anneliese's restless spirit is satisfied. Justified. She and the land want a reckoning for the wrong that was done."

⚜

I go outside, into the night. The cabin feels too close. Too crowded. The air outside ain't any cooler. It's humid-hot and stifling. This heat is enough to drive a person crazy.

The last time the curse came through Tin Mountain, there was a flood. This time, if I had to wager, it's looking to be a drought.

If what Ebba says is true, people are going to die. Lots of people. Unless I can find a way to stop it.

But how? If Granny couldn't, how do I stand a chance?

Ebba hadn't offered anything real helpful—and some of the things she told me made no sense. I go past our sheltering wards and through the trees, along the foraging trail, with a mind to cross the creek and check for Morris up at his still. The moon hangs like a freshly sharpened scythe above my head, lending scant light to my steps.

Suddenly, alongside the spring's warble, a low moan filters through the thicket. I stop short and listen. I hear heavy breathing, like the panting of some wild animal that's been hurt. Up ahead, movement flashes through the cedar boughs.

I slowly creep forward, until what I'm seeing becomes horrifyingly clear.

There, on that same flat, mossy rock where Granny saw the portent of a hard summer to come, lies Val. She's naked, her eyes closed, her hands knotted in her hair. A man kneels between her pale, splayed legs.

He's . . . oh, God. They're . . .

I step backward, bile rising in my throat. A twig snaps. The man raises his head. It's Josiah Bellflower. His eyes are pitch black, with that eerie shine of silver at their center. As he locks eyes with me, a shard of pain drives itself deep through my forehead.

Suddenly, I'm *seeing* again.

Bellflower transforms. His sharp, jib-nosed looks fade and morph until a decrepit, aged creature hunkers over Val, with ancient sagging skin. He smiles, showing blackened teeth. He moves on top of Val. She wraps herself around him, her cries echoing as Bellflower begins to rut inside her. Shadows swirl around them both, hiding them from view.

I turn and run, until I'm back outside the cabin. I heave my guts into Granny's peonies. My head hurts so bad I think it might explode. A trickle of blood runs from one of my nostrils, and I wipe it away with the back of my hand.

What the hell is he? I stopped believing in God and the devil a long time ago, but with the sick feeling in my gut right now, I'd reckon he's something close to the latter. I now know with a certainty that Val ain't coming home. Bad, bad, bad. All of this is bad. And I'm in the thick of it all, not knowing how to fix it.

And then I remember Granny's book.

INTERLUDE

ANNELIESE'S GRIMOIRE

February 15, 1831

It has been a brutal season. Papa died in the earliest days of January, despite my best efforts to save him. A cut from his saw blade festered, and no amount of willow bark or whispered prayers quenched the fever that followed. I could not bring him back from the brink.

Jakob and I are alone now.

Papa provided well for us, but the meager savings he left behind will not last. Each day, I count the coins in his snuff box, and watch them dwindle. I feel guilty eating our porridge, preferring to ration the rest for Jakob, as his appetite is fickle. Instead, I subsist on dried berries, locust pods, and the wrinkled potatoes I manage to dig from the cold ground. I drink bitterbark tea instead of coffee or cider.

I need to find work.

I have been consulting my Oma's Zauberbuch for recipes and charms that might fetch a price. It is so curious, this book. It ever shows me what I need and has done so since I was a girl. The book also warns me to be cautious, for it is a small leap from cunning woman to witch in the eyes of many.

Yet, with Papa gone, I must put aside my fears and set myself to the only work I know to do.

February 20, 1831

I have labored day and night, crafting my charms and cures. Yesterday morning, I packaged them neatly in bottles and burlap, loaded up our rickety wheelbarrow, and bade Jakob to mind the cabin.

Last night, when I trudged back to the hollow, weary and out of breath, my cures were all gone and the wheelbarrow full of food. It was a fruitful day. I will go to town twice more this winter. Jakob will soon be feasting on schnitzel and sweet pastries instead of bland gruel.

April 3, 1831

The women have started to come to our cabin.

They are secretive, covering their hair and faces with shawls and cloaks as they knock upon our door. News of my gifts has spread—that they stretch beyond the provenance of simple tinctures and remedies. The women make their petitions in low voices. Some wish to lure men to their beds. Some, to be rid of their unborn babes, saying they are bone tired, and their husbands will not leave them be. Some, their bodies marked with angry purple bruises, ask to be rid of their husbands entirely.

I listen to their woes and their desires, tell them to come back in a day or two, then watch them leave through the window. They spit at the ground over their shoulders when they depart, shamefaced and furtive.

Yet, the women are pleased by my work. They pay me well. My cheeks are full and round as apples again and my clothes are growing snug. When the last snow melts and the dogwoods bloom, I will buy fine fabric and soft leather at the mercantile, to sew new spring dresses for myself and lederhosen and moccasins for Jakob.

We are as rich as we could ever hope to be. We are happy.

April 30, 1831

This morning, in the wee hours, I was awoken by the sound of hail. It was as if a giant had dropped a pailful of stones on the roof, so sudden was the squall. The wind howled and shook the cabin, yet Jakob slept through the storm, peaceful as a lamb.

I wish I could say the same. It has not been a fortuitous beginning to Walpurgis.

As dawn grayed the sky, the storm ceased. I crept out of doors, my feet skidding on shimmering orbs of ice. A horrific sight awaited me. My new hen, a beautiful black speckled bird, lay on the ground. I rushed to her side, the other hens clucking as I knelt over her. She was dead cold. Stricken down by a hailstone.

I gently pressed my palm to her breast and felt the faintest stir of life. I closed my eyes, willing her to be healed. A moment later, she warmed, her heart beating strong and sure beneath my palm. She scrambled to her feet and rustled her wings, preening proudly as she tilted her head to look at me with gimlet eyes. I spread a handful of corn on the ground, and she fluttered over to peck at it, drawing the others to do the same. I smiled, pleased that my gift is of such a practical use.

After I had gathered a few eggs in my apron pocket for our breakfast, I felt a *presence*. I cannot say what it was, only that I had the uncanny notion that I was being watched through the dense thicket bordering our homestead, though nothing moved among the shadows.

May 2, 1831

All my hens are dead. Torn to little more than feathers. They were beyond my powers to restore. I suspect a fox.

May 3, 1831

I had a visitor today. A minister. He sat with me and read verses from his Bible. We talked for a good long while. He is from out east—Massachusetts or Maryland, although I cannot recollect which. He has promised to come again. Entertaining him demanded only a cup of tea and a listening ear, although I have little use for his teachings. He is called Nathaniel Walker.

May 7, 1831

Mr. Walker came again, as promised. This time, he brought sweets for Jakob and two red hens for me, as I had spoken to him of our unfortunate massacre. It was a disarming gift. He helped me build a sturdy slat rail fence around the henhouse—one high enough that a fox would have little chance of breaching it. After, we sat by the fire and talked long into the evening. He showed an interest in my work, asking me about the bundled herbs hanging from the rafters and their various uses.

He is congenial and kind, with blue eyes that sparkle when he laughs. I find myself wondering what could be possible between us. I have been lonely, I suppose.

May 25, 1831

Nathaniel and I have become lovers. We first came together late one night when another storm raged outside the cabin. After we had enjoyed a warming draft of cider, I was of no mind to send him out into the weather. It has been the coldest spring I can remember. I suppose it is only natural we craved one another's warmth and closeness.

Nathaniel has been with me every night since.

May 27, 1831

Something strange and unsettling has happened.

Last night, Nathaniel drifted to sleep beside me. He usually leaves well before dawn crosses the windowsill, but as the morning light touched his fine features, his sleeping countenance briefly flickered and changed. I sprang from the bed in horror. Where my handsome lover had been, a demonic creature had taken his place, with clawed hands and fanged teeth. And then, just as suddenly, his beauty was renewed, his dark hair falling across the pillow, his eyes opening wide.

Fear roiled through my body as Nathaniel reached for me. Horrified, my mind at war with the wanting in my body, I bade him go, pleading an excess of work. He rose, stretching luxuriantly.

I quelled my distemper and allowed him to kiss me.

Was his transformation merely a trick of the light, or something more? Even as the comforting noonday warmth floods through my windows, a dark chill settles in my marrow. I know not what it means, but I am troubled all the same.

TWELVE

DEIRDRE

1881

Deirdre closed the grimoire, her mind clouded with warring thoughts. Outside the train car, the trees rushed by in a haze, blinking gold and green.

She thought of the glinting shine in Ambrose Gentry's eyes, his gleeful, hungry grin reflected in her mirror. His words in her head, promising to pursue her like prey. Had it merely been her imagination? Was Gentry only a lustful man driven by covetousness . . . or something far worse?

Deirdre gathered her cloak around her shoulders. A chill ran through the train car. She took a drink of tea to warm herself and opened the grimoire again. The scent of dried geraniums wafted out. Each time she opened the book, the scent changed slightly. Sometimes it smelled like dirt or fresh-mown hay. Other times it smelled like ashes and fire. And the words themselves shifted and moved. Things were never in the same order. The book seemed to know her thoughts and reflect them back to her.

She'd opened the book three times since she'd left Tin Mountain. But each time, the feeling of dread grew stronger. As much as her curiosity drew her to read on, to learn more of Anneliese's story, she feared the knowledge within. Ever since her vision of Anneliese in Sutter's holler, vague imaginings had haunted her. The surge of *knowing* that had come over her that night had diminished, but she had the sense that if she chose to call up that knowing—that greater power—it might consume her.

She feared that giving herself over to this strange new knowledge would be like turning on a tap that she wouldn't be able to shut off again.

A rustle of sound caught her ears. Deirdre startled. No one else was in the compartment she was traveling in. Pa had used his standing as an engineer to secure a first-class ticket, and the only other passengers, an elderly couple who had boarded with her, had gotten off at Cape Girardeau. She slowly turned, her heartbeat thrumming in her ears.

There was no one there. Just the swaying gimbal lanterns and row upon row of scarlet banquettes.

She went back to her reading, hurriedly skimming over Anneliese's journaling and concentrating on the innocent recipes at the back of the book. As the train curved on its route eastward, the steady clatter of the tracks and the rhythm of the train soon made Deirdre drowsy, and in the plush comfort of her seat, she drifted off to sleep. Her dreams were troubled. In them, she was trapped in a never-ending forest of looming trees, pursued by an unseen creature, who snarled and snapped. She awoke sometime later, her stomach knotted with fear.

"Miss? Are you all right?"

Someone grasped her shoulder. Deirdre flinched and let out a shaky breath. It was only the railway steward. She nodded. Her head swam with the motion, and she closed her eyes to stop the spinning. A high-pitched whine started up, somewhere deep inside her ears.

"Are you sure you're well? You're a bit peaked." The young man's voice rang hollow and distant, as if he were at the end of a long tunnel. "I can escort you to a sleeping car if you'd like."

"I'm well. I'm only . . . very tired."

He smiled down at her kindly. "Long journeys are wearing. If you'd care for anything, just ring the bellpull." He motioned at the length of braided rope behind her and then pushed his cart down the aisle, teacups rattling in time with the train's jostling.

Deirdre closed her eyes and leaned against the banquette. She felt so very tired. Her nights spent caring for little Collin had finally caught up with her, it seemed. She waded off into sleep again as if it were heavy, soft fog. When she woke, a blackness had descended outside the windows, dousing whatever landscape lay beyond in night.

The same rustle of sound she'd heard earlier came from behind, as if someone were shaking the pages of a newspaper. Deirdre turned. A man sat two rows back and to the left of her, the dark crown of his head just visible. She must have slept through a stop, and he'd gotten on then. Yes, surely that was it.

As if the man felt her eyes on him, he slowly raised his head. Glinting green eyes met her own. An icy cold finger of fear laced its way through the hair at the nape of Deirdre's neck, prickling her skin. A frail whimper escaped her lips.

It was the preacher. Gentry. Somehow, someway, he'd followed her. Just as he'd promised.

THIRTEEN

GRACELYNN

1931

I wake, my neck cramping from the awkward way I'd fallen asleep, folded against Aunt Val's mattress in the loft. A trail of silver moonlight shines across the open pages of the grimoire and Anneliese's looping script. It's late or early. I can't reckon which.

There's something oddly familiar in the way Anneliese describes Nathaniel Walker's arrival—how he'd just shown up, bringing troubles and poor weather in his wake. The disturbing vision Anneliese had was also familiar—I'd felt the same fear in that revival tent when Josiah Bellflower and I locked eyes. Walker and Bellflower couldn't be the same person. It was impossible. He'd be well over a century old.

Just then, a loud crash sounds from the kitchen, like every pot and pan we own's been knocked asunder. I jump to my feet, my heart pummeling, my head clouded with images of demonic, wrathful lovers.

I climb down the ladder and creep along the hall. The kitchen door stands wide open, slammed back against the shelf above the sink. Broken crockery lies on the floor, and a trail of muddy footprints leads to the pantry.

A low groan carries from the other side of the room.

Caro comes up from behind me and takes hold of my elbow. She's shaking. "Might be a hobo," she rasps. "I'll get the shotgun."

"We ain't got no more shells, remember? Granny used 'em all the other night," I whisper back. "'Sides, I think it's Morris. Them look like his boot tracks."

A hand snakes out around the pantry door. "Gracie, it's me. Help . . ."

It's Morris, all right. Caro and I nearly knock each other over in our rush to the pantry. Morris is in a bad way. Even in the weak light, I can see that his face is bruised as dark as a storm and his nose is all off-kilter. Worse than that, though, his breathing is labored and shrill. Broken ribs, I'd wager.

"Lordy, what happened to you?"

"I got jumped. Me and Seth separated at the fork last night. They was waitin' for me in the trees."

"Who?"

"Harlan's gang, all hooded up. Three of 'em."

"Goddamn Northrups. Let's get you on your feet, so I can give you a look-over. Help me, Caro."

I wedge myself behind Morris and lift under his arms as gently as I can, using my legs and hips for leverage as Caro steadies him from the front. He whimpers like a hurt animal. We half carry him to the table and carefully ease him down.

Caro lights a lamp and I split Morris's bloodstained shirt with kitchen shears. Bruises bloom like scarlet and purple flowers over his pale skin. "Put some water on to boil, Caro. Fetch the dried tansy from the pantry, along with some willow bark and whiskey."

"Yes'm." Caro slams the kettle on the stovetop and starts stoking the flames.

I ain't never set ribs before, only watched Granny do it. I'm scared I might hurt Morris worse. I'd wake Ebba, but knowing her, she'll probably want to fetch Doc Gallagher, and the last thing we need is the whole town knowing the Northrup gang jumped my cousin.

Caro brings a shard of willow bark, some dried tansy, and the near-empty fifth of Jack Daniel's we keep hidden for times such as these. I hand Morris the bottle, and he takes a long swig. "Now, chew on that willow bark," I say. "It'll help with the pain."

A few minutes later, the kettle starts whistling. I crush the tansy between my palms, into a bowl, then pour boiling water over it. The sharp, green scent steeps out of the leaves, clouding the water yellow. After it's cooled a bit, I soak a washrag in the water, wring it out, and use it to wipe the caked blood from Morris, gently, but with purpose, so I can see where the hurt lives.

Once I've got him cleaned up, I feel along Morris's side, pressing in gingerly, watching his face. He cries out in pain, my fingers hovering over a spot just below his right armpit. Caro's scared eyes hold my own. Morris bites down on the willow bark as tears run down his cheeks. I ain't never seen my cousin cry.

"Steady, Morris," I say, trying to soothe him. "You'll be all right, hear? Hold real still." I prod again, closing my eyes to concentrate. Morris howls. "You've got two broken ribs. You're lucky, though. One's broke so bad it could've punctured your lung. It's gonna be real sore. You'll need to lay up as long as you can, but you gotta remember to breathe deep now and then, even though it'll hurt like hell. Otherwise, the pneumonia'll set in. Caro, go get a sheet from the clothesline and tear it into strips. We need to wrap him up tight, put that arm in a sling to keep them ribs in place."

"Jus' do what you need to do, Gracie," Morris gasps. "And hurry."

After we've got him all bandaged up and tucked into my and Caro's bed, I can see Ebba stirring in the yellow morning light on the porch. I go out to tell her what's happened. She sits in the rocking chair next to Granny's daybed and buries her face in her hands, muttering in Swedish. Granny sleeps on, her jaw slack, her lips dry and chapped around the edges.

"Deirdre knew this would happen," Ebba says with a sigh. "She tried to talk sense into Rebon when he first started building that still years ago."

"You know how Rebon was. Morris is a Doherty, too, Ebba. He does what he wants and damn the consequences."

"You're the same way, Gracelynn." Ebba smiles wryly. "We should go to town. Tell the sheriff."

I stiffen beside her. "We should, but Sheriff Murphy won't do anything. We ain't gonna say nothin', Ebba. You and me both know who did this, and why we best lay low."

"Northrups."

"Yup. They'll kill Morris just like they killed Rebon. And we gotta protect Seth, too. It's best for everybody involved if we let Morris heal up and just stay quiet."

Ebba clenches her fists. "Ain't right how Al Northrup runs this town. Back when I was a girl, Bill Bledsoe—"

"Was high and mighty but stayed out of hill people's business. I know."

"Trouble's all around us, Gracie," Ebba says. "Just like fifty years ago. And more trouble's on the way."

❦

The sun gives one last defiant blaze before folding into the darkness of the hillside. Abby just stands there, arms draped over the lighthouse railing, staring down at the trees. She's sullen and quiet, like the tar's been whipped out of her. The beacon whooshes overhead, the *whup-whup* of the lantern motor the only sound between us.

This is the first chance I've had to get away. Three days have passed since Morris got jumped. Hot, rainless days spent changing his bandages, watching over Granny, and building up our store of ointments and tinctures, even though the demand for our cures dwindled with Bellflower's arrival, just like I was afraid it would.

"Morris got jumped the other night," I say. "Harlan's doing, no doubt. Busted two of his ribs and knocked his nose out of joint."

"You sure it was Harlan?"

"Who else would it be, Abby? I'm real worried. Things are goin' sour in as many ways as they can. Val's taken up with that new preacher, and I ain't seen her in days. Doc Gallagher's been checking up on Granny—giving her fluids—but she's still sick and showing no signs of getting better."

"Your granny will pull through. She's too stubborn not to." Abby grins at me, but it's a nervous grin that doesn't reach her eyes. Her curls fall like a dark veil over her face. She clears her throat. "Pa's worse. He's hockin' up blood now."

"I'm sure sorry." I want to reach for her hand, but something stops me. I rake in a breath, and my stomach tumbles. Troubles everywhere. Troubles all around. And this heat, thick and heavy as a wool coat, driving all sense away and making folks mean. Fights are breaking out all over town, and Sheriff Murphy's jail's already full-up.

It's the curse. It has to be.

Earlier, after I'd fed and tucked Caro in and after Ebba fell asleep, I went up to the loft to study the grimoire. I've learned a lot already. I skipped the recipes I've learned at Granny's feet, and I'm reading Anneliese's journal entries instead. Her death seems to be at the root of the darkness that still haunts Tin Mountain. She and the townsfolk had mostly lived in accord until Nathaniel Walker showed up.

Why is it that most of a woman's troubles in life have to do with a man? I wonder about my mama a lot—just how much better her life would have been if she'd never met Shep Doherty.

I can't help but worry about Val. It seems she's the one Bellflower is after, and she's falling right into his trap, just like Anneliese did with Nathaniel. She's been taken in by his glamour. His pretty lies. A woman past her prime with fading looks makes for an easy mark, after all. She's always been vain, and a man like Bellflower could exploit that for his own gain.

Abby flicks her cigarette butt over the edge of the lighthouse balcony and fixes me with a stone-faced glare. "I seen somethin' last night, Gracie."

"What?" I whisper.

"I ain't sure what I'd call it. A haint, maybe? I'd just gotten Hortense in the barn for the night, and heard a sound like heavy footsteps, comin' from the holler. I looked down and I saw a flickering light through the trees. At first, I thought it was just a hobo camp. That's when the screaming started. Next thing I knew, somebody took off up the hill. Looked like they were lit on fire. But it weren't like no fire I'd ever seen—the flames were all blue and cold. It ran plumb up to the old Sutter cemetery, shrieking, and then just . . . disappeared. Things got real quiet after that. Even the damned cicadas quit their racket." Abby lights another cigarette, her hands shaking. "It took a long time for me to calm down. Reckon I ain't calm yet."

"Lands, Abby, that's quite a story."

"That's what Pa said, too. 'That's quite a story, there, Abigail.'" She laughs drily and kicks the toe of her boot against the metal balustrade. "You believe me, though, don't you, Gracie?"

Abby ain't one for tall tales, and after what I seen the other night between Bellflower and Val, I'd believe anything. "I sure do. Maybe it was Owen Sutter's haint. Folks say he set himself on fire after he murdered his family. I'm seeing things, too, Abby. And I'm just as scared as you are."

"Feels like the whole world is going crazy in this heat, don't it? Like hell just decided to come right up topside."

I grunt in affirmation. I used to think them old stories about curses and haints around Tin Mountain were falsehoods. Somethin' for the old men on the mercantile porch to chew on, along with their tobacco. I ain't so sure about that anymore. This mark on my back, for one thing, that still stings and burns every time I open the grimoire, reminds me of what happened to Anneliese—of what could happen to any woman who chooses to walk a different path. Tin Mountain is a boil, festering.

"You ever think about leaving Tin Mountain after your daddy's gone?"

Abby shoots me a scolding look. "Where in hell would I go?"

"I . . . I been saving up money since I was a little girl. I got almost two hundred dollars. Maybe, after Morris is healed up and Granny's better, maybe we could leave. Together. Go to California. Start somewhere fresh."

Abby smirks. "*California*, huh? Jus' what do you think's better about California than here?"

"The weather, for one thing. And there's plenty of work there. All kinds. With that damned preacher's healin' services, Granny's lost almost all her customers. If I find work out west, I can send money back home, like Seth's pa. Morris won't have to run his still no more, and Caro won't have to work in the fields. This place . . . it's never been right. There are better places, where the land ain't poisoned."

There's a long breath of silence before Abby speaks again. "Gracie . . . I need to tell you somethin' that I been meaning to tell you for a while. Pa aims to see me married, before he passes."

"What? I didn't even know you were courtin' with anybody."

"He wants me to marry Harlan. Says it will secure things for me, after he's gone. The Northrup money, you know. Harlan's been around."

She might as well have hauled off and punched me in the gut. I swallow the bitter spite in my throat like it's a shot of quinine. "Abby, you can't. Him and his gang nearly killed Morris. The Northrups killed my uncle for hiding Al's cut of the profits from that still. Everybody knows, they just keep it quiet to save their own hide. The Northrups are bad all the way through."

She turns to me, tears welling up in her eyes. "You think this is what I want? I don't feel nothing for Harlan. I just want to make Pa happy and have a little peace from my thoughts, Gracie. If I marry Harlan, maybe I'll get right in the head."

"What do you mean? There's nothin' at all wrong with your head. And what kind of thoughts are you talking about?" Suddenly, my pulse is thrumming at the soft way Abby is looking at me.

"Don't you know, Gracie?" She reaches out and takes my hand.

"What?" I ask, like an idjit. My skin is lit up with the feel of Abby's hand in mine.

"I don't want Harlan. I don't want *no* man. Because I'm in love with you."

"You . . ." My legs wobble beneath me and my heart slams into my throat.

"I know . . . I know it's wrong. I've prayed my heart out, not to be this way. But I can't help the way I am."

I could almost laugh. I let go of Abby's hand and wrap my arms around my waist to stop my trembling. "Wrong? Abby, I—"

Her lips are on mine before I can finish. I give a startled grunt of surprise. She wraps me up, pressing me against the hard stone of the lighthouse, her warmth and her curves and everything that makes her *Abby* soft against my front. And oh, God, kissing her is *good.* Better than Granny's peach cobbler and ice cream. Her lips are questioning, soft. My hands don't know where to go, I just know they belong on her, and so I pat at her awkwardly because my head is all fuzzy and I never been kissed until now. She gives a throaty laugh and pulls back to look at me, the air between us hot as stoked coals.

"I weren't expectin' that," I murmur. "But it was a good surprise, all the same."

"It's all I been thinking about," she says, her head dipping to my throat. She kisses me there, my pulse dancing under her tongue. "I been thinking about a *lot* of things I'd like to do with you, Gracie."

"So have I." Shame rears up, threatening to throttle my joy, and I push it away. This is right. It has to be.

Abby unbuttons my dress with sure fingers. My stomach somersaults. I freeze in place, panic skirting through me as an old, unwanted memory comes crawling through my mind. But this ain't that. This is Abby, and Abby's touch is what I crave more than anything. She pulls my slip down over my shoulder, then lowers her head and warms my skin with her mouth. My breath hitches as her hands rove over me. I want her. Every bit of her.

"You look like the moon," she says against my skin. "So pretty. So sweet."

I close my eyes, and open them, delirious with wanting. Then I see him. In the tree line below, watching us, his face lit up pale with unearthly light. Bellflower. He smiles mockingly, then touches his finger to the brim of his hat.

I tangle my hands in Abby's hair, fear washing over me like cold rain. "Abby. Abby—"

A ragged, wet cough rattles up from below, followed by the crunch of pea gravel. We spring apart. "Aw, shit. That's Pa," Abby rasps.

I duck around the lighthouse's curved side and hastily button up my dress. I glance to where Bellflower stood a moment before, but he's gone.

"Abigail? You still up there, girl?" Her daddy crosses the yard below us, his kerosene lantern swinging in the dimness. He peers up at the lighthouse, his face gaunt in the yellow light. He's lost so much weight he looks like a scarecrow missing half its stuffing. "Supper's gettin' cold."

"I better go." Abby reaches for my hand. "But I want you to know I love you, Gracelynn Doherty. Even if it's sinful. I can't help how I feel."

Fear and desire make a confusing tangle in my chest. I'm intoxicated with the feel of Abby's kisses, her love, but I'm also afraid. Bellflower saw us. He knows what we are, now. And if I've learned anything about preachers, demon possessed or not, they've got no use for our kind of love.

But I also know that no matter what it takes for Abby and me to be together—I'll do it. I'll protect her, no matter *who* tries to tear us apart.

FOURTEEN

DEIRDRE

1881

Deirdre woke, her head pounding in time with the sound of the train's rattle and clack. She pushed herself up onto her elbows and the pain behind her eyes throbbed in response. She was undressed, down to her shift. When had that happened?

The last thing she remembered was the sight of Gentry in the rail carriage. She blinked in the dim, coppery light. Early morning. Sunrise. How had she lost so much time?

"Ah, you're awake." The woman's voice came from the shadows. As her form unpeeled from the murk, Deirdre glimpsed a starched pinafore and cap. A nurse. "You're likely to have a mighty headache," the nurse said, placing a cool hand against Deirdre's forehead. A sharp, antiseptic smell came from her skin. "Chloral hydrate does that. It should go away within the next few hours."

"Chloral hydrate?" Deirdre had no idea what that meant.

"It's a sedative. You don't remember what happened, do you? The medication sometimes brings confusion. You were disturbed by something you thought you'd seen. The steward heard you screaming. We had to isolate you in a private carriage."

"Where is he?"

"The steward?"

Deirdre winced. "No. The man. That preacher."

The nurse placed her cool hand on Deirdre's. "There were no other passengers in your car."

"I saw him. He was real as you. I *saw* him." Deirdre vibrated with agitation.

"That's what you've been saying, over and over." The nurse pressed her lips together. "You were only hallucinating. Once you've arrived in Charleston, Dr. Phipps will give you a referral to a doctor—an alienist—"

"He was there. He was!"

"Delusions can seem very real. People with disorders of the mind often see people who are not there."

Disorder? There was nothing wrong with her mind. Nothing.

The nurse stood with a crisp rustle of sound. "I can show you the railway manifest if you don't believe me. You *were* the only passenger in first class. Now, if you don't calm yourself, I'll be forced to sedate you again for your own good, Miss Werner."

Deirdre sagged against the thin mattress. There was no use arguing. She thought of what had happened to poor Tessa Ray—her ravings and screams. If she didn't pipe down, they might put her back to sleep and escort her straight to a hospital once they got to the next stop. Best to go along. Be amenable and keep her wits. She pushed the heel of her hand against her eyes. "Could I have some water, please? My mouth feels like I swallowed cotton."

"Yes. I'll be back shortly with water and coffee. Sometimes it helps ease the pain. The porter will bring your valise so you can dress."

The nurse left the car, letting in the clatter from the vestibule. The sound set Deirdre's teeth on edge. She knew what she had seen. Gentry had followed her. Somehow, he'd disappeared. But Deirdre knew he would be back—just like he promised.

❦

Four days later, Deirdre arrived in Charleston, tired to the bone. Her mind still swam with train tables and all the transfers she'd had to make, but to her great relief, she'd seen no more sign of Gentry. She climbed down from the streetcar she'd boarded at the depot, and found herself on a wide boulevard lined with strange trees. They stood as tall as the loblolly pines back home, but instead of branches, they had feathery, fanlike tops, blown back like hair in a gale. Odd. The air was thick with moisture and smelled of salt.

The streetcar driver tipped his hat to her and handed down her carpetbag from the luggage rack. "School's just down the way, around the corner from the church, miss. You'll see it. Big double house behind an iron fence, with balconies and a cupola."

Deirdre had no idea what a *coopla* was, but she nodded her head like she understood, and handed him a quarter dollar. "Thank you."

He drove off, and she shouldered her valise. The boulevard moved like a river, flowing with carriages and streetcars and people on horseback going about their business. Deirdre hurried on her way, glancing down every alleyway and shadowed corner, expecting to see Gentry's menacing presence. Charleston was big enough that she could get lost in the crowd if she had to. Unlike Tin Mountain, she could disappear. Be someone else. The thought livened her.

Maybe Charleston wouldn't be so terrible. She need only be here until the end of summer, after all, and then she'd return to become

Robbie's bride at the harvest. She could hardly wait to write to him of this strangely beautiful city, with its rows of colorful houses.

But even in her best traveling clothes, she felt out of place. The women here wore light-colored muslin dresses to fight the heat, their heads adorned with straw hats tied under their chins with bright ribbons. Deirdre, in her dull, faded brown homespun was a sparrow moving among doves. Unremarkable. She was also miserably hot. By the time she made it to the corner and passed the towering, whitewashed church, she'd already sweated through her drawers. Her thighs chafed and stung. Her head pounded from the heat.

Up ahead, she glimpsed a large mansion through the fanlike trees, with a pretty glass tower on its roof that reminded her of the top of the Liberty Lighthouse. A knot of anxiety clenched in Deirdre's stomach as she neared the gate and saw just how fine the house was—all Roman columns and porch rails hung with ferns. She smoothed her plain skirts and went up the porch's steps. A plaque nailed to the clapboards next to the door said:

MISS MUNRO'S FINISHING SCHOOL FOR YOUNG LADIES OF CHARACTER

Deirdre looked over her shoulder once more, pulled in a shaky breath, and knocked.

Two girls answered, giggling as they jostled one another. One was fair haired, with a round face and a comely figure to match. The other was tall and slender as a coachwhip, with dark eyes and brown hair done up in long curls. The blonde swept her eyes over Deirdre and scowled. "I'm sorry, Miss Munro isn't hiring any help."

"I . . . I'm not here for a job. Miss Munro should've had a telegram from Hannah Bledsoe? I've a letter from her, too." Deirdre reached into her pocket and offered Hannah's letter of referral.

The blonde snatched it from her hand, raising her brows. "Wait here," she said.

The girls turned as one, slamming the heavy door shut behind them. Deirdre slumped, her shoulders rounding forward. She had no mind what she might do if they wouldn't let her in. What if Gentry found her, out here alone?

Run little rabbit, run.

Minutes passed, soupy hot and slow. A bead of sweat crept down Deirdre's temple, and she wiped it away.

The door swung open again. The blonde motioned her inside, her demeanor lit with frustration. The other girl had disappeared. "Come in, *Miss* Werner. I'll show you to your room. Miss Munro will call you in for a conference this afternoon."

"Oh, thank you." Deirdre bustled over the threshold, relief flooding through her. "And it's just Deirdre," she said with a smile, hoping to warm the girl's icy manner.

"Miss Munro asks that we not address one another with our Christian names, Miss Werner. But I'm Phoebe Darrow."

"Pleased to meet you."

Phoebe sighed. "Likewise."

They went through a vestibule lined with empty cloak hooks into a large, squarish foyer with hallways shooting off in three directions and a staircase at its edge. The house was fine enough on the inside to match the outside, if a bit plain, but cobwebs hung in the corners. Deirdre could hear muffled voices coming from behind the closed doors along the halls. She wondered how many students lived here, and whether she'd find friends among them.

Phoebe motioned toward the staircase. "You'll have to room on the top floor. The attic. It's the only dormitory with an open bed."

Deirdre cast a wary eye up the dizzying rectangular spiral above her. The steps seemed to go on forever. But she was a mountain girl. She could climb. And she reckoned it would be good practice for when she became Robbie's wife. There were even more steps to the top of the lighthouse.

She hefted her valise, heavy with her clothes and the added weight of Oma Anneliese's grimoire, and followed Phoebe, her dress snagging on the sharp corners of the balustrade as they went up, up, up.

By the time they reached the fourth landing, her legs had gone as soft and useless as bread left too long to rise. She stopped to reclaim her breath in the heavy, Carolina-wet air. This wasn't anything like walking up the slow and steady climb of Tin Mountain. This was terrible. She clawed at the high neck of her bodice, desperate to cool off.

Phoebe shot an impatient look over her shoulder. "You'll have to get used to going up these stairs. Scrubbing them, too. We don't have housemaids, only kitchen help."

"Didn't reckon so, given all the cobwebs."

"Miss Munro won't favor your sassy mouth." Phoebe huffed another annoyed sigh and flounced to the third door on the right. "This is it."

Deirdre trudged down the hall, her lungs still heaving, and followed Phoebe into the room. It was spare, but brightly filled with afternoon sun. The clip-clop of horses' hooves came through the window on a sea-rich breeze. Two beds stood on opposite sides of the garret; on one of them sat another girl.

She raised her neat brown head from a book. Dark-lashed eyes blinked behind wire spectacles. She was the prettiest thing Deirdre had ever seen, with a narrow, pointed chin and freckles sprayed like stars over her nose.

Suddenly self-conscious under the girl's quiet regard, Deirdre ran a hand over her sweating brow. She must look a sight.

"I've brought your new roommate." Phoebe's lip curled. "This one's from the sticks. You should hear how it talks."

It. Deirdre clenched her teeth. She had the feeling if she didn't stand up for herself from the start with Phoebe, things would only get worse. "My name's Deirdre, like I told you. And you should know, Miss Darrow, if you aim to cast aspersions, I give as good as I get."

Across the room, a tiny smile lifted the corner of the pretty girl's lips. Deirdre couldn't mark whether the smile was friendly or merely amused.

"Dinner's at seven." Phoebe crossed her arms and eyed Deirdre's rumpled clothes. "Surely, you've brought something better to wear? What you've got on now won't do."

"I'll manage." Deirdre set her valise on the bed by the window. The springs creaked in protestation. Phoebe gave a curt nod and stalked off.

Tears pricked at the corner of Deirdre's eyes. It wasn't right, coming to this big city school with these rich girls who thought themselves better than she was. *They* didn't need someone else's charity in order to be here. She should have been bolder—should have run to Robbie and eloped. He'd have protected her from Gentry.

"Phoebe will come around," the other girl said softly. "She just thinks she's in charge, being one of the oldest. And she's having trouble finding a suitor. You're very pretty, and she's jealous. That's all."

"That ain't no reason for her to be so mean. I can't help how I look."

"That *isn't* any reason for her to be so mean. You'll need to use proper grammar here. Miss Munro doesn't tolerate country talk, even if it's how you were raised. Phoebe was rude and didn't introduce us. I'm Esme Buchanan. From Missouri. You?"

"Deirdre Werner. Tin Mountain, Arkansas. Just over the border between our states."

Esme smiled and closed her book. "Well. We're compatriots, then."

"What brought you all the way here?" Deirdre started unpacking, shaking out her plain dresses. Everything was hopelessly wrinkled.

"My grandmother insisted on sending me here," Esme said, coming to her side to help. "Mostly because I was getting on too well with our gardener. I've something you can borrow. We're the same size, I think."

At first, Deirdre's pride reared up, then embarrassment. None of her dresses were good enough, then. "That would be real kind of you."

"I was new once. I remember how it feels to be so far from home." Esme went to the end of her bed and opened a leather trunk. She started pulling out beautiful dresses, perfumed with lavender and as fine as anything in Hannah Bledsoe's wardrobe.

Hannah had given her money—tucked it into her hand before Pa drove her to the station. Nearly twenty dollars. She would put some of it toward summer muslins and the new corset she'd already been needing.

"What's your favorite color?" Esme asked. "Blue? Yellow?"

Deirdre smiled. "Blue."

"I figured as much, with your eyes. I've got just the thing. And we'll need to do your hair. I plait well. Would you like braids? They'll tame your curls in this heat. It's really something, isn't it? It took me a time to get used to it. But the rain is a blessing when it comes. Cools everything down. And best of all, there's the ocean. From the top of the cupola, you can see the whole harbor. I'd never seen the ocean till I came to Charleston."

So, the *coopla* was the tower. The tension drained from Deirdre's shoulders. Maybe it wouldn't be so bad here after all, so long as Esme stayed as nice as she seemed. She never knew if kindness would last with other girls. She glanced outside the window, at the waving, strange trees. "What are them funny-looking trees called?"

Esme laughed. "Those trees are called palmettos. Or palms. You'll get used to them, too."

FIFTEEN

GRACELYNN

1931

Abigail Louisa Cash loves me. I can hardly believe it.

I gather myself in one of Granny's crocheted afghans and go out to feed the chickens, my head and my heart abuzz from the night before. A fool grin is still plastered on my face. Circe, our prize laying hen, cocks her head at me and clucks.

I reach into my pocket and spread millet on the ground. The other hens, each one of them named for a famous witch or wise woman, come chattering out of the henhouse in a line, followed by Gentry, the proud little rooster who *thinks* he runs the place. I squat and watch them peck.

Gentry. That name. It's what Granny called Josiah Bellflower, the night she shot at him.

"Mornin', Gracie." I turn to see Morris limping toward me. His face is still swollen, and his right arm'll be bound up in a sling for a while, but it's good to see him on his feet again. I only wish Granny was. She's wasting away to nothing, lying in that bed.

Morris lowers himself gingerly onto Granny's bench under the peach tree. I brush off my hands and go sit next to him.

"You're lookin' mighty thoughtful," Morris says.

"I got lots on my mind, I reckon."

"You're gonna be worn plumb through if you don't stop workin' so hard. You should give Caro more of the chores."

"She works hard enough."

Morris sighs. "Me being laid up ain't helping."

"Now, stop that. You'll be back to work soon as you're healed. You can't rush things. Your body needs to rest."

"How's Abby? Ebba said you went up to the lighthouse last night."

"Her pa's near the end."

"That's too bad."

"Yeah, it's hard. What's worse is that he wants her to marry Harlan Northrup before he passes."

Morris whistles, low. "Well, that's some horseshit."

"That's what I said, too. I don't know how I can stop it, but I aim to try."

Morris heaves a thoughtful sigh. "I don't know about that, Gracie. Keep that business between Abby's pa and Harlan. Best stay out of it."

"It's more complicated than that, Morris." The question I want to ask him is right there on my tongue, but even though I know he's the safest person in the world to ask, I still take three quick, shallow breaths before the words leave my mouth. "When did you figure out that you and Seth were more than just friends?"

"I can't think of a specific time that I knew. He was just my favorite person to be around, and I didn't feel no pull toward girls like most boys do. Then one night, we were rasslin'. We'd had some moonshine. It made me brave. I kissed him and he kissed me back. It just felt natural. Right."

"Sounds nice."

"Why are you asking me about that, Gracie?"

I toe the ground with my bare foot, making circles in the silt. Embarrassed, I look down at my hands. "Because maybe I feel the same way about Abby."

Morris smiles. "I knew it. Them's the berries, Gracie."

"She told me she loved me and we kissed last night. It was the best thing that's ever happened to me, Morris. I want her to go with me to California, once things settle."

"Listen. I'm real happy for you, but Abby ain't never gonna leave Tin Mountain. You know that. Her kin's always been here, and she's already taken over as lighthouse keeper. 'Sides, the world's not made for people like us to have a happily-ever-after like normal people." Morris shakes his head. "Much as I love Seth, someday I'll have to let him go for his good as well as my own. Two men living together? One of them colored? They'd kill us." Morris barks a humorless laugh. "Best thing to do is have your fun now. But when it's time for you all to part, and she marries Harlan or somebody else, don't you dare be mad at her."

I swallow the catch in my throat. "That don't seem fair or right at all."

"What is, Gracie? Ain't much about life that's fair when you think about it. Look at Granny, laying in there, half a heartbeat from the end. Hell, look at me." He gestures to his busted nose. "Life's just one burden after another, till we die. But it's the happy things—the good things—that make it all worthwhile. Things like kisses."

"Morris Clyde, I never knew you for a philosopher." I jostle him gently.

"I'm smarter than I look." Morris leans his head back against the peach tree's trunk and closes his eyes. "Lands, I'm sure tired."

The wind kicks up, blowing the sheets on the clothesline. For just a second, I imagine a shadowy figure beyond, where Granny's vegetable garden falls off into the woods. I strain my eyes and study the cedars, but nothing's there.

I'm nerved up by everything lately.

The sound of tires crunching on gravel carries up the mountain. Somebody's coming. Ain't nobody up on these curvy roads this early unless they're aiming to meet Jesus.

Headlights sweep across the front yard.

I stand, a twist of dread in my gut. I shake Morris, and he startles awake. "Somebody's here."

"What?"

"I think it's the law." I peer around the side of the house. The hulking outline of a car sits there, with a single domed light on its roof. "It is. We need to hide you."

"Maybe they're just here to ask about who jumped me, Gracie."

For Pete's sake. Morris Doherty might have a brain for philosophy, but when it comes to common sense, he'd drown faster than a turkey in the rain. "You think the Northrups ain't got the law in their pocket? I'd bet all the money I got that Harlan and his daddy reported your still. We gotta hide you."

Morris lumbers to his feet, all stiff and sore. He leans on me for support, and we make our way around the side of the cabin, Morris's breathing labored from the effort. When we get to the back porch, I can see Ebba stirring through the screens. "The law's here," I whisper.

"What?" Ebba blinks at us in the dim light and wipes the sleep from her eyes.

"There's a car out front. Looks like a copper. I'm gonna hide Morris under the porch. Don't answer no questions until I get in the house, hear? And don't let Caro pipe up, neither."

Ebba waves us away and pulls on her housecoat. A booming knock comes, loud enough to shake our little cabin to its foundations. My mouth goes dry.

"Get under the porch," I whisper to Morris. "All the way to the back. And don't you dare move until I come back and say it's all right." Morris stumbles to his knees and crawls under the porch, wincing as he works himself backward on his one good elbow. I peer under at him. Sure enough, he's fairly disappeared into the shadows. "Good. I'm gonna go in now."

"Be careful, Gracie."

"I will. Now shut up and keep still and pray they ain't got a dog."

I ease up onto the porch, stepping over the loose boards. I pry open the screen door, making sure it don't slam behind me. Granny's breath rasps softly from the daybed.

I creep past Caro, who's sound asleep in the main room, and stop and listen, waiting for the right moment to make my entrance so I don't get a gun pointed at my face.

"Now ma'am, we know Morris Doherty lives here." The cop has a voice like metal scraping over rusty gears.

"Yes." Ebba's nervous. "But I told you. I ain't seen him for over a week. At least I think it's been a week."

I grit my teeth. I need to get out there. "Is somebody here, Ebba?" I holler.

"Who's there?" the copper barks. "Come on out. Slow. Hands up."

I push through the curtain, my sweetest smile pasted on my face as I raise my hands and walk slowly into the kitchen. The lawman's cold eyes skim over me, his hand on the pistol at his hip. I see from his armband that he's a US marshal and not one of our local deputies. Northrup sure enough called in the cavalry. "Miss Gracelynn Doherty, sir." I offer my hand.

The marshal ignores it, his mouth set in a line under his mustache. "You Morris Doherty's sister?"

"I'm his cousin."

He reaches into his pocket and unfolds a piece of paper. "I have a warrant here for his arrest."

I wrinkle my forehead, feigning confusion. "What are the charges?"

"Operating an illegal distillery, in violation of the Volstead Act."

"Lands, this is the first I've heard about a still." I laugh and go all wide eyed. "I ain't seen Morris for over a week. Last I heard, he went to Blytheville to visit a girl he's been courtin' with." Ebba glances at me and I subtly jab her with my elbow.

"We've found the still, and I have a reliable witness's report that says he's the one who runs it, ma'am If you wouldn't mind, I'll take a look around the property. Are there any other people living here, Mrs. Doherty?"

"It's *Miss* Doherty," I say with a scowl. "I ain't married. My cousin and grandma are still sleeping, in yonder."

The marshal raises a dark brow under the brim of his hat. "The two of you stay put. Don't leave this room." He unholsters his pistol and makes a beeline for the pantry. He rattles through Granny's carefully organized apothecary supplies. I reach for Ebba's hand and squeeze it. He's looking for Morris's hooch, no doubt. Even though it's supposedly legal for folks to possess liquor, just not to make or sell it, I'm more than a little thankful Morris finished off that fifth of Jack Daniel's.

The cop moves on to the main room of the cabin, where Caro is stirring. I pray to God, or whoever else might be listening, she don't smart off. He herds her into the kitchen, and she meets my eyes, ginger hair disheveled. She starts crying. I hug her to me and shush her, best I can. The marshal's footsteps creak overhead. He's in the loft. A few minutes later, the screen door slams, and my heart takes a swan dive into my stomach.

"Where is he?" Caro asks.

"Under the back porch," I answer, my tongue thick. "I told him to keep quiet."

"What are we gonna do, Gracie?"

"You just let me do all the talkin', kid, and try to stay calm."

We sit around the table, listening. Any moment now, I'm expecting a gunshot. The seconds drip by, thick as cold bacon grease. Finally, I hear the creak of the screen door's hinge once more. A single set of footsteps echoes through the house. I let out my breath, daring to hope.

The marshal strides back into the kitchen. He shakes his head at us. "Did you say he was headed for Blytheville, Miss Doherty?"

I nod, maybe a little too quickly. "Yep, that's what he said. I don't expect he'll be back anytime soon."

"I'll take you at your word and head that way. Any idea where he might be staying?"

I muster another smile. "I wouldn't know, sir. His girl's daddy weren't too keen on them courting, so I'd imagine they're layin' pretty low."

"We've notified the local sheriff and they'll be looking for him. What's his girlfriend's name?"

"Charity McCoy," I blurt. If there's really a Charity McCoy in Blytheville, she's gonna be mighty confused when this copper comes knocking.

He hands me an official-looking card with his name and a telephone code: *United States Marshal Carl Pettigrew.* "Aiding and abetting a suspect is against the law. I expect you'll call me if he turns up."

"Oh, we will," Ebba says, fixing him with a cold stare.

"Ladies." Marshal Pettigrew lifts the brim of his hat and leaves, letting a wash of humid air in through the kitchen door. We hear the engine turning over, and then the crunch of tires as he turns down the road.

I cross my arms over my chest to still my quivering. "Once that marshal gets to Blytheville and he don't find Morris, he'll be back. I only said what I said to buy us some time."

I think about California. I think about the money that's taken me years and years to save. I think about Abby's kiss. I think about Granny and little Caro, whose mama ain't fit for shit and might be gone forever.

I think about that demon preacher and the rash burning on my back. But mostly, I think about Morris, and how if he stays in Tin Mountain, it'll mean jail or Al Northrup's hillbilly justice.

Right then and there, I know what I need to do.

✦

We sit in silence, the three of us piled in Seth's old Ford, none of us daring to say what we most want to say. Morris slumps against the window, his eyes on the dirt road as we chug our way down the mountainside. It's still dark, and if we're lucky, no one else will be out this early.

When we get to the logging depot, Seth parks the truck and cuts the engine. We sit there for a minute, the air thick with the scent of fresh-mowed timber.

Seth clears his throat. "Pa gave me all the rail connections. I wrote it all down for you." He hands Morris a folded piece of paper. "He says there's a stop just outside Billings. That's where the ranch is. You'll need to bail out before you get to each depot, so nobody sees you've stowed away. Wait till the train is going slow, though, and try to land on your good side."

Morris nods. "He knows I'm coming, then?"

"I called him last night from the post office."

I panic for a minute. "But the operators . . . you know Opal Richards just works that switchboard so she can be the first to spread gossip."

"Don't you worry, Gracie, I was careful. Pa knows. He's anxious to catch up with my *cousin* Myrtle. Opal ain't smart enough to figure the real story out."

"Lands, Seth, couldn't you have picked a better name than *Myrtle?*" Morris shakes his head.

"Ain't no time for bickering," I scold. "Come on. Let's get you on that train."

We fall out into the morning air. It's already humid as hell. Seth hauls Morris's knapsack out of the bed of the truck, packed with enough food and water to see him through the journey, along with my savings—all one hundred eighty dollars—and a hunting knife just in case somebody has a mind to rob him of it. Two trains sit on the tracks, one pointed north and the other south. The north-facing train has three boxcars, but only one of them is open. I walk toward it and hoist myself inside. It's empty apart from a pallet stacked with square bales. The scent of dried alfalfa and fescue pricks at my nose, making me sneeze.

I check behind the bales to make sure there's no one else stowing away. Even though I spent most of my time in the first- and second-class carriages as a child, I'd occasionally ridden in a boxcar to get back home. It'd only taken one encounter with a territorial hobo to show me I needed to check every inch of a car before bedding down. Being picked up and dumped out of a moving train was not a pleasant way to wake up.

After I've searched the car, I motion for Seth and Morris to come over. "This'n is empty. Hurry up, now."

Morris turns to Seth. He whispers something in his ear, and then they hug for a long time. I swallow the lump in my throat, all the while nervous as a long-tailed cat in a room full of rockers. We need to hurry. The loggers could show up for work at any time. Finally, they stop canoodling and amble toward the tracks. With the way he's leaning on Seth, I can see Morris is still hurting bad. With any luck, this train will make a long run, and he won't have to hop on another one for a while. We're doing the best we can. The rest is up to Morris and fate.

Seth hands up Morris's pack and then helps lift him onto the edge of the car. I take his good arm and try to pull him inside. "I got it, Gracie," he says, waving me away. "I need to be able to do the rest on my own."

Once he's inside and hidden behind the hay bales, it's time to say goodbye and I ain't good with sentimental bullshit. "When you get to Montana, you better write to me."

"How? They'll see my name on the envelope."

"You're Seth's cousin *Myrtle*, dummy. Remember?" Morris has never been the brightest bulb in the room, and that's part of why I'm so worried.

"You take care of Caro and Granny for me, 'cause Lord knows Mama won't." Tears glisten at the corners of his eyes. "And Gracie, if they . . . If they catch me, I'll be okay, hear?"

"Now, don't start that. They won't. Just use the sense God gave you."

He laughs. "If there really is a God, He wasn't too generous when it came to me." Morris smiles sadly. "I know this ain't easy. And I know what it cost you to do this for me. Thank you."

I try not to think about anything other than Morris getting to Montana safe, working cattle with Seth's pa. I can always make more money. But the feeling deep down in my gut, that scrapes at me like a rusted nail, tells me that after today, things are gonna get harder than they've ever been, and it's real likely this is the last time I'll ever see Morris. A tear snakes its way down my cheek, and I wipe it away, annoyed.

"Don't cry, Gracie."

But I already am, and then Morris is crying, too. There ain't enough time or enough words to get to the heart of what we need to say to each other, so I give him an awkward half hug and stand to go. I glance at the sky, starting to lighten to a grayish pink above the ridge. "I love you, Morris Clyde. You take care of yourself, hear?"

Morris chokes on his words. "I love you, too, kid."

Before it becomes too much, and I lose my resolve, I turn and hop out of the boxcar. Seth stands there, his arms crossed. "He gon' be all right?"

"Yep," I say. "He will. You will, too. You better get on home before the town wakes up, though."

Seth nods and wipes at his eyes. "I'd give you a ride, but . . ." He shrugs.

"I know." A white woman riding in his truck ain't the kind of trouble Seth needs to borrow. "I could use the walk to stretch my legs. It'll take some time to chew on things, I reckon."

"I hear that." Seth runs a hand over his hair and gets behind the wheel, his eyes wet at the rims. "Be careful, Gracie. Stick to the road. And I ain't forgot about your star map. I'll get it to you soon."

"I'll hold you to that. Tell your mama and them little sisters I said hi." I wave him off, waiting until his taillights fade to two dim red eyes in the distance. I square my shoulders and head for home, ready to face whatever comes next, even if thinking about it scares me near out of my skin.

SIXTEEN

DEIRDRE

1881

Deirdre raised a tentative hand and knocked on Miss Munro's office door. She'd done her best to make herself presentable—changed into her least wrinkled shirtwaist and her best walking skirt, though it had already seen far too many seasons.

A moment later, the headmistress answered. The only resemblance Miss Munro had to Hannah Bledsoe was the color of her hair, although her fallen-leaf auburn was streaked with wide bands of silver. She motioned Deirdre through and bade her sit before a wide desk bedecked with one of the new typewriters Deirdre had only ever seen in a catalog. She leaned forward to study the monstrous thing. Her fingers ached to touch it—to test out its keys.

Miss Munro cleared her throat. "Typewriting is taught on Wednesdays, Miss Werner."

Deirdre sat up straight in the ladder-back chair and clasped her hands on the desk to still their shaking. The headmistress swept her skirts aside and sat across the desk from Deirdre, blinking at her over half-moon spectacles. "Do you know your letters?"

"Yes'm. I read the Bible every day, and I can even multiply and long-divide."

Miss Munro pursed her lips. "Excellent. Some country people never learn how to read, so I must ask, you see. As a finishing school, we do not engage in remedial education. We read the poets and great works of literature here. A well-bred woman must be well read, I always say."

Deirdre ducked her chin, not sure how she should respond.

"Miss Darrow showed you to your room, I take it? And you found Miss Buchanan welcoming?"

"Oh, yes." Deirdre beamed at the mention of Esme.

"Very good." Miss Munro extended a piece of paper. "This is the daily schedule for girls in your level—the senior cohort. We begin our mornings at seven o'clock, with a light breakfast in the main hall. After that, we do chores. Your level oversees cleaning and polishing the stairwell treads, risers, and banisters. Afternoons are for studies. You'll see the classes listed. Miss Nancy Caruthers is captain of your cohort. I've arranged for her to sit next to you at dinner this evening."

At the mention of dinner, Deirdre's stomach growled. She took the schedule from the headmistress. As she examined the neatly typed list, Deirdre's eyes swam. There were so many items on the page the letters moved over the paper like fleas on a white cat.

Miss Munro rose, the soft fabric of her day dress whispering against the edge of the desk. "Dinner is at eight o'clock every evening. You'll hear the dressing gong ring at seven. You may retire to your room until then, and rest, as you've no doubt had a taxing journey." She motioned Deirdre into the hall, where she fixed her with an unflinching gaze. "My niece has a caring, congenial nature. She's explained your situation to me, Miss Werner, and I'm very sorry for your troubles, but I must warn you that we hold our girls to the highest standards. I've devoted my life's work to turning out young women of character. The schedule is rigorous and there will be no tolerance for rule breakers. Your being here is a charity. Do you understand?"

Deirdre had never felt the weight of her own poverty more. "Yes'm. I understand."

"Yes, *ma'am*. We speak proper English here."

Deirdre bobbed her knees awkwardly. "Yes, *ma'am*."

"Your curtsy needs improving." Miss Munro looked down her long nose and sniffed. "Cotillion is on Wednesday evenings, before dinner. We'll have your country chaff worn free soon enough."

⋄

Deirdre batted the stodgy wet air with the lace fan Esme had lent her. The sultry heat had persisted into the evening. At least her neck was blessedly cool, as Esme had braided her hair into a high crown and coaxed her fringe into neat curls across her forehead.

Though she looked the part of a fine-bred town girl, Deirdre's first formal supper had been a failure. She'd nearly toppled her chair trying to seat herself at the long, silver-laden table. If it weren't for Esme adjusting the cumbersome, bustled skirt and helping Deirdre lower herself, she'd have ended up on the floor.

And there were too many forks. Deirdre hadn't a mind as to why one person needed so many to eat a single meal. Everything at Miss Munro's school seemed too *much*. From the number of courses that stuffed her belly as tight as one of the Rays' gilt hogs, to the layers of petticoats she wore beneath her borrowed gown.

As they made their way out to the veranda for after-dinner cordials, the sound of high-pitched laughter mocked Deirdre. She turned to see Phoebe and her dark-haired companion staring at her from the doorway, whispering behind their fans.

"Ignore them," Esme said, weaving her arm through Deirdre's. "We'll go sit on the side porch, where it's quiet."

Esme led Deirdre to a palm-shrouded corner where a wicker swing hung from the porch's ceiling, overlooking the boulevard. Deirdre moved aside her skirts, and sat on the swing next to Esme, this time with a bit more grace than before.

"See. You're doing well," Esme said, laying her hand on Deirdre's. Her hazel eyes glimmered in the glow from the gas lamps along the street. "Tomorrow may be difficult. It will be your first full day, and you'll likely be tired. Did Miss Munro give you the schedule?"

"Yes."

"Well, so you'll have an idea of things. We may be separated for the better part of the day, but I'll do my best to watch after you."

"You've been so kind to me."

"I like you," Esme said, opening her fan. "It's good to see an earnest face. Many of the girls put on airs—Phoebe, Nancy, Constance—who is named well, because she's Phoebe's constant shadow." Esme rolled her eyes. "They certainly didn't make things easy for me when I was new. I hated Charleston at first. And I missed Sam dreadfully. I cried for an entire week."

"Your gardener?"

"Yes." Esme batted her fan more briskly. "Sam's married now. To a blacksmith."

Deirdre paused for a beat. "I didn't know women could be blacksmiths."

"I've never met a woman blacksmith in my life, though I suppose they might exist." Esme laughed and closed her fan. "But women can certainly be gardeners."

Oh. *Oh.*

Deirdre blushed and looked away. She'd heard of such things, of course, but didn't quite know what to say. "I'm sorry, I . . ."

"Don't worry. You can't make me feel more ashamed of Samantha than my own family has made me. I'm recovered. We get on with things and do what we must as women. Have you got anyone back home?"

Deirdre smiled. "I do. His name's Robbie. Robert Cash."

"That's a fine name."

"I think so, too. I need to write him—let him know I've arrived."

"Oh, that's perfect. We can go together to post our letters on Friday—that's when we're allowed our afternoon outing. I still write to Sam. She's with child and terribly lonely in her marriage, although the thought of having children underfoot gives her some solace for the future. Tell me about your Robbie. Is he fair? Dark?"

"Dark, with curly hair. Gray eyes like a storm."

"He sounds handsome." Esme glanced at Deirdre's hand. "Has he proposed?"

"Not formally. He still needs to ask my pa. He's promised me, though, and Pa has no objections."

"Promises are a fine thing. Still, you should enjoy the dances. Miss Munro puts on three balls a year, and the next is coming up in August. It's the biggest. Many of the girls meet their beaus that way."

The thought of entertaining another man's interest made Deirdre's heart clench. She couldn't—wouldn't—betray Robbie like that, but she might enjoy the dancing. She had a feeling it would be required of her under Miss Munro's charge, and she'd always looked forward to the barn dances back home.

A flicker of movement turned Deirdre's head. A figure stepped from the shadows pooling beneath the houses across the boulevard. It was a man, dressed in black evening clothes. He moved oddly, strolling silently across the cobblestones as if he were wading through a heavy current. He paused beneath one of the gas lamps, his face hidden by his hat. A shudder of fear crawled up Deirdre's arms and across her shoulders, until it settled beneath her collarbone and set the skin there to tingling. It was *him*. She was sure of it. A whimper escaped her lips, and she clutched Esme's sleeve.

"What? What's wrong, Deirdre?"

As if he'd heard them, the man lifted his head. Two flashes of silver shone beneath the brim of his hat.

"Tell me you see him, Esme. You must see him. Don't you?"

"Who?" Esme asked, squinting and sitting up.

Deirdre squeezed her eyes shut and then opened them again. He was still there, leaning against the lamppost, one long leg cocked at an angle. Deirdre pointed, her finger trembling. "There. There's a man with a top hat, beneath the lamp."

"Don't point. It's rude." Esme gently took Deirdre's hand and lowered it. "And besides, there's no one there at all. It's only a shadow."

Gentry was most certainly still there. He was *real*, though his form cast no shadow on the ground. "He's there." Her voice keened high, growing frantic. "He followed me all the way from Arkansas."

Esme stood abruptly and moved in front of her, blocking Deirdre's view. "I do believe the drink has gotten to you. You've likely never had Madeira before, have you? Or perhaps you're taking ill." Esme put her hand to Deirdre's forehead and frowned. "No fever. You haven't had any laudanum?"

"No," Deirdre said, standing on shaky legs. "No laudanum." She peered over Esme's shoulder. Gentry was still there. Waiting, like a cat in the shadows. She willed herself to be calm. If no one else could see him, she'd need to learn to manage her reactions. She'd need to master her fear, or she'd end up in an asylum. "I think I'm only overtired."

"Are you sure you're all right? You're pale as a sheet. Perhaps we should get you to bed."

"Mmm." Deirdre nodded quickly, her pulse still thrumming. "Yes. Bed sounds good. Will you help me take down my hair?"

"Of course." Esme smiled, but Deirdre noted a wariness in her manner that hadn't been there before.

As they walked past the other girls, languidly sitting in the rattan chairs that lined the porch, humming with talk of bouquets and summer teas, Deirdre felt Gentry's eyes burning into her back. Pa had been wrong to send her away. Leaving Tin Mountain hadn't solved one thing. Gentry had followed her, and now, she had no one at all to protect her.

She had a mind that devil would follow her wherever she might go.

Once in their room, Esme lit an oil lamp and helped Deirdre undress down to her shift, then untangled her braids while she sat at the small vanity, rubbing her scalp with nimble fingers to ease the ache of her heavy hair. Then she took up a silver brush, and raked it through gently, until Deirdre's hair made a wild, crimped halo around her face.

"There," Esme murmured, her hands resting on Deirdre's shoulders. "You look like Circe." Their eyes met in the warped glass. Esme's glittered with life, her pupils wide and sparkling.

"Who?"

"The beautiful witch from the *Odyssey*, who seduced Odysseus and turned his men to pigs. You'll read it in classical literature. It's an epic poem. Quite exciting."

A draft came from the window, surprisingly chill. Deirdre shivered. She wondered if Gentry was still out there. Wondered if he could scale the ivy-covered wall. Wondered if she might find him leering over her bed in the night with his eyes well-deep and full of dark promises.

"Might we close the window?" Deirdre asked softly. "I've taken a chill."

"If you'd like."

Deirdre settled on her lumpy mattress and pulled the covers to her chin. Esme turned down the light, and soon the creak of the other bed came from her side of the room. Within moments, Esme fell asleep. Deirdre listened enviously to the steady rasp of her breathing. She had the urge to cross the room and curl next to her new friend so she might enjoy the comfort of her closeness, but she resisted.

Instead, Deirdre forced her eyes to stay open, though tiredness weighed down her limbs, leaden and heavy as bricks. The palmettos cast strange patterns on the plaster walls—their fronds like sinister fingers, reaching to grasp at Esme's sleeping form. She listened to the great house settle and tracked the waning and waxing light until morning came. Finally, just as sleep began to take her into its arms, the gong downstairs rang seven times, summoning thirty girls from their beds.

SEVENTEEN

GRACELYNN

1931

As I walk home from the depot, I notice something about the hills. They're quiet, watchful, with nothing stirring but the sound of the wind through the cedars. I usually find that kind of quiet peaceful. But this morning, something feels off.

For one thing, it shouldn't be this hot this early. I take off my cardigan and use the sleeve to mop at the sweat dripping from my temples. The sun is crawling above the tree line now, burning the sky a sickly orange. I head for the shady shelter of the woods. A few minutes later, the train's whistle sends up a lonesome call. Morris will be on his way soon.

I try to put my worries about Morris aside and set my mind to all the things I need to do when I get home. Caro's work trousers need mending, and then I'll make up some bland hardtack to stock the cupboards, just in case winter comes in as hard as Granny said it would.

I'm halfway across the Ballard Creek bridge when I hear the singing. It's high and clear. A child's voice. I stop and listen. It's pretty. An old folk song about fairies in the firelight. Curious, I follow the sound through the trees, the sun slanting in low beams through the branches like light streaming through the windows of a church.

I get worried, thinking somebody's young 'un might've wandered off and got lost. It wouldn't be the first time that had happened in Sutter's holler. I pick up my pace, following the sound toward the bluff, craning my head to see over the edge of the holler.

"Hello?" I cup my hands around my mouth and call out. "Are you lost?"

All of a sudden, the song stops, like somebody's turned the dial on a radio. By now, the birds should be awake, but all's quiet apart from the spring's distant trickle.

I ignore the electric feeling in my skin and pick my way down into the holler. The locust tree at its center looms overhead, with twisted, thorny branches thick as a man's waist. Across the way, the ruined log house that once belonged to Granny's kin sits low in the holler. There's a crumbling chimney at each end, the stone streaked with mud dauber nests. The swaybacked roof stretches between them, with the barest hint of the old log walls and foundation visible through the brambles of poison oak and pigweed. I cross the clearing and carefully climb the rotted steps. "Hello?" I call through the door. "Anyone in here? I heard your song. It was real pretty."

I don't get an answer, so I step under the bowed lintel. Inside, the air is rich and loamy, damp with rot. I blink as my eyes adjust to the light. It's built almost the same as our cabin up the mountain, but bigger. An altar of sorts stands in the corner, next to the hearth, branches stacked to form a bower. Animal bones and feathers adorn it, and a slab of rock sits at its center. There's a dark stain on the rock's surface.

It looks like blood. A low creaking sounds from overhead. I look up. Totems like the ones we wove to ward off Bellflower hang from what's left of the ceiling.

Suddenly, the dense heat flies away, replaced by the icy cold of a chilly January day.

"You finally came."

I startle at the sound of a woman's voice behind me, my skin prickling. I slowly turn.

At first, I think I'm seeing my reflection. Only there's no mirror. I shake my head, disoriented. The woman looks a little like Granny, gone back in time. She's wearing an old-fashioned nightgown, her dark-red hair loose in a frizzy halo around her face. This feels like one of my dreams, but I know I'm awake, because I feel a slow trickle of sweat running down my spine.

"Do you know who I am?" Her voice is soft and childlike, but her blue eyes carve into me with an ancient *knowing*, sharp as two pieces of cut glass. She takes two steps toward me, holding out her hand. "Do you know who I am?" she asks again, and this time her voice echoes all through me.

My heart thrashes like a trapped animal, because I do *know* who she is. I want to run. Everything in me screams to go. But my feet are rooted to the spot. She closes the distance between us, bringing the scent of charred embers with her. She leans forward and her lips meet mine. This ain't a kiss like Abby's, all flower-soft and testing. Her mouth is cold and hot at the same time, like an icy, burning brand.

A rush of memories flows through me with her breath. Only the memories aren't mine, they're hers. A log cabin, spilling chimney smoke into the winter air. Lovers in a tangled bed. A line of torches, moving down a hillside. A little boy crying for his mother. A crowd of men, jeering for the woman's death. Then nothing but fire, fear, pain. So much pain—hotter and keener than in any of my dreams.

Anger comes next, searing my veins with a white-hot power that burns fiercer than the fire that killed her and sets my heart to a purpose. Vengeance. Redemption. Justice.

I open my eyes.

Anneliese. My name is Anneliese.

Her voice is a frail, fey whisper in the loamy air of the cabin, but she ain't there anymore.

She's all through me.

I go outside, my legs wobbly, the taste of ash thick on my tongue. There's a new magic to the dappled light shining through the cedars. The cicadas drone loudly around me. I touch the trunk of the locust tree and feel its old pain. It was put to a purpose it never wanted and cursed because of it. Anneliese was a part of the land and it loved her— as much as it loves every bramble of blackberry and wild running thing that refuses to be tethered.

That land is a part of me. Part of *us*.

And it wants a reckoning for the wrong that was done on it.

EIGHTEEN

DEIRDRE

1881

Summer rolled on for Deirdre in a haze of longing for home, though home didn't seem like an auspicious place. She'd written Robbie three letters but had yet to receive a reply. Pa had written twice. In his letters he'd been spare with his words except to say the constant rains had rotted every crop the Rays and Nilssons grew. Children fell ill with typhus, and some had died. Reverend Stack was stricken down during a church service and passed two days later. *Bad heart,* the doctor had said. Deirdre had no quarrel with that. It was long past time for Old Stack to stand in judgement before his maker.

According to Pa, Ambrose Gentry had moved his ragtag brush-arbor congregation to Reverend Stack's Lutheran church that next Sunday.

Somehow, he was able to be in two places at once.

He was still stalking her. Taunting her. Deirdre had learned not to react to her visions of him, at least in a way that others might see. Still, her skin nearly crackled when she sensed his presence. She'd gotten brave and tried touching him once—to see if he was corporeal. He'd laughed when her hand glided through him, leaving an oily sensation on her fingertips. He usually appeared to her at night, hidden in the shadows, the silvery glint of his eyes the only thing visible. But right now, in broad daylight, he sat on the corner of Esme's bed, watching Deirdre while Esme snored on, none the wiser.

Deirdre glared at him and shut the grimoire, the skin on her neck prickling. "Why won't you leave me be?" she hissed.

Gentry smiled his mocking smile. "Now, where would be the fun in that?"

"What do you want?"

"I think you know, little rabbit. Tell me you don't dream of me. Tell me you don't want the same thing."

Deirdre blushed. "I don't."

Gentry stood and walked toward her soundlessly. As he approached, the shadows around him blurred and shifted. He reached, gently cupping her jaw with his hand. His touch sent discordant tendrils of horror and shameful lust through her all at once.

"Our kind have always belonged together, Deirdre."

"What are you?" she whispered, flinching away.

Everything and nothing. What you desire and what you hate.

His voice swirled like smoke in her head. Deirdre scrambled backward on the bed, the grimoire clutched to her chest. She pinched her eyes shut. "Go away. Go away. Land sakes, leave me be."

His laughter echoed in her ears, but when she opened her eyes, he was gone.

Esme blinked awake, as if she'd heard Gentry's wicked laugh. She stretched slowly, regarding Deirdre. "What's the matter? You're all pale."

"I'm not feeling well." It wasn't a lie. Her stomach always went bilious when Gentry's specter was nearby.

Esme uncurled from the bed, slowly, like a cat. She was dressed only in her corset and drawers. Deirdre couldn't help but admire the swell of Esme's breasts as she raised her arms in a graceful stretch. Esme was lovely, like a rose in an oil painting, rendered in soft shades of pink and white. Deirdre envied her, but not maliciously. It was more like a covetousness that bordered on infatuation.

"Hadn't we better dress for dinner?" Deirdre asked, sliding the grimoire under her pillow.

"I suppose it's nearly time," Esme said, yawning. "These afternoon naps are never quite long enough, are they?"

As if on cue, the dressing gong rang down the hall.

Deirdre shrugged off her day dress and petticoats, then unhooked her new corset and let it fall to the floor. Esme padded across the room, watching her through heavy-lidded eyes as Deirdre slid her shift up and over her shoulders and then replaced it with a freshly laundered one made of fine, sheer voile.

"I've been wondering something. Is that a birthmark? On your back?"

Deirdre's cheeks warmed. She hastily pulled the shift to cover the mark. "No. It's a scar. It came on after a rash this spring."

"Well. It's beautiful." Esme smiled. "Let me help you re-lace your corset."

"All right."

Esme picked up the corset, and wrapped it around Deirdre, bringing it up snug beneath her breasts and pulling the laces tight. "That book—the one you were just reading. Old, isn't it? If it's what I'm thinking it is, my mother had a book like that. My grandmother passed it down to her. Mama studied it, just like you, until Daddy forbade it. Said it was evil and took it away."

Deirdre brightened. "Really?"

"Yes. It's a common enough thing among women, I think. Hers had recipes and charms. What does yours have in it?"

Deirdre remembered Pa's admonition to never show the book to anyone outside their family, though she longed to share everything with Esme. "Only recipes."

"Don't worry, I won't tell anyone if it's more than a cookbook." Esme smiled teasingly at Deirdre and bit her lip. "Are there any love spells?"

Deirdre grinned. "A few."

"How delightful. Perhaps we should try them out." Esme hummed beneath her breath, resting her hands briefly on Deirdre's hips after she'd tied off the corset laces. "All done. I think you should wear your yellow batiste tonight. It's lovely on you."

As Deirdre finished her ablutions, the temptation to share the grimoire with Esme grew stronger. After all, Esme had shown nothing but kindness to Deirdre, and had shared so many of her own secrets—even Sam's love letters and poetry. Some of Sam's poems were scandalously funny and described salacious, erotic things.

Surely it would do no harm to share the innocent parts of the grimoire with Esme.

That night, after dinner, when the house went quiet, Deirdre slid the grimoire from beneath her pillow. Esme was resting against her headboard, feet propped casually on the mattress, crafting a letter on her lap desk, likely to Sam.

Deirdre thought of the unanswered letters she'd sent to Robbie and vowed to send no more until she received a reply. She had the feeling he was cross at her for leaving, even though she'd done her best to explain why she had to go without saying goodbye.

She crossed the room barefoot, the grimoire in hand. Esme looked up from her writing, her eyes sparkling with candlelight behind her glasses. "Well, hello."

"I can show it to you, if you'd like. My book."

"Oh, I would most certainly like," Esme answered eagerly. She folded the unfinished letter, then set the lap desk aside and patted the mattress. "Come sit."

Deirdre tucked her nightdress beneath her and sank down next to Esme. Being this close to the other girl, with the weight of the grimoire in her hands, made her pulse race a bit faster. She cast a wary glance across the room, where the shadows leapt long. No Gentry, thank heavens.

Esme scooted closer, until their thighs touched, and her warmth bled through Deirdre's cotton nightdress. She pulled in a quick breath, opened the grimoire, and laid it across both their laps. There was no defiant clap of thunder, no unearthly show of supernatural displeasure. Only Esme's soft gasp as she gently turned the fragile pages.

"Why, Deirdre, this is just marvelous! Is this German?"

"Yes. That passage is a recipe for a tea to soothe menstrual cramps."

"How useful!" Esme turned the pages, pausing now and then to exclaim over Anneliese's artistry. When she came to the drawing of the blazing tree, her eyes widened. "It's just like the mark on your back."

"I suppose so. My pa says my Oma had the same mark."

"Fascinating." Esme turned the page. "Oh, look." Her fingertip hovered over a drawing of a young woman gazing into a mirror, a lit candle in her hand. "That's called mirror scrying. Some use it to see the image of their true love on the winter solstice. I did it once, right here in this room. It works."

Deirdre smiled. "I'd imagine you saw Samantha."

Esme dipped her head, suddenly demure. "No, I didn't see Sam. I was disappointed at the time. Thought it false. I suppose one can't know whether or not such portents are true until they've played out and come to pass."

Deirdre's curiosity was piqued. "Tell me who you saw. What did they look like?"

After a moment or two of silence Esme raised her head. Her eyes were soft, limpid, flashing with sparks of golden light. "You wouldn't believe me if I told you."

"Oh, now you're just being difficult. I've shared my book with you, so you must tell me a secret. Tit for tat. Was it a man, or another girl?"

"Fine then. I'll tell you." Esme's voice had taken on an uncharacteristic tremble. "A girl. A woman, really. Dark hair. Blue eyes. Skin as fair as a lily petal."

The air in the room suddenly became heavier. "I . . ." Deirdre looked away from Esme, searching for the right words to say.

Surely Esme didn't mean *her*. But what if she did?

"Deirdre?" Esme's voice pulled her from her thoughts. Her eyes searched Deirdre's face. "It's silly, but . . . I believe that woman I saw in the mirror was you. On the day you arrived, I felt a pull. A strong one. I thought it a passing fancy. It wasn't." Esme's words tumbled out in a rush. "Please don't be angry with me."

Deirdre leaned back against the headboard in shock. She had certainly felt a pull of her own upon meeting Esme, though she hadn't known how to name the feeling, exactly. Time had only deepened her infatuation. She never had such stirrings for Ingrid. Never wondered what it might be like to kiss Ing's mouth, never watched her undress the way she watched Esme, though they'd undressed in one another's presence many times, and had even bathed in the creek together.

No, what she felt for Esme was more than friendship, but dare she be so bold as to confess it?

"Sometimes . . . I think I might have feelings for you, too, Esme." The words left her mouth before she could stop them.

A whoosh of breath fluttered beside her. Esme laughed. "Really?"

Deirdre closed the grimoire, put it aside, and turned to Esme. The thrill of something dangerously new flittered through Deirdre. She gazed at the pillowy softness of Esme's lower lip and had the urge to take it between her teeth but bit her own lip instead.

Esme lacked the same self-denial. When she reached for Deirdre, all her doubts ended with a whimper and a sigh. They tumbled together onto the mattress, Deirdre's pulse quickening as Esme's hands roved over her. Their lips met, and Deirdre welcomed Esme's kiss, sweet and teasing at first, then more urgent. A fierce hunger, a need to feel the press of Esme's bare flesh against her own, made her fumble with the ribbon on Esme's nightdress, finally succeeding in freeing the knot. She pulled the thin fabric down to kiss the freckled, soft skin on Esme's shoulder, in the same way Robbie used to kiss her own.

Robbie.

It was as if a bucket of cold water had washed over her.

Deirdre pushed away from Esme, her face on fire. "I . . . I can't do this."

"If you don't . . . if you don't feel the same, after all, I'm content with things as they were."

"No, no. It's not that." Not when her desire burned like fever beneath her skin. "It's Robbie. Do you think this is a betrayal?"

Esme sighed and sat up. "I suppose it is."

Deirdre lay there, staring at the ceiling. "Do you think it would hurt him? If he knew?"

"How would he ever know?" Esme laughed. "I'll have to marry, too, someday. Otherwise, I'll never receive my inheritance. I'll be betraying my future husband every time I lay with him, because I'll be thinking of you in order to endure it."

"I don't want to think of that—you with someone you don't love." Deirdre reached out, traced the arc of Esme's spine with her fingertip. "I don't believe these feelings will go away. Do you?"

"No. Not for me." Esme looked over her shoulder. Raised an eyebrow. "He'll never guess unless you tell him."

"Then show me."

Esme leaned down, gave her a testing kiss. "Are you sure?"

"Yes," Deirdre said, reaching for her. "I'm sure."

Falling. Soaring and falling and rising again. That's what it was like. Flying. Deirdre lay back on the mattress, wrung out with pleasure. Their nightclothes lay in a heap on the floor next to Esme's bed as dawn curled pink and gold through the windows. The light touched Deirdre in all her soft places, painting her in blushing shades that Esme traced with her fingers.

Deirdre had quivered, and arched, then begged. She'd fallen apart beneath Esme's sure touch and finally learned what all the fuss was about. *A paroxysm.* That's what Esme had called it, after Deirdre had cried out and Esme had clapped her hand over her mouth to keep her from waking the other girls.

"I never . . . with Robbie . . . ," she panted.

"I'm not surprised," Esme purred, pleased with herself, her hand making lazy circles on Deirdre's belly. "Men only care about themselves. Most of them, anyway. Sam's husband is the same. They'll never know a woman's body like another woman does."

Then Esme had done it to her again, as if to prove things. This time with her mouth.

Now, it was Esme's turn. Deirdre landed teasing kisses along the curve of Esme's hip, watching the steady rise and fall of her breasts as she grew bolder and moved Esme's legs apart to taste her. "Yes, darling . . . yes. There. That's it."

A few moments later, Esme turned her face into the pillow and let out a muffled moan, her thighs clamping tight around Deirdre's head.

Deirdre smiled. Giving pleasure was as much a reward as receiving it.

Downstairs, the gong rang. They lay together for a few more moments, tangled in the sheets, then rose and bathed themselves at the washstand. As she dressed for the day, the world seemed brighter to Deirdre. She glanced in the glass—noted the roses blooming in her cheeks. The fool smile etched on her face. How marvelous it was, to not have to worry about vinegar rinses, or bitter teas and babies, or anything but soothing this ache of fierce wanting with delicious, easy bliss.

It was an awakening. A revelation.

Esme had told her to think about Robbie if she felt guilty, but she hadn't thought about him once. Instead, she'd imagined she saw darker eyes, watching from the shadowed corner of the room. Jealous eyes that witnessed and waited, like a snake coiled to strike.

NINETEEN

GRACELYNN

1931

Town feels different today. The people look strange. They shimmer around the edges, with colors haloing their bodies. Some glow red, others green or blue—like them fancy pictures of saints the Catholics are always handing out. Strangest of all, I can hear their thoughts as I brush past them . . . only they're garbled, and cut in and out, like a staticky radio.

That hog'll be . . . for butcherin' come fall.

If . . . don't . . . drinking all our milk, the . . . are gonna starve.

Sure wish it would rain . . .

This new power running through me is unsettling. I think of my encounter with Anneliese's spirit and wonder if every day of life had been like this for her and will be for me, now that she's touched me. Part of me hopes my heightened senses will be like a surge of electricity during a storm—something that will wear off with time and lessen, but I also wonder what *else* I might be able to do.

I lean against the corner post of the mercantile to catch my breath. The old men on the porch have their instruments out today. They're taking turns pickin' and grinnin'—a congenial war of sorts between their idle talk of the weather, the raucous chorus of mandolins, banjos, and fiddles sharper in my ears than it ever has been before. A thread of perspiration winds down my neck like a serpent. It's infernally hot, now that the sun has climbed higher than Old Liberty. Part of me wants to run up the mountain to Abby and forget my troubles. I could lose every thought to the feel of her lips on mine. But getting lost in her kisses won't help matters. Won't take away this cursed drought or heal Granny.

I need to find that preacher.

I reach inside my dress pocket and rub two coins together. Enough to buy a Coca-Cola to slake the dryness in my throat. I push open the door to the mercantile and blink as my eyes adjust from the bright burn of outdoors.

Penny, the shopkeep's teenage daughter, lounges against the counter, all daydreamy and doe eyed. She sees me and glares. Penny and her kin, like most of the rest of Tin Mountain, only speak to me and Granny when they have to, but they're always happy to take our money, just the same.

"Afternoon, Penny. I was wonderin' if you might have a cold Coca-Cola in the back?" I pull a nickel from my pocket.

"Yep. We just got a truck yesterday."

"I'll take one."

"Yep," she says again, wiping a strand of sweat-soaked hair from her forehead and sighing.

"Say, you happen to see that new preacher lately? Bellflower? I need to talk to him about something."

Penny frowns. "I dunno. Saw him going toward the creek this morning." She takes the money from me, and her fingers brush mine.

A pinging shock buzzes through me as her thoughts land inside my head. *What's she want with Reverend Bellflower? She ain't pretty enough to turn his head.*

I roll my eyes. "I ain't interested in him that way, Penny."

The words leave my mouth before I think. Penny's wide-set brown eyes go a little wider. If I can hear someone's thoughts whenever I touch them, I'm gonna need to be more careful about what I say in front of people. She moves to the back of the mercantile and tosses a wary glance over her shoulder, like she's afraid I'll walk off with half the store while she's in the other room. When she comes back, she uncaps the bottle and hands it to me. Our fingers brush again. *Whole family's nothin' but a bunch of inbred corncob hillbillies.*

I smile and choke back a laugh. If she knew what *I* knew about her family tree, she wouldn't be so proud. Midwives hold more family secrets than a priest at confession. "Was Bellflower with anyone when you saw him?"

"He was with your aunt Valerie."

"I think they're courtin'. Seems to be pretty serious." I take a swig of my cola, enjoying the way it burns a sweet path over my tongue. It's a rare treat, one I'd normally feel guilty about indulging, but seeing as I just gave Morris all my savings, I don't feel too bad.

"Ain't Val a little old for him?"

I smirk. "I do believe he's much older than he looks."

Penny huffs and crosses her arms. "You need any other groceries? You were just here the other day." That's her not-so-subtle hint for me to get on down the road.

"No, I sure don't. But thank you anyway." I raise my bottle and down the rest of the soda, slamming the empty bottle on the counter. "Mighty obliged."

I step back onto the porch, ignoring the dry-leaf rasp of the old codgers in their rocking chairs, and barrel right into Harlan Northrup. Goddammit. The last person I want to tangle with today.

"Whoa there, Gracie. What's your rush?" He grins at me with his crooked yellow teeth, steadying me with a hand on my arm. His thoughts tunnel through my brain, unbidden. *Look at the sweat runnin' between them little titties. Bet they're pink as a pig's nose.*

I gotta figure out a way to control this mind-reading thing. Find a way to turn it off. There're some folks' thoughts I *never* want to hear, and Harlan Northrup is one of them. "What do you want now, Harlan?"

"I was just wonderin' about your cousin. Heard he got into a fight the other week."

I feel the color drain from my face. He's taunting me. I think over my words, knowing whatever I say next could make the difference for Morris. I decide to go along with what I told the marshal. "I ain't seen him. Last I heard he was headed to Blytheville. He's seein' a girl there."

Harlan smirks. "A girl, huh?" His fingers squeeze my arm. *She thinks I don't know Morris Doherty's queer as a two-dollar bill?*

Bile crawls up my throat. Just then, I wonder if Morris got beat up because he didn't give the Northrups their full cut of money from the still—or because he likes boys. One is just as likely as the other.

"You and me both know he ain't in Blytheville." Harlan grabs me hard by the elbow and marches me under the mercantile's eaves. He boxes me in, hands on either side of the wall behind my shoulders. The cedar shingles dig into my back. My eyes frantically scan for help, but everyone has disappeared. I could scream, but it's likely no one would come. Northrups get to do whatever they want in this town.

"You sure are pretty, Gracie," Harlan hisses, his oily dishwater hair swinging forward as he leers over me. "But you're stupid. I saw you put Morris on the train this morning. Can't mistake the sound of Seth's old truck. I was at the Bakers' house. Heard it go past. Followed you."

Oh, shit.

Harlan revels in the panic on my face. He grins and licks his dry, chapped lips. "I think I can keep quiet about Morris, though. For a price." His hand snakes down and runs up my skirt, grabbing at the flesh above my knee and pinching. *Bet she's such a cocktease 'cause she's still a virgin.*

I shut my eyes, willing myself not to hear the flood of his filthy thoughts. His thumb wanders toward the hem of my necessaries. The world behind my eyes goes a dizzying shade of red and I freeze. Not this. Not again. "I won't say a word to anyone," Harlan says, panting in my ear. "No one has to know a thing, not even my pa. We can just tuck away, right over here behind the mercantile, and take care of things real quick."

Anger and disgust flood through me. No, he's not going to have me. Not here. Not now, not ever. I can't believe that Abby's daddy wants her to marry this slobbering fool. My eyes snap open. I'm ready for a fight. Ready to pull the trump card I've been holding close to my chest for months now. "You were at the Bakers' place, huh? At four o'clock in the morning? You're still sneakin' in little Corinne's window at night, aren't you? She's just thirteen, Harlan. She's too afraid to tell anyone, lessen her daddy lose his job."

His lips peel back. "You little bitch." He pulls his hand from under my skirt, and I let out my breath. "You don't know nothin' about me or my business."

"I know lots of things about you. Know you jumped Morris and know your daddy murdered my uncle Rebon, too. If I ever find out where his bones are, I'll call the *real* law and you and your gang'll have hell to pay." The fire surges through me and I don't hold it back this time. It curls in my fingertips and slows my heartbeat until my blood pulses like a low, wet wave in my ears. "You best stay away from Corinne, and you damned well better stay away from Abby. You ever touch her the way you just touched me, I'll kill you, Harlan. Real slow."

Harlan laughs. "I'd like to see you try. Sounds like somethin' I could charge folks real good money to watch. Especially when you lose."

Heat tingles in my fingertips. I shove against his skinny chest, hard as I can.

Harlan gasps. *Little bitch burned me. What the fuck's wrong with her eyes?*

It's my turn to smile now. His fear is as delicious as a ripe pear. He walks backward, real slow. I want to charge him like a rabid dog.

"Hey now, what's going on here?"

I'd know that deep Kentucky drawl anywhere. Bellflower rounds the corner of the mercantile as if he's been summoned. Even though he's the man I came to town for, at the sight of him, a wave of nausea breaks over me and I get a little dizzy.

Harlan squares up to face him. "This ain't none of your concern, preacher man. Stick to your camp meetings. This is town business."

A strange dark mist curls around Bellflower, just like when I saw him with Val, tendrils of shadow reaching toward Harlan. I wonder if Harlan can see it. I shake my head. I'm beginning to wonder how much of what's happened in the last few days is real and how much is a delusion.

Bellflower's eyes harden under the brim of his hat, cold as two black stones in a river bottom. He stalks closer, anchoring himself between me and Harlan. His scar twists as he smiles, drawing his lips upward in a cruel line. "You ought to get back to work, hadn't you, son?"

Harlan stills, hands dropping to his sides. His jaw goes slack, and his eyes fall vacant. I ain't never seen a Northrup cowed so quickly. "I reckon I oughta get back to work," he intones dully.

"Go on then. Get out of here and don't you dare bother this girl no more. You hear me?"

Harlan grunts and shuffles off. I draw in a belly-deep breath. The suffocating air sears my lungs. "What'd you do to him?"

Bellflower ignores my question and takes a step toward me. The shadows swirling around him recede. "Did he hurt you?"

Why the hell is he so concerned about my well-being? "No. And thanks for your concern, but I can take care of myself."

"Oh, there's no doubt about that." Bellflower chuckles. "I've seen your like before."

"Have you? 'Cause I swear I've seen your ilk, too, and it ain't no better than Harlan there."

Aunt Val rounds the corner, a fishing pole propped against her shoulder. Bellflower glances heavenward and sighs. He's tired of her already. That didn't take long.

She sidles up to him and scowls at me. "Why'd you come to town today, Gracelynn? Ain't you got things to do up at the house?"

"Maybe I wanted to bend Reverend Bellflower's ear for a minute. And ain't *you* supposed to be working?" I echo. "You're always telling me how lazy I am, and yet here you are whiling away the days with your new man. Does Hosea know? Reckon he'd be mighty upset, since you've kept his bed warm for so long."

"You watch your tongue, Gracie. Show some respect." Val lifts her chin. "Hosea knows I've been called to help Josiah with his ministry. Besides, things ain't like that with Hosea. People just talk."

I cross my arms. "Well. Caro's doing the work of three right now, because of your *calling*. The law's after Morris, 'cause of the damned Northrups. Everything's gone to hell up on the mountain. Granny's so sick she can't even get out of bed."

"Mama's sick?" There's not an ounce of surprise in her voice. She shifts and looks away from me.

Now I'm wondering if *she* had something to do with Granny's fit. I can't be sure, but I've learned the best way to catch Val in her guilt is to be direct—to accuse her as if I already know what she's done. "Yep. She almost died. But you knew that already, didn't you, Val? What'd you do?"

"I didn't do a damn thing, Gracelynn."

"Valerie," Bellflower says, his voice warm. She turns to him, her mouth going all slack like Harlan's had. He reaches out to push a wayward strand of brassy hair back under her scarf. "Why don't you go and fill the lamps for our service tonight, hmm?"

"I . . . I . . . ," Val stammers, then nods her head, transfixed by the gleam in Bellflower's eyes. "All right, Josiah. I'll go do that."

"Good girl," he croons. He whispers something else in her ear. She giggles and turns to go, walking with a lift in her step.

Bellflower cuts me a conspiratorial grin. "She's so full of faith, isn't she? Every prophet needs a willing . . . acolyte. Val is simple. Easy. You're not simple at all, are you, Gracelynn?"

You're a challenge. And I haven't been challenged in so very long.

His lips aren't moving, but I can hear his voice in my head, clear as day. It's worse than when Harlan put his hands on me. The sick feeling wells up, sending my guts into a twist.

"Stop it," I hiss, gritting my teeth. "Get out of my head."

Bellflower snaps his fingers. The air stills, like time itself has stopped. The old men on the mercantile porch fall silent, their mouths frozen open, mid-conversation. "If you want me out of your head, you'll take the time to listen to what I have to say, won't you? You've been wondering why I'm here. What I want."

Sheer terror floods through me. I'd had my doubts about who and what he was before—had wondered if everything I'd seen him do was akin to a magician's illusions, or a figment of my own imagination. But whatever he is, it's powerful. I need to use my wits. Disarm him like he's trying to disarm me. "Sounds fair," I say. "And you're right. I been mighty curious about why you're here. What you want."

"We'll get to why I'm here and what I want . . . later. I like to take my time with such things."

"I saw you that night in the woods. With Val."

"Oh? What did you see, Gracelynn?" He tethers me with his eyes. Something within me weakens under his gaze, and I fight his strange allure, clenching my teeth.

"I saw you . . . change. Become someone else." My heart beats so hard I can feel it in my throat, but I refuse to let him see my fear. "I reckon maybe you've had a lot of faces over the years. Names, too. Nathaniel Walker. Ambrose Gentry."

"You *are* a smart girl," Bellflower says coldly. His smile turns malicious.

"People tell me that."

"I'd just bet they do." The tip of his tongue snakes out, flicking over his lower lip. "This town, though." Bellflower gestures at the run-down buildings, gone silent. The air is so heavy and hot I can barely breathe. "Smart hasn't gotten you far in a town like this, has it? Petty, small-minded people, with their dreary church socials and gossip about the neighbors. No. You're meant for greater than this, Gracelynn. I know you want more. I can give you more than you ever thought possible. *Make* you more."

"You gonna take me up on a high hill and show me all the kingdoms of the world? You should know I don't like heights."

"Spirited, aren't you?" Bellflower laughs, and it runs all through me. "You'll find you may have need of me, soon. But I am a gentleman with an abundance of patience. I've waited a long time for you. Half a century. A few more days will do no harm. I'll come to you again, and we'll talk like this. Just you and I."

A cloud blots out the sun, sending Bellflower into shadow. Down the road a coonhound starts howling. Another starts up. A low humming rings in my ears. I close my eyes and shake my head to clear it. When I open my eyes, Bellflower's gone. The old men on the mercantile porch pick up their frozen conversations mid-sentence. Kids run laughing and shrieking out of the schoolhouse. It's like a still frame turned into a movie. People walk past me, looking at me as if I've gone crazy, standing dazed in the middle of the road.

Not a single soul knows what just happened but me.

༺❀༻

The next morning, when Caro sleeps long past the time she's usually expected in the fields, I don't wake her. I ain't sure how I'm gonna support all of us, but I'll be damned if I make that young 'un toil in the sun anymore. Ain't nothing growing in this hateful, cursed drought, anyway.

I stoke the fire as low as I can to keep the heat out of the house as long as possible—just enough to scramble some eggs and brew coffee. My mind goes spinning back to the day Granny took ill. I want to believe that Val is innocent—that she wouldn't hurt her own mother. But what brought it on? I sort through the day, remembering. I'd given Granny a cup of coffee not even a half hour before she sickened, and I'd cut it with ground acorns and chicory root, something all hill people did in lean times. Me and Ebba had both had the same coffee in the days since. And we were both fit as fiddles.

Maybe Granny had eaten something poisonous? I look through the greens wilting next to the sink. There's nothing that could cause an accidental poisoning—no water hemlock, jimsonweed, or death camas. Besides, me and Granny are careful. She knows everything that grows in these hills and has taught me the same. She would never knowingly eat something harmful.

My eyes drift to the open cupboard and land on the sugar dish. Only one person in this house likes sugar in their coffee. Granny.

I take the sugar bowl down and look inside. Nothing but pure white granules. I dip my finger in the bowl and taste the sugar. There's a metallic twinge to it. Not arsenic, then. I poke my finger deeper. I feel something hard, buried in the sugar. I hook it around my fingertip and pull it to the surface. It's a nail, bent at an angle and rusted red. I reach in again and find another. Then another. I drop the sugar dish. It shatters, spilling a handful of nails and sugar onto the floor.

I'd read in the grimoire that iron is poisonous to witches. It leaches into their blood and blunts their powers. Makes them weak. Enough iron can kill a witch. It's the reason Granny never cooks with cast iron unless it's enameled. She claims raw iron takes the charm right out of her work.

Given her guilty air earlier, it must have been Aunt Val who put the nails there. It makes me so angry I could spit.

But why would she want to hurt Granny? Had Bellflower made her do it?

I clean up the mess in the kitchen, then go out to the sleeping porch, bringing Ebba a plate of eggs and coffee. She's curled on the rug next to Granny's daybed, sound asleep. Apart from going home briefly to tend to her goats, she's been here every hour since Granny fell into her coma. I can't help but be reminded of a loyal dog. Stubborn as she is, Ebba's good people. The best.

Granny's color looks a little better—pink instead of gray. She just looks like she's sleeping, instead of near the brink of death. It gives me hope she'll come through.

Hope's all I have to bank on right now.

I leave the food for Ebba to find when she wakes, then climb back up to Val's loft. The grimoire's still open on the mattress, beckoning me. After my encounters with Anneliese and Bellflower yesterday, the call to turn its pages and seek its knowledge is even stronger.

As I search the fragile pages, the scent of dandelions wafts out. A few pages on, I find an ancient drawing—more primitive than Anneliese's finely drawn illustrations—that sends the all-overs through me. It looks like a human at first glance, but there's something about it that's wrong. Uncanny. The eyes are set too far apart, and the fingers end in daggerlike claws. The word *incubus* is scrawled above it, and a description:

> An incubus is a demon in male form who seeks sexual congress with a woman. Incubi are inexorably drawn to witches, and the attraction a witch feels for an incubus is nearly irresistible. Each time she succumbs to the demon's

seductions, her gifts diminish, until she is left entirely weak and powerless. When the inevitable pregnancy occurs, the witch's health will falter—and the birthing process will be arduous. The infernal offspring of this union is called a cambion. When a witch births a cambion, her descendants are forever tainted with demonic blood.

As if an unseen hand is guiding me, the crinkled and worn pages lead me onward, to passages about the gifts witches might possess. Divination. Healing. Clairvoyance. Even the ability to resurrect the dead. Only the most powerful witches were able to do so.

I remember Anneliese's account of reviving her dead chicken. I wonder if she'd ever brought anything else back to life. If she'd been powerful enough to raise the dead, why hadn't she been able to prevent her own death? If Nathaniel Walker was one of the incubi, in the guise of a man, he might have stolen her abilities.

I've been too intent on easy answers to pay Anneliese's journal entries much mind. Now, I go back to them, because if I have to outsmart Bellflower, I need to learn about the past and why he keeps coming back to plague Tin Mountain and my family.

INTERLUDE

ANNELIESE'S GRIMOIRE

June 1, 1831

Morning. I have discovered what Nathaniel is—his true nature. The last time we lay together, the things he forced me to do . . . I cannot speak of them. I will not. And his eyes. The darkness behind them! How had I never noticed it before? I must have been under a glamour. A wicked spell. I must do what I can to protect myself and Jakob.

June 3, 1831

Eventide. Nathaniel tried to come to me once more, last night. Though my powers are diminished, I warded the cabin door and all the windows as best I could with blessed asafetida and oil of cloves. He paced about the porch and begged me to open to him. His footsteps were as loud as ten men. I held Jakob on my lap, shushing him until Nathaniel departed. I've no doubt he will be back. I am sore afraid.

June 9, 1831

Zenith of night. As I suspected, Nathaniel returned. I did not open to him. When I was sure he had departed, I found a parcel on the porch, wrapped in brown paper. I had a suspicion it might be charmed, so I doused my hands in oil and opened it out of doors. It was a length of fine white silk—enough to make a bridal gown, and a letter. A proposal of marriage. I stoked a fire in the yard and burned both.

June 13, 1831

Reddest dawn. Nathaniel returned for my answer last night, howling for me at some unholy hour—three or four in the morning, by my reckoning. Through the door, I shouted, "I will not marry you, Nathaniel Walker! Not in this life nor any other." As soon as I spoke the words aloud, a ragged scrabbling began in the walls, as if a thousand rats had been let loose in the timbers. I clapped my hands over my ears to drown out the sound, to no avail. Nathaniel roared such foul, disgusting things I shudder to remember them. Jakob woke, and ran to me, terrified. I soothed him as best I could and prayed to any god who might hear for Nathaniel to depart and leave us be. I must try to reclaim my power, though I fear it may be too late. He has taken almost all of it.

June 23, 1831

Overnight. My worst suspicions were confirmed. I am with child. Nathaniel's child. Already, I can feel what little power I had left draining from me. This fiendish creature, this cambion growing in my womb, will take all that I am for sustenance.

July 7, 1831

Today, I am rid of my pregnancy. My usual methods did not work, so I had to employ . . . other means. I am weak. Tired. Conflicted in feeling. There can be no doubt the child was wrong in a way that could not be overcome. Still yet . . . I grieve. If it were not for Jakob, I would not have had the courage to follow things through. I must protect him.

July 17, 1831

Half past midnight. He knows. Nathaniel knows.

August 2, 1831

Elizabeth came to me today, bringing milk and cheese. The mercantile will no longer sell to me. The women have stopped coming to my door. If it weren't for dear Elizabeth's true Christian charity and my little hens, we would feel the bitter bite of hunger once more.

Elizabeth told me the rumors have grown fierce. A wasting disease has claimed the lives of some of the village children. Nathaniel is blaming the plague on me from his pulpit.

"He's saying Jakob is the child of the devil, Anna," Elizabeth said with a shake of her head. I laughed at this. If only I could tell her the truth!

"It is no laughing matter. I fear what he might do. You should take the boy and leave."

But I cannot. I will never leave my home. This land is a part of me. I will remain—even if death comes to claim me.

August 17, 1831

I have had another vision. Nathaniel will come for me soon, with his cold demon heart. He will have his vengeance for my refusal to bear his unholy child. The townsfolk are his willing hands—the very same people I helped and healed are now my accusers. The scent of excrement and offal assails me each time I go out of doors and their wicked, common words are etched in my memory. All the power I have left is in my blood and in the land. For Jakob's sake and for my progeny's sake, I will sacrifice. I have seen the far-off future. I have seen my daughters— my legacy. They will bring a reckoning to Tin Mountain and purge the land of this oppression. This is not the end.

TWENTY

DEIRDRE

1881

Deirdre stood on tiptoe, grasped the banister for balance, and swiped at the stairwell's corners with her flannel-wrapped broom handle. There. Finally. No more cobwebs. A satisfied smile curved her lips. It was the day before Miss Munro's summer ball. While Deirdre's chore list had grown longer by the week, the added work kept her from worrying about things at home and kept her eyes from the shadows.

He was there, now, his specter hovering on the second-floor landing, watching her go about her work. Deirdre frowned up at him. Willed him to go. He was ever toying with her, like a cat with a mouse. She shut her eyes as his sinuous voice wound through her head, promising foul, decadent things.

She thought of Esme's lips.

Esme's hands.

Esme's whispered words in the night, driving away her fear.

Phoebe Darrow came stomping down the stairs, a mop bucket in her hands. She passed right through Gentry's specter, none the wiser, and set the bucket in front of Deirdre. Water sloshed over the edge, soaking the floor. "It's your turn to mop the landings, Miss Werner. And be sure to get the corners."

Deirdre propped her broom against the wall and began dusting the trim work above the stairs. "Miss Caruthers told me to dust. Mopping the landings is your task this week."

Phoebe drew herself up, crossing her arms. "You'll need to do both today. I have a carbuncle on my knee."

Deirdre knew Phoebe was lying. She always had an excuse for not doing the harder chores when they came on rotation.

"I'll get to it, *if* I have time. It's better to mop after you dust, anyhow."

Phoebe looked Deirdre up and down, and leaned close, her voice low. "I heard you," she rasped. "Last night. And the night before that, too."

"What are you talking about?"

"You and Esme."

Blood rushed to Deirdre's face. They had tried to be quiet with their lovemaking, but the plaster walls were thin, and their beds squeaked terribly. "You don't know a thing about me and Esme."

Constance chimed in from three steps below. "I heard you, too." She doused her cloth with lemon oil and began polishing the freshly dusted balustrade. "We know the real reason Esme was sent here, after all."

"It was Miss Munro's or the asylum for her," Phoebe said, tsk-tsking. "That's what they do to girls like you. They put them in asylums and give them ice-cold baths. Whip them until they're right in the head. It's worse than prison, they say."

Deirdre had heard of such things. She thought of Tessa Ray and wondered if her screaming had ended within the walls of that asylum or only gotten worse.

"Don't worry," Phoebe said, her voice wistful. "I won't tell Miss Munro about you and Esme. If you'll take on my chores. But out of concern for your soul, you should know the thing you're doing with Esme, it'll send you straight to hell if you don't repent and turn away from your sin. My daddy's a preacher. He's taught me all about it."

"Seems to me your daddy wouldn't take the time to tell you about such things if he weren't worried about *you* falling in with the same lot."

Phoebe pressed her lips together and her face went as scarlet as the flannel in Deirdre's hands. "I know what else you get up to. The other girls say you have a book in your room. A devil's book. They say you're a witch."

How had anyone found out about the grimoire? Esme would never tell.

"People sure do say a lot here, don't they?" Deirdre said tightly.

"The Bible has a good bit to say about witches, too. 'Thou shalt not suffer a witch to live,'" she intoned. "Maybe you and Esme are doing more than gobbling each other late at night. Maybe the devil is in there with the both of you."

Deirdre bristled. She glanced up at Gentry's shadow, saw him smirk.

Down the stairwell, Constance had disappeared, just as she always did when Phoebe took one of her mean spells, though she was ever willing to stir the pot. She and Phoebe were alone.

The other girl's feet perched at the edge of the landing. A sudden urge came over Deirdre to shove her—she could almost see Phoebe losing her balance and tumbling down, her dress tangling around her legs as she tried to catch herself. With the water-slicked floor, it would seem an accident. Deirdre took a step forward, fingers flexing at her sides in readiness. The temptation to shove Phoebe was so keen it nearly made her delirious.

Do it, she heard a voice whisper. *No one will ever know it was you.*

No. She willed Gentry's reckless persuasion out of her head. Her fingers relaxed and she stepped backward, pressing her shoulders against the wall, just in case the temptation overtook her again. How foolish it would have been to follow her impulse!

"What's wrong with you?" Phoebe hissed. "You're always staring at me. Maybe I should tell Miss Munro, after all. It makes me and the other girls nervous, having your sort around. You might get ideas."

Deirdre choked back her laughter. "You've nothing to worry about, Miss Darrow. I would never. The thought makes me positively bilious."

Phoebe sputtered with indignance, her face reddening even more.

Just then, Nancy Caruthers, their cohort's captain, came around the turn on the balustrade. Her narrow features creased into a frown. "What are we on about, ladies?" she asked crisply. "I see neither of you are working. Miss Werner, back to your dusting. Miss Darrow, come with me. There's something we need to discuss."

Phoebe hurried off behind Nancy, shooting a scowl over her shoulder.

Wretched cow. How dare she threaten to report Esme! Something had to be done about Phoebe, but it needed to be something that couldn't be traced back to Deirdre.

Deirdre waited a few moments until the sounds of the other girls had grown distant and the anger coursing through her diminished. She flew to her room and closed the door. Esme was still downstairs, helping her own cohort arrange flowers for the ballroom. She pulled the grimoire from beneath her bed and removed its tapestry cover. The book had been tampered with—she could see from the way its metal closure had been refastened—clumsily, with the clasp only halfway threaded through the eye. She had suspicions Constance had snooped in their room, at Phoebe's bidding.

It was well past time for some sort of recompense.

Deirdre tucked herself into the narrow space between her bed and the window and opened the grimoire. She rested her hand over the surface of a page and closed her eyes, moving her hand slowly over the parchment. She'd learned this was the best way to use the spell book. It already knew what she wanted, what she needed, just as it had when she sought it for the purgative teas she'd drunk after her trysts with Robbie. She'd never used the book for anything other than simple charms and tisanes. The closest she'd come to actual conjuring was when she and Esme dabbled with the divination methods—crystal and rock scrying— which they had only done in good fun.

Pa's admonishment to do no harm rattled her. What if her intentions *were* to do harm? Would the book still obey her?

Deirdre closed her eyes and turned the page, passing her hand over its surface again. "Show me something I might use, book. I only want to teach Phoebe a lesson. Only to humble her."

Suddenly, almost as if she were dowsing for water, she felt a tug on her finger. She opened her eyes.

A simple drawing of a common white mushroom lay beneath her fingertip.

In the shadows, the darkness smiled.

⟡

The next morning, Deirdre woke before dawn and crept down the gas-lit streets to the park across from St. Michael's church. Deirdre easily spotted the mushrooms in the damp, musty reaches of the oak grove, where they sprouted like pale, squat parasols. She plucked one carefully, then wrapped it in a handkerchief and secreted it in her pocket. Gentry's specter perched on a moss-draped oak branch, watching her. Always watching.

Later, as the girls gathered for breakfast, Deirdre made sure to sit next to Phoebe. The other girl was in high spirits, her cheeks flushed with excitement as she chattered to Constance about her new ball gown and the young men she hoped to dance with.

Once Constance had excused herself from the table, Phoebe turned to Deirdre, as if just noticing her presence. "I have a conference with Miss Munro tomorrow," she said giddily. "Miss Caruthers's fiancé proposed by letter. She's departing after the ball to plan her wedding. It seems I'm next in line to be our cohort captain." Phoebe raised her teacup and sipped from it. "I think you know what that means, Miss Werner."

Deirdre pressed her lips together. "I certainly do." More work. More chores. As captain, Phoebe would have an added measure of power over Deirdre. If she refused to comply with Phoebe's orders, she might tell Miss Munro about her and Esme, which would mean expulsion and a train back to Tin Mountain for Deirdre. For Esme it would mean much, much worse. An asylum. Deirdre would never let that happen.

"I'm glad we understand one another." Phoebe smiled at her, cat-like, and went to fetch more toast from the buffet.

At last, Deirdre had her opportunity. She glanced from side to side, furtively. Most of the girls had left the breakfast hall and had gone back to their rooms. No one would see. Quickly, she pulled the handkerchief from her pocket, broke off a piece of the mushroom's cap, and crumbled it in her hand. She sprinkled the mushroom into Phoebe's porridge, gave it a quick stir, then washed her fingers in her finger bowl.

It should be just enough to make Phoebe sick. Just enough.

A few moments later, Phoebe returned. She shoveled the tainted porridge into her mouth with her toast and chased it with the rest of her tea. "We'll get started with the new chore list on Monday. I've some mending I need done as well. You wouldn't mind taking it on, would you?"

"Of course not," Deirdre said, lifting her chin. "I'd be happy to."

"Good." Phoebe stood from the table, her eyes cold. "I've not the slightest notion what she sees in you."

After Phoebe had rustled off, an uncomfortable feeling settled between Deirdre's shoulders. This vendetta of Phoebe's seemed personal. More than shallow bullying. Was there some history between Phoebe and Esme? Esme had never hinted as much, but there was a provocative tone of jealousy in Phoebe's parting words.

Later that day, Deirdre and Esme were perched on ladders, hanging crepe paper bunting from the ballroom's doorframes under Miss Munro's supervision, when Constance rushed in, her face ashen. She took Miss Munro aside and whispered in her ear.

The headmistress pressed her fingers to her lips and shook her head, then hurriedly trailed Constance upstairs.

"What was that about, I wonder?" Esme asked, pinning her end of the swag on the doorpost. "Constance seemed upset."

"I wouldn't know."

"Oh well. We should start getting ready as soon as we have this done. I've the most wonderful idea for your hair," Esme said. "I saw a drawing in *The Delineator* I've a mind to copy."

"Mm." Esme's words faded to a low hum in Deirdre's ears. She swallowed to quell the sour taste in her mouth. What if she'd given Phoebe too much? She disliked the girl, but she'd merely wanted to teach her a lesson and enjoy the ball without her meddling and judgement. Pa's warning about coming to the book with intention vexed her once more. Perhaps the book knew the depths of the darkness in her heart and had reflected it back to her.

If she could poison someone, what else might she be capable of doing?

"Deirdre. Are you listening to me?" Esme's voice rose in irritation. "I asked if you had a corsage in mind for tonight. If not, I can make you a posy with the leftover roses from the centerpieces. The white ones would look grand with your green dress."

"Yes, that sounds splendid. I . . . I need to go to the washroom." Deirdre climbed down from the ladder, nearly stumbling on the bottom rung.

"You're all out of sorts. Are you falling ill?"

"No, it's only my menses," she said. "They've come in hard this month. I'll be back in a moment."

Deirdre rushed up the stairs, her skirts gathered in her hands. On the second-floor landing, she heard a hoarse gagging, followed by a groan. She shuffled silently to Phoebe and Constance's door. It was open a crack. She carefully leaned forward to peek inside.

Phoebe lay on the bed, atop the covers, her shift drenched with sweat. Her face glowed a sickly, yellowish white. Miss Munro sat on the edge of the mattress, mopping her forehead with a cloth. Suddenly, a gut-wrenching spasm shook Phoebe. She leaned over the bed to vomit into the basin on the floor. Miss Munro turned away, squeezing her eyes shut. The stench wafted through the door and assaulted Deirdre's nostrils—it was rancid, sour. Bile.

She had done this. Out of a sense of petty vengeance.

A low, menacing chuckle came from the end of the hall. Deirdre whirled to face it.

Nothing was there. Not even the shadow she'd come to see as a constant companion.

Miss Munro threw open the door. "Miss Werner. Why are you loitering? We only have a few hours before the ball."

"Is Phoebe taken ill?"

"Yes." Miss Munro crossed her arms, pushing her sleeves up past her elbows. "No sign of fever, so it's likely nothing to be concerned with. If she's not better by evening, I'll send for the doctor."

"Might it have been something she ate?" Deirdre could have slapped herself. Why had she asked that?

"Did you not have the same thing as she at dinner last night? And breakfast?"

"Yes. I—"

Miss Munro waved dismissively. "It's likely the heat. These digestive complaints happen often in summer. Not to worry. Miss Darrow may well make a full recovery in time for tonight. Miss Brewster has been relieved from her other duties and will tend to her." She gave a curt nod. "Now, back to work. As soon as you've completed your chores, you may retire to your room to rest before the ball."

The headmistress strode away, her back straight as a ramrod. Deirdre sagged against the wall, her eyes smarting with unexpected tears. Guilt and shame coupled with her fear. If anyone ever found out what she'd done, it could mean a punishment worse than expulsion from the school. If Phoebe died, she'd be a murderer.

Unless the grimoire might hold an antidote. Hope bloomed in her chest. It had given her all the knowledge she'd ever sought, so why not that?

Deirdre pulled in a rallying breath and turned to go when she sensed eyes on her back. She looked over her shoulder.

Constance's pinched, wren-like face peeked out the dormitory door. "You. This is your work, isn't it? You and your witch book."

Deirdre hastily wiped at her eyes. "I don't know what you're talking about. That book was my grandmother's. It's only recipes and such."

Constance scowled. "Recipes for poison. I know what you did. I know what you are. And if Phoebe dies, you'll wish it were you instead of her."

TWENTY-ONE

GRACELYNN

1931

After Anneliese's final journal entry, there's an illustration of a crescent moon, and a single line of script before the grimoire falls away to the blank pages at the end. The words are rushed and nearly illegible, written in dingy, brown ink:

> The curse can be broken only by the maiden, the mother, and the crone, who must speak Nathaniel's true name thrice to cast him out.

His true name. As I'm pondering the words, a soft knock comes at the kitchen door. It's mighty early for company. I climb down from the loft, tiptoeing past Caro. I open the door to find Calvina Watterson, Mr. Bledsoe's maid, huddled against the porch post. She has dark purple circles underneath her eyes, and the rims around them are all red, like she's been crying.

"I came about Mama," she says, her voice choked by a sob. "I didn't know who else to turn to."

"Lands, Calvina. Come on in."

"I ain't got long to chat. Mr. Bledsoe'll be expectin' me soon."

"Of course. Just sit for a spell and tell me what's happened."

Calvina bobs her head and steps over the threshold. I pour her a cup of chamomile and catmint tea. Her hands shake as she takes it from me. Her fingers brush mine, but her thoughts are so faint I can barely hear them. "You want cream?" I eye the empty spot next to the stove where the sugar dish used to sit. "We're all out of sugar."

"No, them's precious things. I like it plain, anyways." She takes a long sip and studies me over the rim. "It were all a show, that night when that preacher healed Mama, Miss Gracie. She felt real good for a few days, then took a hard turn—got down in her hip worse than I ever seen."

Dammit. I knew Bellflower's gifts were a sham. A demon's parlor trick, just like his good looks. He's toying with the townsfolk—using them. But to what end?

"I found her after I got home from Mr. Bledsoe's last night. She'd been tryin' to bring food in from the springhouse when her hip gave all the way out and she fell. She said she drug herself along the ground for a bit, then got tuckered out. She laid there all day, in that hot sun." Calvina's breath hitches. She takes a long swallow of tea before she speaks again. "She's at Doc Gallagher's place now. He said it's a broken hip. They're taking her to the big hospital today, soon as they can get an ambulance down from Springfield. It ain't lookin' good, though. How am I supposed to pay for a funeral? Mama deserves better than to be laid in some potter's field."

"Lord, Calvina, don't think like that." But I know she's right. A broken hip at Elmira Watterson's age is likely a death warrant.

"That preacher—he's bad, Gracie. Real bad. He's got the whole town in a thrall. They're goin' to that tent every night now, hoping for a blessing from the Lord, but there ain't nothing but death in that man's hands."

"I know it."

"Mama ain't the only one to get a false healing. Nadine Clark's baby boy died. He'd been sick with some sort of colic and that preacher laid hands on him. He seemed to get better, but two days later, his mama found him cold in his crib. And two more young 'uns he touched have the pellagra so bad Doc Gallagher don't think they'll make it to September."

"Lands."

"Now, I know your Granny has *ways*. Ways she don't like to talk about. That's the real reason I'm here. I wondered if she might do some work for Mama. For me."

Calvina ain't heard about Granny, then.

"She's in a deep sleep. Not been well lately."

"I'm sorry to hear that. Should I come back tomorrow?"

"You could, but I don't think she'll be awake then, neither. Nothin' like this has ever happened. Granny don't get sick. You know that." I bite my lip and look out the window. A hot, dry wind wafts through. "You believe in generational curses, Calvina?"

"Yes, ma'am, I sure do. The Bible talks about 'em plenty."

"I think that preacher man means to do more than mislead people. I think whatever's comin' is worse than a few hot days in May or false healing services for show. Promise me, if folks start talking nonsense about me or Granny, you'll tell me."

"They're already saying plenty." Calvina pushes away from the table and gathers her thin cardigan tight around her bony frame. "But I'll never hear a bad word against Miss Deirdre in my presence, and I won't listen to no bad talk about you, neither. I promise you that." She arches a brow. "My gran had powers, too. Visions. She saw an angel once.

Came right in through the window to claim my uncle three days 'fore he died. He'd been in an accident and got the gangrene, real bad. When his body passed, my gran weren't surprised, 'cause she'd already seen that angel take his spirit, while he yet breathed."

I think of Granny in the other room, hovering between life and death. I hope no damned angel comes through *our* window. I ain't ready to say goodbye.

"I better head to work. Them hospital bills won't be cheap." Calvina yawns. "If you find some way to help Mama, even if other folk cast aspersions, I'd remember the effort kindly."

"I'll see what I can do." I go to the pantry to fetch a muslin sachet filled with lavender and clary sage to help soothe her sleep, then see her to the door. As she pushes through the garden gate, something catches my eye off to the side, swinging from the maple tree in front of the fence. It ain't one of our grapevine totems. It's something else.

As I get closer, I see that it's a rustic dolly, made out of burlap, with corn silk for hair. Somebody's hung it with a makeshift noose from one of the lower limbs of the tree. There's a piece of paper tacked to the skirt.

It's not the only time ne'er-do-wells and bored young 'uns have done such things on our property, but this is more than stealing a chicken or dumping pig innards in our garden. This is hanging me in effigy. A chill walks across my shoulders. I tear the piece of paper free.

It's a misspelled warning, written in a messy, childlike scrawl:

Witch's hang eazier then they burn.

I crumple it and throw it in the ditch, where the scorching wind picks it up and carries it off down the road. Everything that's happened lately has me wound up tighter than a cheap dime-store watch. Morris. Harlan Northrup. Granny. Bellflower and Aunt Val. Ma Watterson. Now this. Heat rises in my belly like a pot set to boil over. I was afraid before, but now I'm mad.

I think of Anneliese's story. There ain't no way to prove it, and it had been a mere guess at the time, but given Bellflower's reaction yesterday when I'd spoken Nathaniel Walker's and Ambrose Gentry's names, there's no longer any doubt the three of them are one and the same. Anneliese's demon lover has come back in another guise, and after our encounter, it seems he's got his sights set on me now, instead of Val. But if he thinks I'm gonna succumb to his seductions like Anneliese, or bow down to his threats without a fight, he's got another thing coming. I may be new to witching, but I wasn't born yesterday.

TWENTY-TWO

DEIRDRE

1881

Deirdre flew up the stairs, Constance's accusation still ringing in her ears. She felt a headache coming on, as they often did with her menses, sending shards of spiking pain behind her left eye and sharpening her panic. *Had* she made a mistake? Plucked the wrong sort of mushroom? It was possible—she was in a different climate, with unfamiliar flora and fauna. Deadly mushrooms easily mimicked their less lethal cousins.

In her room she hurriedly brought out the grimoire, flipping through its pages and pacing the floor. There had to be an antidote—something that might undo her foolishness. Deirdre's finger traced line after line of Anneliese's trailing script, willed the grimoire to show her the answer. She would do anything to make this right. Anything.

It's too late. There's no antidote for Amanita bisporigera—*the destroying angel. Aptly named, don't you think?*

Deirdre whirled on Gentry. His specter lounged against the wall, arms crossed, his eyes cold and filled with malice.

"You. You made me do this, didn't you?"

Gentry laughed. "No, little rabbit. It was you. Only you. We are two of a kind, you and I. Always doing whatever it takes to get what we want." He pushed off from the wall, and walked toward her, soundlessly. "You wanted that girl. Wanted her sweetness on your lips. Did you truly think no one would ever find out about the two of you? Phoebe is only the first of many who will judge you—who will condemn you for your lust. Will you poison them all?"

"It's not lust. I love Esme. There's nothing wrong with what we've done."

Gentry chuckled softly. "Would your steadfast Robbie agree? And to think you once judged your poor, sickly mother a whore. *Your* sin is far worse, little rabbit. It's driven you to murder. 'The wages of sin are death.'"

His words filled Deirdre's ears, taunting her with guilt and shame. "Hush up. Just go away! I'll fix this. I will."

Gentry laughed again and faded from view just as Esme swung open the door, clutching a handful of white roses.

"Deirdre, are you all right? I was worried when you didn't come back downstairs."

Deirdre shut the grimoire in frustration and sank onto her bed, defeated. "I'm sorry . . . I've a headache coming on."

"It's all right. Nancy helped me hang the rest of the bunting. Who were you talking to just now?"

"No one."

"I could have sworn I heard you talking to someone. You sounded agitated." Esme sat next to her, the usually sweet scent of the roses made metallic and harsh by the headache. "You aren't the only one who's feeling ill. Nancy told me Phoebe's sick, too. I hope it isn't catching."

"That's too bad. I hope she recovers in time for the ball. Fetch me a cool cloth for my head, would you? I'd like to lie down for a spell."

Esme did as she asked, then curled next to Deirdre. "My poor darling," she said, smoothing the cloth over Deirdre's eyes. "Rest well."

As she fell into a fitful sleep, Deirdre doubted she'd ever rest well again.

❧

Deirdre stood before the photographer's floral backdrop, doing her best to not sweat away the layers of powder and rouge Esme had painstakingly applied. The first attempt at the photograph hadn't gone well—a gnat had landed on her nose, and Deirdre had swatted it away just as the shutter closed, ruining the dry plate exposure.

The sounds of the orchestra warming up drifted from the ballroom into the main hall. Outside, the young men Miss Munro had invited— the sons of Charleston's best families—were gathered on the veranda, enjoying cigars and brandy.

Deirdre's pulse beat behind her eyes. Maddening pain. The kind that could only be made better with morphia and lack of worry. She had neither.

"Now, Miss Werner, is it?" The photographer's tinny voice interrupted her thoughts. The gnat buzzed near her ear. This time, she did not swat it away. "Turn to the side. Just a bit. Hands clasped softly in front of your waist. There. That's it. Your gown is lovely. Lovely. Nose to the light. Now, take a deep breath and hold it. Don't move, not even a blink."

He went behind his tripod, took off the lens cap, then put it back on again. "Perfect, Miss Werner. Absolutely perfect."

Deirdre exhaled with relief. "Thank you."

As she passed through the atrium, Deirdre overheard a thread of a conversation, ". . . still feeling poorly. Weak. The doctor thinks it might be a poisoning . . . Miss Munro will be questioning girls tomorrow . . ."

The other girls were talking. Gossip about Phoebe's illness would spread quickly and gain steam in the crowded ballroom. Deirdre strove to keep her head. With Constance already suspicious, she'd likely be questioned first. She'd need to slip away tonight, at some point, and find a place to hide her book.

The string quartet entered the foyer and sat before the hearth, striking up a bright tune. The last few girls joined the receiving line. Miss Munro bustled toward the door. She looked years younger tonight— her usual grim demeanor lightened by her lilac dress and the soft curls framing her face. The hired footmen brought on for the evening threw the entryway doors wide, and the young men filtered through, dressed in white tie, with waxed mustaches and pomaded hair.

Deirdre gracefully curtsied and smiled, practicing the refined manners she'd learned over the past few weeks, but inside, she was filled with turmoil. She offered her dance card to her suitors and tried her best to remember their names as they exchanged pleasantries about the weather and the tides.

As for Esme, she was in high demand and had a full dance card within the first half hour. The orchestra struck up a Viennese waltz, and the first of her partners, a tall, strapping fellow with a riot of blond curls and broad shoulders, led Esme to the dance floor. Deirdre tried her best not to be jealous. Their hidden afternoon kisses and whispered secrets would have to come to an end eventually. They'd both marry soon, as they must, and their forbidden love would become a memory left to grow bittersweet, like overripe fruit on the vine.

A Mr. Briggs came to claim Deirdre for the first dance, and though she tried her best to follow, she found him an awkward partner, as he was three inches shorter than she and unsure on his feet. He sniffed constantly, and the sour scent of kippers wafted from his mouth.

As Esme spun by in her own young man's capable arms, she caught Deirdre's tortured gaze and giggled. Thankfully, the music died down and it was time to switch partners.

"Might I borrow you again later this evening, Miss Werner?" Mr. Briggs asked.

Borrow. As if she were a library book on lend!

"I'm afraid my dance card is full for the night, sir."

The orchestra struck up the next dance. Deirdre searched for Esme in the crowd. Where had she gone? The pressure in Deirdre's head roared. Made her senseless. Clumsy. Her new partner sensed her distracted manner and excused himself mid-dance, much to Deirdre's relief. As she hurriedly crossed the floor, she thought she saw Gentry, leering from the side of the ballroom.

She found Esme on the stairs. Her face was pale as a tomb, her mouth set in a grim line.

"Esme! I wondered where you went off to. What's wrong?"

"I've just been up to check on Phoebe. She's taken a bad turn. Miss Munro has sent for the ambulance, but by the time it gets here, it may be too late."

Deirdre gasped to keep from screaming. "Too late?"

"She's dying, Deirdre. And Constance told Miss Munro you poisoned her."

TWENTY-THREE

GRACELYNN

1931

When I get to Hosea Ray's pasture, just after sunset, there's a bus parked outside Bellflower's tent and a long line of people waiting to be let inside. It seems all of Arkansas has turned out for the good preacher's healing touch tonight.

I duck my head to hide my face beneath my scarf and push through the dense crowd. The congregants' voices clatter in my head as I brush past the thicket of humid, sweating bodies. At least I can't hear their thoughts. Inside, there ain't any seats left, so I wedge myself against the side of the tent, where the menfolk stand with their hats in their hands.

He's fancied the place up. There's an altar on a rough-hewn platform, with lilies wilting in the heat, and an upright piano at the side of the altar. Candles blaze from every surface, dripping wax and smoking up the air. Next to the pulpit sit two tin buckets, covered with flour sacks. There's still not a single cross or Bible in the place. It might have the feel of a church, but it's anything but.

Bellflower shows up a few minutes later. Aunt Val hangs on him, all tarted up in cheap blue satin, her mouth and fingernails lacquered red. My teeth clench. I could choke the life out of her for what she's done to Granny.

She looks up at Bellflower with adoring eyes as he pries her hands from his arm. He gestures toward the piano with his sharp chin, and Val obediently goes to the piano and sits. She starts pounding out the opening chords to a hymn. I never even knew she could play.

With the townsfolk distracted by the music, I slowly move forward.

Once I'm near the front, Val lays off the music and Bellflower takes his place behind the podium. A hush falls over the tent.

"Good people of Tin Mountain," Bellflower intones, his flint-dark eyes sliding over the crowd. "I have heard a rumor there may be witches in our midst."

My pulse quickens. At first, I think he's seen me. But as his gaze scrapes past me, I realize this is all just part of his act. I release a shaky breath, settle my hip against a tent pole, and draw my scarf tighter around my face.

"The book of Exodus has much to say about the dangers of consorting with witches," Bellflower continues. He stalks back and forth on his makeshift stage. He enjoys this. The attention. The power. "Whether you believe in darker powers or not, the evidence of evil is all around us. This drought," he says, throwing his hands wide, "is a sign of sinister influence. What other plagues might follow? I received most unfortunate news this morning. The baby boy I healed from a pernicious colic last week has died. His dear mother found him in his crib yesterday morning. There will be more deaths, my brethren. Just as there were fifty years ago. Some here are old enough to remember."

A few of the elderly people nod sagely.

Bellflower places a hand over his heart and drops his head in mock sympathy. "These plagues are no coincidence, my friends. Evil lives in Tin Mountain. It was brought upon this land by witchcraft and divination—the devil's tools. Evil wears many guises." He shrugs. "Some beautiful. Seductive and sweetly innocent. But no matter how appealing evil may seem on the outside, the destroyer seeks always to undo the work of the good. Witches are the Enemy's helpmates."

My hands ball into fists at my sides. He's using his illusions of healing and godliness to convince people to turn against us. How many more people will he fool—how many more have to die—before they see him for what he is?

"But I have good news, my children. Witches aren't the only ones who have powers." He ceases his pacing. "I was given a greater gift, in my youth. My dear, sweet mother was afflicted by a witch's curse. From my earliest memory, she was racked with fits that bent her back and sent her into such painful spasms that she begged for the mercy of death. I prayed fervently for her to be healed. And one day . . . one day, I was heard." Fake tears glisten in Bellflower's eyes. He pulls in a deep breath and lets it out.

I can tell he's covered this ground before. The speech is practiced and polished, like he's repeated it over and over for years. I wonder how much of it—if any of it—is true.

"An angel came to me, in the night. He touched me and made me a promise. If I would help purge the world of witchcraft, he would heal my mother, and give me the gift of healing so that I might bless others. Friends, that angel made true on his promise. And I have made true on mine. I have spent my entire ministry chasing down evil and delivering those oppressed by the dangers of witchcraft."

He bends to pick up one of the tin pails. At first, I think it's just an offering bucket, but I hear a faint rasp of movement coming from inside. "You have seen me heal. You have seen me prophesy, and tonight, you'll defy death with me." Bellflower thrusts a hand into the bucket.

Paulette Kennedy

He lifts a snake—a copperhead, its brilliant brown and orange body twining up his arm. "To drive out evil, we will dance with the devil's serpents, brothers and sisters."

Aunt Val starts playing the piano again—a wild, careening version of "Go Tell It on the Mountain." I move forward with the rest of the crowd with a spiteful determination to expose him for what he truly is.

The other congregants reach into the buckets and take up snakes—there are water moccasins and rattlesnakes, too—and start dancing with them. The music gets louder and the tent heaves with people drunkenly spinning in circles and speaking in tongues as they sway.

I tie my scarf tighter around my face, covering everything but my eyes. Curiosity propels me to the altar. I reach inside one of the buckets, feeling the dry, cool softness of a snake's scales slither over my hand. I grasp the copperhead, and hold it close to me, humming to it, trying to calm its frantic thrashing. It strikes me anyway, as is its nature. But I don't feel the sharp sink of fangs like I should—only a pinch.

I tickle the snake under its chin. It lets go, then strikes again, its jaws closing over my thumb. I turn the snake and look inside its mouth. I knew it. There are two gaping holes where its teeth should be. It's been mutilated. That bastard has pulled out its fangs. A snake represents original sin, but the only sin here is Josiah Bellflower's charade.

I pull in a deep breath and the heat in my bones begins to sing. As if he can feel the shift in energy, Bellflower turns to me. I push the scarf off and stalk toward him, unafraid. Aunt Val must see me, too, because the music dies, and the wild dancing slowly comes to a stop. The tent goes quiet. I turn in a slow circle, brandishing the snake in front of me before I bend to gently release it.

"It's all a lie. Look at your snakes. He's taken their fangs. They aren't biting you because they *can't*. There's no miracle here, just meanness and a good pair of pliers."

Some of the townsfolk look down at the snakes they're holding, but most of them just stare at me like I've got two heads.

"Are you going to tell them what else you've done, Josiah Bellflower? I know who you really are." My voice is strong. Sure. "I know what you're tryin' to do. You're a deceiver. A liar."

Bellflower snaps his fingers. Everything goes still. People freeze in place—caught up in his trance. It's suddenly so quiet in the tent, the only sound I hear is the pounding of my heart.

"Ah, Gracelynn. So glad you could come. What do you think? I'm coming up in the world, aren't I?" He points at a weedy-looking man with a camera, sitting in the front row. "That man's a reporter from the *Gazette*. He's working on a front-page story about my ministry."

"That's what you're after? Fame?"

"No. Although it's a pleasant distraction. All of this," he says, sweeping his arms at the frozen congregants, "is just a game to me. Theater. A farce. It means nothing." He stalks toward me, his eyes lit with that unholy, silver light. "Has she told you yet, Gracie?"

I step backward. Fear threatens to throttle my breath, my voice, but I won't give him the pleasure. "What are you talking about?"

"Your beloved Granny. Has she told you the truth?"

"Well, seeing as she's in a coma, thanks to Val, she can't tell me much of anything right now. So, I guess that leaves you, though I'd be as foolish as your congregation to believe a word that drops from your poisoned lips."

Bellflower laughs, throwing his head back.

I glance at the piano. Aunt Val's hands hover over the keyboard, her mouth agape. A water moccasin is curled around her ankle.

"Does Val know you're just using her?"

Bellflower sighs. "She gets plenty from our arrangement. She's ravenous. I hardly sleep."

"So, what's the point to all this, Bellflower? I reckon if you wanted to kill me, you would have done it by now. Yet, you seem set on turning all these townsfolk against me and pinning this drought on me and Granny. Why?"

"The ends necessitate the means."

"Is that what you said when you killed Anneliese?"

A shadow passes over his lean face. "*I* didn't kill her. *They* did."

Now it's my turn to laugh. "So, you're the sort who believes your own lies. You'd make a good politician. You should take that up instead of preaching. I've heard the pay is better."

It must be my laughter that does it. His face hardens. He snaps his fingers again, and a cacophony of sound erupts behind my ears. The congregation comes back to life, shouting and hollering their *amen*s and *hallelujah*s. Bellflower steps behind the pulpit again.

His eyes glint as he gives me a smug grin. "Brethren, did I not just proclaim that evil seeks to undermine good?" he booms. "Here we have one of the very witches who plagues your town. She wishes to cast doubt into your heart. To seduce you from the truth with her beauty and her lies." Suddenly, I'm surrounded. Bodies press against me. Voices crowd my head, all talking at once, like a hillbilly Tower of Babel:

I always knew something weren't right with that girl.

Her and her granny are in league with the devil.

She's always thought she's better than us.

She killt that woman's baby.

I clap my hands over my ears, but that doesn't stop the flood of accusations and threats as the townsfolk close in. It's not my powers this time. It's Bellflower. He's forcing their words into my head, amplifying their voices, making me crazy.

I underestimated him. He ain't raising a congregation, he's raising a militia. A wave of panic winds up my spine, and all my earlier sureness flies away. I've gotten in over my head, coming here, where he has control of the chessboard.

"Bring her to me, brethren," he commands, a wicked smile curling the corners of his mouth. "I'll drive out the demon who vexes her."

The men hem me in, leering. Somebody swipes at my scarf, grabbing the tail. It's still knotted under my chin. I yelp as I feel it tighten like a noose. It's Harlan Northrup. I can smell the sweet-sour tang of the sawmill on him. He winds the scarf around his wrist like he's winding cotton, pulling me closer and closer until I nearly taste the tobacco on his breath and his hands close around my arm. "You little bitch," he whispers. "Let's see how uppity you are now."

I claw at the fabric, wheezing as my air bottoms out. Nobody comes to help me. Nobody cares. Just as my vision starts to flicker and go dark, he releases me. I haul in a breath, my throat stinging with pain. I frantically look for a way out, but there are hands everywhere, grasping at me, pulling me forward. Bellflower steps down from the altar and stares at me a long while, then reaches out, stroking his hand along my neck. At his touch, the pain flees. So, there's something to his *healing* touch after all, even if it's a false balm that fades away with time.

"Kneel, sister," he commands gently. "And I will pray for you."

"No," I rasp. "I'll never kneel before a man. Especially you."

"Spoken like a true Werner." He leans close to me. "Kneel, you foolish girl, or I will set them on you like dogs. Just as I set them on Anneliese. Take the hand that I extend to you and live."

"No."

"I can hurt you more than you ever knew you could hurt."

I bark a hoarse laugh. "Go on. Sic your horde on me. You can try to hurt me. But I already know what it means to hold pain deep inside, Bellflower. My daddy taught me just how much a soul can suffer."

You should have never been born, you worthless chit. His last, whiskey-soaked words to me, the night before he found his death. The heat sears through me again. I narrow my eyes and focus all my will. My head throbs so strongly, I think it might crack open. There's a loud crash behind the pulpit. The acrid scent of kerosene fills the air, followed by a sickening flare of yellow-orange light.

"Fire!"

TWENTY-FOUR

DEIRDRE

1881

Death was in Phoebe's room. It hung heavy in the fetid, stinking air. The breeze from the open window did nothing to quell it. Deirdre blinked and pulled in a tight breath, covering her nose with her hand to block the stench.

Phoebe wasn't moving. Her skin looked twice as yellow as it had that morning, and her eyes were sunk deep in their sockets and smudged with grayish purple. Esme knelt next to Miss Munro, her ivory skirts pooling around her. "Phoebe, it's me. Esme. Can you hear me?"

The dying girl let out a rasp of rancid air and turned her head slightly toward Esme. "Why . . ."

As Deirdre watched the two girls, an uncomfortable suspicion needled her. Something about the way Esme spoke to Phoebe seemed much more intimate than she ever knew them to be.

Constance burst into the room, carrying a ewer of water. She shoved Deirdre to the side and the pitcher sloshed, splashing water onto the floor. "What's *she* doing in here?"

Miss Munro stood and crossed the room, taking the ewer from Constance. "Never you mind, Miss Brewster. Now go to the rectory and wake Father Sunderworth. Have him bring the Eucharist. It would bring Miss Darrow much comfort to have him here."

Constance scowled at Deirdre, her nostrils flaring, and turned on her heel. Miss Munro shook her head with a weary sigh. She poured warm water in the basin, dipped a fresh cloth into it, and wrung it out, then handed it to Esme. "Miss Buchanan, if you could relieve me for a few moments, I'd have a word with Miss Werner in the hall."

Deirdre's stomach tumbled to her feet. She followed the headmistress out, her feet clumsy. Miss Munro gestured to the settee at the end of the hallway, overlooking the school gardens. Deirdre reluctantly sat, pushing her sweaty palms across her lap, over and over. From downstairs, a cheerful polka floated up. The lively music was an ironic counterpoint to the deathly atmosphere of the room down the hall.

"Someone mentioned you might have had something to do with Miss Darrow's sickness." Miss Munro peered at Deirdre over her spectacles. "I'd hope not. But if so, you'll need to confess it to me now. If she expires and the coroner comes, I won't be able to protect you from an investigation. But, perhaps, if you might have done something accidentally . . ."

Should she confess what she had done? A cold sweat broke out along the nape of Deirdre's neck and ran down her back. Just how much could Miss Munro do to help her? Certainly, she had some level of influence with her money and standing, but would it be enough to keep Deirdre from the courtroom or the gallows?

Tell her nothing.

Deirdre jolted at the velvet deep whisper in her left ear. Her head jerked toward the open window. The wind had picked up, whipping the linen curtains to the side and bringing the scent of confederate jasmine with it. She expected to see Gentry, but his shadowy form was not there.

"I . . . I don't know why Phoebe . . . I mean to say, Miss Darrow, has taken ill, ma'am. I wish I knew."

Miss Munro cleared her throat. "Miss Caruthers told me the two of you had some sort of quarrel yesterday, in the stairwell. And Miss Brewster mentioned a book in your room. A magic book, of some sort. With spells."

Deirdre's forehead pinched at this. "Constance shouldn't have been snooping in our room. I only have a journal with a few family recipes. Nothing bad or evil."

"Will you fetch it for me, so that I might have a look and put these rumors to rest?"

"I . . . I can't." Deirdre bit her lip.

Miss Munro sighed and rolled her head on her delicate neck. "Miss Werner. If you refuse to cooperate with me, I'll have your room searched this very moment."

She'd have to bring it, then. Have to show her. She had marked the page with the mushrooms with a length of satin ribbon. She could remove it, of course, but she couldn't tear the pages free. Miss Munro would know. Dammit. Instead of dancing, she should have done what she'd planned and hidden the book in the gardens. "I'll go fetch it, then."

"Very good. I'll wait here. Don't tarry too long."

Deirdre made her way up to the top floor, her knees trembling. She pushed open the door to her room and startled. Ambrose Gentry stood there, handsomely dressed in evening clothes, facing the window. He turned, his lips quirking up at the corners. Deirdre whispered a curse beneath her breath.

"Ah, there you are. You look stunning in green, Miss Werner."

He walked toward her, and for the first time, she heard his footfalls on the floorboards. His shadow stretched out long behind him. Deirdre reached out and poked a finger at his lapel and instead of the usual oily mire, felt fine summer wool. He laughed and grasped her hand in his. She jerked away at the feel of his cool flesh. He was truly here. Not just a figment of her imagination or the menacing specter that haunted her from the shadows.

"How did you get here?"

He shrugged. "I walked in the door. With all the other eager young men downstairs, it was easily done."

Gentry clasped his hands behind his back and paced back and forth. Gone was the simple country pastor, along with the slow as molasses drawl. Instead, he held a veneer of city polish, a brash confidence befitting a well-to-do gentleman. He was ever a mimic, blending in wherever he found himself.

"Why are you here?"

"I've only come to help you. That's what pastors do, Deirdre. They help."

Deirdre lifted her chin and laughed. "Is that so?"

"There are pressing matters to discuss. Like that poor girl you poisoned, two floors down. The ambulance won't arrive in time. There's been a streetcar accident downtown, and many people are injured."

The sick feeling twisted in Deirdre's gut. "I didn't mean to hurt her."

"Ah, but you *did!* You have a vengeful streak, Deirdre. All the Werner women have it. But you, my dear—you have it in spades." He waggled his finger at her. "They'll hang you for it, you know."

"You said you were here to help. I ain't seen much help in what you're saying at all."

"First things first. Your spinster schoolmistress wishes to see the grimoire, yes?"

"Yes."

"Well, let's see it. Bring it out."

"I'm not supposed to show it to anyone, leastwise you."

"But you've already broken the rules. Showed it to Esme. You're not in a position to quarrel with me, Miss Werner, as I'm your only ally. I'm the only one who knows what you've done, and I'd wager you'd like to keep it that way. The clock is ticking. Remember poor Phoebe."

Driven by guilt, Deirdre knelt at the foot of her bed, keeping a wary eye on Gentry. She pulled the tapestry satchel out and took the grimoire from it.

"Open the book and tell me what you see."

Deirdre took a breath and opened the cover. The page was blank. She turned the next page, then the next. All were empty of their spells and charms. Instead, there were only the neatly written and festively illustrated recipes. Not for poison at all, but for gingerbread and spiced cider, kuchen and schnitzel. It was just as she'd told Miss Munro—a journal with family recipes. But how? Deirdre almost laughed with relief.

"What do you see?" Gentry asked slyly.

"Nothing. Nothing at all apart from a few recipes. Did you do that?"

He chuckled. "It's a mere glamour. A trick of the eye. It won't last long, but it will last long enough to save you."

"But Constance looked at it. She told Miss Munro there were poison recipes inside."

"That silly girl didn't see a thing. When she tried to open the grimoire, the clasp cut her finger and she jumped to her own conclusions. The grimoire does protect itself . . . and its owner."

"If that's so, then why did it let me poison her?" Deirdre asked.

"Free will is free will, and you willed that girl to suffer." He shrugged. "Your father tried to warn you to come with intention. The grimoire merely bowed to your urges."

"If I show it to Miss Munro, then, it will look as it does now?"

"Yes. That prickly schoolmarm will never know it's more than a rustic country cookbook. But that's only half of your problem solved, my dear, because your rival is still dying." Gentry walked to her and offered his hand, helping her to her feet. His earlier effusiveness had fled. A sober look shone in his gimlet eyes. "Do you know what regret feels like, Deirdre? True regret? Because I do. I let someone die once, when I might have saved them. You will regret it if she dies. It will haunt you all of your days."

"It's too late for me to do anything about Phoebe. There's no antidote. What's done is done."

"But it's not too late for *me* to save her . . . if you'll make me a promise and bind it with your blood."

"What kind of promise?"

Gentry circled her. "What I desire most, little rabbit. Give it willingly, only once, and I will trouble you no more, until I return in half a century to reap what I have sown. Fifty years is a long time, Deirdre. You'll grow old and live out the simple country life you've always wanted."

"You want me to barter my soul. That's it, isn't it?"

Gentry laughed. "No. I do not want your soul. I want something much simpler. Something much sweeter." He trailed his fingers over the mark on her back, where her ballgown dipped low, then wrapped his arms around her possessively, his breath hot on her neck as his hands roamed up her bosom to her throat. "Think of the noose, Deirdre."

Deirdre nearly swooned, her knees weak with sudden, shameful desire and fear. What would it hurt? To give in to his seductions, only once. Then she'd be free to live out the rest of her days, unblemished by the stain of murder.

"Yes. Yes. I'll do it." Deirdre turned in his arms, trembling. "I'll lie with you. And I'll do so willingly."

Gentry smiled. "Good."

And then he kissed her.

All Deirdre's rationale, all her tenuous morality, crumbled completely in the wake of that kiss. He claimed her mouth with a hunger that sent fire through her body, made her arch her back and whimper. She curled against him, her every nerve alight. More. She wanted more. What had come over her? Only the day before she'd feared him—been disgusted by his presence. And now, she ached for him with a fervor that frightened her.

He laughed. "I knew you wanted me just as much as I want you." He placed a finger on her fevered mouth and pulled away. Deirdre sighed in disappointment. "I promise, I will make true on my word. But now is not the time. Now, we must save that poor girl you've poisoned, and for that, I need your blood, my darling. Only a little."

"Yes, of course," Deirdre said. As if in a trance, she went to the desk she shared with Esme. Esme's pearl-handled letter opener lay atop the blotter. Deirdre took it up, its slender blade gleaming in the wan lamplight. "What should I do?" she asked drowsily.

"Just close your palm over it and draw it through. Your tender flesh will yield."

Deirdre did as he asked, wincing at the bite of the blade. He was by her side in a flash of movement, eyes aglimmer with their queer silver light. Blood filled Deirdre's hand and dripped to the floor.

"Promise me," he urged.

"I . . . I promise."

"Yes," he hissed, and hungrily brought her palm to his mouth. A heady rush of lust swam through her at the feel of his tongue lapping against her skin. When she pulled her hand away, the mark had already healed, though it still burned beneath the newly formed scar that stood in a red crescent on her palm.

"I'll look forward to our reunion, Miss Werner. I'll come to you again when the time is right." He gave her a wicked smile, full of carnal promise . . . then stepped into the shadows. He was gone.

Deirdre clasped the grimoire to her chest and hurried downstairs.

"There you are!" Miss Munro stood to greet her, a look of irritation etched on her face. "I was about to come looking for you. A lay pastor arrived from St. Michael's. I had to show him to Miss Darrow's room. He's praying with her now."

"I'm sorry. I had to go to the washroom." Deirdre offered the grimoire to Miss Munro and stepped back, her arms crossed over her waist. The headmistress opened the book, turning the pages faster and faster. When she got to the end, she scowled as she read. For a moment, Deirdre worried the book had betrayed her. But when Miss Munro closed it with a decisive thwack, then returned it to Deirdre, she smiled warmly.

"Just as you said, Miss Werner. Only recipes. And a rather good one for gingerbread I might ask to borrow for the holidays."

A wash of relief went over Deirdre, and she beamed, dropping a perfect curtsy. "Thank you, ma'am."

"You may return to the dance, if you wish."

"I . . . I couldn't do that." She had to make sure that Gentry would make good on his word. "Not with Phoebe in such a state."

A few moments later, Esme emerged from Phoebe's room and stepped into the hall. Deirdre took note of the redness in the corners of her eyes and the deep rivers her tears had cut through her powder and rouge. "The pastor asked me to leave, so that he might say prayers for Phoebe's soul," Esme said. "She's no longer awake. It won't be long."

"Well." Miss Munro cleared her throat. "I'll pay the orchestra and dismiss our guests before I notify the coroner. We can't have all of Charleston gossiping about a hearse showing up during a party."

After Miss Munro swept downstairs, Esme's quiet weeping became heaving sobs. Deirdre did her best to soothe her distress. "There, now. Don't cry."

"I can't help it." Esme hiccupped and wiped at her eyes with Deirdre's offered handkerchief.

"I've never seen you so upset. I didn't realize you and Phoebe were that close."

"Well. We were at one time. I was her . . ." Esme bit her lip and turned to the window.

"Her *what*, Esme?"

"Friend. Her first roommate."

"You were more than roommates, weren't you?" Jealousy and anger overtook her. She grasped Esme by the shoulder, turning her. "I might have known that was the reason she's been so cruel to me. She was jealous!"

"Oh, Deirdre." Esme sank onto the settee and rested her head in her hands. "Please don't be angry."

Deirdre sat next to her, holding the grimoire on her lap. She felt as if something inside her had shattered into a thousand brittle pieces.

"After Sam, I was terribly lonely. One night, Phoebe confessed that she'd never been kissed. One thing led to another, and—"

"I don't need to hear more." Deirdre put up her hand.

"Things went sour after that. I blame her religion, mostly. She knew her father would never approve of our friendship once he found out about my inclinations. Last winter, after returning from Christmas holiday, she started shunning me and took the room downstairs with Constance."

"That hypocrite," Deirdre said, seething. Her guilt over poisoning Phoebe thinned with her jealousy. "She threatened to tell Miss Munro about us! Held it over my head."

"I was afraid you'd be angry. And you are. I don't love her. I swear it. But she's dying. Am I not supposed to make peace with her and with myself for what happened between us?"

"Her bullying isn't the worst of it. She's been sending Constance to our room to snoop. She told Miss Munro I have a witch's book and that I poisoned Phoebe. I could be hanged for that, Esme!"

"Why, that's ridiculous. You'd never do such a thing."

Deirdre's guilt once more pricked her conscience. Esme thought better of her than she deserved.

"It's going to be all right. Just calm yourself and we'll find a way through this. You've done nothing wrong."

But she had. And then she'd trusted Gentry—put her fate in the hands of a liar and a demon. She could almost feel the noose tightening around her neck, choking the life from her. And what would come after? Surely hell awaited a murderer—especially one who had just sold her fate to a devil. Deirdre longed to run, to hide. But where could she go where Gentry wouldn't find her?

"Esme . . . I need to tell you—"

Just then, hasty footsteps echoed on the stairs. Likely the coroner. Panicked, Deirdre shut the grimoire and put it aside. Miss Munro and Constance emerged from the stairwell, a man dressed in black following them. His round face was reddened by his climb up the stairs. He seemed quite agitated. "As I've said, Miss Munro, I do not have a lay pastor named Gentry in my parish, and I did not send anyone else. I've no idea who's in that room, but he is not from St. Michael's." He stalked down the hall, Miss Munro and Constance bustling behind him. Esme and Deirdre rose as one to follow.

As they neared the death-shrouded room, Deirdre's ears began to ring distantly. "Esme, what does the pastor in Phoebe's room look like?"

"He's tall, young. Good looking. He was very charming and gracious to me." Esme gave her a puzzled look. "Why?"

Miss Munro opened the door to Phoebe's room and gave an astonished gasp. "Oh, my heavens."

Had Phoebe expired? Deirdre worked her way forward until she could see inside, expecting the worst. The ringing in her ears became a scream. She thought she might faint.

There Phoebe sat, reclining against the headboard, a Bible propped on her lap with the bloom of life in her cheeks. "I've just had the strangest dream," she said, stretching as if she'd woken from a long Sunday nap. "I dreamt that I died, but an angel came and kissed me and brought me back to life."

TWENTY-FIVE

GRACELYNN

1931

I run from the flaming tent into the night, careening with the rest of the townspeople in a panicked, tangled herd. Sparks spiral upward, embers popping as they consume what's left of the tent. People bat at their flaming hems and hats. The acrid scent of burning oilcloth and singed hair assaults my nostrils.

"Where's Harlan?" Al Northrup stumbles toward me like a drunk. His beady eyes are red and swollen. He grasps me by the shoulders and shakes me. "Goddammit, girl, I asked you a question. You seen my boy?"

"Not since he tried to choke the life out of me."

"Goddammit," he swears again, pulling off his hat to swat out a stray ember on the dry grass. The fire is spreading—snaking away from the tent's tattered remains and winding through the alfalfa in flickering rivers. The wind picks up and fans the flames. A nearby blackberry thicket starts to burn.

"Somebody get the fire brigade!" Northrup yells, and then stumbles off, baying Harlan's name. A pack of three men tumble into a farm truck and fly off toward town, sending up a spray of gravel and dust.

I should run, but my feet are rooted to the spot, as if I'm in a trance. I've never seen a brush fire before. It's oddly beautiful. Hypnotic and horrifying at the same time. The flames almost seem alive. Hungry. I lift my hand and the flames climb higher.

Did I do this?

"Gracie!" I shake off my sense of wonder and turn to see Abby coming toward me, tears running down her soot-covered face. I didn't even know she'd been in the crowd. She grabs me by the arm and starts pulling on me. I can't hear her thoughts, but her frantic eyes tell me all I need to know. "We got to get out of here. Fire's spreadin' fast."

Sure enough, a hard puff of wind comes and the fire surges forward. An ember lands in one of Hosea's peach trees, and a loud pop sounds as the branches ignite. Heat sears the air, and a low roar starts to build around us.

"Come *on*, Gracie!" Abby cries, fear stitched over her face. "Do you want to die?"

In the distance, the fire brigade's sirens sound. Their reedy, high-pitched whine brings me back to my wits. We take off and head up the mountain. When we get to Granny's cabin, I look east, where the sky has turned a noxious shade of orange. The campfire scent of burning timber is everywhere.

Ebba meets us at the door, her eyes wide. "Gracie! Come! Deirdre is having fits again—seizures."

I push past her and go through the cabin to the back porch. Granny's wrists and ankles are tied to the daybed with scraps of fabric, her back arching as she spasms. Her eyes are open, fixed on something in the distance. A low moan comes from her mouth. I cross the room and kneel at her side, stroking her hair back from her forehead. I don't know what to do. But at my touch, she calms, her chest rising in gasping breaths and then steadying. The seizure abates, the tremors cease. Granny's eyes roll back and then close once more.

"She woke for a bit. Spoke to me." Ebba works her jaw in agitation. "Something about the curse. I gave her some broth and water, then the fits started. I had to tie her down so she wouldn't hurt herself."

"She was awake? Where's Caro?"

"I sent her to fetch the doctor."

I nod. Ebba's done the right thing. "I don't know how fast he'll get here, what with the fire down at the Ray place. A lantern fell over in Bellflower's revival tent. Whole place went up. Aunt Val was there. I think she made it out all right, though." I hope. I hadn't seen her in the ruckus that followed.

Ebba paces back and forth, muttering to herself, her frail arms crossed over her waist. She's got something on her mind. Abby's busy in the kitchen, clanging around. Now's just as good a time as any to let a certain elephant come barreling into the room.

"You're gonna wear a hole in your boots, Eb," I say. "Got somethin' gnawing on you?" I lower my voice. "Maybe now's the time to tell me what else you know before the whole town burns down?"

Ebba whirls on me, her turquoise eyes bright. "You have the gifts of a wise one. A true witch. But they are untested. You don't know how dangerous those ways can be, *lilla flicka*. I was worried about this."

"If I don't figure out how to stop this curse, I'm afraid that demon preacher ain't gonna be satisfied until Tin Mountain is a pile of cinders and me and Granny are burnin' right along with it. So, if you know anything that can help us, I need you to tell me before it's too late."

Ebba shakes her head. "It *is* too late. It's already started." She jabs a finger at my forehead. "You were there when that fire started, yes? Think, Gracie. Think. This is what he wants. To trap you. Just like he trapped Deirdre. Just like he trapped Anneliese and all the witches

218

before her. He's a trickster. A seducer." She jabs her finger at my forehead again. "You're not strong enough to unmake old mistakes. Only Deirdre can unmake what she promised. And it will likely kill her."

Anger flashes through me. Even though Ebba means well, even though she just wants to protect Granny, I'd love to throttle her right now. "Ebba," I say slowly, gentling my tone, "Granny can't do a single thing right now to help. I need you to help *me*. Think of the past. You say she made a mistake. Tell me what she did."

"I promised her. I promised her with my own blood." Ebba shows me her palm. A pale scar crosses it. "I told her I would never tell anyone. That includes you, Gracelynn. *Especially* you!" She turns and stomps outside, the screen door slamming behind her.

Looks like I'll have to figure things out on my own.

I leave Granny and climb into the loft. I relight the oil lamp and put my hands on the grimoire's cover, then close my eyes and pull in deep breaths, focusing my thoughts and intentions. "Help me, Anneliese," I whisper. "Show me what to do."

The book seems to hum under my fingers. Heat trails up my arm. I blow a puff of air from my lips and open the book to the page with the spell for undoing a curse. The script begins to shift from dull brown to a brilliant crimson red, the lamplight glistening on it. I realize it's not ink at all. It's blood.

A vision slams into my head: Anneliese sitting at a table, the grimoire open in front of her. She dips her quill in a saucer of blood and scrawls across the page. She looks up from her writing, her blue eyes blazing into mine. Her lips never move, but I can hear her bell-like voice in my head. *Look above the blood moon and see what is written there, Gracelynn. Before it is too late.*

And then, the vision is gone, leaving me breathless, with another splitting headache and a slow trickle of blood streaming from my nose. I wipe it away and look at my scarlet-streaked fingers.

Blood moon.

Outside the window, there's no moon in the sky—it's full dark with only the flicker of distant flames glowing against the horizon.

Maybe Anneliese means the blood moon in the book. There's a drawing of a moon after one of her journal entries.

I hurriedly scan the pages until I come to the section Anneliese wrote shortly before her death. Beneath the words, the illustrated crescent moon glows a lurid red. I read the entries again, quickly, eyes darting over the words, hoping to parse some meaning, but my mind is so addled that none of it makes sense. I try different combinations of words and letters. The closest I come to finding anything coherent is when I combine the fancy first letters of each entry on the page to spell M-E-Z-R-O-T-H—which has absolutely no meaning to me. It's just nonsense.

My eyelids droop with exhaustion, but I don't want to sleep, just in case the fire spreads and comes up the mountain. I need to stay awake, at least until Caro comes home. I close the grimoire and climb down the ladder. Ebba must be over her snit. She kneels at Granny's side, holding her hand. I hear her singing softly in Swedish. If Granny dies, it's gonna hurt Ebba as much as it'll hurt me. The two of them are like sisters.

I find Abby out on the front porch, sitting in the swing. She cradles a cup of coffee in her hands, and she slowly rocks back and forth, tipping her feet from heel to toe. I sit down next to her, and she sighs, leaning her head on my shoulder. The thought-reading power seems to have gone, and I'm thankful for that. Out over the ridge, the fire still burns bright against the indigo-violet sky. It's eerie, because up here on the mountain, it's quiet, peaceful. Even the mockingbirds are singing.

"Think they'll put it out by morning?"

"I hope," Abby says. "I'm worried about it coming up the mountain if the wind shifts."

"Surely it'll get to the crick and stop?"

"Not afore it burns through Hosea's orchard. He's gonna be hell to deal with after this, Gracie. Bellflower better hope his pockets are deep enough to pay the Rays for the damage."

Abby's still blissfully unaware of what Bellflower truly is. I take the cup of coffee from her and drink. It's full coffee for once, not cut with anything. Ebba must have brought it from town. The bitter taste clears some of the muddiness from my head. My eyes still sting from the smoke, and I'm so bone tired I could fall over. Still, being here with Abby provides some respite.

"This fire might put a halt on my weddin'. Pa had arranged things for this Sunday, after church. You'll be there, or at least come to shivaree us, won't you?"

And just like that, my peaceful respite is over. I think of the way Harlan's fingers crawled up my skirt in town. How he made me twist and choke in the tent tonight. I stand up from the swing, the hot coffee sloshing over the rim of the cup. I don't even feel it scald my hand. "You're actually goin' through with marrying that bastard?"

"Gracie, I have to. It's what Pa wants." Abby tries to grab my hand. I push it away. "He's only got a few days left, according to Doc Gallagher. He's wasted away to a scrap of what he was. He ain't even eating now."

"I'm sorry to hear that, Abby. But does your pa know he's marryin' his only daughter to a rapist?"

"Harlan can be a little forward in his ways, but to say he's—"

"No." I don't let her finish. If Abby's gonna marry this bastard, she deserves to know the truth. "He knocked up little Corinne Baker. She came here last month, asking for Granny's secret tonic."

"What?"

"It's a purgative tonic, to end a pregnancy. If you take it early enough, it works."

"No." A horrified look passes over Abby's face. "She's just a baby herself."

"Yup. I sat there and held that little girl's hand while she cried and told me how scared she was that her daddy'd find out about Harlan sneakin' in her window. She was even more scared of the hellfire she'd face if God wouldn't forgive her for killing her baby. I told her if God couldn't forgive a scared kid for doing what she had to do, he'd better not forgive Harlan Northrup, 'cause that ain't the kind of God I want to believe in."

My lip trembles and I start to cry, tears of anger and frustration bubbling over. I wipe them away angrily. "But she ain't the only one. He cornered me outside the mercantile yesterday and shoved his hand under my skirt. Touched me. He wanted to do a whole lot more."

"Gracie, I'm so sorry. I didn't know."

"Well. Now you do. And since you were at that camp meeting tonight, you saw for yourself what he did to me there. So, no. I won't be comin' to your wedding, Abby. I won't bless your marriage to a man cut from the same cloth as my daddy. In every way."

It takes a minute for my words to hit Abby fully. I can see the shock wash over her like a cold rain. "Gracie . . . Your pa did that to you? Why'n't you ever tell me?"

"Because it ain't something I care to remember. Or talk about."

No. I don't want to remember, but I do anyway.

I remember the night Shep Doherty came in from a drunken tear and found his way to my bed. I'd just turned thirteen three weeks before, and I'd shot up like a spring sapling. Before he'd done what he'd done, he'd whispered my mother's name—as if looking like her gave him the right to touch me.

"Things didn't go farther than groping. But I think they would have." My words sound distant, hollow. It's easier to imagine I'm talking about somebody else. "I was just thankful the whiskey made his dick so soft he couldn't do more. He never touched me again . . . not in that way. But he still found ways to hurt me—sometimes with his words. Sometimes with his fists."

Abby's eyes fill with sympathetic tears. "I'm so sorry."

"I started skipping out on school and going on the train almost every day after that. Pretended I was an orphan. The rich people treated me good—paid for my dinner, gave me sweets. The whole time, I was stealing from them when they had their backs turned. I didn't like it much, but I had to. I swore, once I had enough money saved up, I'd stay on that westbound train until it got to California. Then, he up and died and I had to come here."

Abby takes my hand. "And if you'd never come here, we'd have never met."

"You're right, I reckon." I smile at her. "I just wish we could be together, Abby. *Really* together. I hate it that you're marrying Harlan. I wish there was some way . . ."

"I can't talk about it, Gracie." Abby's voice cracks. "What good does it do to think about the might-have-beens? That lighthouse won't make me a living, and I can't run our farm by myself much longer. It's too expensive. Harlan has more than enough money to take care of things. You'll get married, too, someday, Gracie."

I laugh. "No. No I won't. I'll stay single, just like Granny."

"And you know how people judge her for it—for having Val out of wedlock and everything."

I let go of Abby's hand. "My being single or married ain't gonna change a thing about our standing in this place. They've always judged us. They always will."

"Well. I'd better get back home. With Pa sick the way he is, I don't like to leave him for very long."

"Okay." I turn away. "Go on, then." I try not to cry. All of this is too much. There's a beat of silence, then she takes me by the arm, turning me.

"Gracie?"

"What?"

"After you get some rest, come up to the lighthouse. Real early, before daylight. Pa ain't up by then . . . and well, I'd like to . . ." She smiles shyly. "I'd like to finish what we started the other night."

I touch my forehead to hers and close my eyes. "Maybe after Caro gets home, I can sneak away."

"I'd like that a lot."

⚜

It's three in the morning when I creep down the ladder. Caro is in bed, sound asleep, one leg thrown over the covers. She hadn't been able to find Doc Gallagher, but Granny had made it through the night without having another fit, and I'd finally gotten a couple hours of rest.

I silently slip on my boots and head out the kitchen door. The smell of charred timber hangs in the air. Down over the ridge, the sky still blazes orange. Now and then, the fire catches on a tree and shoots up a column of explosive flame. It's almost enough to make me turn back and go inside—but this might be the only chance Abby and I have to be together, and I can't deny myself the one bit of sweetness I have left in my life.

I head up the hill, my back to the fire and my eyes on Old Liberty's steadfast beam.

When I reach the stone tower, the door is open, just a crack. Flashing yellow light seeps out. That must mean Abby's upstairs. Waiting for me. My heart beats faster at the thought.

I take the stairs up the tower two at a time. It's so stifling that I have to pause to catch my breath at the top before emerging into the lantern room, shielding my eyes from the white-hot light.

The French doors leading to the outer gallery are open. She must be waiting at our dangling spot. I undo my braids and shake out my hair, letting it flow long and loose down to my waist. I imagine Abby's fingers tangling in it as she kisses me. Out on the gallery, I have a bird's-eye view of the fire. It's huge, and dangerously close to the lights of town. The height coupled with the scent of smoke makes me dizzy.

A part of me worries that this was all my doing. I wonder if that surge of power I'd felt back in Bellflower's tent created the blaze. If I could start a fire through sheer force of will, what else might I be capable of?

I turn from the railing and make my way around the curved side of the lighthouse to our dangling spot, but Abby isn't there.

"Abby?" I call out. "You out here?"

I edge further along the metal catwalk, until I'm halfway around the side. Still no sign of Abby. The beam whooshes over my head, lighting up the forest below. My pulse quickens. Something ain't right about this. She's playing a game. She must be.

"Abby?" I call out again. "Now, it's too early in the morning for games. You wanted me here, and I'm here."

There's no answer. I start imagining the worst—that she might have lost her footing and fell, or worse yet—jumped. I'd never known Abby for the melancholic sort, but with her pa about to die and a marriage to Harlan Northrup on the horizon—

A wave of nausea hits me at the thought.

Suddenly, a loud rush of wind comes from above, like the rustling of a large bird's wings.

Everything goes still. The air. The trees. My breath.

I turn slowly, already knowing what I'm going to see. *Who* I'm going to see.

Bellflower.

Sure enough, he's standing there, smiling his devil smile. "Here we are. Alone at last."

"*You,*" I growl. I back away from him, until I'm up against the stone wall. "Where's Abby? What did you do with her?"

"I haven't harmed a hair on her head. She's sound asleep, poor thing. She found her pa passed out cold, and forgot all about you. It won't be long now," Bellflower says with mocking sadness. "Hours, not days."

I try to rush back to the tower doors, to run to Abby, but Bellflower snaps his fingers, and it's as if I've run into a brick wall. Suddenly, I can't move. I'm like one of his congregants, frozen in time.

"You're not going anywhere, little rabbit. Not until I've had my say."

"What do you want with me? What do you want with my family?" I manage to squeak out.

"I've been tied to your family for many, many years. Over a century. We'll get to all that soon. Now. Will you promise to be still and listen?"

"Yes," I say weakly.

He snaps again, and my invisible bonds release. I pull in a deep, heaving breath, and nearly retch. Bellflower closes the distance between us, and reaches out to touch my cheek, whisper light. "You're very special to me, Gracelynn. Precious." He studies me for a moment, his eyes hooded and dark. "I'm here to help you, not hurt you. I've already done you a favor. Gotten rid of a little problem of yours."

Despite the heat, a chill creeps across my shoulders. "What are you talking about?"

"That Northrup boy. Harlan. He meant to ravage you." Bellflower scowls. "Repugnant. They just found his body, charred almost beyond recognition, but it is him, I assure you. He'll trouble you—and your lovely Abigail—no more."

"You started it, didn't you? The fire."

"Perhaps." Bellflower shrugs. "Or perhaps you did. You're certainly capable of it." He glances over his shoulder at the fire, which has gone completely still in his eerie thrall, flames shimmering in place. "Fire purifies, cleanses. It's beautiful."

"Is that what you told Anneliese before she burned?"

"Anneliese. Anneliese." He sighs in irritation. "Her name wasn't Anneliese. That's just what that ridiculous German boy Friedrich called her.

226

"Her real name was Betsy. Betsy Sutter. And she was meant for a greater purpose, just like you are—a purpose she denied."

"You're talking in circles, Bellflower. I ain't got the patience for your riddles."

"How about a story, then? People tell all sorts of stories about the Sutter family, don't they? The most well-known tale is that Owen Sutter killed his family after he discovered his wife had a lover among the Natives. Ridiculous. Then, there's the myth he committed incest with his oldest daughter and the guilt destroyed him. Also false." Gentry's lips curl into a smile. "Or my personal favorite—that he made a deal with the devil, and it drove him mad. There might be a thread of truth in that one." He winks.

"Betsy was special from the moment she was born. A true witch, with raw, innate powers. Her blood *sang* with it. I came to Sutter's Hollow when I felt the tug of her essence. At first, I was formless and hungry, only a spirit in the ether. I played games with the Sutter girls, ripping their bedclothes off at night, cackling in the wee hours of morning. I haunted them in many forms. A black dog. A maiden dressed in green, swinging from the highest branches of the locust tree. A cantankerous, foul-mouthed old woman with an affinity for Scripture. They nicknamed her Mary." Bellflower chuckles to himself. "Playing Mary was my favorite game. She was how I knew I had a gift for ministry."

"Pardon me, but you're not makin' a lick of sense."

"In time! All will be clear in time." Bellflower paces back and forth in front of me like he does when he's preaching. "Soon, word of the 'witch' haunting Sutter's Hollow spread. Old Owen was driven mad by the attention. He hated my games. Hated it even more when I came to his wife late at night and made her quiver and moan in ways he never could. He begged me to depart—to leave his family alone. So, I made him an offer. I'd depart, if he'd promise his youngest daughter to me when she came of age."

"Anneliese."

"Betsy," he corrects. "Beautiful blue-eyed Betsy. Owen knew what I could do if he denied me. I played my part. Hung back and watched, quietly. It wasn't *my* fault Owen's madness made him mean. When his killing notions took root and came to fruition, I protected Betsy. Delivered her safely into the hands of young Friedrich Werner, then wandered from town to town out east, toying with the locals, until she was ripe for me. Only, instead of a bodiless spirit, I came back as—"

"Nathaniel Walker."

"Yes. You're very clever. Nathaniel was a young, naive pastor that made a deal of his own with me and invited me in." Bellflower passes a hand over his face, and his dark eyes change to blue as his dirty blond hair shifts to black. "I healed his beloved mother and then took his body for my own. I've been inhabiting it ever since."

"For what purpose? Just to seduce some pretty country girl?"

He raises an eyebrow. "Do you know what an incubus is, Gracelynn?"

My mind flickers back to an image in the grimoire, crudely drawn. The creature that looked like a human but seemed a bit . . . off. "A demon who seduces women—especially witches."

Bellflower gives me a dazzling smile. "You *have* been studying! I'm so proud. And why do they want to lie with a witch, specifically?"

"To create offspring."

"Yes. A cambion."

"What does that have to do with anything? You still haven't told me what you want with me. Why you keep turning up, like the worst kind of bad penny."

He's talking in circles. Confusing me, making my head spin.

"I'm still not following."

"I wanted Betsy because I wanted progeny from a natural-born witch. First, there was Betsy, who betrayed me. Then Deirdre, who *tried* to betray me, and failed, poor thing. She never even *thought* about you." He sighs wistfully. "Your grandmother was a beauty in her youth. I enjoyed our time together.

"Betsy and Deirdre were both special. In different ways." Bellflower stalks toward me. "But you . . . you are exceptional. Diluted a bit by your father's inferior blood, but still remarkable." He reaches out, his fingers grazing the jagged scar that Shep Doherty laid across my forehead when I was eight years old. "You don't even know what you're capable of. But I do. Together, we'll do great things. Together, we'll have everything we've ever wanted."

"We? If it's sex with me you're after, you should know I don't care for men. Never have. Never will. I ain't having your demon babies, neither."

Bellflower laughs. "I wouldn't think of such a thing. It would be . . . wrong. Even for my kind. I do have a moral compass of sorts, you know."

"Well, compasses don't work here. Not even the moral kind. Enough with talking in circles, Bellflower."

He begins pacing again, his hands clasped behind his back. "We'll get to the point, then. I'd like to make you an offer."

"There's not a thing you could offer me that I'd want."

He cocks a brow at me. "Not even an immortally long life, with more power than you ever thought possible?" Eerie shadows dance across his face, sharpening his features. "Protection for your family? Your darling grandmother's life? She made me a promise when she was young. A promise I've come to collect on. *How* I do so is up to you."

My guts plunge to my feet. "What are you talking about?"

An amused smirk spreads across his face. "Deirdre swore an oath to me many years ago, and offered you up as the binding, long before you were ever born."

"Granny would never do such a thing."

"Oh, but she would. In her youth, Deirdre was lustful. Wrathful. Driven by her own impulses. She poisoned a girl and the girl nearly died.

Deirdre would have hanged for it if it weren't for my help." Bellflower shrugs. "I happened to be there in her time of need. I *healed* the girl. She lived on, well into her golden years, because of the power I took from Deirdre's blood oath. Best of all, it got me what I wanted most. You."

"You're lying," I growl. "Granny doesn't poison people and she'd never give me to you. Granny is good. The best person I've ever known."

He laughs. "What is the difference between good and evil? Truly? It's all a matter of perception. Every bit of it. Wars. Plagues. Famine. Saints and sinners. Angels and demons."

Bellflower passes a hand over his face and his rangy good looks flicker once more. The ancient man I saw ravishing Val in the forest stares at me with dark, deep-set eyes.

"This Nathaniel vessel I inhabit has grown weak. Decrepit." He passes his hand over his face once more and his glamour is restored. "I can still disguise myself—take on any form, any shape I please. But it's no longer enough. I want an amplifier. A young, vital vessel—an ongoing source of power created by my own design. The daughter of a cambion is a rare thing. *You* are a rare thing."

"Daughter of a cambion?"

"Your mother. Ophelia."

Something has shifted in Bellflower's demeanor. He glowers at me darkly. Threateningly. My head starts to swim. The longer I'm around him, the weaker I get—like he's draining me. I back away from him as a knife blade of pain pierces my temple. I wince and knot my hands in my hair. I'm suddenly as helpless as a newborn kitten. I cry out and collapse in a huddle on the metal floor, the pain shooting through me.

"You are as much mine as you are Deirdre's. I don't like hurting you." Bellflower sighs.

"I will make the pain stop if you invite me in. Allow me to inhabit you, Gracie—let me use you as a vessel, just as I did with Nathaniel. I will protect you from death, from sickness. I will even restore Deirdre to health. No one you love need suffer, ever again."

"No," I say through clenched teeth. "Never."

Bellflower scowls. "Your free will is beyond tedious. A flaw in the design." He twists his wrist, and my back spasms and arches in response. Pain colors my vision red. I scream. The shadows flare around him. Tendrils of oily smoke surround me, stealing my breath. "Foolish girl. You choose to barter away your life?" His voice reverberates through me.

I pull myself to my feet, and sway shakily. There's a flash of movement, and Bellflower shoves me to the lighthouse railing, his hand knotted in my hair. The ground swirls below me. "Think of your granny. Think of little Caro. She's going to flower into a lovely young woman soon. Perhaps, when I've used up her mother, I'll have my fun with her."

A righteous anger surges through me. "No! Don't you dare lay a hand on her."

"Then give me what I want!" he roars. "Let me in! Deny me not!"

"I'll never give you what you want!"

"Then I'll find another way to take what was promised to me, witch," he hisses.

He pushes me, hard. Suddenly I'm falling, falling, fast as a stone.

❦

"Gracie. Gracie! What's gotten into you?"

Abby's voice is a distant echo. I suck in my breath, panting. The wind whistles in my ears, but I'm not falling anymore. I'm still at the top of the lighthouse, back pressed against the stones, shivering so hard my teeth chatter. I'm cold. So cold.

Abby comes to my side, her eyes wide in the flashing light. "Are you okay?"

"V-vi-vision. B-bell . . . flower."

"What?" She presses the back of her hand to my forehead. "Lands, you're burnin' up with fever. Let's get you home."

"Oh . . . kay."

Somehow, we make it down the tower steps, and into her pa's truck. Abby starts it up and puts it into gear. Every muscle in my body aches. I feel like I'm dying.

When we get back to the cabin, Abby helps me up to the porch, and I collapse onto the porch swing. She covers me up to my chin with a quilt. "I'll go in. Fetch Aunt Ebba."

"F-f-ever-few tea and white . . . w-willow bark. In the p-pantry." A wave of nausea hits me, and I lean over to retch between my knees. Nothing but bile comes up. I didn't eat dinner last night. The thought of food brings on another spasm, and I gag.

Abby and Ebba come rushing out. Ebba offers me a mug of something tepid, herbal, and bitter. Feverfew. She places a cold washrag on my neck. "It's like an oven in the house. Best to keep her outside, until the fever breaks. Val was here, Gracie. Looking for you. She took Caro with her."

Bellflower's threats ring in my head. Caro . . . I should have never left her alone. "We have to . . . we have to find her. He'll take her. He will."

"Darlin', you can't go anywhere right now," Abby says, smoothing my hair. "You've got to rest. You ain't makin' any sense."

I raise my head, look out over the ridge. My vision blurs and comes into focus, then blurs again. A serpentlike line of yellow light crawls up the mountainside. "Is that f-fire?"

It sure looks like fire. But in my feverish state, I can't be sure of anything.

"No. That ain't fire, Gracie," Abby says. "It's headlights."

TWENTY-SIX

DEIRDRE

1881

Deirdre focused on the unlit candle, stilling her breath. *Light.* Flame suddenly flared, igniting the wick. She closed her eyes. *Dark.* The candle extinguished, just as if she'd blown it out with her breath. She smiled. It was getting easier every time.

"You're getting good at that," Esme said. "I'm a little jealous." Moonlight streamed through the cupola windows, cloaking her in silver.

"It's easy."

"Because you're talented, if a bit cocky. But I love you all the same."

"Then come here and kiss me," Deirdre teased, biting her lip.

"Oh. I'll do much more than that." Esme stepped over the chalk circle and knelt, gently wrestling Deirdre to the floor. They tangled together, giggling.

Life had taken on a languid rhythm. It was easy to forget about the promise she'd made to Gentry. His shadowy specter no longer menaced from the corners or haunted her dreams. Almost every night, she and Esme stole up to the cupola. By candlelight, they'd study the grimoire and practice its spells. Then, as the tides rolled and whispered in the distance, they'd make love and nap, until the silent, blue hours gave way to morning.

After their first flush of shared passion, Esme lay next to Deirdre and coaxed a dark strand of hair from beneath Deirdre's shoulder. She wound it lazily around her finger. "Lionel Faulkner is coming to call again next Friday. He wants to take me to Folly Beach. Will you come along as chaperone?"

"Of course. I'll pack us a picnic. Do you think he'll propose?"

Esme's cheeks dimpled. "What makes you think he'll propose?"

Deirdre sighed and rolled her eyes toward the window. A thin ribbon of pink light shone on the horizon. "Don't you see how he looks at you?"

"Like I look at you?" Esme nuzzled Deirdre's cheek with her nose. "Why do I have to get married, when life is so perfect already? We could choose to be spinsters, you know. Living alone. Working our magic. We could even open an apothecary."

"With what money, Esme? Do you think your daddy would hand over your inheritance if you were living with a woman? We have to marry. Besides, I *want* to marry Robbie." After she'd sent Robbie a letter with the photograph from the ball, he'd finally responded. In his long-awaited letter, he'd confessed his longing for her and ended the letter with heady promises and a lock of his hair. All Deirdre's worries had flown away, and she was eager to return to Tin Mountain at summer's end.

"Oh, Robbie. Always coming between us." Esme wrapped a leg over Deirdre's hips and straddled her possessively. She took the ribbon from her hair and loosely bound Deirdre's wrists with it. "There. Now you're my prisoner. I'll keep you in this tower forever. That way, you'll never leave me."

"You're silly," Deirdre said, laughing lightly.

"Am I?" Esme gave a wicked grin and nipped at Deirdre's earlobe. "More greedy than silly. I don't want to give you up."

As Esme moved down her body and resumed the tender onslaught Deirdre had come to crave like butter on warm toast, she closed her eyes and gave herself over to her lover's touch once more. Within moments, she fell apart like a row of knitting dropped from a needle.

❧

Deirdre and Esme stumbled up the stairs of the schoolhouse, sun drunk and eager to shake the sand from their clothes after their Friday at the beach with Esme's beau. They had picnicked on cucumber sandwiches and seltzer, then walked the strand arm-in-arm, as the surf pooled around their bare feet. Esme had marveled at the creatures in the tide-pools, and lifted out starfish and sea urchins, offering them to Deirdre and Lionel to examine before gently setting them back down for the tide to reclaim. It had been the kind of lovely day that felt like a dream.

Charleston had broadened her world and made her see that life outside of Tin Mountain was rich and full of possibilities, though the draw of home was nearly as sweet now that Gentry had gone and Robbie had renewed his promises.

Later that day, as Deirdre sat on her bed crafting a letter to Robbie while Esme napped, clouds gathered outside the window and a fickle wind tossed the palms to and fro. It was nearly September, and Esme had warned her about the massive storms that roared through Charleston with the fall. As rain began to spit at the windowpanes, a knock came at their door. Deirdre rose from her bed and went to answer it.

Phoebe Darrow stood in the doorway, raised from the dead with a demon's kiss and hearty as ever. Deirdre's stomach lurched. What did she want now? "Good afternoon, Miss Darrow."

Phoebe gave a contemptuous sniff and produced an envelope from her pocket. "Telegram, Miss Werner. It arrived this morning, while you were away."

Deirdre took the envelope from Phoebe, who quickly went on her way. A twist of dread snaked through Deirdre. Good news hardly ever came by wire. She sat on the edge of the bed and held the envelope gingerly. She could sense the wretchedness of what lay inside through the thin paper.

Esme stirred and sat up, rubbing the sleep from her eyes. She came to Deirdre's side and looked over her shoulder. "What is it, my love? Why don't you open it?"

Deirdre drew in a quick breath and tore the envelope open. There were only two lines on the paper:

Your mother is dying (stop)
Please come home (stop) Pa

"It's Mama." The solidness of Deirdre's world dissolved. Gentry's healing powers had been false. Mama's recovery from the consumption had been a ruse. And now, she was dying, with so much left unsaid between them. She and Mama had too many wounds to heal. Things to mend before she passed.

She had to get home.

Esme climbed onto the mattress and wrapped her arms around Deirdre from behind, resting her pointed chin on Deirdre's head. "I'm so sorry, my darling."

"I have to leave," Deirdre said quietly. "Tonight."

"Of course you do. Especially with this storm coming." Esme glanced toward the window. The sky had taken on a greenish hue. "It looks to be a bad one. Do you have enough money?"

"I . . . I don't know if I have enough." Pa hadn't sent money with his last letter, and with the expense of her new Charleston wardrobe, her savings had dwindled to the five dollars tucked beneath her underthings in the dresser. She had no idea how much a train ticket would cost. Pa had arranged all that last time.

"I can give you the money to get home. And back again, too, once things are settled."

Back again.

Deirdre pulled away from Esme's clinging hands and took the carpetbag from beneath her bed. She packed the grimoire first, then began filling the valise with her clothes.

"You *are* planning on returning, aren't you?"

She pressed her lips together and turned away from the pleading tone in Esme's voice. "I'm not sure. Pa's getting old. He won't be able to work much longer. And Robbie's waiting for me . . . we're supposed to have a harvest wedding."

Esme burst into sudden, dramatic tears. "Deirdre, you can't let this tear us apart."

A shard of anger broke off in Deirdre and settled in her belly, hardening her. "That's a mighty selfish thing to say, Esme. Given the circumstances."

Esme rushed to her side, grabbed her by the arm, and tried to turn her. "I'm sorry, Deirdre. I shouldn't have said that. Just promise me you'll come back."

Deirdre whirled on her. "For what? I love you, too, Esme, but this will never work. We've always been on borrowed time. We don't live in a world where we can be together. It's impossible. Can't you see that?"

Esme's tears began in earnest then. She sat at the foot of Deirdre's bed, clad only in her bloomers and stockings, and buried her face in her hands. "I could come with you, couldn't I?"

Deirdre tried to imagine Esme in Tin Mountain, with her city ways. Esme might think it a novel thing, for a few days. Until the boredom set in, and the resentment began to fester. She thought of how lonely Hannah Bledsoe was in that big house at the end of Main Street—shunned by the other women because of her money and fancy clothes. An orchid in a field full of cow parsley. Women like Esme and Hannah were always bending to every fickle wind. Too soft, too tender. The Werners were hard, like cedar and pine—solid and evergreen. Mountain people. No. It was time to end things. What she'd had with Esme was a shining seduction. A feverish fantasy, gone on too long.

"You can't come with me, Esme. You'd hate Tin Mountain. You belong with Lionel, in a big house surrounded by fancy things. After you're married, I'll come visit you, I promise."

"It's that easy for you to leave, then?" Esme cried, her face red and angry as she stood to face Deirdre. "You can't wait to get back to your blessed Robbie and that sad little one-horse town. Well, let me tell you something, Deirdre. I've seen visions in a dream. I've seen the far-off years and the loneliness they hold for you. You'll rue the mistakes you've made and the day you left the one who truly loves you."

Deirdre's skin prickled. The way Esme spoke made her words sound almost like prophecy. Like a curse. "Are you cursin' me and speaking death over my head, Esme Buchanan?"

"No, Deirdre. You've already cursed yourself. Now, if you mean to leave, don't linger on. Just go."

༺ঙ৯༻

Deirdre wasn't a thief, but she was desperate. She tapped gently on Miss Munro's office door. When she didn't hear the headmistress's usual crisp greeting, she nudged the door open with her toe. Just as Deirdre had hoped, she was still out on her Friday errands.

Deirdre shut the door softly behind her. She'd heard talk from the other girls that Miss Munro kept a stash of money in her desk. Though it pained her to do so, she went through every drawer, quickly rifling through the contents. Finally, in the second drawer from the bottom, she found a leather pouch. It was so heavy the strain of lifting it taxed her wrist. She opened it and found it full of silver dollars. She counted out ten of them—that would surely be more than enough to get her back to Tin Mountain on a second-class railcar. She secreted the money in her dress pocket, then shoved the pouch back into the drawer and closed it.

Luckily, with the impending storm, there wasn't a soul to see her go out the front door and down the walk. When she reached the gate, she turned to look at Miss Munro's Finishing School for Young Ladies of Character one last time. She'd learned plenty during her time at Miss Munro's—how to appreciate works of philosophy and poetry by Ovid and Homer. She even had enough Latin now to pray properly with her dying mother. But even with her improved knowledge and manners, she'd never belonged here, among the pampered, indolent girls who'd grown up at the end of long oak alleys with servants to attend their every need.

They'd reminded her she didn't belong, nearly every day.

Esme came to the dormer window in their room, watching her like a half-lit haint. Deirdre lifted her hand. Esme stared at her for a long moment, then the curtain fell back into place.

It was all for the best, her leaving. For both of them. Deirdre squared her shoulders, took a deep breath of the salty, rain-laden air, and walked away.

TWENTY-SEVEN

GRACELYNN

1931

The line of trucks threads up the mountain, roaring in an angry rumble. They're led by the sheriff's patrol car, a flashing red light on its roof.

"What d'you think's happened?" Abby asks.

"I haven't the foggiest," I lie. If what Bellflower told me in that vision is true, Harlan Northrup is dead and Abby's about to find out her wedding's been called off in the worst way possible.

The patrol car whips up the drive, spraying gravel. Aunt Val crawls out of the back seat. Caro tumbles out after her. Caro's face is swollen and puffy, like she's been crying. "Gracie!" she hollers. "You gotta get—"

"Hush your mouth!" Val scolds, jerking Caro's arm.

Caro starts whimpering. It takes all I have not to launch myself over the porch rail and slap Val all the way to Sunday.

The sheriff steps out as a truck pulls up alongside his car. A group of men haul ass out the tailgate. They've got burlap hoods on. A few of them have shotguns. My heart jumps like a jackrabbit. The men stomp through Granny's garden, crushing her tender peonies with their boots. Sheriff Murphy clears his throat, a wary look in his eyes. "Miss Doherty?"

"You know who I am, Sheriff . . . ," I slur. The fever is just beginning to break, but my head's still muzzy with it. Sweat beads along my hairline and rolls down my face. "How can I help you?"

"I've come with a warrant for your arrest."

I could almost laugh if I felt better. "On what charges?"

"Arson."

I raise my pounding head and look him straight in the eye. "Arson? First off, I didn't start no fire. And I didn't have nothin' to do with Harlan, neither."

There's a rumble from the crowd of men. Some of them start cussing.

Murphy frowns. "Harlan Northrup?"

It takes me a minute, in my state, to realize my mistake. Goddamn this fever and my addled brain. The only reason I'd known anything about Harlan was because Bellflower told me he was dead in my vision.

A vision no one else saw.

"How'd you know about Harlan?" Sheriff Murphy takes two steps toward me. I see the metallic glint of handcuffs in his fist. "We just found him dead in Hosea Ray's field about half an hour ago."

All the air leaves my lungs, like somebody's kicked me in the gut. I've just incriminated myself.

Abby wails and the sound cuts through me like a knife.

My mouth has gone dry, but I swallow hard. "You're accusing me of murderin' Harlan now, too? That's what this is about? How'd you get a judge to sign that warrant so soon? There ain't even been time for an investigation."

This is all Bellflower's doing. I can see his hand in all of it. Folks need a good reason to kill a witch in these times—saying she casts spells ain't enough. Murder and arson would be.

"Several witnesses came forward. Saw what you did. Now you can go willingly, ma'am, or you can go at gunpoint. Those are your choices." He reaches for me, and I jerk backward, but then realize if I resist, it just makes me look guiltier.

"All right. I'll go willingly. But I want a lawyer. I ain't answering any questions until I have a lawyer." I offer my wrists and the cold metal slides over them as the handcuffs click into place. I turn back to look at Abby and Ebba. "I want y'all to bear witness. You tell the world if anything happens to me, you hear? Y'all stick together. Take good care of Granny, Ebba."

Sheriff Murphy jerks on my cuffs hard enough to make me stumble. The crowd of masked men jeer. Caro breaks free of Val and runs to me. I try to push back the tears as I lean down and whisper in her ear. "Now, you go on up to Ebba and let her take care of you. Stay away from your mama, you hear? No matter what she says. She's not right in the head these days. And you stay *far* away from that Josiah Bellflower. Promise me. He's rotten to the core."

"I will, Gracie, I promise."

"I love you, kid."

The sheriff jerks my arm, pulls me away.

"Gracie!" Caro hollers again, and the sound of her little voice is almost enough to do me in.

Murphy leads me right past Val on the way to the patrol car. She won't look me in the eye, but I speak to her anyway. "I hope you're happy, whorin' yourself out for that devil," I hiss. "Because that's what he is, Val. He don't care a lick about you."

Val smirks at me, then starts twisting and yelping, pulling at her dress. "Oh, Lord, she's burning me up! Just like she burned Harlan!"

And then it's on. They're all shouting and carrying on. Somebody throws a handful of pea gravel, and it glances off my forehead. Blood trickles into my eye, but I can't wipe it away, so it just flows like water from a tap until it turns my vision red and runs over my lips. Sheriff Murphy pushes my head down and shoves me into the back of his car. The seats still smell like Aunt Val's cheap rose perfume. It makes me gag, and I vomit on the floorboards.

Their ways may have changed, but everything else is the same.

They'll find a way to burn me, just like Anneliese.

Just like Bellflower wants them to.

❦

I swim up from sleep, my back aching from the razor-thin scrap of mattress. I smell fresh-baked biscuits. My belly claws with hunger. The vomiting has passed, but they ain't given me hardly anything to eat in four days, only a few crackers and tiny sips of tepid water from a ladle shoved through the bars. Sheriff Murphy's deputy, Jimmy Adams, sits at his desk, eating biscuits and gravy, staring at me as I go to the corner of the cell and piss in the coffee can they've given me as a chamber pot. I've seen circus animals treated better than this.

"You gonna feed me today?" I ask, wiping myself with a scrap of newsprint. "Can't have your accused dying of starvation before you get the satisfaction of your hillbilly trial. Skinny as I am, it won't take much longer."

The deputy stops chewing and squares me up with his eyes. "You hush your mouth, girl. You'll eat when the sheriff says you can eat."

I shake my head and stalk back and forth. The scent of ashes and smoke comes through the tiny, barred window above my head along with the oppressive, relentless heat. "They finally get that fire out?"

"Not 'fore it got to town. Barely spared the Bledsoe place."

My trial is in two days. I'm imagining most of the witnesses will be against me, and Bellflower will be judge, jury, and prosecution.

The door to the jailhouse swings open. I blink at the sudden intrusion of light. Abby steps into the jail, dressed in black. She never wears black. She smiles at me sadly, then approaches the desk.

Adams shoves in another mouthful of food. "Mornin', Miss Abigail. Ain't your daddy's funeral today?"

"I'm on my way to the cemetery now. I just came to check in on Gracie. I mean . . . Miss Doherty."

"She ain't supposed to have no visitors."

"I brought her somethin' I been meaning to give her. That's all."

"What is it?"

I peer through the bars as Abby pulls a rolled-up piece of paper from her dress pocket. She unrolls it and hands it to the deputy. "It's just a star map. I reckon she can see a scrap of night sky from her cell. Might help her pass the time."

Adams rolls it back up and hands it to Abby. "Fine. You got two minutes, girl. Lemme pat you down, though, first."

Abby raises her arms as Adams pats her up and down, taking his time around her bosom. I glare at him.

"That's enough, Jimmy," Abby says, crossing her arms over her chest.

Adams gives a stiff nod. "Two minutes."

"Yes, sir."

She rushes toward me, her eyes shining with tears. "Gracie, ain't they feedin' you?"

"Nope. Hardly a crumb." Adams has gone back to his breakfast, his back to us, fat rolls hanging over the top of his pants.

Abby follows my gaze and shakes her head. She leans close to the bars, and I take her hand, just long enough to squeeze her fingers. "I'm real sorry about your daddy."

She nods. A tear breaks loose and traces down her face. "It was peaceful as it could be."

"Still . . ."

"Yeah." She swipes at her eyes.

"I wish I could have been there with you. Wish I could be there today when they lay him under."

"It's okay. I'll be all right."

"I know you will be. You're a mountain girl, Abby. We're made tough."

Her lip trembles. "I reckon."

"How's Granny? Caro?"

"Aunt Ebba's still there, keepin' watch. I called on them yesterday. Doc Gallagher came up, checked on your granny while I was there. She's doing good. Still asleep, but stable."

Relief floods through me. "I'm glad for that. Caro?"

"Feisty. That girl has a mouth on her, don't she?"

I grin. "The only thing she got from her mama, 'sides that shock of red hair."

"Val's gone plumb crazy. Out hollerin' on the square, preaching louder than Bellflower."

I roll my eyes. "Figures."

"I got something for you." Abby squats and pulls something from her shoe, fast as lightning. "Seth Cornelison came up to the lighthouse. Him and his family are moving out west. To Montana. He drew that star map he promised you, and said he wanted you to have it." She hands me the rolled-up paper she showed the deputy, but now there's something inside it. I sneak a quick glance. It's a carpenter's nail set, sharpened to a point. That must have been what she had in her shoe. I furtively stash it inside my brassiere just before Adams turns around.

"You've had enough time, girl," Adams barks.

I reach through the bars and grab Abby's hand. "I love you," I whisper.

"Me too." Her eyes spill over again. "Just . . . be careful."

Abby turns away and I watch her go, my heart thudding in my chest. She just took a big risk doing what she did. I'm so filled with love and longing I could cry. But I ain't got enough water left in me for crying.

I sit down on the narrow cot and unroll the star map. Seth labeled everything neatly, but some of the names of the constellations are off. Where the Big Dipper should be written, he's got *Billings*. And where Orion is, *Ranch*. And finally, above Cassiopeia, *MD Safe*.

Realization dawns over me. Morris Doherty. Safe. It's a note, letting me know that Morris made it to Billings. Of all the things going wrong in my world, something is finally going right. Maybe in Montana, Seth and Morris can be free to be themselves. I lay down on the cot, flattening out as my bowels gripe again and a wave of dizziness washes over me. The metal shank rests cold against my breast. I'll have to be careful to keep it hidden until the time is right. But for the first time in days, I have hope.

TWENTY-EIGHT

DEIRDRE

1881

Deirdre arrived at the depot in Rogers, tired from the long journey. She was stunned by how quickly the new town had sprung up around the rail line. There were shops and a stagecoach stand, and the beginnings of new houses all around. Pa had told her many times of the power the railroad held—to build new cities and destroy old ones—but she'd never seen it for herself. It was astonishing.

Famished and thirsty, she walked to the café near the station for a cup of tea and a pastry. She was hurriedly finishing her meal when she caught a glimpse of Robbie outside the window. Deirdre's heart soared. She left a dollar on the table and rushed outside.

"Robbie!"

He turned, his eyes lighting with recognition. "Deirdre Jane? Is that you?"

She picked up her hem and ran toward him. He caught her in his arms and picked her up, laughing. "Why, I hardly recognized you. You sure are a sight for these sore eyes! I just came to get some roofing nails for Pa. Lands, this place has grown, hasn't it?"

She buried her face against his chest and sighed. She was home. Home, and in her husband-to-be's arms. If it weren't for the circumstances, she could have laughed for joy. "Oh, Robbie. I've missed you."

He chuckled warmly. "I've missed you, too. I thought you weren't coming home until later this fall, though."

"I got a telegram from Pa, telling me I needed to get home. Mama."

He nodded. "I can take you, if you like. I don't have a wagon, just my horse, but as long as you don't have much in the way of luggage . . ."

"Just my bag! I left it inside the café. I'll just be a minute."

Deirdre rushed inside to get her bag, and Robbie met her at the corner, where he sat astride his handsome Appaloosa mare, Georgia. He offered his hand to her, and she lifted her skirts and swung up to sit in front of him, hanging her bag from the saddle horn.

He nudged Georgia with his heels, and they were off at a trot. Deirdre sighed and leaned back against Robbie, his warmth and strong arms a sturdy support. Before long, his hands began to wander, and though Deirdre's mind had been far from lovemaking when they'd first reunited, his touch soon sent an undeniable flare of desire through her. When they reached the covered bridge that stretched across Ballard Creek, freshly repaired after the floods, Robbie abruptly pulled Georgia to a halt.

"Why are we stopping?" Deirdre asked. "I should get home, Robbie. Mama—"

"Just for a few minutes, Deirdre," he whispered against her neck. "A few minutes won't change a thing, I promise. The stage would have taken twice as long."

He dismounted and helped her down. They walked beneath the bridge, hand in hand. Once they were well hidden in the shadows,

Robbie kissed her, his mouth searching and soft. She sighed, her hands tangling in Robbie's hair. His kisses had improved by a mile.

He pressed her against the wall of the bridge and began undoing the buttons on her shirtwaist. "I need you so much, Deirdre."

"Here?" Deirdre asked nervously, clutching her blouse closed. "What if someone passes by?"

"They won't. Not at this time of day."

"I . . . Robbie, I just don't know—"

"Shhh," he whispered, silencing her with another kiss. This one was deeper, hungry, hard, and demanding. Deirdre whimpered as Robbie opened her shirtwaist all the way. She cast furtive eyes to either side of the bridge, ears perking for the sound of hoofbeats.

"You're so beautiful," he murmured. He kissed the soft flesh between her breasts, then lifted his head. His eyes glinted in the low light. For a moment, just a moment, his countenance flickered, and he looked like someone else.

Suddenly, he grasped the hair at the nape of her neck, crushing her lips to his as he pulled her to him. Desire flooded through her. She closed her eyes as the ache between her legs became a torrent of want.

"It's time, Deirdre," he growled. "I've waited long enough."

Deirdre nearly swooned as Robbie raised her skirts and found the opening in her drawers. He had never touched her like this. She threw her head back, gripping his shoulders as he worked her with a sureness unlike anything she'd ever experienced. When she shattered, moments later, he lifted her against the bridge's wall and took her. She clawed at his back and clung to him as he watched her with unwavering, depthless eyes. It was exciting—dangerously so—to be made love to in such a salacious way. When she found her pleasure again, she could have sworn she heard Gentry's laughter echoing along with her cries.

After her trembling ceased, he lowered her gently onto her feet. Robbie's eyes, storm gray and searching, met hers in the darkness. "I suppose I've missed you," he said, laughing shyly.

"I've missed you, too. But now that I'm back, we won't never have to miss each other again."

"That's right," Robbie said, his smile dying. He turned his back as Deirdre buttoned her blouse and smoothed her crumpled skirts. Guilt warred with her lustful satisfaction. She thought of Mama, sick and dying at home. What if their little tryst had cost her more than a few stolen moments?

Just as she feared, when Deirdre saw the darkened windows of the cabin, she knew she was too late. She gave Robbie a hasty kiss, hoisted herself from Georgia's back, shouldered her bag, and broke into a run.

She found Pa on the porch, his head cradled in his hands. At the sound of her rushing through the grass, gone long and weedy, he lifted his gaze and stood. He was thin. Haggard. "Deirdre . . ."

Pa opened his arms and she rushed into them. His ribs quaked and he shook, crying and murmuring in German.

"How long?" she asked, pulling back.

Pa blinked, his eyes red-rimmed and bleary. "Two days. Funeral's tomorrow."

Her shoulders fell. Denying herself with Robbie wouldn't have made a difference, after all. "Can I see her?"

Pa nodded. "She's laid out in the parlor." He cleared his throat and threw back his shoulders in his proud Werner way. "I'll start some tea. Are you hungry, poppet?"

Deirdre's stomach gave a hearty rumble despite her grief. The food in the café had been middling and spare, and her shoulders ached from sleeping on the cramped second-class banquette, wedged between the other passengers. "I reckon so. After I take my time with her, 'course."

Pa nodded brusquely and opened the door. The cloying scent of lilies crawled up Deirdre's nostrils. It was always lilies or roses at a wake—their strong, sweet perfume helped mask the stench of death.

She took off her lace gloves and pulled in a steadying breath. Regret and guilt clashed within her. The last words she'd spoken to Mama had been harsh. And Mama's to her. Their relationship had always been contentious, fraught. But for all that, Deirdre still knew the softness within Mama's hardness. The calm way she delivered babies and soothed mothers. The way she'd come into Deirdre's room for evening prayers, and her patience with teaching Deirdre about the saints and how to read the Bible.

She followed Pa inside, steeling herself. He'd done things well. Candles were lit on the mantle and black crepe draped over the mirrors and windows. The fine casket sat upon trestles, smelling of freshly hewn pine. Mama's head rested lightly on a lacework pillow, her garnet rosary wound around her crossed hands. But she was a husk of the robust woman she'd once been. Beneath her finest calico, the jut of her hip bones was visible. Her collarbone and wrists were as fine and brittle as a sparrow's bones. Her lips were chapped and slightly parted, enough so Deirdre could see the blackness within.

Pa cleared his throat. "I'll leave you to it."

Deirdre put her fingers to her mouth and squeezed her eyes shut for a moment, gathering her senses and her words. Perhaps Mama's spirit still lingered here. Perhaps she might glean some solace from saying what she'd meant to say had Mama still been drawing breath.

She leaned close to the casket, so Pa wouldn't hear from the kitchen. "Mama," she began, "I'm sorry I didn't make it home in time to see you. I tried. I promise I did."

The clock on the mantle ticked on, measuring the time that Mama would never experience again. It was surreal, how everything continued, how everything kept *on* after a person died. Shouldn't time stop for grief, even for a moment, so one might catch their breath before things started moving again?

Deirdre tilted her head back. A long, wavering sigh escaped from her mouth. "I've learned a lot since I been away. A lot more than manners and fancy talk. I've learned about life and how people love each other. And even though the secret I kept for you tore me up inside, I think I understand." A long-held tear flowed down her cheek.

"I fell in love in Charleston. I never thought I could hold space for more love in my heart than I felt for Robbie, but I fell in love, all the same. There's a girl—she's so pretty, Mama. Sweeter than clover spun honey. Her name's Esme. She's upset at me for leaving her, but I had to.

"I understand now how you could love Pa and Arthur. Both. There's all kinds of love, and one ain't any better than the other. And I also understand that bein' a woman ain't the easiest thing, and sometimes a woman's got to find her peace and happiness wherever she can. I forgive you. And I hope, wherever you are, you can forgive me, too."

Deirdre wiped the wetness from her eyes and bent to kiss the cool dryness of Mama's forehead. "I love you, Mama. And I'm so glad to be home."

⊱⊰

Deirdre sat across the table from Pa, trying not to look at Mama's empty chair. He slid a mug of steaming tea toward her. She stirred milk and two spoonfuls of sugar into it and swirled a circle with her spoon. Her hands shook. "Did she go easy?"

Pa nodded, working his top lip under his teeth. "Easy enough. I had the priest come down from Blue Eye. He heard her confession and gave her the last rites, the way she wanted."

"She looks good, Pa. You did good."

Pa made a sharp sound at the back of his throat, somewhere between a laugh and a cough. "I ain't never seen a corpse look good, Deirdre Jane. But folks always find the need to say that, I reckon." He smiled for the first time since she'd arrived. "How was the school?"

"It was good, for the most part. Met some friends. Learned how to dance and talk right." Nevertheless, her hill cadence had already come back. Her vowels were longer than the June solstice. It was good to be home and among people who weren't always putting on airs. Charleston was pretty, but it wasn't where she belonged.

"I'm glad," Pa said, nodding again. "I didn't want to tell you this while you were away, but Hannah Bledsoe's little one died. Took sick with some sort of fading malady."

Deirdre sat back in her chair with a hard huff of air. She thought of the soft, warm smell of Collin's baby-soft skin, the giggles and coos she could coax from him as she rocked him. She took a swallow of her tea. It was sad, but babies died all the time for all sorts of reasons. It was part of life.

"June. That's when her young 'un died. Your Mama took sicker than I ever seen her around then, too. I quit the railroad to take care of her. I've a mind they'll let me come back after everything's settled, though."

Deirdre searched the corners for shadows. She absently stroked the healed-over cut on her palm. She wondered about Phoebe. If Mama's healing with Gentry didn't hold true, Phoebe's might not, either. The thought blackened her mood even more.

Pa brought a loaf of molasses bread out from the hearth, and they sat together in amiable silence as they ate. After they finished, Deirdre fidgeted in her seat, the question she most wanted to ask on her lips for a long time before she put it forth. It was hard to speak of her own future, with Mama dead in the other room. "Robbie brought me home. I saw him in Rogers. Goodness, has Rogers grown, just like you said it would." She took a sip of her tea. "Has Robbie been by yet? To ask for my hand?"

Pa wrinkled his brows. "No, poppet, he hasn't. And there's something I need to tell you, but I didn't want to say it in a letter." He reached out, his calloused hand warm over Deirdre's, which had suddenly gone cold. "He's married Ingrid."

Everything slowed down. "Ing?"

"I'd hoped he'd tell you himself. They got hitched a month or so ago. I was afraid Maja was gonna have to get her shotgun out. Ingrid's bigger than the broad side of a barn with his child. I'm sorry, poppet. There are other fine men. Better men than Robbie. Why, there's a young engineer . . ."

Papa's words faded as a thousand feelings ran through Deirdre at once. Anger. Embarrassment. Hurt. She stood from the table, shaking.

Pa shot up from his chair. "What's the matter, Deirdre Jane? You look like you're going to be sick."

"I . . . I just need to take the air, I think."

"You want me to come out with you?"

Deirdre shook her head. "No. I need to be by myself for a while, Pa. I'll be back afore dark to help with supper."

She tied on her cloak and went out, tearing through the grass and up the rain-slicked hillside before she could lose her nerve. The lighthouse loomed over her, the cozy stone shack at its base streaming a friendly column of smoke from its chimney. Georgia was tied to the hitching post, her spotted flanks shining with sweat. He'd ridden hard after leaving her. Ridden hard to get back to Ingrid.

Deirdre stalked to the door and raised her fist, giving three brisk knocks.

Ingrid opened just as she raised her fist for the fourth. Her great belly nudged outward, round and full as a bushel bale. She smiled. "Deirdre. I didn't know you'd come home."

Deirdre opened her hand and sent a stinging slap to Ingrid's cheek. The other girl stepped back, her eyes widening.

"How could you, Ing?"

"How could I what?" Ingrid lifted her chin. Deirdre's handprint blazed red against her pale skin. "I was with his child before you even lay with him."

"*His* child. And how can you be sure it's his? I know you."

Ingrid smirked. "What does it matter?" Ingrid said haughtily. "All of our farmhands have gone. Left to work for the railroad. Only my brothers are left to see to our farm. Robbie was here, and you were gone. I had to marry someone, Deirdre. You'd have done the same, if it were you."

"No, Ing. I wouldn't have." Deirdre fought back the tears prickling at the corners of her eyes. She wouldn't give Ingrid the pleasure of seeing her cry. "No wonder you didn't write to me in Charleston. No wonder you were so keen to have me do the vinegar rinses. How long have you secretly hated me?"

Ingrid pressed her lips together. "I don't hate you. I never could. Life's just easier for girls like you. Girls with pretty faces and straight teeth. All you need do is blink your eyes and men fall at your feet. For me, I always had to give more than a smile to turn a man's head. You can't see how you're the lucky one." Ingrid rubbed her belly. "But you needn't worry about Robbie. I make him plenty happy."

"Is that so?" Deirdre pulled the barb of hurt free and used it as a weapon. "He picked me up at the station. Pulled the wagon over on Ballard Creek and showed me just how much he's missed me. He probably still smells like me, if you doubt it."

Ingrid scowled. "I never meant to hurt you, Deirdre. But you'd do well to stay away from my husband."

"He wrote to me. Sent me a lock of his hair. Told me he loved me." Deirdre hated the tremor in her voice. The desperation.

A tear leaked out of Ingrid's eye. How dare she cry!

In the shadows behind Ingrid, Deirdre caught a flicker of movement. Robbie emerged from the murk. He laid a hand on Ingrid's shoulder. "Ingrid, let me talk to her."

"No. Anything you can say to her, you can say in front of me, husband. We both deserve as much."

Robbie's eyes hardened. "Go back in the house, Ingrid."

Ingrid gave an exasperated sigh, and turned away, muttering as she waddled back into the cottage. Robbie took two steps toward her, and Deirdre stepped backward. He smiled sadly.

"I'm sorry, Deirdre. I didn't know how to tell you. I was only with Ingrid once. And then . . . this."

"How long have you known about the baby?"

He sighed and rubbed a hand over his hair. "She told me in May. Right after you left."

"I hate you," Deirdre spat. The tears came boiling out of her eyes, hot and fast. "If you only knew what I've given up for your sake."

"I'm sorry. I meant everything I said in my letter. I did. We could still do everything we did before. Ingrid will never know. I don't love her." He took another step toward her. "You're all I think about. Those sounds you make. Your body." His hand brushed her waist and she flinched away.

Disgust rolled through Deirdre. "I wanted to be your wife, Robbie! I wanted to have your children. Now I can't stomach the sight of you. The two of you deserve all the unhappiness that will surely befall you." The words held all the gravity of a curse.

"Don't you dare speak those words over me and my house, Deirdre Werner."

"Are you afraid of me?" Deirdre barked a laugh.

"Maybe I am. A little. People talk. Say you brought on that flood and everything that followed."

Deirdre lifted her chin. "I want my portrait back. I paid good money for that."

Robbie reached into his trousers pocket and produced the cabinet card she'd sent him. "I keep it with me all the time. You sure looked pretty."

Deirdre snatched the photograph, remembering how she and Esme had argued over Robbie's loyalty on the day she left Charleston. Dearest, darling Esme. Steadfast and true. Deirdre swallowed back a sob.

"I'm real sorry about your ma," Robbie said.

"So sorry you had to pull me over on the side of the road to have one last poke! All you think about is yourself. You always have. I hope Ingrid knows how faithless and feckless you are."

"I didn't mean it to be like that. I don't know what came over me back there, on that bridge—didn't even feel like I was there, just like I was watching." Robbie reached for her again. "Ain't there any way we can work through this, Deirdre?"

"No. And don't come calling for my help when Ingrid's time comes. Maja delivered every one of her babies on her own and so can Ingrid."

Deirdre turned on her heel and walked away, her back straight and proud.

Once she was in the cool safety of the cedars down the mountain, she fell to her knees and sobbed out her hurt and grief. This was all Gentry's doing. She'd fallen into his trap, into his web. It had been him, there on the bridge, taking hold of Robbie's body so he might trick her and take what she'd promised with her own blood. She was sure of it. She saw his hand in everything now—how he'd used Phoebe to drive her and Esme apart. How he'd manipulated her to poison Phoebe so she might weaken to him. She was too foolish, too lovelorn and impulsive to see it before. Rage pummeled through her. She screamed, the torn edges of her voice shattering the silence and bouncing off the trees. High above her, a limb cracked, and then crashed to the ground.

TWENTY-NINE

GRACELYNN

1931

I wipe the sleep from my eyes and blink at the wan light coming through the tiny window above me. It ain't yet dawn, but the moon is a waxing crescent, casting everything in the jail cell in an eerie gray pallor. I sit up, my head throbbing from hunger and dehydration.

If I've counted the days right, it's the morning of my trial.

Yesterday afternoon, I overheard Sheriff Murphy talking in hushed tones to his deputies. They ain't got permission from any prosecuting attorney to try me for any sort of crime. There's been no hearing. No formal charges. It's because they ain't got proof, just circumstantial evidence. But they're gonna do it anyway—in a kangaroo court of their own making, with Bellflower as magistrate.

Everything to this point has been set up by Bellflower. The deaths after his false healings. The fire. Harlan. All arranged to turn the townsfolk against me. He wants to make me desperate, so I'll cave to his will. Become his vessel—whatever that means.

I'm still pondering things as I rise and pace my cell like a cat in a cage, running my hand along the bars. I've tried and tested them all, focusing my will. I try again, clenching one of the bars until my palm stings and burns. Iron.

As dawn pinks through the window, I sit and stand, stretch and flex muscles that are so tight and dry they might snap. In the distance I can hear the steady rhythm of hammers. I wonder if they're building a gallows for me. Or a pyre. Will there be a jeering crowd, calling for my death, like there was for Anneliese? Will the whole town turn out to see me hang or burn?

I palm Abby's shank, rolling it back and forth in my fingers.

Sheriff Murphy's keys rattle in the lock. As I hide the shank inside my brassiere, he comes in, dressed in a freshly pressed uniform. He's carrying a tray of food, and my mouth waters at the smell.

"I brought you a proper breakfast, Miss Doherty. You'll need it for what's to come."

I rush to the bars like an eager dog. He slides the tray through the opening beneath the bars, then hands a steaming mug of coffee through to me. I fight the urge to fling the hot liquid in his face. But I ain't strong enough to try anything foolish right now. Besides, I could use the coffee for my headache.

I wolf down the food. It's the best thing I've ever tasted in my life. Scrambled eggs with cheese mixed in. Bacon. A side of buttered grits with gravy. I gulp the coffee and it scalds my tongue and throat, but I don't care one bit. I feel almost human again.

After I've finished, I pick my teeth with my fingernail and push the empty tray back to the other side of the cell. When the sheriff shuffles over to collect it, I ask for more coffee, and he shakes his head. "Trial starts in half an hour."

"Ain't I gonna get to talk to a lawyer before I go? The accused have a right to representation."

"It ain't that kind of trial, girl, and you know that. Al Northrup wants justice for his son, and he means to get it however he can." Sheriff Murphy pulls the brim of his hat down over his forehead. "If I were you, I'd start prayin' now."

Deputy Adams and Hosea Ray come in a few minutes later and haul me out of the piss-scented cell. They push me outside, where the brightness of the morning sun blazes into my eyes, blinding me and washing the dirt road in purple and red spots.

"Climb up in the back there," Murphy says, motioning to Hosea's truck.

I put a knee on the tailgate of the Ford and crawl up. Jimmy Adams follows and sits down next to me on one of the hay bales stacked along the side. The scent of chicken feed and sweat rolls off him. He wraps an arm around my hip, snugging me up to him. "Jus' in case you think about tryin' anything funny," he says, and laughs. He's breathing heavy as his fingers start kneading my thigh through the filthy fabric, hard enough to bruise. I'm glad I can't hear people's thoughts anymore. I'd hate to hear the smutty thoughts he's likely thinking.

When the truck starts moving with a lurch, my guts tumble. I ate too much, too fast, after not having food for days. I lean over and vomit, my breakfast landing on Jimmy Adams's polished shoes and splashing on the bed of the truck.

"Dammit, girl, why'd you up and do that for?"

I wipe my mouth on my shoulder and raise my head. He's bent at the waist, fumbling with his handkerchief and cussing under his breath. The sausage-pink sliver of flesh above his collar is vulnerably soft. I could stab him with the shank and launch myself over the edge of the truck bed, hit the ground with a roll, and make a run for it before Hosea could throw the truck outta gear.

I could. Right now. If my hands were free.

I been too afraid to try anything since they came to arrest me—too afraid I'd make things worse for myself.

At this point, I figure I've got nothing to lose.

While Jimmy Adams mutters to himself and wipes my sick off his shoes, I pull in a deep breath and close my eyes. The tree scar on my back warms, radiating threads of heat all through my bones. I imagine the handcuffs unclasping. Falling free.

I will it so hard, I feel it happening.

A stunned gasp escapes my lips. I wriggle my fingers and move my wrists apart. They're no longer fettered. Somehow, someway, my hands are free.

But I'm smart enough to play like they're not. I squelch my sense of wonder and steady my breathing, as much as I can. I'm trembling all over. Adams looks at me, his expression of irritated disgust slowly morphing into something else. Fear.

"Your eyes. Land sakes, girl. What the hell . . ."

I spring back to give myself room to strike and pull the shank free from my bodice. Without hesitating for even a breath, I stab at his fat neck. But I don't allow for how much my hands are sweating, and the blow lands crooked. He yelps in pain and stumbles backward, but there's just a thin trickle of blood running down his collar, not the flood there would have been if I'd aimed true.

"Sheriff!" he hollers. "Stop the truck. Prisoner's escaping!"

I haul myself over the side of the truck bed, hitting the rocky ground hard. I roll to the ditch and stumble to my feet just as the Ford grinds to a halt.

There's the sharp bang of a pistol shot, and a bullet whizzes past my head. Sheriff Murphy is the best shot in Tin Mountain. I got lucky. But my luck won't last.

I still have to try. For Caro. For Abby. For Granny. I make for the trees and run as fast as my legs can carry me, knowing any minute now I'll feel the burn of the bullet that'll end me.

THIRTY

DEIRDRE

1881

A month after Mama's funeral, Deirdre shrugged off her melancholy as best she could, dressed in her Sunday best, and walked to Hannah Bledsoe's house. She was shocked at what she saw. Long grass grew along the porch, and Hannah's prize rosebushes were choked with weeds, their buds long spent. The windows were dim and shuttered, as if the great house lay under a spell.

Deirdre grasped the circlet in the lion's mouth on the front door and rapped three times. No sound came from within. Deirdre knocked again. On the third knock, the door flew open. Deirdre had expected to see Mary's freckled, smiling face, but another maid stood there—this one tall and thin, with stringy auburn hair and deep hollows beneath her cheekbones. Her belly poked beneath her crooked sash. She was pregnant.

"Hello, I'm here to see Mrs. Bledsoe?"

The woman laughed, a dry cackle that shook her bony frame. "Don't you recognize me, Deirdre?"

Deirdre stumbled backward in surprise. Familiar green eyes blinked at her slowly. "Hannah?"

"Come in, silly goose," Hannah said in what was meant to be a coy manner, but instead had the opposite effect.

She followed Hannah into the dark house. Inside, filth surrounded her. Empty milk bottles sat near the door, seeping viscous liquid onto the Oriental rug. Maggots crowded one of the bottle necks, writhing in an orgiastic mass. Deirdre's gorge rose at the sight.

"I do apologize for the mess!" Hannah said lightly, over her shoulder. "Mary quit months ago, so I've had to mind things on my own."

"Where's Mr. Bledsoe?"

"He's likely still out west. He's invested all we have in the Frisco rail line. I haven't seen him since the baby died."

"I was sorry to hear about that, ma'am," Deirdre said, genuinely. "Collin was a fine boy."

"Oh, yes, yes he was." Hannah sighed heavily and led Deirdre through to the parlor. The tabletops were stacked with unopened mail and newspapers. Empty cups tinged with dry tea and plates crusted over with food lay atop every surface. Deirdre gingerly pushed aside a tin of cookies to sit, and a mouse crawled out, squeaking at her in irritation before scurrying away.

She had seen grief. She knew the bitter taste of her own melancholy. But never had she fallen to this depth.

"I'm so sorry, Mrs. Bledsoe. But this ain't somethin' I was expecting to see." Deirdre gestured at the once-fine surroundings. "Are you all right?"

Hannah sat heavily on the cluttered divan, tears springing to her eyes. "No. Isn't it obvious?"

"I can help you set things back to right. That's why I'm here. To show my gratitude for what you did for me, just like I promised. Pa's headed out west again and I need the work."

"Did you like Aunt Beryl's school?"

Deirdre blushed, remembering Esme and the lazy Charleston afternoons they'd lain tangled together. "Yes, ma'am. I sure did. I learned a lot. And I'm much obliged to you for sending me there."

"I heard about your mother's passing. I'm so sorry about that."

"Well." Deirdre cleared her throat. "She's in a better place. No longer in pain."

"That's what folks say. But all I can think about is my baby in the cold ground. I want to dig him up sometimes. Did you know, Deirdre? I read in the magazines that Mr. Lincoln did that with his son, after he died. That he went to Willie's tomb, took him out of his casket, and held him. Talked to him. Couldn't let go. My daddy didn't much care for the man, but I understand why he would do such a thing. It's so very hard to let go."

Deirdre didn't quite know how to respond. "But it looks like you've got another on the way. Won't take the place of Collin, but it'll surely help you mend."

"I'm not sure it works like that. Besides, this one's different. It's not Billy's baby. Nobody knows that. Nobody even knows I'm expecting."

The color drained from Deirdre's face. "Hannah . . . I . . ."

"Oh, what have I done!" Hannah burst into tears, hiding her face in her hands.

"Who . . . whose baby is it?"

"It's the groom's baby—Mr. Blake. We got to talking one night, over whiskey, shortly after you left for Charleston. I'd been so lonely, so sad. And he listened." Hannah's mouth wrenched. "Being with him chased the misery away for a little while. The loneliness. Shouldn't I have a little bit of happiness, Deirdre?"

"I think . . . I think I know some manner of what you're talking about." Deirdre thought of her sweet stolen moments with Esme, and how delicious it had been to give in to her urges. But Deirdre had no husband to bind her. She was free to do whatever she wished. Though her husband was absent, Hannah was still a wife. "Where's Mr. Blake now?"

"Oh, he left, of course. They always leave, don't they?" Hannah's lip trembled and her skeletal hand rubbed her belly. "I wasn't expecting this. Especially so soon after Collin. By the time I figured it out, it was too late to do anything about it. No one knows except you. No one else can ever know. My daddy would disown me if Billy divorced me. I don't know what he'll do if he comes back and finds me like this."

"I see."

"Now that you're here, things will be all right, won't they, Deirdre? You'll help me figure it all out?"

Deirdre glanced out the hazy windows, at the rubbish crowding the edges of the room. The scent in the house was overpowering—moist and heavy, like meat gone to spoil. It would be a daunting task, recovering the house from Hannah's melancholic neglect. But what else could she do? Being Hannah's companion would give her purpose. And money, besides. Money that might someday return her to Charleston, where she could live with Esme and her husband—if Esme could ever forgive her for the way they'd parted. She'd write to her. Beg for understanding. There might be a chance. Hope was all she had left to cling to.

She reached out to grasp Hannah's frail hand. "We'll fix things, Hannah. We will."

❧

A month later, Deirdre was cleaning the larder when she realized she'd missed her menses. A few days after that, a rank biliousness relieved her of her appetite. She'd rinsed with vinegar water after she and Robbie had been together the last time. Had been drinking her tea. But the signs were unmistakable. She was with child. Panic set in as she realized what it meant, and the true nature of the promise Gentry had made to her:

In fifty years, I'll return to reap what I have sown.

Deirdre was certain Gentry had possessed Robbie on that bridge. Spilling his seed into her. Now, this child—whatever it might become— was growing inside her. She was tempted to take dire measures as Anneliese had to prevent its birth, but she could not bring herself to destroy what was half her own. Instead, the drive to nurture the life growing in her strengthened every day. She would not let Gentry lay claim to what was hers. She would find a way to protect her child.

❦

Deirdre told no one about the baby. Not even Hannah. Her breasts grew heavy, pendulous, and tender. Her wherewithal ran low. One frigid afternoon in December, as Hannah lay soaking in the bath, Deirdre raised a question. "Would you think about hiring more help, Hannah? It's becoming hard to manage things, just the two of us. Perhaps one of the girls from town might come by once or twice a week to help? Just for the day."

"Oh?" Hannah sat up, water splashing over the edge of the tub. "Who did you have in mind? It has to be someone who can keep my secret."

"I saw Ebba Nilsson at the mercantile a few days ago. Ingrid's younger cousin."

"That strange child? Does she still not speak?"

"No. Not English, anyway. That's why I thought she might be suitable."

"I suppose it couldn't hurt, if you think she'll keep quiet."

Deirdre went to fetch Ebba from the Nilssons' farm that same week. Maja came to the door, her careworn faced creased with deep

266

wrinkles. She offered Deirdre a seat by the fire and a mug of spiced tea. Deirdre tried not to look at the rag rug in front of the fire where she and Ing had often played with their dolls as little girls. Losing Robbie had hurt. But not as much as losing Ing. She'd been tempted to go back up the hillside to apologize for the harsh things she had said. But the thought of seeing Robbie again made her blood boil. Her hatred—and her pride—ran far too deep.

A few moments later, Ebba stepped into the room. She'd grown taller, and had lost some of her fey, childlike whimsy. She'd be a handsome woman, someday. She shyly came to Deirdre's side, and Deirdre offered her hand. Ebba took it and smiled. "*Tack*, Deirdre."

"She's been good help to me with Ingrid gone and Petr abed with a fever," Maja said, swaying heavily to the hearth. She plucked the lid of the crock and stirred the hearty-smelling pottage within. "But, if Mrs. Bledsoe pays her well, the money will help us more."

"Hannah pays more than what's fair," Deirdre offered. "Ebba will have money to spare and enough to save for a healthy dowry, someday, too."

Maja nodded brusquely. "Good, good. Off with the two of you, then."

It would be the last time she'd see Maja alive. A week later, Petr died, and Maja sickened from caring for him. She was dead within a week. The eldest Nilsson boy, Erik, followed soon after. By taking Ebba from the Nilssons', Deirdre had not only given her work but had likely saved her life.

Ebba was a hard worker. She seemed to hear Deirdre's thoughts before she spoke them aloud and would rush to her side to help in whatever task she needed. When Hannah's time came, one late February afternoon when the sun blinked dimly through the trees, Ebba helped boil water, gather linens, and sopped Hannah's brow as the labor pains became fierce. Deirdre coaxed Hannah through the pushing, but unlike little Collin, this baby came headfirst and easy into the world.

It was a girl—fat and healthy, with a mass of red hair and an angry little face to match. Hannah was distant. She refused to hold or even name the baby, so Deirdre named her instead: Valerie.

When Ebba was emptying Hannah's chamber pot a few mornings later, she found an empty bottle of laudanum and brought it to Deirdre. In a panic, Deirdre flew upstairs, woke Hannah from her catatonic sleep, and shoved her fingers into Hannah's mouth until she vomited.

Hannah apologized, over and over, her voice slurred and heavy. "I just want to sleep, Deirdre, why won't you let me sleep?"

When Deirdre found her the next day, cold and still and pale as the grave, she shook Hannah, slapped her face. Cried her name, over and over, and even pounded her breast in a vain attempt to start her heart. It was too late. Hannah was dead, just as she'd seen in her vision on that stormy night months ago.

Before she sent for the coroner, a revelation came to Deirdre, growing and spreading like a quick-rooting tree. A way she might undo the past and the desperate promise she'd bound with her blood.

Deirdre handed little Valerie to Ebba. "Take the baby to the carriage house and keep her quiet," she told Ebba. "No one can know she's here. And no one can *ever* know who she belongs to. Do you understand me, Ebba? Especially Mr. Bledsoe."

"Yes, Deirdre. I will be secret," Ebba said, speaking the first words Deirdre had ever heard her say in English.

The next day, Deirdre found an attorney's calling card beneath the blotter on Mr. Bledsoe's desk. She went to the post office straightaway to send a telegram. When Billy Bledsoe came home four days later from California to bury his wife, his black hair had gone white, and Deirdre never knew the man to smile again.

THIRTY-ONE

GRACELYNN

1931

I don't get far. Just as I reach the edge of Sutter's holler, all the strength goes out of me. My side howls with pain. My knees give way and I collapse in the underbrush on all fours. Sheriff Murphy and his men approach, crunching through the underbrush. This is it. This is where it ends.

"She's over here, Sheriff." That's Hosea Ray. "I think she's hurt."

"Good! Little bitch stabbed me!" Adams bellows. He stalks over and yanks me up by the elbow. I spit in his face. He wrinkles his nose and clenches my arm so tight I just know he's gonna break it.

"That's enough, Jimmy," Sheriff Murphy says. "Turn her around and I'll cuff her again."

I laugh. "You mean you ain't gonna shoot me while I'm an easy target?"

"If I wanted you dead, girl, you'd'a been dead with that first shot. We're takin' you back to town, and you're gonna act right this time, hear?"

"I'm dead now or dead later. If it's all the same to you, I'd rather face your gun than burn."

Sheriff Murphy just grunts and cuffs me. I can barely walk, but they pull me along until we're out by the open road again. It's high noon and the sun is hot as shit.

They haul me into the cab of the truck, and this time I'm wedged in so tight any hopes of escape are impossible. I rock my head back against the seat. Stars flicker behind my eyelids.

Sheriff Murphy nudges my chin with something cool. I open my eyes. It's a flask. "It's just water, girl. Drink up."

The water is crisp and cold, soothing the dry scratch at the back of my throat. "Thank you," I manage, licking my lips to moisten them.

He grunts again and shoves the flask under his seat. Hosea starts up the truck and heads toward town. I try to use my magic again, but in the suffocating heat, my thoughts bounce all over the place. My concentration breaks every time Hosea hits a rut in the road. I'm weak. Wrung out like a mop. A few people linger alongside the road, watching us go by. The church steeple rises in the distance. Sure enough, on the square, right in front of the statue of Andrew Jackson, they've got a new scaffold built, a gallows at its center.

So, I'm to hang, not burn.

"That's just for me, ain't it? Don't I feel special. First time there's been a hangin' in what, twenty years, Sheriff? And a woman, at that!"

Hosea pulls up in front of the church steps. Bellflower stands there, all dressed in black robes, like he's done this before. When I climb out of the truck, he looks down at me coldly. "Now that our lady of the hour has arrived, shall we begin?"

The church is packed, the pews so crammed that wives are sittin' on their husbands' laps. Everybody's turned out for the spectacle. Heads swivel toward me as I'm led up the aisle, flanked by Bellflower and Sheriff Murphy. They sit me down at the front of the church, at a table facing the pulpit.

"Can you at least uncuff me now?" My voice shakes, betraying my nerves. I've never been more terrified.

"Not with what you pulled in the back of that truck," Sheriff Murphy says.

I scan the crowd for any friendly faces, and finally see Abby toward the back. She meets my gaze and gives me a sad smile. She looks pretty today. She's wearing a different black dress that does wonders for her figure. A wave of sadness washes over me. If I end up dyin' today, I'll be glad we had what we had. I never thought I'd fall in love or feel any kind of wanting after what my daddy did. But I'd felt it with Abby.

Ebba and Caro aren't there, and I hope that means they're keeping vigil with Granny. All I've done is worry about home since I got arrested.

Bellflower knocks a gavel against the pulpit. "Good people of Tin Mountain, we have gathered to bear witness against the enemy in our midst. Miss Gracelynn Doherty has been accused of arson, murder, and witchcraft. Let it be known that as a god-fearing people, it is our duty to cast out transgressors. We must purge the canker of evil before it festers and grows."

Somebody cries out. It's Aunt Val, standing off to the side of the altar. She grips her stomach like she's in pain and howls. More theatrics.

Bellflower points at Val and shakes his finger. "See how the witch tortures this woman. How she suffers in the grip of wickedness?"

A murmur goes up from the crowd. Before long, other people are twisting in their pews and crying out. Some start speaking in tongues. It takes everything in me not to roll my eyes. These people have gone insane. Every last one of them.

Bellflower hammers the gavel on the pulpit like he's driving nails into my coffin. "Do we have anyone who would bear witness?" he intones.

"I will." A woman stands off to my left. It's Nadine Clark, the woman whose baby died of colic after being *healed* by Bellflower. A baby I'd delivered two months ago, healthy and perfect.

She comes forward. Bellflower holds out a book—most assuredly not a Bible—and Nadine puts her hand on it. He murmurs something and she nods, then takes a seat next to the pulpit, crossing her legs at the ankle. She seems calm and sure of herself, and it frightens me more than Val and the folks who went into hysterics moments before. Calmness is credibility.

"Mrs. Clark, can you tell me how you know the accused?" Bellflower asks.

"She delivered my baby and checked in on us after his birth."

"And was there anything unusual about her behavior when she attended you?"

"No . . . not then. She was nothin' but kind and helpful."

I wrinkle my brows. *Not then.* What the hell is she getting at?

"I see. But in the days after?"

Nadine's lip trembles. "It was around the first of May when things took a turn. Danny started runnin' a temperature and got sicker as the days went on. And . . . and I started *seein'* things."

At this, a hushed murmur comes from the crowd.

The first of May was when Bellflower showed up. Walpurgis Night.

"What did you see, Mrs. Clark? Can you describe it to us?"

Nadine crosses and uncrosses her ankles and fiddles with the clasp on her handbag. "Well, I suppose it sounds crazy, but I started seeing *shadows* around Danny's crib. A cold draft would blow through the room, even though no windows were open. I'd hear whispers in the night, and felt a dark presence, like somebody was at the end of our bed, watching me and my husband."

272

The hair stands up on my arms.

"Go on," Bellflower urges. His eyes glint in the red-stained light coming through the window depicting Christ's Passion.

"Danny just kept gettin' sicker, no matter how hard I prayed. His fever would come and go, and he coughed constantly, all through the night. Wouldn't nurse, neither."

Nadine's lip trembles again and a tear breaks loose from her eye and plops onto her lap. Even though she's helping convict me, I can't help but feel sorry for a mother who's lost her only child.

Bellflower hands her a handkerchief and she dabs at her eyes. "And then one morning, just before dawn, when I went in to check on him, he was floatin', pastor. Above his crib.'

"Come again?" Bellflower cranes his neck, confusion etched across his sharp features.

"He was floating. Levitating, like. Just a few inches off the mattress. That's when I knew the things I'd been seein' and hearing were real and that Danny's sickness weren't only of the flesh, but an *oppression*. That's when I brought him to you."

There's more murmuring from the crowd. Bellflower comes out from behind the pulpit and starts up his characteristic pacing. He raises a hand to hush the noise. "And the boy got better, after I'd laid hands and prayed over him, yes?"

Nadine nods. "Yes. For a couple days. He was himself again. It was a miracle." She breaks into tears again, her mouth forming a pained rictus. "And then I found him one morning. All cold and still. I tried to wake him. Held him, rocked him. But he was already gone."

I clench my fists behind my back. It sounds like some sort of ague—a common fever that could have likely been cured if Nadine had come to me or Doc Gallagher instead of believing in Bellflower's nonsense. So much senseless death. So much suffering.

Anger surges through me, steaming like hot pavement after a cold rain. I stand, my knees shaking. They won't give me a chance to speak my mind, so I'm gonna take it myself.

"Nadine, I'm real sorry about your loss. But I didn't have nothin' to do with Danny's sickness or death. Or any of the other things you just talked about. Me and Granny have always been good to you. You know that." I jerk my chin toward Bellflower. "This man's got y'all fooled. If Satan's in this so-called courtroom, he's working through Bellflower. Or whatever his *real* name is."

A roar goes up from the townsfolk, bouncing off the high ceiling of the church. Bellflower frowns at me and stalks back behind the pulpit, banging the gavel. "The accused will not speak unless called upon to do so."

Sheriff Murphy grabs me by the arm and pulls me back down into my seat. "Girl, if you don't behave and hush your mouth, I'll put a gag on you and tie you to this chair."

"So that's the way it is, huh?" I hiss. "They can say whatever they want about me, but I can't defend myself? You're a fair-minded man, Sheriff. Always been a good man, by my reckoning. I delivered every one of your young 'uns and every one of 'em's still alive. Can't you see how wrong this is?"

Sheriff Murphy just looks away, shamefaced.

Bellflower dismisses Nadine and calls Al Northrup to the stand. He looks like he ain't slept in a month of Sundays. Here we go.

"Mr. Northrup, my condolences on the loss of your son." Bellflower is doing the fake sympathy thing again, his voice all syrupy sweet. My bile rises. "Can you tell us what happened on the night of the fire, to your best recollection?"

"I . . . um, I was there with Harlan and his girl. Abigail. We was just watchin' the service when I noticed Miss Doherty. She come walking through the crowd. Somethin' weren't right about how she moved."

"In what way?"

"She slithered, like . . . like a serpent on two legs."

Oh, good Lord.

"Is that so?"

"Yes, sir, and when she got to the front, and was facin' you, I saw her eyes go all white. Then the fire started."

This makes me even more nervous. Everything else he's said is hogwash, but this . . . this could have the ring of truth to it. My eyes must do something strange when that fiery surge washes over me. More than one person has said the same. It's the truth in the middle of the lies that'll prove to be my undoing.

"And after the fire started, you lost sight of Harlan?"

"Yes, sir. And that girl, she was just standing there, off to the side, watching as everything burned. She was smiling, almost like she was proud."

"Thank you, Mr. Northrup. I won't ask you any further questions. You've been through enough."

One by one, Bellflower calls more witnesses. People I've tended while sick. Men and women Granny has known since they were babies. They tell their tall tales—each one wilder than the next. A man, made of shadow, walking backward through a cornfield. A cat with human eyes. Children bitten and scratched in their sleep by unseen entities. Blood coming up from wells and springhouses instead of water. A black wolf with glowing, red eyes.

The specter of a beautiful woman, singing in Sutter's holler.

I believe that story, told in a soft, hesitant voice by little Corinne Baker, because I've seen her, too. Anneliese.

The rest are Bellflower's parlor tricks.

The same kind of nonsense he told me he manifested with the Sutters: Disembodied voices. Doors slamming of their own accord and bedclothes stripped from virgins' beds. Unseen lovers in the night.

With each witness, the tension grows inside the packed church. The sun drops low in the sky. The light fades to a sickly yellow green, like it does before a storm. I blow at the hair falling into my eyes, sweat beading along my brow and sliding down my neck. Somebody throws open one of the windows, and a blast of humid, dense air rushes in, sending the chandelier above the center aisle rocking.

Bellflower looks straight at me with a smug grin. "I call Miss Calvina Watterson to come forward and bear witness."

I swallow hard. Calvina may be the only person he'll call that might speak up for me. I hope she'll hold true to her word.

She makes her way to the front, dressed in black with a corsage pinned to her dress. It's a mourning bouquet; orchids tied with black ribbon. Her mama must have died, just as she feared. My heart jumps to my throat.

She takes a seat at the altar and pokes a stray strand of hair behind her ear. She won't meet my eye. It ain't a good sign.

"Miss Watterson, is it true that your mother passed away yesterday?"

"Yes, sir. She did. At the hospital up in Springfield."

"I'm so sorry to hear that. And what was her cause of death?"

"She had complications of a broken hip. Arthritis."

"But lately, she'd made a full recovery, isn't that right?"

Calvina's eyes dart to me, and then flicker away. "Y . . . yes. For a bit. After your healin' service, sir."

"Can you tell us what led you to believe Miss Doherty might have had something to do with the recent fall that brought about your mother's death?"

He's leading her—coaxing her to say what he wants. I stand up. "You're full of horseshit, Bellflower."

"Goddammit. Sit down!" Sheriff Murphy yanks me back down onto the hard wooden seat.

"So sorry for the interruption, ladies and gentlemen." Bellflower smiles beatifically. "Now, could you please answer the question, Miss Watterson? You told me that your mother saw something right before she fell. Something unnatural. It swooped down from the trees."

Calvina grips the handkerchief so hard her brown knuckles turn white. "I can't recall, sir. Things have gone fuzzy the past few days."

At this, Bellflower frowns. "Are you sure? Because I remember quite well. When you came to me, just last night for counsel, you told me a creature that looked like Miss Doherty, but had leathery wings and sharp talons, came swooping out of the pines. Your mother took off at a run, tripped over a stone, and fell."

Calvina presses her lips together and looks away. "I don't know about that." For once, I wish I could *really* read people's minds, so I could know what Calvina's thinking.

Behind me, the talking gets louder. Some people start moaning and carrying on again.

One lady near the front points up at the ceiling. "I see a creature! Can't you see it? Up there by the light. It's perched atop of it!"

Sure enough, the chandelier starts swaying harder, as if something or someone is pushing it back and forth. The wind has died, so it's not that. I wonder if it's another of Bellflower's distractions.

Bellflower bangs the gavel. He's getting frustrated. Angry, even. For the first time, he looks to be losing control. "Miss Watterson, did you or did you not tell me that a foul, demonic creature accosted your mother?"

Calvina starts crying then, fat tears rolling down her face. "I can't do this," she murmurs, just loud enough I can hear her. "I won't."

"What did you say? You must speak up, Miss Watterson."

Calvina stands, her eyes wide. "I said, I can't do this! *You* put those words in my mouth, sir. You said you'd pay for my mama's funeral if I promised to—"

Bellflower pounds the gavel on the altar. It flies out of his hands. The chandelier above starts twirling in a mad circle. Something's happening here, and it's not me making it happen. Not even Bellflower. Not this time. I wonder if it's Anneliese.

"Sit down!" Bellflower commands.

Calvina shakes her head and stabs her finger at the townsfolk. "Now, y'all listen, and you listen good! Miss Doherty and her granny ain't never been nothin' but good to me and everyone else in this town. This man's a false prophet and he's got you half blind and foolish with his lies, and y'all better wake up, 'cause if you hang that innocent girl, you'll bring a curse down on this town, the likes of which you never seen. Now *that's* a vision I had from the Lord Himself. You can mark it."

Calvina shrugs like she's satisfied and steps down from the altar. I smile at her, tears of gratitude filling my eyes. She nods at me as she walks down the aisle and out the door. After she leaves, everybody starts talking at once.

Bellflower glowers at me, his eyes boring holes into mine. I don't flinch. I don't even blink. He tries to retain order, tries to refute Calvina's testimony, but the cacophony of voices drowns him out. The energy in the room has changed. He's losing control of his flock for the very first time.

There's genuine fear and hysteria now. A pair of young girls fall out of their pew, howling and clawing at their hair. One of them faints. A froth of spittle bubbles from her mouth. Aunt Val comes screeching out of the corner, her arms covered in oozing, red scratches. She latches on to Bellflower's arm. He pushes her away, a look of disgust on his face. "She sent her creature down from the rafters. It did this!" she cries, holding out her arms for the congregation to see. Blood drips from the scratches. If she did that to herself, I can't help but admire her dedication to her act. Damn.

Some menfolk take out their guns. This ain't good. All it'll take for this to turn into a massacre is one idjit hillbilly popping off a shot. Next to me, Sheriff Murphy cocks his sidearm. I turn my head to see I'm facing down the barrel of a gun.

"Better my gun pointed at you than theirs."

He ain't wrong, but my trust of anyone in authority here has long since gone.

Bellflower finally manages to calm the rabble. The church goes silent again, apart from the wild creaking as the chandelier sways above our heads. Sheriff Murphy slowly lowers his pistol. I pull in a shaky breath.

"I now call the accused to testify," Bellflower intones. "Miss Doherty, if you claim to be innocent of the crimes of which you are accused, now is your opportunity to prove it."

How on earth can I prove anything? Especially when Bellflower already wants me dead so his demon can claim my body? This is just part of his sideshow game.

I stand once more and move forward, feeling a hundred pairs of eyes pinned on my back. I fold myself wearily into the chair at the front of the sanctuary and try to focus my hunger-crazed mind. Whatever I say or do next, I need to be careful and choose my words wisely.

Bellflower steps down from the pulpit to stand in front of me. He regards me coolly. "When did you come to Tin Mountain, Miss Doherty?"

"In the winter of my fourteenth year."

"And how did you come to live with Deirdre Werner?"

"She's the mother of my aunt by marriage. Valerie."

"So, you bear no blood relation to her?"

"No. I do not."

"Interesting." Bellflower walks back and forth in front of me, three times. "Miss Doherty, will you stand, and turn your back to the congregation?"

Acrid, cold fear winds up my throat. I sit, stock-still, afraid to move.

"If you are innocent, you've no reason to be concerned by what I've asked. Now, please stand."

I reckon I don't have much of a choice, so I do as he says. When I feel his hands, cold on the back of my neck, I freeze. Then, in one motion, he rips the flimsy jailhouse shift I'm wearing down to my waist, exposing my back to the crowd. There's a collective gasp. Bellflower runs his fingers up my back, tracing the treelike lines of the witch rash. Where his fingers touch my flesh, it burns like fire.

"Deirdre had the same mark," he whispers in my ear, his hand resting between my shoulders. "So did Betsy."

"Leave her alone! Don't you touch her!" It's Abby. She rushes up the aisle, her eyes feverish. She nearly gets to Bellflower before Sheriff Murphy wrestles her away. "Get your hands off me!" She thrashes, wild as a bobcat. "Gracie!"

Murphy wrangles her outside, into the churchyard.

Suddenly, a loud groan sounds from above, metal twisting and screaming as it's wrenched from wood. The chandelier crashes to the floor, landing on some of the congregants. They fight their way out from underneath it. I see blood on the floor.

Everything devolves into chaos. Val pulls on Bellflower's arm, and while he's swatting her away, I see my chance. I run for the door at the side of the altar and into the rectory, then outside. Humid air hits my face like a wet mop. Storm clouds boil on the horizon. Big ones, all gray green and lit with lightning. People stream out of the church like they're running from the devil. I reckon they are, they just don't know it. High above, in the steeple, the bell starts tolling erratically. The air crackles with static.

I'm too weak to run, so I hide instead, tucking behind a gravestone at the rear of the church. I've never been the praying sort, but I pray now. I don't know what else to do. I never wanted any of this. Bile rises into my throat, and I retch onto the parched ground, vomiting raggedly.

And then I see Abby. She stumbles through the churchyard and its helter-skelter stones. Her eyes are wet with tears. "Gracie!" she hollers. "If you can hear me, you've gotta run! They're gonna kill you if you don't. I'm so sorry! I'm so, so sorry. I should have spoken up for you sooner!"

I rush out from between the graves. "Abby!"

When she hears me, she turns, smiling as she starts toward me. Then, her smile fades as footsteps beat through the cemetery behind me. Abby screams. "No! Leave her alone!"

Someone grabs my wrist, wrenching my arm. I howl as the fine bones shatter.

"Here she is! I got her!" Al Northrup bays. "You're gonna pay for what you done to my boy, you little whore," he hisses, rank spittle hitting my face. "Right here and right now."

THIRTY-TWO

DEIRDRE

1882

Deirdre's labor pains came on late in the day as a storm crackled over-head, lightning cleaving the sky over the mountainside. The first cramps hit her low in the back, just as they did with her menses. She was able to walk them out easily, so she drew more water from the springhouse, stoked the fire to make tea and porridge, and watched the clock.

Within a few hours, the pains had worsened. They now felt like hammer blows. She chewed on a shard of willow bark to ease the pain, but it did little to help. The next cycle was fierce enough to pull the first childbirth cry from her throat. Valerie startled in her sleep at the sound, little fists flying above the top of her crib.

Apart from hasty trips to the mercantile, for which she wrapped herself in shawls and corseted herself tightly to hide her growing belly, she had sequestered herself in her cabin with Valerie after Hannah's death, keeping Hannah's secret and her own well tucked away. Winter was colder and fiercer than any winter on record, and Pa had wired her to say he would remain in Colorado until summer. At first, she'd found this fortuitous. It was one less lie she'd need to tell. Now, with late spring in full flower, and not even a letter, she was certain he had fallen to some wilderness calamity and would never return. She was likely an orphan now.

How would she bear this baby on her own, in secret, without anyone knowing? What if something went wrong, as it had with Hannah the first time? She didn't think the baby was breech—she'd felt little feet wedged between her ribs often enough in the past few weeks to gather the baby was pointed in the right direction—but still, she was afraid.

She might make it to the Nilsson farm before her pain grew so keen it tied her to the bed. Ebba lived there alone now. Deirdre had always trusted Ebba. Could trust her to help bring the baby. But then Ebba would be party to her secret. Gentry might come back and use Ebba just as he'd used Phoebe and Esme.

The thought brought a clench of raw grief and regret as the next spasm seized her. A moment later, a warm trickle ran down her thigh. Her waters had broken. She lifted her skirts to inspect them. Clear, no hint of black or green. It was a good sign.

The cabin had grown far too hot. She'd stoked the fire to excess. She stripped down to her shift and contemplated throwing open a window to let in the cool, rain-soaked air. If she did that, somebody down the hill might hear her labor cries and come nosing around.

No one in Tin Mountain could ever know about the baby.

But *he* would know about the baby.

She still dreamt of him sometimes. Her shadow demon. Still imagined him watching her as she lay alone in the darkness, awaiting his seed to flower fully in her womb. He'd said he'd return in fifty years, but what if he refused to wait? What if he appeared as soon as the child was born, to spirit her away to some snarling netherworld?

It was a girl. She was sure of it. Had dreamt of her, too. The beautiful woman she would become.

Her stomach hardened and clenched once more, stealing her breath. Deirdre grabbed hold of the bedpost and worked her way to the floor, on her hands and knees. She rocked slowly, rounding out her spine and arching like a mad cat, measuring her breath and counting through the pains. The shaking time would come next, and her body would take over for her then.

Valerie stirred in the crib, letting out a long, reedy cry. Deirdre swore. She worked her way up from the floor and crossed to the crib, picking the baby up and shushing her back to sleep. The child was always restless. She was thin, too. Deirdre had been tempted to bring Valerie to her own breast for sustenance, but was afraid it might trigger an early labor, so she'd had to suffice with syrup-sweetened goat's milk from Ebba's farm.

Just as Valerie had settled, a knock came at the door. Deirdre froze, her breath hitching with another contraction. The knock came again, louder this time. Valerie woke fully, her face reddening as she wailed.

"Deirdre! It's Ebba."

Oh, how happy the bright sound of Ebba's voice made her! But Ebba couldn't know about this baby. No one could know about this baby.

"Deirdre! I know. I have known about the baby all this time. Open this door!"

She crawled to the door and pressed her forehead to the cool wood. "Is there anyone with you?"

"No."

Deirdre cracked open the door. Ebba stood there, an angry look furrowing her brows. She clutched a hatchet in her hands. Deirdre's eyes widened.

Ebba shrugged. "To cut the pain. Or cut down the door if you refused to open." She strode past Deirdre. Shoved the little ax beneath the bed, then went to Valerie's cradle and began rocking it with her foot. "You are stupid, doing this by yourself."

"How did you know I was with child?" Deirdre worked her way slowly to the bed and crawled atop the eiderdown.

Ebba tapped her head with her finger. "I know things and see things. Just like you."

Deirdre moaned as another cramp claimed her breath. She opened her knees. "Come have a look, down there," Deirdre managed. "Tell me if you can see the baby's head."

Ebba washed her hands in the basin, then knelt between Deirdre's legs. "Yes. I see her hair. Almost time?"

"Yes. Almost time."

Within minutes, Deirdre was trembling from head to toe. The urge to push overrode everything. Ebba urged her on, with gentle words and singing, until, with a triumphant last push, the baby slipped free. It was a girl, just as she'd known it would be. Deirdre rubbed the baby briskly to warm her and brought her to her breast, unexpected tears springing to her eyes. "Fetch the scissors, over there, Ebba. Pour boiling water over them, and bring them, along with a length of twine. You remember what we did with Hannah?"

"Ja. Tie the cord in two places, tight. And cut between the knots?"

"Yes, I'll help you through it."

An hour later, Deirdre was weary, but wrapped in a kind of drowsy, lovesick fog. She looked down at the perfect baby sleeping in her arms, her crisp cupid's bow mouth, and the feathering of blonde eyelashes resting on her cheeks. She had little hair, but what she did have was fair as Ebba's. She wasn't a monster at all—just another sweet, innocent babe who had never been asked to be born. Deirdre stroked her cheek gently, pushing back the stab of bittersweet pain that coursed through her. Her eyes darted to the corners, searching among the shadows, dreading the glint of silver she might see lurking there. But thankfully, blessedly, Gentry did not appear.

Valerie woke and gave a short, sharp cry. "Bring her to me," Deirdre said. "I can feed her from my breast now."

Ebba rose from the rocking chair next to the bed and brought Valerie. Deirdre guided her to her breast. At first, the baby seemed unsure what to do, as Deirdre had only ever fed her the goat's milk from a false teat. But soon, she'd latched on, her little mouth fierce with hunger until she was milk drunk and satiated.

Deirdre's mind spun with possibilities. She might raise them like sisters. Twins. She could tell people their father was dead—a young man she'd met out east and married there. After a time, no one would be able to tell they were three months apart. She could even leave Tin Mountain and start fresh somewhere else with both girls, but with no money and no husband, it would be hard going. Esme had not responded to Deirdre's letters, but Deirdre felt no animosity. That chapter in her life had closed. She was on her own. Always would be.

Keeping the babies wasn't a possibility. She would steel herself and do what must be done. The grimoire had shown her. The sooner she followed things through, the easier the loss would be to bear.

⁕

Deirdre opened the grimoire, lit a candle for each cardinal direction, then stood next to Ebba on the wide, flat rock where she and Robbie used to tryst. The moon shone high overhead, casting enough light to see by. Her baby lay sleeping in the center of the stone, swaddled in white fabric, and protected by the pentacle she'd drawn across the stone with salt and imbued with prayers to her mother's God and the Virgin who bore Him, and to the older gods of her ancestors.

She hoped it was enough to keep whatever darkness might be lurking in the shadows well away.

Deirdre held a knife high to the heavens, where the blade might catch the moonlight and be purified by it, then read the incantation from the grimoire, written in Anneliese's hand.

"I stand today and ask for the gods' favor and the blessing of the eternal Mother. I mark a sign of my sacrifice with willing blood, so that they might find my purpose true and strong."

Deirdre drew the knife across her palm, once, then again, in the shape of a cross, blotting out the scar she'd made when she'd bound herself to Gentry.

Ebba sang out in Swedish, raising her hands heavenward.

"As the Virgin blessed her own beloved Son, I bless my own flesh and bind it with my blood. For protection and a shield against those who would seek to harm her—in body or in spirit."

Deirdre knelt on the stone, and using her thumb, made the sign of the cross on the sleeping infant's forehead. "My shield I place on you, for as long as you live, my daughter. May you be protected and hidden from evil, as long as you live." She kissed her baby's small hand, and stood, turning to Ebba. "Give me your hand, my friend. Swear to me that you will keep your vow of silence for all of your days."

"I swear it, Deirdre."

Deirdre made a shallow cut on Ebba's palm. The girl winced, then smiled. They pressed their bleeding palms together, locking eyes. "By the blessed mother Mary," Deirdre said.

"And the blessed mother Frigga," Ebba echoed.

"So mote it be."

Deirdre and Ebba stood looking at one another for a long moment, the heaviness of their oath lingering between them. They were sisters now, bound by a blood covenant.

Finally, Deirdre spoke. "Tomorrow will be harder."

Ebba nodded, her eyes filling. "Hidden things have a way of turning up, Deirdre. But we will try."

"We will. We must."

❧

By night, St. Louis was silent, the city hunching over the river and its barges. Deirdre stepped from the paddle steamer. Ebba followed, carrying Valerie. "The orphanage is around that corner, next to the cathedral. I can see the spire from here," Deirdre whispered, low enough that the few people on the pier wouldn't hear her. "St. Mary's."

They walked solemnly, in silence, until the cathedral loomed in front of them. Next to it was a three-story brick building, with a statue of the Virgin Mary behind its gates. A single light shone through one of the downstairs windows. They went up the steps. At their knock, a world-weary sister answered, blinking at them with tired eyes.

"May I help you?"

Deirdre motioned toward Ebba. "I've brought my sister's child, and my own. As neither of us are married, we are destitute and cannot afford to raise them properly."

The nun raised a suspicious brow. With Ebba being only twelve, the lie was a little far-fetched. "We've only room for one infant, not two. With the winter being as harsh as it was, we've too many orphans and not enough beds."

"No." A wave of panic flew through Deirdre. To her great shame, she began to cry. "Please. Can't you take them both? They're good babies."

The elderly sister sighed, her eyes softening "I cannot. I can sense your desperation, my child. But please know that the baby you choose to give up will be cared for and loved. Infants are easily placed in good homes."

Deirdre looked down at the child of her own flesh and blood. In fifty years, Ambrose Gentry would return to collect on her foolish debt. To collect her only daughter and the promise she'd made out of desperation.

She only hoped the ritual from the grimoire had worked. Hoped it would hold. She supposed she would know in fifty years' time.

Deirdre took one long last look at her daughter. She was sleeping, breathing calmly in and out. She'd never know the difference. She'd grow up far from Tin Mountain. Safe from curses and oaths and vengeful demonic preachers. She kissed the baby softly and handed her to the nun. "Please take care of her. Her name is Ophelia."

THIRTY-THREE

DEIRDRE

1931

Deirdre woke, shrugging off the heavy mantle of time and the trance she'd fallen under. Old memories taunted her. A tear traced the line of her cheekbone and slipped into her ear. Esme. Mama. Ophelia.

She'd dreamt of her daughter most of all—willowy and tall, with fair hair and clever blue eyes. It had been foolish, giving up Ophelia. It hadn't done a damn thing to undo the oath she'd made. Ebba had been right. Things hidden always had a way of turning up.

Deirdre had suspected Gracie might be her own from the moment she'd arrived on Tin Mountain, skinny and underfed, with that tangle of blonde hair and those blue eyes—the Werner eyes. And now she knew the full measure of the folly she had created. She'd protected Ophelia with her ritual and her words. But she hadn't thought far enough ahead—that Ophelia might have a daughter of her own.

But *he* had, and he'd tricked her.

She had to protect Gracie.

"Deirdre, are you awake?"

Deirdre turned her head. Ebba floated into focus. Her oldest friend. Her truest friend. "I need water, Eb."

Ebba brought a glass and Deirdre drank it down, chasing the dryness away. She sat up, her head swimming. "How long was I asleep?"

"Over a week. Where did you go, Deirdre?"

"The past, mostly. Spirit walking. Remembering what I've done. But it's time now, Ebba. Time for me to set things right and give Anneliese her reckoning and cast that demon out for good." Deirdre stood, steadying herself against the bed frame. "He said he'd come back to reap what he'd sown. And he has." Deirdre shook her head. "I've been watching from the spirit realm. Tried to intervene, at the church. I bought Gracie some time, but we have to hurry."

Ebba sprang up and rushed to her side. "You are too weak, Deirdre. You must rest first. Eat."

"Dammit, I'm a mountain girl, Ebba. I've *never* been weak. Now get me my grimoire."

❧❧❧

Deirdre knelt on the ground, the heavy, wet wind lashing her hair. All her regrets crowded around her—her grief over giving up Ophelia, her selfishness, how easily she'd fallen into that demon's cunning hands.

Even if it took every last breath, every last drop of her blood to make things right, she would.

For Gracie.

Deirdre opened the grimoire. The flaming tree stretched across its pages. She gently ran her hands over it. Heat bloomed beneath her fingertips.

"I'm sorry, Anneliese. I'm sorry I wasn't strong enough. I'm sorry I disappointed you. But I need you to help me now. I need you to show me what to do so that this spell won't be in vain and I might undo the mistakes I've made, for once and for all."

Anneliese's voice rang out, bell-like and pure inside Deirdre's head.

Willing blood, Deirdre. Willing blood. Be strong. Invite me in and I will do the rest.

Deirdre nodded. "I understand." She prayed to the old gods and the new, and called upon her ancestors for strength, women whose names she knew only from the grimoire. Their voices became a chorus in her head, drawing power from the earth and the air. The clouds above churned and heaved, like a womb ready to give birth.

Deirdre kissed the knife's blade and raised it high.

And then she bled.

THIRTY-FOUR

GRACELYNN

1931

It's my twentieth birthday. I just now realized it. In my mind, I replay everything I might have done differently over the past twenty years, if I had the chance. I might have spoken up sooner, in that courtroom. Might have never come to Tin Mountain. Might have left on a train to San Francisco long before my daddy died. Might have never been born at all.

Surely that would be better than dying like this.

Al Northrup steers me to the scaffold. The townsfolk are gathered there, faces colored by the eerie, greenish light of the impending storm. Al grasps a handful of my hair and hauls me up the steps.

"I didn't kill your son," I say through clenched teeth. "Bellflower did."

"Shut up," he mutters. "You'd say anything to save your skin."

Thunder crackles. Old Liberty stands in the distance, lit up by lightning. Its beam is dark for the first time in almost a hundred years. I glimpse Abby in the crowd, her face streaked with tears. She tries to fight her way to the scaffold, but the men hold her back, jeering.

I whisper *I love you* as my heart begins to skitter out of control.

I'm going to die and there's so much I didn't get to do. So much I never got to see and feel.

A cold, piercing rain starts up, stirring the dust and bringing a hot metallic smell like cordite. The townsfolk cheer and start to dance. The long drought is over. Praise the Lord.

On the other side of the square, I see Bellflower. The crowd parts for him, a look of reverent awe on their faces as he climbs the steps and comes close, his breath like sulfur. He ties my hands with a hank of rope. My broken wrist yelps in pain. "You foolish girl," he rasps. "I tried to make things easy. I would have protected you from them. Taken you gently. Easily. Now the simpletons will have their show."

He turns to the crowd. "Good people of Tin Mountain, see how the heavens open and smile upon you! And this is but the beginning. This act of justice will purge the evils of witchcraft from Tin Mountain forever and bring prosperity to the land once more."

The crowd cheers. Then they start chanting. At first, I can't make out the words. Then they get clearer, louder: "Hang the witch!" A rotten egg lands at my feet, foul and stinking. More sour food and offal hits me. The rain turns to hail, pelting my face with ice, and the sky roils above me. Al Northrup brings the noose down over my head and steps away.

It's just me and Bellflower. He turns to me and smiles.

"Do you have any last words, Miss Doherty?" he intones. "A confession will bring rest to your soul. I can offer you forgiveness. Peace."

"I don't want your kind of peace."

"Very well." He tightens the noose under my chin. Panic claws up from my belly. I try to slow my breathing, try to concentrate and call up any power I might have left, but it's like trying to scrape up hard dirt with my fingers. My palms are slick with sweat. A whimper escapes my lips.

"Don't worry. It's not a long enough drop to break your pretty neck," Bellflower whispers in my ear. "Only long enough to steal your breath until I've claimed you. You will be my greatest miracle yet. A resurrection."

"A resurrection of somebody they wanted to kill," I rasp. The noose digs into my tender skin. My vision blurs. "You've made them hate me. You think they'll celebrate my resurrection? You didn't think that through very well, did you?"

He laughs. "I've glamoured this entire town—bent them to my will. I can glamour them again. They'll worship you. Adore you. Together, we'll do great things. You'll see." I think of Granny and Caro. If he takes over my body, what will happen to them? Whatever's left of me once he's taken possession of my body won't have the strength to protect them. After all, whatever humanity remained within Nathaniel Walker had done nothing to save Anneliese.

I have to try. I have to fight.

I close my eyes. I breathe in. Every breath is precious right now. Every beat of my heart has new meaning. Every second loaded with a thread of hope.

In my head, I pray, because prayer is all I've got left right now.

Anneliese, help me . . .

God, if demons are real, maybe you're real, too, even though you were never there when I was a child—when I needed you most. Help me now . . .

An eerie sense of calm descends over me. The sound of the crowd fades to silence. A vision plays out behind my eyes. It's Anneliese, writing in the grimoire by candlelight. Her quill flies over the paper. Her childlike voice chimes in my head:

His name. You already know his true name, Gracie. Speak it. Drive him out. Banish him. You will know when the time is right. I will do the rest.

I remember now. The night before I had the awful vision of Bellflower at the lighthouse, I'd pleaded with the grimoire for help. At first, I thought the fancy letters in Anneliese's journal entries had spelled a nonsense word. Could it have been a name instead? Could it be *his* name?

I open my eyes. Bellflower is staring at me, his hands raised to the sky and his eyes flickering with an eerie silver light. Shadows snake out from his body and move up mine, trailing an ice-cold path across my skin.

"Mezrith," I whisper, testing the word on my tongue. No, that's not right. "Merthoz."

"Mezroth . . . ," I whisper. That's it. "Mezroth."

The air stills. Bellflower's eyes go wide. His glamour flickers and the truth beneath his beauty shows itself for a hairsbreadth of time. A few people up front gasp. They see it, too.

"Shut up," he growls, low and menacing. "Shut up, you stupid girl."

"Mezroth!" I say again, louder. I could almost laugh, I'm so giddy. Maybe I've gone mad.

Lightning dances overhead. Suddenly, it's like all the oxygen has been sucked out of the atmosphere. And then I see it.

Anneliese's reckoning.

◦◦◦

The hail has stopped. The rain has stopped. Everything has stopped, except for the clouds, churning above. And for once, it's not Bellflower—Mezroth—who's responsible for the stillness. A strange, high-pitched scream like a train whistle comes from the southwest. The townspeople turn as one, no longer interested in my hanging. "Cyclone!" Hosea Ray yells. His hat lifts from his head and blows away.

I work my hands free, just as the wall of the wind hits, full-on. Everyone scatters. The storm sends down a rippling rope of wind, chewing up everything in its path. I claw the noose from around my neck, pull in a wheezing breath, then scramble beneath the scaffolding. I wrap my arms and legs around one of the posts.

Everything is chaos. The roar is deafening as the tornado passes overhead. Crashing wood. Shattering glass. Groaning metal. My ears pop and my head pounds with pressure. I scream along with the wind. I scream until I don't have any breath left.

And then, almost as quickly as it started, the storm stills, bringing with it an eerie calm.

I crawl out from beneath the scaffolding and see a wasteland where the town once stood. Wreckage is everywhere. Cars and trucks are tossed about like children's playthings. The church steeple is on its side in the middle of the square, its century-old bell cracked. A single cow moos forlornly in front of what's left of the mercantile. There are people lying everywhere. I work my way through the wreckage. The first person I come to is Nadine Clark, her right ankle bent backward at an unnatural angle. I kneel at her side. She looks up at me. One of her eyes is swollen and red.

"Gracie . . ."

"It's okay, Nadine. You just stay still. I'll get help."

"I think it's broken. My ankle. I got hit in the head real hard, too."

"I can see that. Other folks have things a lot worse, though, so I need to check on them. I'll come back to you, I promise."

She grips my arm. "Please . . ."

I gently pry her fingers from my arm. "It's all right. You just stay here. I'll try to find Doc Gallagher."

All around, people cry out for help. I can't do much with a broken wrist and no medical supplies, but I tend to the injured as best I can. A few townsfolk stumble out of what's left of their houses to help. I want to leave, go back up the mountain, but I dread what I might find. Our cabin has survived many a hard storm, but this is unlike anything I've ever seen.

All of a sudden, a single truck comes rumbling down the street, painted with Norse sigils. Goats bleat from the back. It's Ebba.

She slams on the brakes and jumps out, spry as a jackrabbit. "Help me, Gracie. Help."

I rush forward, still not quite believing I'm alive. Everything feels like a dream.

Ebba opens the passenger door, and Granny nearly falls out into my arms. She blinks up at me, and smiles. "Gracie."

I almost start crying. "Good to see you awake."

"Good to see you alive. We have to hurry, though. He's coming. Get me on my feet."

Ebba and I help her out of the truck. Her left wrist is bandaged, blood seeping through a hastily tied dressing.

"What happened?"

"The ritual. The reckoning. It required a little blood, that's all," she says weakly. "But we're only half done."

Suddenly, the hair on my arms stands up and a strange chill raises goosepimples on my skin. Granny's eyes widen and fix on something behind me. She gasps.

I look over my shoulder. A man stands in the middle of the road. He's handsome and sly, with dark hair and flashing green eyes. I don't know who he is. Until he laughs. No matter what guise he takes, the laugh is always the same. He snaps his fingers, and the rest of the town goes still. People freeze in place, their mouths agape at the destruction around us.

"Ambrose Gentry," Granny says coyly, "the years have been kind to you."

"I wish I could say the same for you, my love."

"I was *never* your love." Granny shakes free of me and Ebba and walks slowly toward him.

"Still, we had our moment, didn't we? And it was worth it, don't you think? She's exquisite," he says, looking at me.

"She is. But she was never yours. Never will be." A tear threads down Granny's cheek. She brushes it away angrily. "You tricked me. First, with your words. And then, on that bridge."

"Neither one of us was pure, Deirdre. You know that." He smiles sadly. "You tried to trick me as well. Hid *our* child away with your powers. It would have been easy for me to destroy you if I'd wanted to. I didn't want to. It was more fun to let you think you'd won."

"Oh, Ambrose. We aren't finished. Not yet. *She* isn't finished." Granny reaches out, cups his jaw. He closes his eyes, and turns into her hand, kissing her palm. She stands on her tiptoes, whispers into his ear, and then kisses him, full on the lips. The air crackles with witching. The years suddenly fall away, and a young woman stands in Granny's place, voluptuous and auburn-haired, her fair skin as smooth as mine. Anneliese.

The sun blazes blood red along the horizon, coloring everything scarlet. "You've come back, Betsy," Gentry says, opening his eyes. They've gone from a lurid green to a depthless black. His youthful glamour fades, until an ancient, decrepit man stands before us. "I suppose you want your vengeance."

"It's time to reap what you've sown. Just as you vowed. You're not the only clever one, you know."

Ebba and I come to Anneliese's side. She reaches for my hand, and then Ebba's. "Mezroth, I banish thee," she says softly.

"Mezroth, I banish thee," Ebba echoes.

I draw in a breath, his cursed name ready on my tongue.

Mezroth's countenance flickers. He transforms once more and I'm almost undone. This time, it's Abigail looking at me, beseeching and soft. "Gracie, I love you. Don't do this." She reaches out. "Don't you want to be with me? If you let him in, we'll always be together. Just let him in."

"You're not Abby," I say through clenched teeth. "I'll never let you in, you demon!"

He roars in anger. A rush of wind, like the beating of giant wings, nearly knocks me to the ground. I step back in horror, hiding my eyes. Mezroth laughs, shadows unfurling as he rises above me. "Afraid to look upon your maker, granddaughter?"

Panic ices my tongue. I'm frozen with fear. Helpless and small, like a rabbit caught in a hawk's talons.

"Now, Gracie!" Ebba screeches. "Be strong!"

"Mezroth . . ." When I speak his name, the earth shakes, toppling me. I fall onto my bad wrist, screaming as pain lances through my arm like hot metal. I scramble backward, clumsy on the rocky ground. I shield my eyes as the demon's wings unfurl once more. This is it. This is where it ends.

"You stupid girl," he hisses, and hurtles toward me.

"Mezroth! I banish thee!" I scream, with all my might. He howls in agony and drops like a stone at my feet. Writhes in the dirt, clawing at the ground. His now-useless wings fall to tatters, his glamour desperately shifting from one incarnation to another. He tries to rise, then falls. Tries to rise again. He's pitiful—a weakened shade of the arrogant, awesome creature he was just moments before.

Anneliese comes to my side. She takes my hand, helps me to my feet. My skin prickles with electricity. She smiles at me, her eyes filled with love. Gratitude. Peace. Then, she turns to Mezroth, regarding him quietly.

His eyes dim to a dusky blue. Their inhuman shine fades, replaced with something far more tender than I ever expected to see. He's little more than a boy, a youth caught on the cusp of one and twenty. Nathaniel.

There's a sudden heaviness to the air. A pall of sorrow I wasn't expecting to feel.

"I'm sorry," he rasps. "I loved you. I did. Please forgive me."

"I can't, Nathaniel," Anneliese says. "But at least now . . . at least now you can rest. And so can I."

He collapses with a mournful sigh, and begins to crumble like ash, until he's nothing more than gray dust carried off by the wind.

Anneliese closes her eyes for a moment, then whispers beneath her breath. Suddenly, she's Granny again, wearing all of her sixty-nine years once more. She's never been more beautiful.

Sound crashes into my ears. The broken town slowly comes back to life. Doc Gallagher pulls up in his black Dodge and rushes out to see to the wounded. An ambulance whines in the distance. More help is on the way.

Granny takes my hand. I rest my head on her frail shoulder.

"Is it over?" I ask.

"It's over, Gracie. Let's go home."

THIRTY-FIVE

GRACELYNN

1931

There ain't much left of Tin Mountain. What the fire didn't burn, the tornado plundered. Ten people died that night, including Al Northrup and Deputy Adams. Their bodies were found several miles away, in somebody's cornfield.

Ain't nobody seen Aunt Val, though somebody claimed a vaudeville dancer at a traveling show over in Carroll County looked an awful lot like her. That'd be fitting for Val. She was always a good actress.

The townspeople who are left are hollow. Haunted.

They come up the mountain and leave offerings at our door—tokens of apology as precious and rare as a roasted chicken, or a chocolate cake, with a hastily written note attached saying how sorry they are about all of that witch business with that preacher man, and they sure hope Granny gets better soon.

She's still weak. But she's strong. And I know she's gonna pull through just fine.

She was near death when we got back up the mountain that night, but something told me to lay my hands on her, and the healing words came to my tongue. She'd spilled her own blood to unbind the promise she made and summon Anneliese's spirit so that she might have the strength to face Mezroth. I gotta hope that, between the three of us, we drove that demon out for good and set Anneliese's spirit to rest. I suppose we'll see in fifty years' time.

As for me, I'm bruised and broken, but alive, of course. I'm at the kitchen table, writing all this down with my good hand in the grimoire, because I've a mind to teach Caro the ways of witching, and I don't want to forget anything that happened.

There's a knock at the side door, and I figure it's just another delivery of mournful mashed potatoes or contrite corn bread. Caro goes to answer it. She comes back to the kitchen, a look of confusion on her face. "It's some old lady. Says she's from Hannibal. Where's that?"

"It's up by St. Louis. Lots of fancy people live there." I stand and stretch, smoothing out my apron. "Can you put the kettle on, Caro, just in case she wants tea?"

"Sure thing, Gracie."

I go out to the porch. Granny's sleeping on her daybed. I can see the lady pacing out back. She looks nervous as a cat on a hot tin roof, her fancy patent leather heels sinking into the wet ground. I ease the screen door open, so as not to startle her. "Can I help you, ma'am?"

She startles anyway, taking two steps backward and laying her hand across her chest like prissy ladies do in the movies when they're about to faint. Then she starts crying. Hell.

"Are you all right?"

"I'm . . . I'm so sorry. Oh, my heavens." She sinks down onto the steps, her handbag falling from her elbow to her wrist. She digs a lace-trimmed handkerchief out of it and presses it to her eyes. "It's just that you look so much like her."

"Like who?"

"Like my daughter."

⁘

Esme Faulkner sits across from me, her teacup rattling against the saucer as she sips from it. Her eyes skitter toward Granny. "I didn't know if I should come. Didn't know if she'd still be living in Tin Mountain or living at all. You never know when you get to be our age."

"How do you know Granny?"

"Deirdre and I were friends. In Charleston."

I'm wary. It's possible this woman could be telling the truth, but I've never heard Granny mention an Esme. "Charleston? I didn't know Granny lived there."

At this, Esme's lip trembles. "I figured she wouldn't tell anyone about me. We went to the same school there. A finishing school. We became close." She takes a quick sip of her tea.

"I tried writing to her, over the years, but I mustn't have had the right address, because all my letters were returned unopened. After I left school, I married the boy that had been courting me. Lionel. He was good to me. We tried, but we couldn't have children of our own. One spring, we visited my parents in Hannibal. While we were there, we went to an orphanage in St. Louis. There was a little girl there. She was three years old. When I held her little hand, I knew she was Deirdre's."

I raise an eyebrow in disbelief. "You *knew?*"

"Yes. Deirdre and I . . . we have some of the same gifts. Clairvoyance and such." Esme clears her throat and looks away. "I know, it sounds silly, doesn't it? In any case, Lionel and I signed the papers that very day and brought Ophelia home."

"So, you claim you adopted my mother?"

"Yes."

It occurs to me just how much about her life Granny's kept hidden. If she really had a secret daughter, and that daughter had somehow been my mother, it'd mean we're blood kin. Not that it matters much. Granny's my family. Always has been. Always will be.

But knowing this about my mama gets me to thinking about how Bellflower called me "granddaughter" before I sent him hurtling back to hell, what he told me at the lighthouse about Granny, and their strange conversation on the square. Maybe there's some truth in his lies, after all. Had he seduced Granny and fathered a child with her? My mother? I shudder to think I could have any part of *him* running through me.

Esme clears her throat, and I drag myself away from my troublesome thoughts.

"Lionel died the next year of an awful bout of cholera. I auctioned off our low country plantation and went back to Missouri to raise Ophelia near my family. She was a quiet child, but willful. As she grew older, she never saw much sense in social affairs and courting like most girls her age did. She preferred her books. But when she got to be in her twenties, she started running with a rough crowd. Met a girl named Valerie at a dance, who was dating a boy with an older brother. She took off with him. After I threatened to get the law involved, she wouldn't speak to me anymore." Esme rubs her forehead. "He was a drunkard, I think."

"Shep Doherty."

"Yes."

"That bastard's long dead," I say. Esme looks up in surprise, probably at my language. "Sorry. Shep was my daddy, but he wasn't any good. After he died, Valerie took me in. She's Granny's daughter, too. That's how I came to be here."

"Oh my. How strange. But I always knew things would turn full circle, somehow." Esme reaches out and squeezes my hand. "I'm so glad I came."

From across the porch comes a rustling. Granny throws off her covers and sits up, blinking. She rubs at her eyes and squints. "Gracie, who's there? Who are you visitin' with?"

"This lady's from Hannibal. Says she's my grandma, too, and she knew you at school?"

Esme swivels in her chair. "Hello, Deirdre."

All the color drains from Granny's face, and a whimper drifts from her lips. "Esme. After all this time."

❧

I help Granny out to her bench under the peach tree and cover her shoulders with one of her crocheted afghans. The weather has cooled, and we've had enough rain lately that the grass is up to our ankles again and full of chiggers. Esme sits next to Granny, and after I've brought them a few slices of buttered corn bread and more tea, I leave them be. I figure they've got a lot to catch up on, and I'll have a chance to ask all my questions later. Lord knows I have plenty.

Instead, I walk up the hill and knock on the door to the lighthouse cottage. Abby answers. I don't even wait for her to say a word. I just pull her to me and kiss her like there's no tomorrow, like someone that's almost lost everything and everyone she loves.

I figure this is the start of everything good in my life, after so much bad, and I'm not afraid of anything anymore.

Not even high places.

EPILOGUE

GRACELYNN

WALPURGIS NIGHT, 1981

Caro just left, with all her grandbabies in tow, and I'm tuckered out from braiding daisy chains and chasing them around the maypole all afternoon. Somehow, even without a blood tie to Anneliese, one of them has our gift—the youngest—Jessica. It crackles off her like summer lightning. I'll pass this grimoire on to her when it's time, just like Granny did with me, and then she'll add her own knowledge for *her* granddaughter someday, because that's what we do in this family. We carry things through, and then we pass them on.

It's been a curseless fifty years so far, filled with nothing but happiness and love. I have no reason to think the next fifty years will be any different.

Sometime after midnight, I take Abby's hand and lead her to our bedroom up in the loft, where the sweet scent of lilacs comes through the open window. In the distance, an owl hoots mournfully against the trickle of the spring. Underneath it all, a train chugs along with its promise of far-off places. But just like the curse that used to plague this land, the girl who couldn't wait to leave Tin Mountain is long gone.

As I've gotten older, I've come to realize that *home* is less about the place you live, and more about the people who love you. The memories you make. The laughter and tears and all the moments in between.

Home is Esme and Granny, their ashes spread under the peach tree where they used to feed the chickens and steal kisses. They had a whole twenty years of loving before they passed within a month of each other. Peaceful, in their sleep. Home is Morris and Seth, almost two thousand miles away in San Francisco, growing old together in their tiny apartment—and still looking at the same stars I look at, every night.

Home is Caro and her brood of kids and grandkids, and the way she no longer calls me Gracie, but "Mama." I reckon I've earned that honor.

And even though it has its flaws, Tin Mountain is home, too. It always has been. It's the women lining up outside our apothecary, still occasionally paying me with ham hocks and zucchini in exchange for herbal tonics to soothe their babies so they might get some sleep themselves. It's Calvina's tearoom and boardinghouse at the old Bledsoe place, and the memory of Ebba's silly, girlish laughter. It's the monument to Anneliese in the town square that the townsfolk put up as a penance, the year after the storm. It's the way the sun lingers long in summer and the first frost of autumn turns the maple leaves from scarlet to silver.

Like Granny once told me, Tin Mountain is where I belong.

Where I'll always belong.

Home.

AUTHOR'S NOTE

I always knew I wanted to write about home. But I didn't know *how* until I'd left.

Growing up in the Ozarks, I didn't always appreciate the beauty of the landscape. This rocky land, with its lakes, caves, and serpentine rivers shone clearer for me in my rearview mirror as its rolling hills, pastures, and forests were replaced by California's equally beautiful mountains, deserts, and beaches.

A lot of media gets us wrong. Our dialect, our family ties, our resolve and stubborn resilience. You *have* to be stubborn to live in a place like this. Marked by fitful weather that can quickly transform balmy, mild spring days to fickle tempests that bring killer tornadoes and baseball-sized hail, the Ozarks are mercurial. The weather events in *The Witch of Tin Mountain* are only slightly exaggerated—and while they are touched with a hint of the supernatural, I myself have witnessed the kind of weather my characters experience within these pages. This novel was revised during a particularly brutal Ozarks winter, and even though being home added a layer of nostalgia to this work, it reaffirmed that I much prefer California's subtly shifting seasons.

The Ozarks (*Aux Arc*) were first named as such and rudimentarily mapped in the eighteenth century by French and Acadian fur trappers and missionaries, who found this land between mountains teeming with bounty. After the Louisiana Purchase, a variety of European immigrants came west to break ground and stake a claim—stealing from and colonizing Indigenous lands. Native peoples including the Osage, Caddo, Quapaw, Tunica, Kickapoo, and Chickasaw—who had inhabited this lush riparian wilderness since *Homo sapiens* first emerged in North America, rightfully resisted the European settlers' encroachment, and were later joined by the Cherokee, who arrived shortly after the European settlers forced them out of Appalachia. After Andrew Jackson signed the Indian Removal Act, the Ozarks' abundance of caves, hidden hollows, and rocky bluffs aided in the Native peoples' fight to maintain a foothold on their ancestral lands and resist forced relocation. The Arkansas band of the Western Cherokee still remain in the area to this day.

Tin Mountain itself, while a fantastical figment of my imagination, is inspired by the array of tiny towns that sprang up in nineteenth-century southern Missouri and northern Arkansas along rivers and railroads, many of them named for railway moguls. Many of the places mentioned in this book are real: Rogers, Fayetteville, and Blytheville, Arkansas, and Springfield, Missouri (my hometown). While my fictional Tin Mountain would be a bit north of the actual Ponca Wilderness, savvy readers from the area will recognize my renaming of Whitaker Point, also known as Hawksbill Crag, which overlooks the breathtakingly beautiful Buffalo River Valley. The Buffalo itself is a fine river to float down on a hot summer day.

I have taken some liberties with the establishment of railway lines and connections and took marginal liberty with the official founding date of Rogers, Arkansas (which happened about a week after Deirdre's departure to Charleston). The café she eats lunch at in Rogers was also not yet in existence, although the train depot *was*. I have done my best to stay as accurate as possible otherwise. The CALS Encyclopedia of Arkansas (https://encyclopediaofarkansas.net) was a valuable resource for dates, times, locations, and general history of the area that I know well but am often still surprised by.

As for the folklore that inspired me to write this novel, I loosely based the core haunting on the Bell Witch legend of rural Adams, Tennessee. I consulted several sources in my research on the Bell family and their eponymous witch, including *An Authenticated History of the Famous Bell Witch* by Martin Van Buren Ingram, which was written in 1894 and is the closest thing historians have to a primary resource about the haunting. There are a variety of theories about what exactly happened to the Bell family during the early nineteenth century, but as their descendants are still living, out of respect, I will refrain from making my own conjectures about the nature of the haunting. My reasoning behind the fictional Sutter/Werner family's generational haunting/curse is strictly the result of my own imagination. The Bell Witch haunting has inspired many other fictional adaptations, among them *Little Sister Death* by William Gay, which I highly recommend to those interested in American folklore and southern gothic literature.

My decision to set my own Bell Witch–inspired novel in the Ozarks instead of Tennessee reflects the fact that many Appalachians, like my father, migrated to the Ozarks, bringing their stories, music, and history along with them. The two regions are quite similar in topography, socioeconomic status, and cultural heritage. The abundant underground springs and mineral-rich karst geology of the Ozarks plateau contribute to the similarities—and the folklore. Some unique regional phenomena can be confirmed by locals—for example, real places in the Ozarks such as Magnetic Mountain and Magnetic Spring have electromagnetic anomalies that have been experienced by residents for generations. The failure of compasses to settle on a direction in the vicinity of Tin Mountain, however, is entirely my own invention, although paranormal researchers and mystics claim that the convergence of ley lines and iron ore deposits in northern Arkansas work as a sort of magnetic spiritual vortex, and who am I to argue? It makes for a great story.

As for the rest of the strange phenomena occurring in Tin Mountain, a good percentage of the paranormal content was generated by my own family's tradition of oral storytelling and their personal anecdotes. My father, who grew up during the Great Depression, hailed originally from Tennessee, not far from where the Bell Witch haunting occurred. His recollections of his family's log cabin inspired the Sutter/Werner homestead, and some of his strange and unusual stories have made it into the book—the specter of the flaming man running up the hillside that Abby recounts was an apparition he saw himself, as a boy. My dad's recollections about sharecropping, music parties, and foraging for food in the wilderness also gave me firsthand information about day-to-day life for the rural poor during the Depression.

My mother's anecdotes also have a place in this novel. For example, Deirdre's vision of the wolf attacking Gracelynn was a vision my own grandmother had about my mother. (Unlike Gracie, my mother did *not* go to the tent revival she was warned away from!) My grandmother was a deeply religious woman of the Pentecostal faith, who often had visions. One of the characteristics of Ozarkian folk magic and mysticism is its symbiosis with Christianity. If you ever go to a Pentecostal church service or a tent revival in the Ozarks, you'll see exactly what I'm talking about.

Concerning my research on early Ozarks "hillbilly" culture, I consulted Vance Randolph's *Ozark Magic and Folklore*, as well as *Ozark Mountain Folks*. Randolph spent a great deal of time in the Ozarks during the Depression, and his entertaining and unique experiences with the granny women, water witchers, and other hill folk helped to infuse my own work with eyewitness authenticity—including midwives who placed axes beneath the beds of laboring mothers to "cut the pain," as Ebba does within this novel. Randolph was also one of the first historians to catalogue our unique Ozark dialect, vocabulary, and the colloquial speech of rural Missouri and Arkansas. Many of those colloquialisms are featured in this book, and I can attest from personal experience that most are still in use to this day. The Facebook page Dark

Ozarks and the excellent online magazine *StateoftheOzarks* provided many anecdotes that helped shore up the historical detail in this novel. For the history of late nineteenth-century Charleston and its unique architecture and culture, I consulted several online sources, photographs, and maps. *Charleston! Charleston! The History of a Southern City* by Walter J. Fraser Jr. was also very helpful. Miss Munro's school is entirely fictional, although such finishing schools were in abundance in the South during the time in which Deirdre inhabited the city.

For the green witchcraft, herbology, conjure work, midwifery, and magic mentioned within, *Green Witchcraft: A Practical Guide to Discovering the Magic of Plants, Herbs, Crystals, and Beyond* by Paige Vanderbeck; *Old Style Conjure: Hoodoo, Rootwork, and Folk Magic* by Starr Casas; and for Ebba's Norse form of magic, *Trolldom: Spells and Methods of the Norse Folk Magic Tradition* by Johannes Björn Gårdbäck were invaluable resources. I'm also grateful to Astrid Grim for her authenticity read of this manuscript and her guidance with the Nilsson family's characterization and her advice concerning the Swedish language used herein.

Gracelynn's ad hoc "trial" was directly inspired by the Salem witch trials. Truth is often stranger than fiction, and much of what transpired during the actual magisterial proceedings in Salem far outpaces anything I have written. *American Witches: A Broomstick Tour through Four Centuries* by Susan Fair, *Six Women of Salem: The Untold Story of the Accused and Their Accusers in the Salem Witch Trials* by Marilynne K. Roach, and *A Delusion of Satan: The Full Story of the Salem Witch Trials* by Frances Hill were consulted in my research, and they extensively cover the truly fascinating and disturbing aspects of the trials and the unfortunate men and women who were the victims of collective delusion and hysteria. What happened in Salem is a cautionary tale to this day, and a call to employ our own critical thinking and personal judgement in the face of sensation, public opinion, and hyperbole.

In closing, I've always found the thought of angels mildly terrifying. Ever watching. Ever present, ostensibly to protect us but also functioning as supernatural hall monitors, waiting to report our indiscretions to a higher power. The verse in Hebrews about "entertaining strangers" also strikes me as a bit ominous, and that verse inspired my antagonist's various incarnations. Ironically, while revising this novel, I spent the winter at my mother's house, being stared at by her collection of angel statuary in the wee witching hours of morning. (This may also have had a formative impact on my editorial decisions.) However, this novel is in no way an indictment of Christianity, or religion, but of hypocrisy. In my opinion, the most effective tool an evil being, fictional or otherwise, can use against us is our own capacity to judge others more harshly than we judge ourselves.

This novel is a work of fiction. Any errors within this novel are completely my own, and I take full responsibility for any and all historical inaccuracies.

ACKNOWLEDGMENTS

The time period in which I wrote this novel was rife with unexpected challenges. Shortly after Lake Union Publishing acquired *The Witch of Tin Mountain*, I received a devastating phone call that had me packing a suitcase and flying home. Soon after, I became my mother's live-in caregiver while she underwent treatment for cancer. That this book exists at all seems something of a miracle, and there have been many times over the past two years, in general, where I've looked at my relatively new role as a published author with a combination of bemused disbelief and gratitude. This gratitude is extended to the many talented, compassionate, and patient people who have contributed to my success as an author, and I relish the opportunity to thank them on paper.

First, to my agent, Jill Marr, and the entire team at Sandra Dijkstra Literary Agency, thank you for tirelessly championing my work and helping it find its way to readers. You encourage me to reach high and to believe in the worth of my words.

To my acquiring and developmental editor, Jodi Warshaw, who presented *The Witch of Tin Mountain* at her final acquisitions meeting at Lake Union and set me on the path to publication in 2020 with *Parting the Veil*, my gratitude is boundless. You are brilliant and kind, and I will always be thankful for your patient guidance and belief in my work.

Many thanks to the marvelous Melissa Valentine, who took me under her wing after Jodi's departure, and reassured me that this book would receive her enthusiastic support and guidance. I look forward to seeing what we might create together in the future! Special thanks as well to Danielle Marshall, who managed the production of this novel in the interim period between editors and patiently addressed all my questions and concerns.

To the Lake Union author relations and production teams, especially Gabe Dumpit and Jen Bentham, bringing a book to the world is a team effort, and you all make me look good while enduring my incorrect comma usage and emails about pesky internet pirates! Thanks as well to the copyeditor, Kristin Carlsen; the proofreader, Valerie Paquin; and the cover designer, Amanda Hudson, for the gorgeous cover art.

Thanks as always to my steadfast critique partner, Thuy Nguyen, and her unflagging confidence in my abilities. I wouldn't be able to draft a darn thing if I didn't know you were on the other side of the internet, patiently waiting for my pages. We're a dream team, and together, we persevere.

To Maria Tureaud, who reviewed this manuscript and critiqued it with her characteristic honesty and humor. You are matchless. Thanks for shoring up my decisions concerning complex villains and making them even more . . . appealing. *wicked cackle*

I had a brilliant group of beta readers, including Megan Van Dyke, S. Kaeth, and Alex Gotay. Thank you all for taking the time to read this manuscript in its early stages. You'll see many of your recommendations reflected in the finished work. Megan and Alex, special love and thanks for commiserating with me over weird southern colloquialisms, the tendency to use an abundance of superfluous words to convey a simple thought, and the strange naming conventions of our kinfolk. Also, cicadas. A book can't be set anywhere in the South without cicadas.

To my WiM family: You held me up during a very difficult year. Your cards and letters brought smiles and tears, and I can't thank you enough for the gift of your friendship. I love you all.

Special thanks to Jeni Chappelle and the #RevPit editors for continuing to nurture writers and to educate them about the publishing industry and writing craft. You elevate us.

To my "APub debut" family: Jennifer Bardsley, Mansi Shah, Elissa Grossell Dickey, Kate Myles, Eden Appiah-Kubi, and Sara Goodman Confino—thanks for all the support, advice, and encouragement during our debut year and onward. I love you all so much! I hope to meet over a bucket of champagne someday soon. Thanks also to the 2021 Debuts group on Facebook. Wishing you all much success and longevity in art as well as in life.

Thanks to friends and authors Libbie Grant, Aimie K. Runyan Piper Huguley, Jane Healey, and Kris Waldherr, as well as Hester Fox, Lydia Kang, Dawn Kurtagich, Kim Taylor Blakemore, Stacie Murphy, Nicole Eigener, Elle Marr, Barbara Davis, Rachel McMillan, Georgina Cross, Clarissa Harwood, Jessica Lewis, Laura McHugh, Jo Kaplan, Olesya Salnikova Gilmore, Alyssa Palombo, Megan Chance, and Elizabeth Blackwell—all tremendously talented authors who have demonstrated a willingness to give of their time, support, and knowledge. You exemplify humility and gratitude in action. I'll be happily paying your kindness forward for the rest of my career.

A wealth of gratitude to my street team: Desirée Niccoli, Amalie Frederiksen, Harlequin and Astrid Grm (who also reviewed this manuscript for Swedish authenticity), Megan Van Dyke, T. C. Kemper, Ashley McAnelly, J. M. Jinks, R. Singer, Shyla Shank, Alex Gotay, Gabby Barone, Jolie Christine, Pamela Hernandez, Erin Litteken, Thuy Nguyen, Maria Tureaud (your ongoing support is my linchpin!), and Belinda Grant. You shouted *Parting the Veil* into the ether and, therefore, were a huge part of the success that paved my path as a writer.

Most of all, a huge thank you to every reader, reviewer, blogger, bookstagram influencer, and podcast host who read and reviewed my debut and expressed their excitement for this book as well as any others

I might write in the future. From the moment of publication, my words belong to *you*.

And finally, to my family:

Mom, this season of uncertainty has brought us closer than ever. Your bravery, your strength, and your will to survive in the face of astonishing odds has been a beautiful thing to witness. This is a book about *home*, and you have always shown me what that word truly means. I hope you can see your reflection in the words and relationships herein. I love you.

Dad, this book wouldn't ever have existed without your scary stories and tall tales. Perhaps a few of those stories were inappropriate for little ears, but all the same, I'm grateful to you for my lifelong interest in the paranormal and the weird. You were always a little bit quirky and a whole lot of fun. I miss you every single day.

Lula, you'll never know just how much all those frozen toffee lattes helped my mental health over the past few months. Truly. Sisterly love is played out in the little things.

Avery, you are my sunshine. The reason behind everything I do. Your enthusiastic quoting of uncomfortable animal facts helped me to smile and carry on when I felt like crying from overwhelm. Your humor and wit are a gift to this world. *You* are a gift. Don't ever doubt it.

Ryan, I don't know where to begin. There's nothing I could ever say to convey the depths of my gratitude for being the kind of partner who quietly supports me in every way, and who asks "What can I do to help?" without hesitation. You are the Carl Dean to my Dolly. I love you, I love you, I love you. Thank you for being you.

BOOK CLUB QUESTIONS

1. The bulk of this novel takes place during two time periods: 1881 and 1931, while offering interludes from Anneliese's grimoire in the 1830s. Which time period did you enjoy reading about most and why?

2. There are references to the land reacting to the presence of Ambrose Gentry and Josiah Bellflower. How did you interpret the weather and climate phenomena, considering the rumored curse?

3. Community justice of the sort used in Salem, Massachusetts, diminished as the United States criminal justice system developed. But in small, isolated towns in rural communities, vigilantism and revenge justice still happen to this day—in other words, the "code of the hills." Was Gracelynn's witchcraft trial believable to you? Why or why not?

4. When Deirdre uses the knowledge within the grimoire to harm Phoebe, did you feel as if the grimoire was betraying Deirdre, or reflecting her own capacity for wrongdoing back at her? How much does free will factor into Deirdre's choices versus Gentry's influence?

5. Tin Mountain's hypocrisy and corruption are central elements of the novel. The Werner women are often victims

of this hypocrisy. How did you feel about the ending of the novel? Was Gracelynn's forgiveness and acceptance of the townspeople's apologies satisfying or frustrating?

ABOUT THE AUTHOR

Photo © 2021 Paulette Kennedy

Paulette Kennedy is the author of *Parting the Veil*. When she's not writing, you can find her tending to her garden and trying to catch up with the looming stack of unread books next to her bed. Originally from the Ozarks, Paulette now lives with her family and their menagerie of pets in a quiet suburb of Los Angeles. For more information visit www.paulettekennedy.com.